The Color Storm

Also by Damian Dibben

Tomorrow

The Color Storm

A Novel of
Renaissance Venice

DAMIAN DIBBEN

HANOVER
SQUARE
PRESS

HANOVER
SQUARE
PRESS™

Recycling programs
for this product may
not exist in your area.

ISBN-13: 978-1-335-01593-8

The Color Storm

First published in 2022 in Great Britain by Penguin Michael Joseph. This edition published in 2022.

Hanover Square Press
22 Adelaide St. West, 41st Floor
Toronto, Ontario M5H 4E3, Canada
HanoverSqPress.com
BookClubbish.com

Printed in U.S.A.

For Michael and Dick, fathers of inspiration one and two

The Color Storm

PAINTERS AT WORK IN SEPTEMBER, 1510

Venice

Zorzo Barbarelli, or *Giorgione*, aged 33.
Giovanni Bellini, aged 80.
Tiziano Vecellio, or *Titian*, aged 22.
Sebastiano del Piombo, aged 24.

Florence and Milan

Leonardo da Vinci, aged 58.
Raphael Sanzio, aged 27.

Rome

Michelangelo Buonarroti, aged 35.
Pietro Perugino, aged 64.
Lorenzo Lotto, aged 30.

Germany and the Low Countries

Albrecht Dürer, aged 39.
Hieronymous Bosch, aged 60.
Matthias Grünewald, aged 40.

PROLOGUE

Sixty years afterward. Rome. January, 1570.

On the Quirinal Hill, a young man waits at the door of a palazzo. He hasn't knocked yet. He's trying to compose himself. It's cold, colder than any January he can remember. His eyes are sore and his hands—ungloved, one clutching his portfolio, the other the neck of his coat—have turned a kind of iron blue, except at the fingertips where paint is ingrained—Persian red, verdigris green, orpiment yellow—from the canvas he was working on before setting off for Rome, *The Revenge of the Widow Giuditta*.

He was told in the letter that the mansion was easy to find, close to the civic barracks and built in the Moorish style of a Spanish *palacete*, its facades reminiscent of beaten silverwork, but he walked past it several times without realizing. He'd been expecting a splendid mansion—the letter surely implied it—but if it had been once, those days are gone.

He feels duped, after the effort he's spent getting here, inexorable hours rocking up and down in cramped carriages, shoveled around by barking drivers, barely eating or sleeping and shivering for days. Then, when he arrived in the city and panicked about his appearance, about that vital first impression, he spent the last of his money on a new coat—a garment that turns out to be as itchy and ill-fitting as it is ineffective against the wind.

He knocks and after a pause there comes a shuffle of footsteps, a swing of lantern light through the hall window. The door is unbolted and cracked open, just enough for an elderly steward to peer out.

"Domenikos Kopoulos," the young man says, in the habit now of shortening his surname. "From Venice. The painter."

"Yes, yes," says the steward and ushers him inside.

"My apologies for arriving so late." Domenikos peers around, disappointed to find that, like the outside, the interior gives no sign that money lives here. "But in the last letter I received, the lady said there was urgency." He adds, pointedly, "The *lady* provided me with an address, but I still have no name for her?"

He deserves to know by now the identity of who he's dealing with, but the steward holds up both palms and says, "Yes, yes. Wait here." He totters off down a corridor into a room and there come sounds of opening cupboards and rattling glass.

Domenikos looks around. The space is bare, the walls tatty and crumbling. Most worrying of all, not one piece of art is on show, though discolored patches indicate paintings must have hung here once. In her letter to him, signed only as *A Lady Collector,* she praised his work, had a detailed knowledge of it, surprisingly—even what he'd produced in Crete before leaving for Italy. She explained he was suited for the task. She didn't say what that was, though, and offered no information about herself. He presumed—why wouldn't he?—that she was a rich patroness who liked to remain anonymous. In any case, she'd sent a sum of money to cover his traveling expenses to Rome—and that decided it.

"This way, this way," the steward says, pattering back, a silver tray in his hands, a decanter with brandy and two glasses. "Up, up." He starts to ascend the stairs to the first-floor gallery. "She's not been well today, but your arrival will revive her."

Domenikos follows and at once the light in the hall changes; the space fills out with a pearly luminescence, bringing everything, all the decay, into clarity. White flakes dance against the window halfway up the stairs.

"Snow in Rome?" Domenikos says.

Peering out, he finds the city already half-dusted in it. The old Forum has been transformed into a fairy kingdom. Then, casting his eye along the horizon, a surprise: on the crest of the opposing hill is the new basilica of St. Peter. Since he arrived, he's only caught glimpses of it behind buildings, an abstract corner here, a part-section of dome there. He thought it was finished—wasn't everyone saying it was?—but sections remain scaffolded and strewn with ladders and even from the Quirinal he can hear the tap of hammers across the valley.

The steward leads him into a large, dark room. Domenikos notices the fire first, which is housed in a tiled cabinet that comes out from the wall, like an ironmonger's furnace, though more ornate. Its door is ajar and flames rumble within. In shadow on the far side of it, a lady is seated at a table. The steward sets down the tray in front of her and goes to load up the fire with logs, taking a stoker and shunting them into the heart of the blaze, before closing the hearth door.

"Come closer." The lady motions with a gloved hand.

"Signora."

She beckons him again and Domenikos steps forward.

He resists the urge to ask who she is and says, "It's an interesting chimneypiece. Ceramic? I saw one like it in a house on the Black Sea, but never in Italy."

"In Germany they are everywhere. Some engineers came from there to install it," she replies. Her voice is wheezy, like an old squeezebox, and she has an accent Domenikos can't place. "It keeps me alive," she says, and the word *alive* gets trapped in her throat, turns to a cough and it takes her some moments to regain composure. Domenikos tries to see her face, but it's a dark cobweb of lines beneath her headpiece. "How was your journey?" she asks.

"Eventful, cold, painful at times." If he'd found himself in a wealthier place, he'd probably keep any gripe to himself. "I'm not built well for traveling. Or the winter. No fat on me."

"And everyone is talking about you. A young contender for the crown. And a Greek. A Cretan. They call you the Greek, don't they? A nickname is reassuring. It means you're being noticed."

"I hope so. Unless they don't like that I'm foreign."

She gives a nod, of understanding, perhaps. "In Italy—as you can hear—I am a foreigner too." She takes the stopper from the decanter and tries to pour a glass, but she barely has the strength to hold it up and the neck rattles against the rim. Domenikos steps forward to help, but she repels him with a shake of her head. She doesn't offer up the spare glass, nor does he ask.

"I wasn't sure," Domenikos goes on, "from the correspondence I received, what exactly the commission is."

"There is no commission." She puts the brandy to her lips, wets them with it, before taking a sip. "Not in the usual sense. I offer something else. Those are your drawings?" She extends an arthritic fist toward the portfolio. "Let me see. Samuele." The steward collects the folder and places it on the table, along with a lamp. He unties the ribbon of the folio, opens it for his mistress and exits the room. She examines the first work. It's a detailed cartoon of the painting he's most proud of, *Christ Cleansing the*

Temple. Creating it had been a revelation from start to finish. Jesus is steady in the center, like a general, as a maelstrom of confusion sweeps around him. A tale told in color. She stares at it for minutes, eyes blinking, before she touches her gloved finger against the surface texture.

"You sketch in oil?"

"For vibrancy, yes."

She goes through the pictures, two dozen of them that Domenikos selected from hundreds, thousands even, of mostly new work from his three years in Venice, where stories began infatuating him, where the sheer drama of the city inspired him to paint St. Francis and Gabriel and Moses, not as icons like he used to in Crete, but as living, breathing people. Looking around, he notices a canvas on the wall—the single adornment of the room, of the entire house. He squints to see what the subject is, but in the gloom he can make out little more than a portrait of a woman.

"I need no painting from you," she says when she's gone through all the drawings and closed the folder. "It would be wasted on these cataract eyes anyway. I have—what is the best word for it—knowledge. I can impart it to one person only. I considered many before settling on you. These drawings are proof I have chosen well."

"Knowledge?" He only half hides the disappointment in his voice. His debts are on the point of becoming unmanageable and *knowledge* is not what he's traveled for.

"*Rare* knowledge. It would be unforgivable, for those who risked so much in pursuit of it, to take it to the grave with me. And the grave comes soon. I have crossed this continent a hundred times over and my bones are thin. When I try to walk, it's like balancing on ice. Even the children of my contemporaries have begun to die. I have sold everything. The palazzo is empty. All my furniture gone, every painting except the one there. Only this last task remains." She pauses briefly, then asks,

"How much do you know of the painter Giorgio Barbarelli?" She studies him keenly.

"Barbarelli?"

"Of Castelfranco." She waits a beat before adding, "Perhaps more commonly known as Giorgione."

"Giorgione, yes, him I know a little."

"A little?" Not the answer she wanted. "What paintings of his have you seen?"

"I—can't recall if I've seen any."

"None? Do you not have to study great work when you train?"

"Of course."

"You have not seen his *Tempest*, or *Venus Sleeping*? Not the altarpiece of Castelfranco, which you can visit and see the colors as fresh as the day they were ground? And you've been in Venice three years?"

"I have seen many Tizianos," he offers, certain they were contemporaries. "Venice is crammed with them."

"I do not speak of Tiziano." From somewhere in her broken body her voice finds force. "Tiziano had the luck of long life. Luck all through it. He died an old man, in his bed, his family about. I speak of Giorgione. You are a painter who wishes to make his mark on the world; he should be always in your thoughts. He started it all. *He* was the Colorist."

She pauses to get her breath and Domenikos wonders exactly what Giorgione "started." His name rarely came up during his years of apprenticeships. Tiziano, on the other hand, was studied ad infinitum. "When I return to Venice, I shall seek him out immediately. This information you have, it concerns him?"

She lifts the end of her stick and points it toward the single piece of art on show. "That is one of his."

"Giorgione's?"

"It was never finished," she says softly. "It is me." For a moment, just the sound of burning from the hearth, and the tapping of hammers from across the valley. "How old are you?"

"Twenty-eight."

"I was your age, more or less, when I met Zorzo—that was the name we knew him by. Your age when I realized what it is we're all in search of, in one way or another, the subject of every artist's sigh, the reason we wake up in the morning and escape into dreams at night."

"Love?"

"Color."

Hearing this, Domenikos's mouth slowly turns up in a smile.

"Stepping into his workroom for the first time," she goes on, "was like finding myself in another country. I knew nothing of how paintings were made—or how colors were conjured: azurite, crimson lake, pink chalcedony, vermilion, realgar, lead yellow, bone black."

"Yes, yes." Domenikos nods, his enthusiasm growing. "I was the same."

"I knew little of the world either, of the shocks that were about to tear through it at the start of this century, when ideas would light up the continent like fires everywhere. When no one knew if those fires would bring light—or burn us all. When painters were so charged with purpose, so voracious, so rebellious against everything that had gone before, that they described the age as *a color storm*. And I knew nothing of the *new* color, the great secret, the color that would change my life."

"Which color is that?"

"One that had never been seen before. Never imagined either. One that men would die for. He was prepared to die. My love. My other soul."

Domenikos wonders if he heard right. "He was prepared to—?"

A cry goes up from outside, drums start to beat in time and what sounds like a hundred men—the civil guard from the barracks, presumably—begin a march down the hill. As they scour past the palazzo, feet pounding the frozen ground, the floor shakes and dust falls from the ceiling. In the chimneypiece, a log tumbles and flips open the hearth door. A shaft of light is thrown across the room, illuminating the signora at her table.

"Leave it," she says, when Domenikos goes to close the fire door. "Let it breathe. Sit here where I can see you."

Domenikos approaches and takes the chair opposite her. Now he sees her face. Skin like pale parchment, veined and watermarked, stretched over a tiny skull. She keeps her back straight and neck long, though her body, under layers of black tulle, is as thin as twigs. It is like looking at time itself.

"Prepared to die, yes," she says. "Some people are. They're ready to walk into fire, into battle, knowing they'll not return. They're willing to do it—so the rest of us can be safe."

In front of her, the decanter and glass rattle on the tray, the surface of the brandy shivers as the pounding of soldiers' boots reaches its apogee, before beginning to diminish. Down into the valley they go, in their nightly maneuver to guard their city. Domenikos's heart quickens. He feels suddenly grateful he came to Rome, beyond doubt that the journey was worthwhile, sure he's found a kindred spirit. He's desperate to know more of Giorgione now, of what he made, what he painted, what he risked, that six decades later this woman in front of him is still in awe of it. Domenikos feels a light creaking open inside of him, a shiver of excitement—a sensation he hasn't had in months. In years, perhaps.

The signora gives a nod and with her knuckle pushes the decanter toward him, and then the spare glass. "Drink."

Domenikos fills the glass, throws back its contents in one, inhales against the reassuring shock of alcohol and says, "I'm listening. Tell me all about him—all about this color storm."

1

Winter's Envoy

Sixty years earlier

Zorzo has always imagined the little island of Poveglia is the sort of place you'd be able to enter the underworld from. That there might be a hidden fissure in the rock and a staircase that goes deep into the earth. He has pictured descending it, as Orpheus did, or Aeneas, down, down to the fiery realm below.

It's a clod of sand and mud in the south of the Venetian lagoon. There was a town on it once, but foreign invasions more than a century ago have left it almost uninhabited. A *cavana*, church and leaning bell tower sit deserted with their doors smashed and roofs down; while what remains of the town's timber homes have become passing places, or hideaways, for smugglers and vagrants, though even they vanish when the island turns into an unofficial burial ground during seasons of the plague. If you look closely enough at the ground, you can see pieces of human bones in the earth. Only birds—great, cawing factions of herons and gulls, indifferent to the dream of Venice—are constant. For over a hundred years, they've been the true rulers of Poveglia.

Zorzo approaches the island by gondola.

"Let's hope the mist will rise," he said, to be sociable, when he embarked at San Marco. "We've not met before. I'm Zorzo, and you?"

The man seemed to resent the question. "Tullo." He turned his back and jabbed down on the oar.

It was a journey of less than an hour from Venice, but the weather turned in that time. A chilly gust picked up and the sky darkened to the color of aged tin before it began to rain.

"There," he calls to Tullo now, pointing toward an old pier. The wind rocks the gondola and keeps pushing it back, but once it's close enough, Zorzo slings his satchel across his shoulder and jumps ashore. "You'll wait here?" he asks. "I don't know how long I shall be. You'll be all right in this weather?"

The other man yanks tight the mooring and takes shelter under his boat's awning. "It's your money."

Zorzo picks his way through the mud toward a shack set back from the quayside. He pauses at the door, turning his ear to the burr of voices within. Before he first came here, the tavern on Poveglia had such a doomy, secretive reputation that he wondered if it really existed. Indeed, sometimes it didn't: he would make the journey only to find it closed down, or moved from one shack to another.

There's a far-off tolling of bells from the city: midday—though it could be dusk, the sky's so murky. He's arrived early, even though Caspien is invariably late. Zorzo is keen to conclude their business quickly, in daylight, and get back to Venice. He and his team of apprentices are at the final stage of the commission they've been working on, a portrait of a young noblewoman, the daughter of the Count Lippi. They're ready to add her gloves, which occupy the foreground of the picture, and require at least five different versions of black. His *garzoni* are preparing the pigments while Zorzo's gone. More importantly, he's been invited by the Contarini family to a banquet at the Ca' d'Oro that evening. Despite great efforts, he's not gained entry to a single grand event over the summer, but this one could make up for the loss: it will be crammed, surely, with Venice's most moneyed patrons, any of whom might be in the market for a new painting.

Zorzo slips off his ring, a sapphire set in a gold band, the only thing of real value he ever carries on him, puts it in his breeches pocket and enters the inn. Some faces peer around at him from the gloom. Caspien's is not among them. Zorzo crosses the room, moving with what he judges, from his half-dozen trips here, to be the right degree of confidence, and sits in the corner where he has a clear view of the shore through one of the glassless windows. A fire splutters in the hearth and he takes in the usual assortment of rogues hunched around the trestle tables: black-market traders, army deserters, drifters and gamblers. He's reminded of the underworld once more. This tavern could be its antechamber, where dispossessed souls gather to await their fate.

He takes a bundle of papers from his satchel and starts going through them. Workshop bills that need to be paid. His foreman, Janek, has been nagging him for weeks to go through them, and offered many times to do it himself, but Zorzo prefers to keep grim news, the possibility of bankruptcy, to himself—for the sake of morale. "I'll add it all up in Poveglia," he'd told Janek on his way out. "I'll have plenty of time while I'm waiting."

Within minutes of studying the numbers his head is as murky as the weather: rent, interest on loans, insurances, invoices for linseed, canvas, gesso, brushes, quotes for repair work to his roof that he's promised his landlord he's already carried out—all this is before what he might end up spending when Caspien appears. He buys a cup of beer, takes some charcoal from his bag and turns one of the papers over to its blank side. The sight of it, the empty page, calms him. Drawing is the only sort of paperwork worth its while. He angles himself so no one will see—the inn at Poveglia is not a place for artists—and starts drawing the imagined underworld beneath him. He lets the charcoal guide him, down from the tavern, through the crust of the earth. He outlines a chamber of black marble and tourmaline cliffs, with chimney-places alive with giant bonfires. In the foreground, he finds himself sketching a human figure, forlorn against the grandeur of Hades: a warrior, back stooped, armor battered, exhausted by war and endless voyaging. He turns over a second sheet and tries another version, then a third and fourth.

An hour passes, customers drain away, others arrive. A fight breaks out over a sack of eels, a fisherman accusing another man of theft. Weapons are brandished and during a tussle the sack falls and its contents spill, dead eels for the most part, but some live ones too that flap across the floor. *Creatures of the night*, as Zorzo's father always called them. The row is patched up, boats come and go from the pier and Zorzo checks on Tullo several times (still waiting, still unsociable). The rain worsens for spells, lashing down, before lessening again.

By three in the afternoon, he decides he can't wait any longer. He's frustrated he's wasted money getting here, as well as precious time, but needs to be back in Venice to check on his *garzoni*, on the blacks they've been grinding, and get to the Contarinis' banquet. He pays for his beer and is packing up his bag when he notices a boat approaching. It's rocking from side to side, tiny sails frenetic in the wind, a man balancing on deck, a boy crouched at the rudder. Zorzo can tell, even from a distance, that it's Caspien, along with Otto, the young helper who always travels with him. Relief. He goes out to meet them.

Close to the shore, Caspien shouts over the wind, *"Guten Abend, guter Herr."*

Otto leaps into the shallows, disappearing up to his shoulders, before swimming ashore, pulling the boat with him by the tie rope. Caspien always docks halfway along the beach, never at the pier. To make a quick getaway, Zorzo supposes.

"So winter has sent her envoy," Caspien calls. He's lean and angular and has a mercenary's face that's riven with scars, but his clothes are flamboyant, albeit filthy—from his scarlet cloak, fur-lined and belted, to his oversized hat. He talks fast, in a thick Germanic accent, though no one knows exactly where he comes from.

"I thought you were one of the three wise men arriving," Zorzo says, "blown off course."

"Indeed, I follow my own star." Caspien nods before bellowing at the boy, "Not to the rock, it'll slip off! Tie us to that tree there." He jumps down from the craft, takes hold of his trunk and wades up onto dry land.

Some years back, it was Caspien's idea to meet on Poveglia, and the arrangement stuck. Caspien is, in his own words, "wanted" in Venice, though it's never clear by whom or for what. Even so, they could liaise safely enough on the mainland, in Mestre, for example, where there are plenty of out-of-the-way places. But Caspien, Zorzo fancies, likes the drama of the "haunted" island. He's unreliable, a liar by habit, but it doesn't matter to Zorzo. It wouldn't matter if he were a lunatic or a murderer, for Caspien is the best in the business.

"How are you, Otto?" Zorzo asks the boy.

"I am well, sir," he replies, fixing the rope to the base of the branch.

"Is he treating you well?" He means this seriously, but receives another rote, "Yes, sir."

Zorzo is fond of Otto, always struck by how sweet-natured he is despite enduring a thankless life trailing after his master. He's permanently ready at his side but is never shown affection in return. Where the boy comes from has never been explained, if he's Caspien's actual son or just adopted by him. "He is a wandering prince who never ages," Caspien said once, which struck Zorzo as bizarre. But in truth, Otto doesn't seem to grow. He's slight and fragile, but a workhorse of a child.

"Do you not have a coat?" Zorzo says. Otto wears just a shirt and thin jerkin, both of which are soaked through.

"No, sir."

"Don't listen to him," Caspien says, coming out of the sea. "Is he complaining? Anyone would think he'd never sailed before, nor seen the Adriatic rain." He puts down his trunk and shakes the water from his cloak with a tug. "Good evening, Signor Barbarelli. Am I late?"

"Late? Well." Zorzo knows that chiding his supplier would be unproductive, so he says only, "We may have some trouble seeing in this light."

"No matter, no matter. I'll stay for you, *mein Freund*, until morning. We shall buy some Black Sea brandy and play at cards," he nods toward the tavern, "with whatever flotsam has washed up this night."

"I can't wait until morning," Zorzo says simply. "I need to get back." He doesn't mention that neither could he afford to keep the boatman standing by all that time. "Best to do it now It's dry inside."

He turns back to the tavern, but Caspien stalls him. "I'll drink in there, but that's all." He points at the church on a knoll set back from the shore. "There's shelter that way." He leads them to it, before stationing himself on the porch. Zorzo follows. The chapel door hangs open and he can make out the derelict innards, upturned pews and fallen masonry. The boy comes last, heaving the trunk, and sets it down on the flat stones of the portico. It's the case Caspien always travels with, the type that an aged duke or duchess might have carried their jewels and glass in a century ago. A battered block of black oak, two feet wide and one deep, studded with rivets and fortified with iron straps.

From under his doublet, Caspien fishes out a gold chain with a key on the end, looks around to check that no one is watching, unlocks the casket and opens it up. He runs his hand along the grain, undoes more clasps and pulls up the secondary lid to reveal a tray of many square compartments. Zorzo's stomach does a little turn, as it always does. The aromas are familiar and intense: urine-smelling verdigris, nose-burning sulfur and the mulched-leaf scent of madder root. In each stall is a different material, some half-wrapped in paper or pushed into phials: portions of rocks, dull powders, quantities of metal, cubes of caked earth, crushed bone, dried bark—pigments in their raw form, barely giving their secrets away. Zorzo has never lost the thrill of setting eyes upon these apparently plain substances, each one a piece of magic about to happen. He can see—he's spent his life training himself to—the tiny burns of color that come off them, of indigo, ultramarine, vermilion, yellow ocher, burnt umber and malachite. "The destiny of every color," Caspien often reminds him, "is to break free of its ordinary beginnings and dazzle the world."

"So—what are you looking for?" Caspien asks, while his boy sits on the doorstep of the church and wraps his arms around his chest to keep warm.

Zorzo shrugs. "In theory, anything, everything. Supplies are low," he chances a smile, "but so is money."

Caspien screws up his face. "We are all short, Herr Barbarelli. Why don't you tell me what you're *most* in need of?"

"In particular—blue."

"Blue? A fool for blue," Caspien sighs. "As everyone is in this age." Zorzo won't deny it. The right blue, the perfect blue, more than any other color, has the power to stop hearts. Caspien's fingers hover across the compartments, before stopping over one of the stalls. "This is a very good smalt. From Constantinople."

"Smalt?"

"Don't jump to conclusions. It's vibrant, this variety, has a bulk on the canvas, and it dries fast. Very vibrant."

Zorzo looks closer. Other painters use smalt without a problem, good painters, but he always finds it second-rate. It has a manufactured quality and he can never get away from the fact it's essentially crushed glass.

Seeing his client is unenthused, Caspien moves on. "Cobalt," he says, taking up some stones and spreading them across his palm. "Triple the price, but nice and pure. A warm, grayish blue."

"Your boy is freezing," Zorzo says, seeing Otto's skinny arms have now begun to shake. "He should have a coat."

"He *had* one," Caspien bristles. "Didn't you, you rascal, in Rome? And he was careless enough to let someone pilfer it in the Piazza Navona. And now he must learn his lesson."

Being discussed makes Otto tremble even more and Zorzo takes his own coat off and hands it to him. "Wear this for now."

"No, sir," says the boy, his eyes wide.

"Give it back to me when you've dried off. I can live a few minutes without it." Still Otto resists, so Zorzo puts it on his lap. "Take it, please." He waits and eventually the boy has no choice but to put it on. "It suits you." Zorzo smiles. The coat's too large, but it changes the boy, its dark cinnamon trim bringing a distinguished quality to his face. Zorzo picks a piece of cobalt mineral from Caspien's palm and holds it to the light. "Grayish, you say? I'm not sure."

"A difficult customer you are." Caspien takes the stone back and returns it to the stall. "Indigo?" He uncorks a glass phial and shows Zorzo the dried leaves squashed inside. "From the Caucasus. It's a type of woad, I suppose, but could almost be a Tyrian purple. Very regal."

Genuine Tyrian purple, coaxed from seashells, in one of the longest processes in the workroom, would have been of interest to Zorzo. He shakes his head. "Plant dyes—they," he searches for the words, "they lack mystery."

"I'm sure Masaccio never complained about them." Caspien

primly corks the bottle. "Nor Perugino, nor does Michelangelo for that matter." He takes a deep breath and begins again. "Other colors, then. I have a carmine lake that is the best I've had in years. Very dramatic." He unwraps one of the paper parcels to show a wet, crimson chalk. "Kermes beetles, scratched from Prussian oaks. Subtler than cochineal. Exceptional tone."

He's about to show it off, when Zorzo holds up his palms. "Caspien, honestly, I can find all this from the *vendecolori* in San Marco. The reason I come here and wait in the cold for hours, the reason I'm happy to wait, is because you are *the* colorman of Europe and have no equal." This is true: for all his tall tales, Caspien can produce treasure, pigments that are more than just color, that are a mood, or a war, or a woman. "So no more of this dallying." Zorzo taps the bottom of the trunk. "What have you got down here?"

Caspien smiles. "*Expensive* pieces."

"Can a dreamer at least take a look?"

A sharp gust of wind nudges the church door open a little further. A second blast makes the bell in the tower ring. The men peer inside the building as the chimes echo around its walls.

"I didn't realize they still rang," says Zorzo.

Caspien takes another look about, before removing the central section of the tray to reveal a hidden compartment below, lined with velvet, and retrieves a box.

"Lazurite," he whispers, prizing open the lid. "Ultramarine, of the finest pedigree, from the Kokcha mines in Afghanistan."

The hairs on the back of Zorzo's neck lift at the sight: the unmistakably luxurious blue of ground lapis lazuli. This is no pretend pigment, no plant dye or ground glass. But there's barely any left.

"It's all I have," says Caspien. "But I can give it to you for fifty."

"Fifty? That's what I have to spend on everything. Fifty for such a small amount?"

He tips the box to the light and the lapis tumbles like liquid treasure.

"As you're a friend," Caspien says, "I'll throw in a packet of red chalk too, the same that Leonardo uses."

Zorzo calculates in his head. With fifty *soldi*, he could buy a whole palette of colors at any of the material shops in the city and still have enough to pay at least a couple of his bills. But sense has nothing to do with it. The ultramarine cannot be denied. He takes out his purse, counts the money and hands it over.

"Someone is coming." Caspien flinches. "Give me your purse."

Two men approach from the dark part of the island, walking toward the church. Caspien deposits the coins and Zorzo's purse in the box, locks it and draws a dagger from his belt. The strangers don't break their stride or change their course, and only stop when they see there are people on the porch. Zorzo, now at full height, is a head taller than the others. He draws Otto toward him and for a short while they all stand in silence.

"Good evening," says Caspien, keeping his dagger out of sight.

They're militia men, bearded and rough, and are carrying swords, almost certainly army deserters taking refuge on the outer islands, lying low until they've been forgotten.

"If you've come for evening prayers," Caspien nods at the broken door, "you've arrived two centuries late."

They glance at Otto, and then down at the trunk.

"We come for shelter," says one of the men.

"Well, be our guests." Caspien motions toward the church. Still the men linger, five sets of eyes trained on the trunk.

"It is just painting equipment," says Otto, stepping into the light, pointing in turn to Zorzo and Caspien. "This man sells pigments and this one paints with them."

One of the men nods and they slope into the church. Zorzo looks at Otto with renewed admiration—no wonder Caspien keeps him close: how could anyone make trouble in the face of such a boy?

Caspien waits until they're out of earshot before resheathing his dagger. "I take back my words," he says. "Let us resume in the hostelry. There is safety in numbers, perhaps." He unlocks the box and retrieves Zorzo's purse. "Your money, sir." He weighs it in his hand before handing it over. "You're richer than you make out."

"I have a whole satchel of bills that says otherwise."

"Of course, of course." Caspien removes his cap and runs his hand through his matted hair, lost in thought for a moment, then he says, buoyantly, "I was almost forgetting. I have a story to tell you, *mein Freund*. A secret that will entrance you. About a color that no one has ever seen, one that could be even more precious than ultramarine. Shall we go to the inn so I can tell you about it?"

"What do you mean, a color no one has ever seen?"

"I mean exactly that."

This is of interest to Zorzo. Another blast of wind, mightier than ever, sends the bells ringing once more. The tolls drift out across the island and he shivers. He studies his associate carefully before narrowing his eyes in a smile.

"Lead the way."

2

Prince Orient

"Go down to the pier," Caspien says to Otto, "and keep a lookout." For other clients, he means. Zorzo knows his colleague often makes arrangements with several people when he visits Poveglia.

Inside, the men install themselves on a settle close to the fire. There's a friendlier atmosphere than before: the men who'd been arguing are gone, candles have been lit and a party of locals are celebrating the birth of a child. Caspien buys half a bottle of his favorite Black Sea brandy and pours two cups, drinking his own down in one. He gasps at the strength of it, grins and fills his cup again.

"Have you heard of prince orient?" he says.

"No." Zorzo holds the drink to his mouth, enough to feel its heat. "Who is he?"

"Not who, but what. 'He' is a mineral. And a color. From

the Lusatian Mountains in Bohemia. Rare beyond belief. Even lapis cannot compare."

"And what is the color?"

Caspien studies his palms for a moment. "I know you say your funds are low, but you'll not want to miss out on this." Zorzo doesn't follow at first. "Any information I give you could turn out to have great value. The color could not only make you rich, but famous too."

Zorzo laughs. "No, Caspien, I cannot. The money that's left in my purse is to live on. I have mouths to feed—"

"You're married now?"

"What?"

"And children?"

Zorzo looks caught out. "Children? No."

"I didn't think so," Caspien chuckles. "A career bachelor."

The comment is good-natured enough, but it gives Zorzo an uncomfortable prickle, a buried longing being dredged up into the light. "What I meant was I need the money for my staff, for my premises." He pats his bag of bills. "Venice is not a cheap place to live." He looks out toward the city, a blur of campanili in the mist. He needs to get back, to see his black pigments, and get to the banquet. Zorzo downs his brandy and holds his breath against the sting. "How much?"

"I think—another fifty is fair."

"Fifty? Are you mad? No."

"It could earn you a thousand times more."

"I can't give you what I don't have."

"Forty, then."

"Twenty is my limit."

"Thirty and it's yours."

"What is the color?" Caspien keeps his lips shut tight and offers a sympathetic shrug. Knowing he'll capitulate sooner rather than later, Zorzo empties what remains in his purse into his palm. "I should be locked in a madhouse," he says. "Tell me."

Caspien loosens his belt and angles the seat a little closer to the fire. "There's a mine, as I said, in the Lusatian Mountains, a week's journey southeast of Dresden. They began digging it almost two centuries ago. The hills around it are loaded with copper and silver, and this mine proved successful too, at first. They discovered a mineral—close to the surface—not a metal, a rock, like azurite but harder still, hard as diamonds: prince orient. I don't know who first realized its property of color, or how it came by its unusual name—but some weeks after the first haul had been brought up, and they dug down further, miners began to be taken ill." Caspien lays his fingertips on his throat.

"Ill?"

"Peculiar maladies, so go the accounts. Slurred speech, numbness, seizures. They started to die, a few to begin with, but soon dozens, every man and boy that had been down that mine."

"I beg your pardon?" Zorzo puts up his palm to stop Caspien from going on. "This is the mineral for which you have taken my money?"

"No, no," Caspien says hastily, "it wasn't the prince orient. Absolutely not. You see, while digging, they ruptured a seam of quicksilver, which under particular conditions makes a vapor of itself. It's murder to inhale. Nowadays we can explain such a thing, but superstition ruled back then and they believed they'd disturbed the devil. They threw back the haul of precious mineral—except for a small quantity that had already been sold on, which I'll come to presently—and closed up the mine. For nearly two hundred years it lay beneath the ground, winter after bitter winter, forgotten about—until just a year ago."

"And what happened then?" asks Zorzo.

"The mine—indeed, the whole stretch of mountains—fell into the hands of a wealthy merchant from Augsburg, a speculator, an exceedingly rich fellow. His men discovered the abandoned shaft, opened it up and began quarrying once more. The quicksilver must have evaporated over time, for no one has grown ill. They dig there now without peril."

"And who is he, this *exceedingly* rich speculator?"

Caspien peers about the room from beneath his brow—if he were not a traveling merchant, he would surely be an actor—and answers in a low tone, "He is called Jakob Fugger. Do you know him?"

"The banker? I know the name, of course."

"Banks, yes, but mines too, scores of them, nearly every one on this continent and a dozen further afield. He owns iron, copper, silver—and, of course, prince orient."

"Fugger," Zorzo repeats to himself and wonders why his name does not come up more often. In Zorzo's studio—in the studio of every painter in Italy—the names of Europe's powerful financiers are never far from anyone's lips.

"You must have heard of his wife, in your line of work: Sybille Artzi."

"Why?"

"I thought you painters hunted down beauty like they do lions in Egypt. She's a Helen of Troy for our age. A face, they say, that could start a war. Anyway, they've recently bought a palazzo in Venice, and they're on their way to visit it, crossing the Alps as we speak." Caspien holds up his palms for effect. "So good luck."

"Good luck?"

"Making contact with him."

Zorzo waits to hear the rest, but nothing comes. "That is all the information you mean to give me?"

"Rich information," says Caspien. "You have the name of a man, you know where he'll presently be, in your own city, and you have information about a priceless substance."

Zorzo takes a deep breath and exhales. He can't believe he's paid for such a pittance. "So why don't you search him out yourself, if this substance is so precious?"

"I'm wanted in Venice, *mein Freund*, I've told you dozens of times." Caspien pours himself what remains in the bottle. "I don't understand you at all, Herr Barbarelli. I hand you a treasure and you bite my hand."

"What about everyone else you've handed your treasure to for thirty *soldi* apiece? I can't be the only one you've told. You said you've just been in Rome. Were you visiting your prize client?" Caspien has already dropped the name of the famous painter, as he usually does. "You would have told him first."

"If you mean Michelangelo," Caspien purrs, "he is there and you are here."

"But you've told him?"

"I repeat, you are fortunate, Herr Barbarelli: you have a start on the rest. And Venice is your city."

Zorzo laughs. "Truly I am a fool. The rest? How many?"

"One or two. Don't ask for names, for I shall not part with them. But I'll tell you this: if you discover a new color in this age, in this shining new world of ours, your name is made across it. More than that: it is made across time. Imagine, men and women five centuries from now will speak of Zorzo Barbarelli and his miraculous prince orient. What pictures you will conjure! And you deserve it, *mein Freund*—I heard you have talent. Great promise, they say."

Zorzo is taken by surprise. He's forgotten that Caspien has never seen any of his work. Great promise: that most unrewarding of compliments. He wants to remind Caspien that at twenty-four he was selected to paint the doge himself, who famously claimed at the time, "Giorgione records the very atmosphere and temperature of life."

"Well, put me out of my misery," Zorzo replies instead. "What is this astonishing color?"

Caspien draws out another of his dramatic pauses. "That's just the thing. I have no idea."

"What?"

"But I do know the word *color* does it no justice. It changes the very way you see. By all accounts, it has more in common with light." He makes a flourish with his hand. "With *starlight*, they say." He slaps his thigh. "I'm forgetting. The best part of the story. As I told you, when the mine was first dug, two centuries past, a small quantity of the pigment was sold on before the hole was closed up."

"And?"

"That little batch of pigment was acquired by a renowned artist of those times, *exceedingly* renowned: none other than Giotto di Bondone."

"Giotto, really?"

"In Padua he painted some famous murals, no?"

"The Scrovegni Chapel."

"That's it. He used the color there, just once. I believe there are dozens of murals in that church, but he used it in just one of them, a picture of Bethlehem that has a star tracing across the sky. Do you know it?"

"Intimately. I know all the Scrovegni murals. Like every other painter in Italy, I copied them as an apprentice. And wondrous as they are, as the one you mention is, I recall no color within it that changed the very way I see."

"Oh, my good fellow," Caspien laughs. "Aren't those pictures ancient? Isn't time the cruel mistress? She took it away. That, or some thief removed it for himself. But find it again. Find it for all of us. Do it, *mein Freund*, for mankind."

Otto appears. "Someone's arriving," he says, gesturing toward the pier. "Come."

Caspien goes out with the boy and Zorzo follows.

A faint golden light is approaching across the water: a boat lantern that in the afternoon mist seems like an apparition, a young god or goddess advancing in spectral form. Then comes the rhythmic cutting of oars and the barge emerges. It's grand, certainly for Poveglia, with a closed cabin at its center and a team of oarsmen, two at the prow, two at the aft. Caspien smiles: money is arriving.

Zorzo realizes he knows the boat too: it belongs to Giovanni Bellini, one of the brothers he apprenticed for when he first came to Venice. It draws up beside the tumbledown quay and a pair of sailors jump ashore to secure it. The cabin awning is pulled back, revealing Bellini—now eighty—and another man who disembarks onto the pier and busies himself brushing down his velvet cape. Like every painter in Venice, Zorzo knows Vittore di Fonti—and braces himself for some acerbic bon mot to come his way.

Di Fonti has one of those professions that can't easily be explained. He's not an artist but he works with them, as an agent of sorts, a facilitator between patron and those they employ. He's recently become an adviser at the ducal palace for "matters of beauty," as he puts it. It's bad enough that his taste is old-fashioned, that he likes his art to be ornate and decorative; worse, though, he's a snob who is kind only to people who might better his position—a trait that Zorzo abhors.

"Good evening," Zorzo says, knowing he can hardly avoid talking to di Fonti. "We have picked fine weather for Poveglia."

Di Fonti holds his hand up to his face, as if a light were shining in it. "Who is that?"

"Giorgio Barbarelli, sir, Zorzo as some call me, Giorgione others."

Di Fonti pauses a moment at the end of the pier, like some giant, self-regarding raven, before giving the faintest of nods. "Signor."

"What cargo do you bring?" asks Zorzo. "Is it who I think it is, the young Bellini?" The question is amiable, but di Fonti treats it with suspicion, so Zorzo adds, "We are old acquaintances. I used to grind his pigments once. I shall bid him hello."

"Best not to," di Fonti cuts in. "The signor is out of sorts. The rough seas and—the weather as you say. Added to which we are late."

Di Fonti hardly has the power to stop him, but Zorzo is in no mood for polite war. He nods, picks up his holdall, throws it over his shoulder and calls to his boatman, "Tullo, we're leaving at last." Before he goes, he collars Caspien and whispers, "Just tell me this: is it true, honestly, your story?"

"Why would I make up such a thing?"

"I can't imagine," Zorzo replies with sarcasm.

"No, no, I swear it on the boy's life."

"And on your own?"

"On that too, for what it is worth. And here is your red chalk." He pushes the packet into Zorzo's hand. "You see how kind I am?"

"Where's this palace Fugger's bought?" Zorzo's determined to squeeze every last fragment of information from his supplier.

"I don't know, truly," says Caspien.

"And you're going to sell this information to Bellini too? I can't stop you?"

"My dear *Freund*, he's triple your age. Vigor wins this prize."

As Zorzo's about to embark, Otto steps forward. "Sir, your doublet." But there's something about the way the boy looks up at him, holding out the coat with both hands, as though it's a precious relic, which makes Zorzo's heart plunge. The words come out before he's thought about them: "Why don't you keep it until I see you again? I have plenty of others at home." This is not true: he has two more at most, and one of them so shabby he only uses it for traveling.

"It's for him, do you hear me?" he says to Caspien. "And the money I gave you—buy your boy a feast. He deserves it. Let your conscience make you." He jumps aboard the gondola. "Back to San Marco," he smiles at Tullo, "and quickly."

As the boat casts off into the lagoon, Zorzo watches Caspien climb down into Bellini's golden barge with his trunk of materials. Through the curtain, Zorzo can see him open it; Bellini leans forward to look and the reflection of pigments touch upon his ancient face. How marvelous, Zorzo thinks, in the name of color, even at eighty, he still has the spirit to ride out to Poveglia on a squally afternoon.

"Ultramarine!" comes the cry from the boat. He says it like an old general might shout, *"To war!"*

3

The Red House

Going back across the lagoon to the city, Zorzo tries to calculate how many people Caspien might have sold his secret to. Two or three? Half a dozen? More? He might have told every painter in Rome and Florence on his way here. He might offer Bellini even more information than he had Zorzo. Caspien, for all his eccentricity, is enamored of fame. He never seems particularly interested in art itself, never talks of actual paintings, but his eyes come alive when recounting how kings and emperors are pursuing one of his clients, as if Caspien himself were the main agent of success.

"Prince orient," he whispers to himself. The idea of the undiscovered pigment has set his mind racing. The secret mine, the magnate, the connection with Giotto di Bondone. Throughout his life, ultramarine has been the most prized, the incomparable, the king of colors. All the rest have been just background to the main event of a picture: the lapis of St. Peter's robe in Mantegna's *Agony in the Garden*, or da Vinci's spectral lagoon in his *Madonna of the Caves*. Caspien is right: discovering a color greater than ultramarine would make a person famous overnight.

"Prince orient." Zorzo wonders where in the spectrum it might lie. Its name speaks of undiscovered lands and strange, brilliant light. It could be coral, amber or rose-pink, the hue of a Persian sunrise. It could have the honey or cinnamon tones of endlessly repeating dunes, or the vivid cerulean of heat-baked skies. Or perhaps it belongs to the night, to the star-filled orient sky, or to electric winds that ease across the desert. Zorzo is sure that prince orient must be complex, not a bright "throw-away color," as Bellini calls them, buttercup yellow, tangerine or lime green, hues that for all their flashiness have no personality.

Zorzo's home—comprising his workshop and living rooms, as well as quarters for a handful of staff—occupies the north-east corner of Campo San Francesco della Vigna, in the district of Castello, at the tail end of Venice. He arrives back to find all his apprentices have spilled out onto the street, and everyone shouting at once.

Uggo, the thirteen-year-old who keeps watch over the front door during the day and sleeps just inside it at night, is, as always, the loudest. "Give it back to me! Give it back now," he's demanding in his husky, newly broken voice, locking horns—chest out, biceps flexed—with a man twice his size and age, a bailiff that Zorzo has met before. The man has one hand raised against Uggo and holds a portrait behind his back with the other, the piece that Zorzo is currently working on, for which the blacks were being mixed. Other items from the workroom—busts, plaster casts, a metal rule and assorted pieces of furniture—have been thrown into a cart. Two more fellows, the bailiff's assistants, who must witness scenes like this every day, are leaning against it, half amused by the ranting youth, half fed up.

"What's going on here?" Zorzo demands.

"These men came to remove your chattels, sir," Uggo says, panting. "I told them over and over they had to wait for you but they barged in anyway. And then they took that, sir, our portrait, Count Lippi's daughter, and I said it was private property and they must give it back. Paulino tried to reason with them and they thanked him by giving him a punch on the nose."

"What?" Zorzo hadn't seen Paulino behind everyone else and goes to speak to him. He's a pale, dark-haired lad of seventeen, the most delicate of Zorzo's four young apprentices, now more startled than ever. He holds his nose, from which there's a trickle of blood.

"I'm sorry, sir," he says. "I got in the way. It wasn't the gentleman's fault."

"There is nothing to be sorry about. You're braver than us all. Where's Janek?"

"He's upstairs." Then quietly, so the bailiffs won't hear, "Keeping guard over the other canvases."

Zorzo notices Teodor, usually the cockiest of his *garzoni*, and Tulipano, the tallest, are both skulking in the shadows. He turns back to the bailiff. "Signor Rosso, isn't it?"

"Yes," the bailiff says, caught out by the fact Zorzo remembers his name.

"I'd like to say it was nice to see you again, but..." He gestures at the scene. "Do you have the writ with you, regarding my debt?" Rosso produces a now battered sheet of paper and hands it over. "It says here," Zorzo reads, "'removal of goods *only* belonging to the debtor.' You see?" Zorzo shows him. "That painting categorically does not belong to me. It has been paid for and is owned by Count Lippi. That's his daughter you have in your hands. The count is not a man I think any of us would like to quarrel with."

The name seems to spook the bailiff a little, but not enough for him to hand back the canvas. "We just collect. That's what we're told to do."

The comedy of the situation, of men literally fighting over Espettia Lippi, as spoiled and charmless a young girl as Zorzo has ever met, is not lost on him. "Listen here," he says to Rosso, taking him to one side. "I'll do a deal with you." He goes to take the ring from his finger and gets a shock when he finds it gone, before remembering he hid it in Poveglia. He retrieves it from his pocket and, making sure none of his *garzoni* can see, places it in his palm. "This is a sapphire from Kashmir. You can't see in this light, but it's royal blue, the best color the stone can be. It is worth twenty times more than what you've packed in your cart." Actually, it is much more than valuable: it is the only heirloom ever to have trickled down through Zorzo's threadbare, now nonexistent family. "I hold on to the rest, and to the canvas in your hand; you keep the sapphire for a fortnight, as a guarantee. If I have not settled my bill by then, with interest, it is yours."

The other fellows have come to look over the bailiff's shoulder and Zorzo frames it in his eye as a painting, three greedy sets of eyes trained on a blue jewel in a hard-up painter's hand. "As you wish," the bailiff says, scooping it up. "I'll give you a receipt."

As Zorzo waits for it to be filled out, he holds himself steady against the shame of the occasion, keeping upright but loose, to signal to his *garzoni* that problems like this are easily overcome. Although he wonders if they think less of their master, or worse, feel sorry for him. Receipt in hand, he follows everyone back into the house.

It has three stories, is at least a hundred years old and constructed from small red bricks, not unknown in Venice, but uncommon enough for the building to stand out. The *red house* is how Zorzo refers to it when he's giving directions to people. The square in front of it, usually quiet at this time of year, gets busy in the summer, being one of the few open spaces in the quarter. Then, Zorzo's men often work outside and the paintings—at various degrees of completion—are left against the walls to dry in the sun. Zorzo loves watching the faces of locals, who might never possess a canvas in their life, studying them, as if they were some unimaginable breed of thing. He encourages his men to entice them to enter the red house, even when—especially when—they wouldn't be able to afford anything on view. The ground floor is given over to storerooms and a dormitory. The first floor, double the height of the ground, houses both Zorzo's *studiolo* and the main workroom, which extends the whole depth of the building.

Zorzo ascends to it and pauses on the threshold a moment, casting his eye around the room. His apprentices are clearing up and putting the taken items back in their places. At once the edifice of his career seems precarious, on the point of disintegrating to nothing. It doesn't matter that he's worked and worked since childhood, is considered successful, that he has a workshop of his own, where apprentices are willing to come and learn from him, as he did with Bellini. He knows most artists only just get by. They lug their work to market in a cart and sell it for a pittance, do odd jobs painting chests or shop signs, cling to foolish hope, while knowing, deep down, they'll almost certainly be obscure forever. However much Zorzo tries to convince himself he's a class above, the hard truth has just been demonstrated outside his front door. He has no leeway with his finances, no dependable patron to bail him out, nor parents or siblings to borrow from. Worst of all: if he fails, so does everyone in the room. The fear of this never stops ticking through him.

"Are you all right, sir?" asks Janek, the workshop's foreman. He's sturdy, in every way, and while all the other *garzoni* are young, he's thirty-four—a year older than Zorzo—but seems more.

Zorzo gives a smile. "If Signor Rosso and his men had thought of confiscating our pigments," he nods to the shelves where jars of color are stacked to the ceiling, "he'd have done better than an old plaster cast of Hermes and a measuring rule." He stops, turns to one of his boys, the cocky one, who has started plucking a tune on a lute. "Our situation is dramatic, Teodor, but let's leave the musical accompaniment for now."

"Sorry, sir." Teodor puts down the instrument. He's a good-looking lad, with smoky eyes, who fancies himself as a younger version of his master. He has talent but is the laziest of the bunch.

"I need you to find me something," Zorzo says to him. "In one of the cabinets, there's a series of drawings of the Scrovegni Chapel. Do you know which I mean?"

"The Giottos, sir?"

"Precisely. There should be at least a dozen. Find the one of the Nativity in Bethlehem, with the shooting star. Actually, bring them all." Teodor sets to it and Zorzo turns to everyone else. "Do any of you know of Jakob Fugger, the banker from Augsburg? Janek?"

"Fugger, Fugger," the foreman says, trying to look knowledgeable. He's a brilliant manager of workshop logistics but has barely left the streets of Castello, let alone Venice itself.

"I know a little about him, sir." Paulino nods, blushing at being the only one who does. "I believe he owns mines."

"Exactly. I'm told he's bought a palazzo in Venice. That he's coming here with his wife. Tulipano, can you find out?" Zorzo says to a third boy, an excessively tall and skinny youth, nearly double the height of his twin sister, Azalea, at the adjacent working area. "You're the best informed about society's comings and goings." The twins hail from a family that goes right back to the beginnings of the republic, and though they've since lost status, and certainly fortune, Tulipano in particular has a wide-ranging knowledge of the city. "Go to the Archivio Marciano, if you still have your contact there. Find out what you can about Jakob Fugger in Venice. Where his palazzo is, *if* he has a palazzo. Note down anything else of interest, but keep it to yourself, understood?"

"Of interest, sir?"

"Anything—how old, how many children he has, any painters who have been in his employment, information about his mines, his businesses, anything at all. And find out about his wife, Sybille. If only our success was just about painting, eh?" He turns back to the rest, smile still in place, though the shock of the bailiffs is still turning through him. "Now, to the exciting business. I bring a little treasure from Poveglia."

He takes the packets from his pocket, sets them out on the desk and everyone presses forward to look. First he unwraps the sticks of chalk, which are a rich, velvety red, as they should be, the color a vivid encapsulation of the earth from which it's dug. He carefully undoes the other packet. He almost laughs at the sight of the ultramarine: it's so profoundly blue. "That's more like it." They all squeeze in to get a closer look. "Though I wish there was more."

"May I?" says the girl, Azalea. Zorzo lets her come forward to study the pigment at close hand. "Incredible," she says. "There's enough there for a robe or a cloak," she suggests, before borrowing one of Zorzo's own phrases. "That alone can transform a painting."

"Paulino, have you got the blacks ready for me?" Zorzo asks.

"Yes, sir, here." He indicates five little piles of pigment in front of the window.

"Azalea, bring the painting," Zorzo orders. "Let's see them together."

She brings over the small canvas that the bailiff had removed and places it on an easel: the bust of a young lady, almost complete except for the hands in the foreground, which are little more than sketched.

"There she is, our dear Espettia, back from the wars." Zorzo grins, though he can't stop his heart from sinking. The portrait is smaller than anything he's done, ever, not just in size but in ambition. "A compact picture is what we desire," the count said when he interviewed Zorzo to make a likeness of his daughter, who had reached marrying age. "I'm not as wealthy as you might think." Zorzo wanted to explain that small was not necessarily less time-consuming, sometimes the opposite, but knew also he was not Lippi's first choice. Before Zorzo even picked up a brush, Lippi drove him half-mad with the contract: demanding precise stipulations of painting style, the amount of detail to be used, the expression on the face, date of completion, late penalties and on and on. More challenges came when Zorzo turned up for Espettia's sittings in the Lippis' dark and drafty palazzo in Santa Croce. She complained about everything and behaved despicably both to Zorzo's helpers and her own staff. He had to have music played to calm her down.

He put it all to one side, to keep his *garzoni*'s spirits up. He threw himself into the job, resolving to make a success of it, to give the young woman character even as she's spoiled and empty-headed. Zorzo can see now it hasn't worked. For sure, he's managed to paint away her sullenness, her resolute plainness, but he's gone too far. She looks livid, if anything, with an angry kick behind the eye. The only really interesting thing about the canvas is how the waning light through the workshop's diamond windowpanes shines against it in geometric patterns—but they'll be gone in an instant.

"So this is the bone black here?" he asks Paulino, pointing to the darkest of the piles.

"Yes, sir."

"And this the charcoal?"

"Yes, and this the walnut, the licorice, the Anubis and the ebony. These last two here are also charcoal."

"I see." Zorzo is disappointed. He tests the strength of the pigments by rubbing them hard on his fingertips, blotting the multicolored stains already there. None are right, none have the intense, velvet blackness he's after.

"I appreciate it's hard to choose," Paulino says. "They're all so completely different."

Zorzo nearly laughs at how earnest Paulino is, about seven

miniature piles that would look identical to anyone who wasn't in the business. Paulino takes everything seriously, too much so, perhaps. He spends nights at study, trying to make sense of geometry: perspective and vanishing points, Pythagoras, Thales, Archimedes—teachings that Zorzo has little understanding of himself—the properties of circles and pyramids, Euclidean practice and axiomatic forms. And it gives Zorzo no satisfaction at all that despite Paulino's excessive laborings, he is nowhere near as gifted as the wastrel, Teodor.

"Good work," Zorzo says to him. "We'll use the bone as a base, but I don't think we're there yet. The gloves must be so black, so pitch, that the shadows between the fingers are lighter than the rest. Does that make sense?" Nods of agreement. Espettia hadn't worn gloves to her first sitting, but Zorzo had suggested them, as he thought they might add allure, especially with her large ring worn over them. "In any case," he indicates the chosen pigment, "we'll need three times that amount. By morning, all right? And the sapphire in her signet ring." He points to its sketched outline. "We were going to use cobalt. I daresay she doesn't deserve it, but let's grind some of Caspien's lapis instead—just a touch, a little treat for the eyes. Everyone understand? Good. I need to get ready for the Ca' d'Oro." There are murmurs of assent. They know about the banquet Zorzo's attending. All week there's been talk of the Contarinis and the luck the night may bring.

"Sir?" says Paulino. "Could I just say?" He lowers his voice to a whisper. "I hope you don't mind, but I saw what you did." He nods at Zorzo's hand, at the band of light pink flesh where the ring used to be. "I know how precious it is to you. You will get it back, won't you?"

"Of course I shall." He pats Paulino's shoulder, while crumbling a little inside: there's no guarantee he'll see his sapphire again. None either that his workshop will still be running by the end of the year.

He goes to his study next door, which has doubled up as his makeshift bedroom for two years, washes, wipes down his breeches and changes into the best of his two remaining doublets. He empties a bucket out of the window, of water that has leaked through the building from the broken roof above his old bedroom. He goes back to the workroom, thumbs through the sketches he made in Poveglia, of the warrior in the underworld, and chooses the most successful one.

"It's Aeneas. I hadn't even realized until I'd finished drawing it," he says to Janek, who's peering over his shoulder. "It's not bad at all, if I say so myself, even drawn on the back of an invoice. I'm going to try and sell an idea to Signor Contarini. Then we won't need to be disturbed by bailiffs again."

"Sir, the copies of Giotto's murals," Teodor says, appearing with the folder as Zorzo's about to exit. "The one of Bethlehem is first."

"Good, I'll look on my way."

He puts the sketch of Aeneas on top and ties the folio. "Wish me luck, everyone." He exits and hurtles down to the hall. "I'm gone again, my defender in chief," he says to Uggo, scruffing his hair.

"Someone has to be," the boy returns, "with all your faint-hearted painters upstairs." He does an impression and Zorzo's happy to see Uggo back to his old self again, ready to be saucy.

As he heads up the darkening street, Zorzo wonders if Otto would be as amusing if he worked for him and not Caspien.

4

The Bone Queen

Rather than heading straight for the Ca' d'Oro, he goes north, at double speed, to see Leda. He doesn't really have time, but he feels guilty that he's not taking her to the banquet. For him, the evening is work, about making connections, and he wouldn't be able to concentrate with her at his side. However, Caspien's phrase has lurked like a bad smell in his mind since Poveglia. "A career bachelor," he called Zorzo, laughing off the idea that he might have got married. The fact he hasn't has become more and more uncomfortable. People assume he likes to be a bachelor, because he's a convincing one; but really he'd like to mirror his own parents' marriage. They were wed at seventeen and laughed every day, until his mother was taken by sleeping fever when Zorzo was ten and then his father nine years later. They'd wanted a dozen children but managed just one. Zorzo has always hoped to make up the shortfall.

Leda's house is tall and narrow and rises from a lightless canal between the Jewish quarter and the slummish northern ports.

"How are you, Hakim?" he says to her steward, who lets him in. "Is she here? Upstairs?"

Hakim nods and Zorzo cuts through the long ground-floor room where Leda stores her merchandise and ascends to the parlor, which doubles up as her office.

"A surprise visit." He grins, coming in to find her at her desk, counting money. She's already organized five neat stacks from a pile of many dozens of coins and is halfway through the sixth.

"Shh," she says, pausing. "I'll forget. Sit." She continues her count and Zorzo kisses her cheek. "Open the window." She fans her hand against her face.

"Counting money always gets you burning with excitement."

She pauses to give him a reproachful look, then continues. Zorzo unclasps the window latch, pushes it open and looks down the length of the canalway toward the leaning bell tower at the end. He feels as if he's come to say something significant but doesn't quite know what it is.

"What are you doing here, Signor Barbarelli?" she says, starting on a new stack. "A meeting was not agreed for this evening... eight, nine, ten. Nor were you permitted to look so handsome. What is this finery you appear in? A new coat? Are you making money?" She's seen the coat before, Zorzo's certain, but she never misses a chance to be casually dismissive of his profession, of what he gets up to all day. He doesn't mind, though; in fact, he often finds the trait appealing. "Anyway, I've no time for you," she goes on, making a note in her ledger and starting on a new stack of coins. "People are arriving any moment, gentlemen from the navy. I am this close to winning the commission. Buttons for five hundred sailors' tunics."

She's one of barely a handful of women merchants in the city and probably the only one to have built up her business from scratch, rather than inherit from parents or a dead husband. She came from Cyprus. “A lot of olives, a lot of hay,” was all she said about her life there. At sixteen she left, set sail from her homeland in the clothes she was wearing, making all sorts of “improper sacrifices”—as she grimly put it—to get to Venice. “Now I have a palazzo in Cannaregio,” she frequently boasts, stretching the truth, “a dozen men working for me, in the foremost city of the world. But I arrived without a tin pot to my name.” Her business, the production of fastenings for clothes, from hooks to eyelets to laces, took toil to establish and she had to have a thick skin throughout.

Zorzo met her by accident when his boat collided with hers two years ago. He was certain it was the fault of her boatmen—she had a team of men punting at double speed—but she was so dramatic about it, so outraged, he smiled and took the blame. Even after they became lovers, she'd pestered him until he paid for the repair work in full.

Zorzo doesn't know who christened her the *bone queen*, a foreman in her manufactory, perhaps, or one of the shippers she works with. She uses bone to make buttons, of course, but the inference is that the bone came from the remains of the men who crossed her.

She finishes her count, unhooks a ring of keys from her belt (she always wears them, even sometimes to bed), unlocks a credenza, deposits the stacks of coins among the neatly stacked bundles already there, locks it again and makes a final entry into the ledger. “So,” she says, turning to him. “I have half an hour. What would you do with me?” She presses her fingertips into the back of her skull and combs them forward through her hair.

Afterward, lying in bed with Leda, Zorzo feels disappointed in himself. He didn't come for sex, no matter how intense it is, her dress hitched up, his trousers yanked down, her surprising climax coming before his. He listens to a boat passing outside, the echo of oars between Leda's building and the next, and as it disappears around the corner, he wonders if he has time now to bring up the subject of their future. If not to get married—and Zorzo can see no reason why they shouldn't—at least agree they're traveling in that direction. He glances at his bare finger, where his father's ring was until earlier, and has an idea: when he gets it back, he can resize it and give it to her as proof of his commitment.

"Signora, the gentlemen are here," calls a voice from the adjacent room.

Leda claps and jumps out of bed. "Tell them I'll be right down." She goes back to the parlor, over to the mirror glass, tidies her hair and straightens her corset, before liberally powdering her cheeks. She's always been self-conscious of her olive skin in a city besotted with pale complexions. "Wait for me?" she calls to Zorzo and hurries downstairs.

"No, I have to go." He doesn't know if she's heard him. He gets dressed and goes next door to inspect his reflection too. The mirror is Leda's most prized object, costing her a small fortune, but is of poor quality compared with what Zorzo's seen in some patrons' houses. He hardly recognizes the man in it. Hazy in the scratched surface of the mercury stands a specter from the future, an older man than he thinks he is. A quiet and shapeless feeling pools in his stomach. He's lonely. At once, the sensation is overwhelming: he's a family of one. A sole survivor.

He opens the folder he brought and studies the copy he made of Giotto's *Bethlehem*. Of the forty-odd murals in the Scrovegni Chapel, it was the one that first caught his young eye, so it's curious that the original—if Caspien is to be believed—may have contained prince orient. The scene itself is not unusual, a Nativity group at the manger; it's the fireball above that surprised Zorzo, the guiding star the Bible speaks of, which curves across the sky, not serenely, but like a war missile about to strike. He scans each color in the picture, trying to remind himself if any of them seemed out of the ordinary when he copied them.

He looks through the other renderings, all in color—the

wedding at Cana, the casting out of the money changers, Judas's betrayal—and thinks back to the moment he first saw the originals, at sixteen, the shock of color and light when he entered the chapel with his fellow apprentices. He was fascinated by how Giotto had been the original soldier of light two centuries ago, the first crusader, the man who turned his back on the Dark Ages; the first to draw directly from life, to give people breath and muscle, make landscape real, create atmosphere and movement. Before him, no one thought to depict mist, or a sunset, or the cold, let alone emotion. Even now, looking at his sketched copies, Zorzo can't believe how three-dimensional Giotto's characters are: people you'd find in any market square of Europe, gossiping, mocking, trudging through life. He can almost smell the sweat on them from the heat of Judea. The colors are muscular too, browns, ochers and umbers propagated from the earthiness of real life. None give a hint of the exotic, or carry a clue to prince orient.

He looks at the mirror again and wonders if the character of an actual prince gave the color its name. A traveler, perhaps, a desert wanderer. Or the sultan of a Moorish castle, a man of dark and ravishing secrets.

He hears footsteps ascend, not Leda's: they're hefty and forceful. They stop on the landing and a shadow stretches from the doorway.

"You in there?" a voice demands. It's deep and gravelly. There's a pause, before the door swings open and the man enters, stopping abruptly when he sees Zorzo. "Oh." He seems irritated to find a stranger and scowls. "Where is she?" He's maybe ten years older than Zorzo, rangy, perhaps rather self-regarding. His looks are on the turn. His eyes are baggy, lips fleshy and his breath reeks of brandy, even from the other side of the room. Over a dirty chemise, he wears a coat that trails to the floor, with a matted fur trim.

"Leda?" says Zorzo, and his heart races, though he doesn't

really know why. "Downstairs." Not knowing what else to say, he adds, "With the gentlemen from the navy."

"God almighty. Really? I'm late." His vein-laced cheeks turn the color of blood pudding, before a thought comes upon him. "Actually, it's probably for the best she doesn't know. I should be up the Brenta river by now." He gives a smile that reminds Zorzo of a pike fish, with its sharp, brown teeth. "I left something." He goes over to a chair, on the back of which a tunic hangs, obviously his, and he searches its pockets.

Zorzo is riven to the spot. The man doesn't ask who he is. He must assume that Zorzo is part of the household.

"Where is the damn thing?" the man hisses and tosses down the tunic, before going into Leda's bedroom and carrying on looking there, first scouting around the windowsill and then pulling back the covers of the bed. Zorzo tries to reason with himself that Leda is free to do as she wishes. If she has another lover, then that's the consequence of their particular type of relationship. All the same, bile creeps up from his stomach.

The man finds what he's looking for on the floor behind the bed and stands up again. Zorzo notices a tiny glint of gold as he squeezes a ring onto his chubby third finger. Zorzo resents the man for having it, for being careless of it, when he's just handed his own precious heirloom to the bailiffs. The man prowls back into the room and, knowing exactly where everything is, retrieves a bottle of liquor and a cup.

"You?" he says, shaking the bottle above his head but not turning to Zorzo.

"No, thank you."

The man pours a measure, knocks it back, slams down the cup and wipes his lips with the back of his hand. "You haven't seen me."

Zorzo wants to grab him by his shirt and demand to know who he is and what business he has with Leda.

The man goes to the door, but pauses at the threshold. "Do

you have family?" he says. Zorzo shakes his head. "Good for you. It has been decreed that I am a bad husband and father and as punishment I am to take my children fishing. No family? My advice? Keep it thus." He exits the room and thunders down the stairs, leaving his tunic behind.

Some minutes later, Zorzo collects his folder of drawings and goes down to find Leda. She's chatting to the two naval men, all smiles, taking samples from boxes, flirtatiously turning the weight of her hair from one side to the other.

"I have to go," Zorzo says blankly. "A man came. He'd left something. I think it was a wedding ring."

"Excuse me a moment?" she says to the men and comes over to Zorzo. "What is this?"

"He said he'd been a bad husband and father and was taking his children to the Brenta river, fishing. I don't know who he thought *I* was. He didn't ask."

"A wedding ring?"

He watches her carefully. Whatever faults Leda might have, being able to hide the truth from her face is not one of them. For some moments, she wrestles with how to proceed, but eventually her shoulders drop and Zorzo knows she's not going to deny anything. She gives him a sheepish smile and touches her fingers against his arm.

"It's all right. I'm a grown man," he says, looking at his paint-ingrained fingers, trying to keep hold of his emotion. "I'll survive."

"If it makes it any better, he and I were," she gives a coquettish shiver of her curls, "we were involved long before you."

"Why would that be better?" He stays in front of her, head cast down, not knowing how to say goodbye. He recalls the moment they first met, when their boats collided and Leda emerged from her awning like Cleopatra. "That was your fault, wasn't it?" she declared, and he fell immediately for the mischief in her eye.

"I have to go," he says to her now. "I'm expected at the Ca' d'Oro."

5

Men Who Own the World

The sight of the palazzo, lit up with torches, its pale reflection stretching clean across the Grand Canal, forces Zorzo to pull himself together and refocus his attention. Boats queue before the water steps, disgorging their cargo of moneyed Venetians. He cannot waste this evening. Now, more than ever, his face needs to be seen. He needs work. And he needs to get his ring back.

He washes the muck off his boots in the canal before entering the palazzo by the side door. The steward there doesn't recognize his name and Zorzo has to ask him to fetch Carlo Contarini. The man is hesitant, and eyes up Zorzo's clothes.

"I'm invited, I assure you," Zorzo has to say. "Carlo is a good friend."

"Wait here," orders the footman.

Zorzo looks down toward the kitchens where cooks and porters are rushing back and forth through clouds of steam. He's anxious now, like an actor waiting to go onstage. He braces himself for the complicated piece of theater that lies ahead, all the little maneuvers he'll have to make to get in front of the right people, into the right conversations. "Do you know the cardinal of this, the count of that, the duchess of so-and-so?" the chatter will go. "He owns half of Verona, he's the governor of Naples, he ships nutmeg from the Indies. Have you not met Giorgione? He painted the doge at twenty-four. You must have seen his *Tempest*? Ask him what it means." In front of a canvas, Zorzo is at peace, but a party is a battlefield and he never knows—even after they've finished—whether he's been on the winning or losing side.

"Here he is, finally," says Carlo, appearing. "We've been waiting for you. Come up." Zorzo feels even more underdressed; Carlo, always ahead of fashion, wears an olive-green doublet with puffed sleeves that are cut all over in tiny pink slashes.

"Waiting for me, really?" He's flattered, and thinks the evening might at least end better than it started.

"Yes, we need some attractive faces around here," Carlo says. "You should see the cadavers my father's dug up. Accountants and politicians. Did you bring it?"

"What?"

"Your lute," says Carlo. Zorzo is confused and wonders if he's missed something. "Didn't I say?" asks Carlo. "Never mind, we'll find you one."

"You want me to play tonight?"

"You don't mind, do you?" Carlo makes it sound like more of a threat than a question. "Besides, the ladies will love you for it. You know how much they pine for our tall Giorgio." Attendants file past with full platters: quail and pigeon with sugar coating, roasted peacock decorated with its own plumage.

"I'll do what I can," says Zorzo. "As long as I have time to speak to your father."

"What on earth for?"

"I have a proposal for him." He pats his folder. "I'm hoping he might commission me again. A companion piece to the painting he has."

Carlo laughs. "Good luck with that. You know what a miser he is?" He goes into the salon and Zorzo follows.

The supreme of Venetian society are there, at dinner, at play, at diplomacy, in a room that stretches the entire width of the palazzo's *piano nobile*. Zorzo spies Signora Contarini, Carlo's mother, all smiling teeth, in an ink-black gown.

"Remind me," Zorzo says, "the party is in honor of...?"

"The son of the sultan of Hejaz, our esteemed guest for the week. Father has dealings with Hejaz—highly profitable ones—and he's spared no expense." Carlo laughs. "Of course, until the son of the sultan arrived no one knew he was twelve." Carlo indicates a boy in white at the far end of the room, standing in polite bemusement with a retinue of older courtiers.

"You'll be up there." Carlo points to a dais on one side of the chamber where other musicians are playing. "By all means, do your horse trading first."

"How much do you know about Jakob Fugger?" Zorzo asks.

"*The* Jakob Fugger? Well, obviously I hate him."

"Why?"

"For being richer than God and making us all as jealous as hell. Of course I've never actually met the fellow."

"You know he has a house in Venice now? That he's on his way here?"

"No and no. But thank you. I'll have to hunt him down and hear how he does it, conquers the world *sans pareil.* Watch out, Mother's looking this way. I'd better perform some duties."

"Can you tell me some more about him later? I'm as keen as you are to meet him."

"Agreed." He claps Zorzo about the shoulders. "And you'll be paid for your services. I wouldn't like you to think I was taking advantage." He disappears into the crowd and moments later he's laughing with someone.

Zorzo wonders why they're friends. He wonders if they're friends at all. They come across each other here and there and mostly the young noble seems very pleased when they do, giving the impression he looks up to Zorzo, who is five or six years older. "How did you get so handsome?" Carlo often says. Or "Look how the ladies pretend not to look at you, all of them." He appears occasionally at a late hour and insists Zorzo accompany him on some adventure. They might spend all night laughing and drinking, and Carlo might declare undying friendship, only to forget all about it when their paths next cross.

Zorzo takes a cup of wine and as he lifts it to drink, the aroma catches him by surprise: there's no hint of the one-note acidic drafts he's used to. When he drinks, it tastes royal. He circulates in search of the host, and to see if the painting he sold to him three years ago, the *Birth of Paris*, is on show. He observes how different a room of wealthy people feels from the type of room he's used to, or to the inn on Poveglia; how heavy fabrics deepen the sound and how the colors of cloth—vermilion, orchil, dark indigo, cherry red, pearl and madder green—seem exaggerated; how light leaps everywhere from jewels in earrings and neck-chains, sewn into dresses, onto collars and cuffs; and how expensive scents—of chamomile, violet, jasmine and camphor—put him in mind of a flower market, or a cathedral at Easter.

Zorzo can't find his painting, but discovers Carlo's father on the far side of the room. He takes the drawing he wants to show from his folder and goes over.

"How are you, Signor Contarini?" He smiles, catching the host between conversations. "Your party has cheered up this autumn day no end." Contarini looks cornered and Zorzo frets that his boots still smell of the street, but soldiers on. "The Ca' d'Oro must be the most enchanted house in all of Venice." He prefers to keep his compliments in line with his actual feelings.

"Well, try keeping it warm in winter," Contarini retorts, looking around them for someone better to talk to. "That wasn't considered when they built it."

"I've been meaning to speak with you for some time," Zorzo perseveres. "The *Birth of Paris* was a favorite painting, it really was. I don't mind telling you it was painful to part with it." None of this is true. In fact, he struggled, particularly with the infant Paris. He wanted the baby to be blissful, unaware of the great tragedies he'd set in motion, from the golden apple to the war in Troy, but Zorzo never quite managed a living, breathing infant.

"You're not asking for it back, are you?" Contarini says in an accusatory way, which Zorzo puts down to a general possessiveness rather than a particular affinity for the painting.

"On the contrary. I wanted to tell you about its companion piece that I've finally found time to begin. The *Birth of Paris* was always intended as one part of a diptych, the other being Aeneas's visit to the underworld." He presents the sketch. "Paris is the beginning of the Trojan saga and Aeneas the end of it." He's not sure if Signor Contarini is following. "So two paintings, birth and death, side by side."

"You want to double-charge me?" Contarini says, not even giving a cursory glance at the drawing.

"What? No," Zorzo says. "It will be unique, atmospheric. I thought I should at least put it in front of you first—"

"We wouldn't have the space. This house is all corners. I must talk to my guests. It was kind of you to come."

He goes off, leaving Zorzo alone. Zorzo puts the sketch back with his batch of copied Giottos, fastens the folder and glances around at the crowd, to see if anyone witnessed the scene, and to work out whether he should continue moving among them now, in search of employment, or hold back awhile, at least until the guests have drunk more.

He waits for the musicians to break between songs, then walks across to introduce himself. "I'm to join you?"

"Sit here," one of them offers, getting up from his seat, an old chap dressed in the fashion of two decades past, particularly his shoulder-length hair, now a thinned-out straggle. "My backside has gone to sleep."

His companions laugh and Zorzo, though he balked at Carlo's request, is happy now to be among them. He picks up the lute left for him and starts to play. He watches Signor Contarini join his wife and they have a conversation behind the backs of their hands, no doubt at someone else's expense. The feeling of the strings against Zorzo's fingers, the way they tenderly push back, and how sound hums from the body of the instrument, puts him at ease and he brushes aside the incident with the host. As Carlo predicted, now he's up on the dais, a head higher than the other musicians, and the most assured player, guests have started noticing him, certain women in particular. He might usually be flattered and look back, but Leda's rude, hard-drinking lover is still stalking through his mind.

Over a couple of hours, he watches the spectacle unfold. Wine pours from sculptured fountains, while more and more plates are delivered from below and crammed onto the enameled tables that stretch the length of the room. And as the quantity of food grows, the less people seem to eat. Kids' heads, silvered sweetbreads, a pair of roasted swans kissing, a pie shaped like a castle from which a live but almost suffocated bird emerges.

Every now and again, a master of ceremonies clears a space and announces an entremet—dancers, actors and acrobats. A pair of contortionists pass through hoops and three buffoons pantomime a ball game without a ball. Everyone applauds when their ball actually materializes, and everyone can see it's fashioned like a pocket-sized earth. It's a fitting allegory: for the Contarinis and their friends do indeed own the world. The miniature globe is placed on a cushion and handed over to the boy prince of Hejaz.

Zorzo's earlier self, the small-town lad arrived in Venice, would once have been amazed by it all. Today, though, the people in front of him seem themselves small-minded, ruled by traditions and customs and hierarchies, petty in their own way, lacking guts and imagination. He's waited all week, all year, to be here; but at once he doesn't want to horse-trade, as Carlo put it, to strike some middling deal with another Count Lippi. He wants a real victory. A coup. A commission that will take him to the top. "Prince orient," he mouths to himself, entranced more than ever by the notion of a color that is new to the world, of what possessing it would mean.

After the savories, the sweets come—fruit tarts, blancmanges, silver trees pendant with glazed fruits—along with a trio of new guests, all of whom Zorzo knows. Returned from Poveglia and changed into a fresh cloak, Vittore di Fonti comes up the stairs and strikes a pose in recognition of his extravagant lateness, and is met by a round of applause. He goes one better by presenting his companion, Bellini, who soldiers up behind, in plain attire that's just as considered as di Fonti's flamboyance. Zorzo's pleased to see him. Not because his old master is ever particularly convivial, but because he can corner him and find out how much Caspien told him, or even if he knew of prince orient before this afternoon.

Zorzo knows only too well the third person in their party, Tiziano. He was Zorzo's star apprentice until his sudden departure from the red house a year ago. Zorzo studies him as he takes in the crowd; Tiziano's face seeming to shine at the sheer luck of his youth and talent. He's sleeker—Zorzo thinks—better presented, and probably more confident than any of the young dukes in the room. He spots Zorzo, does a mime of plucking strings and comes over.

"They've put you to work?" Tiziano says.

"For my sins," Zorzo replies. "So are you one of di Fonti's 'discoveries' now? He does like to catch a horse after it's bolted."

The young man confides in a low voice, "There's no escaping him. He insisted on collecting me so we could arrive as one. I was ready two hours ago."

"Friend, have you—?" He stops himself. He was going to ask if Tiziano has heard of prince orient, before reminding himself—yet again—they are now competitors. "Have you seen the son of Hejaz?" he improvises instead, nodding at the boy. "Not what anyone was expecting. Try the wine. I'll catch up with you in a while."

Tiziano drifts into the crowd, head up, as if in search of other rare beasts such as himself. It seems to Zorzo like yesterday when the youngster unveiled his painting, his *Man with a Quilted Sleeve*, by the workroom window. It took everyone in the red house by surprise, partly because it had come from nowhere, unsolicited and finished while he was supposed to be collaborating on other canvases; and partly because it was so arresting. That shrewd, teasing face half-turned to the viewer and the gigantic sleeve of blue, the color of a magnificent bruise, breaking through the walls of the canvas. Perhaps Zorzo should have been aggrieved that his student had been so sly, striking out on his own, when he should have been working with the team, but he thought it better to just let success take its natural course. It came to Tiziano Vecellio—or Titian as some of his more pretentious admirers have begun calling him—with breakneck speed. By the end of that month, having gone from being unknown in Venice to sought after by everyone, he departed Zorzo's workroom for good.

The room is newly invigorated with chatter. In the shadows, the head butler snaps his fingers and whistles orders at his staff, to make sure glasses are filled and food brought for the new arrivals.

After three more songs, when the other musicians agree to take a break, Zorzo says, "It's been a pleasure, but at this point, I must leave you to meet some friends." He shakes hands with them and goes in search of Bellini. He's testing a plan in his head, of suggesting to Bellini that they work together to track down Caspien's secret color. The old man is deep in conversation. Zorzo keeps him in his sights and collars Carlo instead.

"So Jakob Fugger, tell me more," Zorzo says.

"Would you paint him?"

"Yes, of course, but that isn't the reason—"

"From what I hear, it's his wife you should take as a subject."

"So I gather."

"A blue-eyed piece of German porcelain. He was, what, forty when they wed and she barely out of puberty. Give me that," he says, taking a salver from a passing maid. "Fig?" he asks, offering them up, but Zorzo shakes his head. "I can't live without them." He ogles the maid as she retreats. "That one is Sicilian, pure fire." He lowers his voice. "But her husband is too, so one must be careful." He laughs, but Zorzo doesn't join in. He has no time for this type of male talk that demeans only.

"You were saying? About Fugger?" Zorzo has spotted Bellini at the top of the stairs, saying his goodbyes to someone.

"I mean the Fuggers are basically merchant class, *parvenus*, as my father would say. He did some kind of business with them ages ago. Textiles, I think. Venetian—Germanic trading the old-fashioned way, caravans across the mountains. But Jakob is in another class to the rest of the family. The richest man who ever lived."

"Really?"

"Look at your face! How innocent our tall Giorgio can be sometimes. And the reason he's richer than God? Because he was actually allowed to use the family money to make more of it. I think he was fourteen when he was subbed his first million. In two years, he'd trebled it." Bellini has now put on his cloak and started down the stairs. "That's the way to do it. Us Contarinis are expected—instructed—to keep money safe, and close. To be gentlemanly with it. That's the curse of *old* money. That's precisely why we'll never become…" he circles his hand as he searches for the word, before settling on, "Fuggerish. More wine?"

"No. I have to go." Bellini has descended out of sight.

"Thank you for coming, my friend. As promised." Carlo produces a little pouch of coins and places it in Zorzo's palm. "You really made the evening sing."

The purse feels heavy enough to contain what he spent with Caspien, but he has another idea and hands it back. "Pay me another way. Ask your father about Jakob Fugger. Anything he knows. Agreed?"

"A deal. Especially if it means setting eyes on the bride."

Zorzo hurries off down to the exit. Bellini's tall, stooping silhouette is retreating along the passage toward the water doors at the back of the house. "Sir, sir," Zorzo calls to him.

"Who is it?" Bellini halts and half turns his head.

"Just an old student paying their respects." Zorzo catches up with him. "It's good to see you, sir. We didn't have the chance to speak in Poveglia."

Bellini's eyes narrow. "Yes, I heard you were there," he growls. He reminds Zorzo of an old lion, a creature that's spent its life guarding its supremacy. "Are you well?"

"Extremely," says Zorzo.

"You don't look it. Are you not sleeping?"

Zorzo thinks about it and shrugs. "Little."

To this, Bellini gives a knowing smile. "How can explorers sleep and risk others finding their treasure?" In the dim hall light, his face is more ancient than ever.

"We're going the same way," Zorzo says. "I wonder if I could ride with you." Depending on how much he finds out, he can always return to the party.

"Which is as good as saying you want something?"

Zorzo laughs, but doesn't deny it. "Be my guest," the old painter says, shuffling on to where his barge is waiting and climbing aboard with the help of one of his boatmen.

On his way out, Zorzo halts, having seen the *Birth of Paris*, the canvas he sold to Signor Contarini three years ago. It's tilted to one side where someone must have knocked it, but—being close to an entrance—it's not badly placed in the house. He straightens it and for a few moments loses himself in the scene. It's better than he remembered: the forest, in shades of peridot and aventurine, has mystery and the figures within it live and breathe, though the baby still floats a little in the air.

"Are you coming or not?" Bellini snaps and Zorzo exits the Ca' d'Oro, climbs down into the barge, takes a seat opposite his old master, his folder on his lap. The boat lurches off.

The interior is almost startlingly luxurious: lined in emerald velvet, lit with gilt lanterns in the shape of dolphins and with deep feather cushions to sit on. Zorzo can only begin to imagine the money that must be passing through his old teacher's workshop. When he was last there a year ago, there were scores of *garzoni*, four times the number Zorzo has: grinders, maquetteers, draftsmen, letterists, everything. At least four large paintings were nearing completion, along with half a dozen smaller ones. Bellini has capitalized on the years of booming fortunes, been at the forefront of the lucky age, when trade ships have rolled in from all corners of the earth at unprecedented rates, and ranks of merchants and bankers have grown tenfold.

"So, my other protégé has left your company, I see," Bellini says, "flown your little nest, as he once did mine." He's talking about Tiziano, it's obvious from the slight edge of bitterness. The youngster used to skivvy for Bellini before he came to the red house and Bellini likes to insinuate that Zorzo poached him, though that wasn't the case. "Did you two have a falling-out?"

"Not at all." Zorzo smiles. He doesn't think he fell out with Tiziano, but neither is he sure. "We're on good terms. We still collaborate."

Bellini chuckles. "First pupil, then collaborator, then victor. Mackerel?" A little silver platter of it has been set up on a makeshift table. Zorzo shakes his head. "I can't eat what they serve at these banquets. It's dishonest food." The statement, Zorzo knows from experience, is the sort of obscure, vitriolic one Bellini makes about everything. "So, what do you want?"

"Does prince orient exist?" Perhaps out of spite, Zorzo's reply is as blunt as the question. Even so, his heart gives a little jump of surprise, at himself, for invoking the name so boldly. He held it back from Tiziano, but knows Bellini has just visited Poveglia. "Which our mutual friend, Caspien, spoke of."

A little breeze passes through the cabin curtains, the flames in the lanterns flicker, and for a moment a charge seems to ring between the two men.

"You must know by now that fellow spouts pure fantasy," Bellini starts to say.

"Because I thought we could strike a deal," Zorzo suggests. "Combine our resources. Two painters in search of a pigment are better than one."

"He's not to be trusted. A waste of a hundred *soldi*, though it's a good story, I'll give him that: the mystery in Bohemia, the quicksilver deaths." A hundred? Zorzo takes some comfort in the fact he bought the information for a third of the price. Unless, of course, Bellini came by three times the amount of it. "Prince orient is a myth," Bellini assures him, "and one as old as Egypt."

"So you'd heard of it before Caspien told you?"

Just for a heartbeat, Bellini looks caught out. "Yes, I know the stories, of course—everyone does, Giotto's falling star. But I can assure you I've studied that picture exhaustively, studied the whole sequence of murals. Caspien said the color had gone. I wager it was never there in the first place."

From his folder Zorzo takes out his rendering of the picture in question and hands it over to his companion. Bellini looks at it, then at Zorzo, more competitive than ever, as if stakes are being raised and he doesn't like it.

"Imagine if you were born in the mountains," Bellini says in a low voice, setting the sketch on his lap. "You've lived there all your life and have never known the sea. And all that time, by means of strange coincidence, no one ever speaks of it. Not once. You can't imagine the ocean, because it's never entered your mind. And one day, by chance, you travel away from that place and come across the shore and the great expanse beyond. What a miracle it would be. How astonishing. Red, green, yellow and blue are our mountains, and orange, pink, ocher, and what you will, the valleys in between. They're the places we know. So what a tantalizing notion, that *another* color, unlike any we could imagine, is lurking somewhere beyond our reach. A tantalizing notion, but a myth." He holds up the picture to Zorzo. "This is where the color was allegedly used. Only here. To describe this fireball and its scorching tail crossing the sky." He indicates with his long index finger. "The color of it had to be different from everything else in the room. Yet, as your sketch shows, and as I've always known, that falling comet is plain burnt umber. Of course, some 'enthusiasts' say the original came away, or was painted over. I don't believe it, that it was ever there, that it existed at all. Color is color and nature can only provide so many."

His old tutor is lying, Zorzo is sure of it. If Bellini truly thought it was nonsense, there wouldn't be such a hostile undertone in his voice. He has the look he had in Poveglia, of a war general who's swamped through bloody battles all his life.

"So you'll not seek out Jakob Fugger when he arrives?"

Bellini stares at him for a moment. "My lad, you have no chance of getting that commission. Not in a thousand years. I doubt I do either, considering who else is in the running. Michelangelo for one, who's probably on his way to Venice as we speak."

"Commission?" Bellini's hand, reaching for a napkin, freezes and the skin around his eyes twitches. He wipes his mouth. "Commission for what?" Zorzo asks again.

"We must be close to your house?" Bellini says tetchily. "Would you mind if we went our separate ways? I'm tired now." He calls up to the crew. "Can we let the passenger off?"

Zorzo is confused, unsure whether Bellini heard his question. "Are you not able to tell me?"

"Let's leave things as they are," Bellini says obscurely and neither of them speaks until the barge has halted by the nearest quay. Bellini is turned from the light and his face is in shadow when he says, "They have their eye on us, you know? The powers that be. They're watching us artists, us thinkers. *I* do not care. I'm too old to care. I'll be cold guts in the ground soon enough. But *you* should be mindful."

"The powers that be?"

"That think *we* are the cause of this strife, all these ill omens."

"Ill omens?" Zorzo doesn't remember Bellini being superstitious, and wonders if old age has brought it on.

"Bad tidings. Strange happenings. Venice is stricken by them. Have you not noticed the flooding of late? Three times this month San Marco has sunk beneath the lagoon and water crept into the cathedral, our sacred heart. But that is just the start of it." In the velvet gloom of the compartment, the outline of Bellini's face looks monstrous, like a gargoyle. "Hares have been seen about the city. Hares? In Venice? Countryside creatures, lolloping through the streets at night." Zorzo can feel the warm, fishy stench of Bellini's breath, and the back of his neck contracts in goose bumps. "And last week, the fellow who brings my chalks from Umbria arrived on the island in the hour before dawn and found every church door wide open. No one about, not a person on the streets, but the doors wide open. Every chapel from Dorsoduro to Cannaregio."

"I don't understand. Why would *we* be the cause of—?"

"Vengeance. All our successes, all our ideas." *Ideas*: he speaks the word with a twist in his mouth. "Artists and philosophers unpicking a thousand years of rules. All those paintings and sculptures and essays, all our wicked thoughts—that declare *man* is the center of it all. Not God. In Castile, you know, they have the Tribunal of the Inquisition for such sinners."

At once, Zorzo finds the air in the cabin stifling. He needs to know about Fugger, ask what his old tutor is hiding, but Bellini lays his great, ancient hand on Zorzo's shoulder and squeezes, too hard to be friendly. "It was good to see you again, my friend. Good night."

Zorzo climbs out of the boat and watches as it casts off into the darkness. As it picks up speed and the oars slick in and out of the water, Bellini's portentous words come back like an echo:

All our wicked thoughts, that declare man is the center of it all. Not God.

6

The Golden Bowl

"I'm listening," Zorzo says. He's hurrying through the streets with Tulipano, the *garzone* he tasked with locating Fugger's house and finding out more about him.

"I have a friend who's an apprentice to a cartographer in the Campo Santa Margherita," Tulipano says. "He knows everything." He tries to find the right page among his scribbled notes and knocks a passerby. "Sorry, sorry." His excessive height and skinniness make him clumsy.

"Go on."

"So he started with mines in Bavaria, the Tyrol, in Bohemia, the Slovene lands, silver, copper, tin, iron. Then everything else followed—manufactories, smelting plants, bronze foundries, road building."

"Road building?"

"To get it all to port, sir, to Antwerp, to Danzig, Lisbon, here to Venice, to sell to the world."

"He built roads to Venice?"

"Who else would? He cut new passes through the mountains. He cut straight through the Urals to the Baltic, through the Pyrenees to Spain. What else?" Riffling through his pages: "Pepper, wine, jewels, soap, glass and holy relics—he trades in all of them."

Zorzo pulls a face. "Holy relics?"

"The bones of the martyrs, splinters off the cross and so forth. And written pardons for sinners, obviously."

"Obviously."

"And now he bankrolls the Hapsburgs, and the Vatican too. He owns everything."

"It sounds like you're quite taken with him, Tulipano."

"No, sir, not at all." The apprentice blushes.

"It's all right, I'm fascinated too. Maybe we need new gods in this age?"

"Sir?" Tulipano is offended now and Zorzo has forgotten how devout the youngster is.

"I'm joking with you. And did you find out about Sybille Artzi?"

"Artzi?"

"Well, Fugger now. His wife, who everyone says is so murderously beautiful."

"Oh, very little, sir." Tulipano leads the way to the end of the path and stops. "That's it, the Fugger residence. It's called the Palazzo Pallido. I came by earlier, but it's closed up at the moment except for some household staff. Although the palazzo is a relatively new purchase, Fugger himself has been back and forth to Venice at different points in his life. He studied here."

"I've lived in Venice eighteen years and I've never seen this place," Zorzo says. "The Palazzo Pallido? Palatial, perhaps, but it doesn't look particularly pale."

"No, sir. I thought the same."

Zorzo studies what must be the back of the building. It's immense, forcefully out of scale and character, surrounded as it is with little tenements and pretty waterways. Its high walls—the color of charcoal smoke—are precipices of small, dark bricks, and set with pious, meanly sized windows. It has nothing of the playful Moorish style of Venice's most famous buildings, like the Ca' d'Oro, with their airy loggias and colonnades. It's more like some Gothic fortress of northern Europe, particularly the tower that rises from the rear like an army battlement. Most of the windows are shuttered, but at least three chimneys exhale perforated bands of smoke.

"It faces the sea, sir, which is also unusual," Tulipano goes on. "The north shore, away from the shipping lines. Nearly every other palazzo of this size is on the Grand Canal. And this part of Cannaregio is pretty run-down."

"Not where you'd expect the richest man in Europe to have his home," says Zorzo. "Which I presume is intentional, privacy-wise. Not everyone who comes to Venice is a show-off." Tulipano giggles at this, being a Venetian. "You're a good lad. Get back to the workroom. I'm going to linger a few moments."

Zorzo waits for more than an hour, knowing Tulipano's right and the master and mistress haven't arrived yet, but intrigued by the noises coming from the house, which seems to have the timbre of anticipation, as if the whole place is holding its breath. It grows colder, as a faint mist rises from the canal.

The chill gets into his bones and he's about to give up his vigil when there comes the toll of a boat bell and a barge steals around the bend. In the fog, it could be a slow-moving whale returning to its home sea. It's loaded with trunks and crates, weighing it down at an angle in the water. A pair of gondoliers power it from the stern, while two more men sit slumped at the prow. These two are splattered all over with dirt and mud, while their eyes are baggy and red from tiredness. The end of a long journey. The barge driver calls. A little window opens, someone peers out and, moments later, there's a whine of metal—shrill and loud against the chill afternoon—and water doors at the base of the tower open. The barge slips in and Zorzo steps back into the shadows. On a little interior quay, a housekeeper is waiting. She's stout, all in black, armed at the hip with a giant bunch of keys. Four or so lads in household livery stand with her.

One of the exhausted men in the boat stands and says to the housekeeper, "This is the first load. The rest will come later, or in the morning."

"The morning? Why not today?"

"The master and his wife may stay the night in Mestre, after all. On the harbor. An issue with," he pauses and wipes the back of his hand across his forehead, "an issue with the mistress, I gather." The housekeeper scowls at this, though she already has what Zorzo's father would have called a face of thunder.

The housekeeper gestures at the cargo and orders, "Take everything to the hall."

"Yes, Frau Bauer."

Zorzo doesn't wait for the unloading. He turns on his heels and hurries across Cannaregio, not back to the red house, but over the Rialto, from where he speeds north. He reaches the port, at the northwest tip of the city, just in time to catch a ferry to the mainland. If Fugger and his wife are holed up in Mestre, he may be able to get a look at them, even find a way to introduce himself.

The boat casts off and his heart thumps. He wonders if he's being too rash, whether he should really be getting back to his workshop and the still unfinished black gloves of Espettia Lippi. He puts his collar up, pulls his jacket tight and watches Venice retreat behind him. He realizes it's been more than a year, maybe more than two, since he's crossed the lagoon to Mestre. When his father was alive, he went all the time to his home in Castelfranco. There is something about the ferry—with its six oars going at once, the speed of it, the huddle of other passengers, everyone on their own mission—that shakes away the anxieties of the last two days: the bailiffs, Leda, the Ca' d'Oro and Bellini. As he settles, a brand-new thought strikes him. Caspien said that prince orient was otherworldly. What if the entity in the sky in Giotto's picture, hurtling toward the earth, actually carried prince orient? He's heard stories of strange bright lights arriving in centuries past, celestial voyagers, some of which fall from the heavens. Caspien also said the mine was shallow, the mineral close to the surface.

The more Zorzo thinks about it, the more it bends his thoughts out of shape. He goes to church, as all men do when required, but he has never truly *believed* in the people from the Bible, not actually thought of them as breathing, striving, struggling flesh and blood—however well artists depict them. To him they're mythology. Jesus Christ, the late-appearing hero of the story, is hardly more credible than, say, Apollo or Zeus. And as for the earlier parts of the Scriptures—the world created in seven days, floods engulfing it, seas parting—wonderful tales all, but beyond logic.

And yet, despite what he thinks in private, one truth is beyond doubt: history has pivoted against that brief moment in time fifteen hundred years ago, that tiny span of three decades, the birth, life and death of one single man. As a result of it, of Christ, the order of the world has changed from one thing to another, maybe not immediately, but eventually and completely. It has even changed time itself, in that it has been counted differently from that moment on.

And now there is this possibility: that an object from the sky, that may have carried within it an unimaginable color, collided with the world at the precise moment the great change commenced.

The moment Zorzo disembarks, it's clear his gamble has paid off. Mestre has usually grown quiet by this time of day, but at one end of the harbor, on the far side of the tavern that Zorzo used to visit, it's thronged with activity. There are three carriages, a pair of traveling carts, stacks of trunks and boxes, at least a dozen panting horses and a swarm of men, all filthy from traveling, like the two on the barge in Cannaregio. Boats are being loaded up. Six men heave an iron chest from the back of a cart and carry it onto the largest barge. It's so heavy the boat tips to one side before they center it and set it down.

Zorzo studies the carriages. Two of them, though dirt-caked like everything else, are very smart, gleaming boxes of dark wood: the new breed of traveling vehicles from northern Europe that people like Carlo spout about—even though he lives in a city of water—with high, slim wheels and ingenious braces to give the compartment a cushion of suspension. Not seeing anyone who might be Jakob Fugger or his wife, Zorzo slips into the tavern.

There's a smattering of dockworkers between shifts, some with their ears pricked to the drama going on outside, some peering through the window at it. No one stands out, though. Zorzo buys a measure of brandy and throws it back, to a satisfying kick of warmth inside.

The door flies open so fast that the handle knocks the wall. A man enters and strides to the bar. He is so imposing, tall and thickset, the floorboards bend to his weight. Thick ringlets of blond hair wind from beneath his cap, and an empty golden tureen hangs from his gloved right hand. It's heavy and large, almost the size of a baptizing font, the type of vessel that a newborn prince might be christened in. "Fill it up," the man says in a foreign accent, banging it on the counter like it's a milk bucket. "Hot water." He casts down some money. The innkeeper seems to resent the man's manner, but the sum of money is undeniable.

Everyone in the room looks over, even those who hadn't been interested in what was happening outside. Against the drab decor of the room, the vessel shines, like an object of the gods that has appeared in the mortal realm. If it's truly gold, it could be worth more than any of the dockworkers will earn in their lifetimes. Though if it crosses their minds to covet such a thing, the stance of the man warns against it. He turns to the room, fists resting on his hips, and everyone pretends they're not looking. His face has the pale pink, ruddy color of pig fat. Both sword and long dagger hang from his belt. They're not ornamental weapons: they've been used, and often, all the shine and decoration rubbed from their hilts.

It takes a while for the innkeeper to fill the vessel, going back and forth to the fire to heat the water in batches. Eventually the stranger gives a flick of his hand to indicate it's enough and tells the innkeeper to follow him outside. Zorzo waits until they've gone before going after them.

The blond colossus leads the innkeeper to one of the black carriages and knocks on the side. "Madam," he says, then he opens the door, takes the tureen from the innkeeper and sets it down on the floor of the carriage.

"*Danke*, Tomas," a woman replies. "Are we crossing now?"

"Shortly," says Tomas. He bows stiffly and retreats, leaving the door open

Crossing? They obviously decided against staying the night here. Zorzo cranes his neck to see. The interior of the carriage is lined in cloth of gold, which shimmers against the candlelight. He can see the white coat hem of the seated woman. She leans forward and her hands come into view. They could be carved alabaster, Zorzo thinks, thin fingers, unnaturally white and glassy—before he realizes she's wearing gloves. She peels them off and sinks her hands—which are pale too, like pink coral—into the water.

Keeping his distance, Zorzo circles the carriage and notices a man, separate from the rest, standing at the edge of the water, half-veiled in sea mist, looking toward Venice—looking in such a way as if he owned the place, or is about to. He too is tall, but he'd still draw the eye if he weren't, even with his back turned. He's not dressed showily, but the black fabrics of his clothes drip with wealth: silks and velvets of pure darkness, not muddy forgeries of color. He wears a chaperon hat, the type rarely seen anymore in Venice. Zorzo wonders if he should go and introduce himself, here and now. He may never get as close to him again, but how would he do it, on a dark quay in Mestre, without sounding desperate, or suspicious? *I hear you possess prince orient. Might I see it?* If nothing else, he should say something to make Fugger turn, so Zorzo can see his face, see the human form of absolute wealth, how money changes a person—but then Tomas appears, Fugger's right-hand man, presumably, and says something in his master's ear. Fugger nods and climbs aboard one of the waiting boats, while Tomas goes to oversee the last of the loading.

From behind, there comes a click. The woman in the carriage—surely Fugger's wife—holds out her palm to the sky. There is a painting, Zorzo thinks: against the bustle of an Italian harbor, the misted thicket of ship masts and harbor cranes, the hand of a lady, the young wife of the world's richest man, comes from a glossy coach to test for rain. She dismounts and Zorzo slips back behind the corner of the inn. She's angled away from him and he can't see her face either.

"Johannes," she says to one of the men who have started unloading trunks from the roof of her carriage.

"Madam?" He's a slight adolescent with a nervy smile: the opposite of Tomas.

"It's not so cold. I won't need this." She takes off her overmantle and holds it out for him. Underneath, her dress is also pearl-white, in satin, a lustrous thing against the drab browns and muddied grays all around her. It's voluminous too, from yards and yards of fabric. She must be one of those ladies who eschew practical clothes for traveling, durable fabrics and dark colors.

"Of course, madam. No rain now either. For that we must be thankful."

She puts her gloves back on and steps across the harbor toward the waiting boats. She looks terrified, her back a stiff board, her ear turning to every noise. She doesn't lift the hem of her gown, but lets it drag along the dirty quay-stones. She's a pale apparition moving through the chaos.

Johannes opens one of the trunks and, to make space for the overmantle, presses down on the clothes inside. Zorzo catches a glimpse of them, folded like giant cushion-cut jewels, their colors—folium violet, Egyptian green, carnelian red—shining like her dress in the dusk. Johannes stows the coat, locks up the casket and hurries to his mistress, who has halted halfway to the water's edge.

"You're nearly there, madam. A few steps more."

"I won't do it." She's taking deep breaths and shaking her head. "I can't."

"You'll be all right, madam," Johannes replies. "It's not the sea proper. A lagoon is calmer than the sea proper. And there's barely any wind now." She rocks on her heels and Zorzo can sense her tension. "Would you like me to hold your arm?"

She shakes her head, steadies herself and glides on toward the barge her husband boarded. He stands in silhouette, facing the port, his eyes trained on her.

"Nearly there, madam," Johannes encourages her. "It'll all be over soon." Again, she reminds Zorzo of a character in a painting he saw once, an empress being led to the scaffold, to her execution. Eventually she reaches the ramp and stops.

"Have fears," her husband says. His voice has a hard, featureless tone. "Have as many as you want. Fear murder, fear plague, fear the devil, but this?" He flicks his head toward the water. "We could have been there by now. Ludicrous." He leans out and takes her by the wrist, but she snaps her hand away. Her resolve seems to strengthen; she puts her shoulders back, mounts the ramp and steps down onto the boat. Tomas embarks after her.

"Well?" Fugger gestures at the captain. "Go. Bring this journey to its end." He moves under the canopy, leaving his wife on the open part of the deck. As the boat casts off, Sybille lets out a gasp, digs her heels in and holds on to the rail. Zorzo steps to the water's edge to watch her. What ludicrous misfortune, he thinks, what cruelty, to have a fear of the sea and be brought to Venice.

When the swaying of the boat evens out, her shoulders relax a touch. She turns to the mainland receding behind her. Zorzo tries a third time to see her face, but all he can discern is a pale question mark against the night. Then the barge shrinks away toward the city.

7

At the Orseolo

"Stop what you're doing for a moment," Zorzo says from the workroom door as soon as he gets back. "Jakob Fugger and his wife have arrived in Venice. This is momentous, just as if a Medici had come to town with a barge full of gold to spend. There is not only a new color at stake, but a significant commission. Quiet, everyone," he says as some *garzoni* start up in a chatter. "And, Teodor, stop looking at yourself. You're the same now as you were a minute ago." The lad blushes, pivots from the mirror and Zorzo turns to another of his men. "Tulipano, is everyone up to date with what you told me about Fugger this morning?"

"Yes, sir."

"Go back to the Palazzo Pallido first thing tomorrow. Keep an eye on what's going on, particularly if the Fuggers leave the building. Either of them. I want to know where they go. Any details may be useful. And be subtle about it." Tulipano nods in agreement.

"As for the rest of you, we have to think of a way to get in front of this man, get his attention. The best option will be to send him something. Ideally we'd create a new piece, bespoke to Fugger, but that will take time, which I daresay we don't have. Janek, is there anything unaccounted for that can go out?" He motions to the racks where work in progress is kept.

"Nothing really suitable," the foreman replies.

"Could we look at least?"

His tone is sharp enough for some *garzoni* to share glances. They watch in silence as the men flip through half a dozen canvases: unfinished, barely started, pictures that never found a home or that were discarded entirely, put out of their misery.

"Ah, perhaps this?" says Janek. "If we worked it up a little." He has pulled out a half-finished canvas of Salome inspecting the severed head of John the Baptist. Much of it is just sketched, but Salome—blue-white skin against a crimson gown—is painted in forensic detail.

"No," says Zorzo.

"No?"

"It's not even mine, really." Tiziano began it when he was working for him, and though, for a while, Zorzo continued where his student left off, he always disliked the subject. As a character of history, Salome never appealed to him; always struck him as just a spoiled princess with no redeeming features or depth. "Bring me the *Knight and Groom*."

"But that's—"

"I know, not ours to send, but we have to be decisive. We have to prioritize. And if that means—" He doesn't finish the sentence, but the implication is clear: though the painting has been promised to someone else, he will use it to get to Fugger. "Or we could just send it on loan as an example," he offers Janek by way of compromise, even though he knows such an approach is also fraught with complication. The foreman goes to get it and places it on the table in front of them all.

The muscles in Zorzo's neck unknot at first sight of it. It has brought him pleasure from its inception and still does. A knight in armor stares at the viewer, his head tilted to one side in anticipation, while his devoted groom—modeled on Uggo—stands in attendance. Though it was all but finished weeks ago and he should have sent word to the buyer already, he hasn't been able to bring himself to let it go. He's grown attached to his two subjects. The knight and groom don't know it, but it's meant to be the last day of their lives. They're going into battle and will not return. As long as Zorzo watches over them, they remain alive.

"Who knows if it's right?" he says eventually. "For now, assemble any others that might do, sketches included, and place them along the wall. In the meantime, I am going to finish this portrait tonight." He indicates the canvas of Espettia Lippi. "Put her gloves on and be done with her. I'll work alone. I brought her into the world and I'll see her out of it. Does everyone understand?" There is a communal murmur of assent.

Zorzo clears a space in the corner and sets down the portrait. He fetches some lanterns, his brushes and the quantities of ground black. He's convinced, if he removes Espettia Lippi from his life, he'll be making way for greater things: the Fuggers and prince orient, a possible victory that will set him apart from everyone else.

He paints in the hub of lantern light in the corner, working into the night as everyone else disperses to their beds, and then waking at dawn to finish. He forgets all his quibbles with the Lippi family, how ungracious they are, how beneath him the commission might be, and follows the example that Giotto left behind: to think only of bringing the breath of life to his subject—sinew, muscle, flesh and bone. Espettia Lippi may be mean-spirited and spineless, but her hands are real. Let them be those of a queen or a grand villainess. They could be Cleopatra's hands, or Boudicca's. Everything goes right. Every shade of black he concocts for the gloves, every touch and turn of his brush, adds truth to the hands beneath. He can sense the carpals and phalanges within them, feel the stretch of ligament, and how the skin sits on top—and her gloves over that. He can feel how they fit her hand, how the satin warms against flesh, how it stretches to catch the light, or folds into darkness. As he works, for hours, stopping only to replace spent candles, Sybille appears to him in a constant dreamy loop, in pearl satin on Mestre's quay, back rigid, the hem of her dress dragging through the dirt, and on the barge, vanishing into the darkness across the lagoon.

Zorzo's last job is to add the jewel to Espettia's ring—on her index finger, worn over the glove. He already has a small quantity of Caspien's ultramarine mixed for it. He takes up a brush of sable marten hair that he saves only for very particular and delicate tasks. He dips the tip in thinner, wipes the excess on a cloth, slides the belly evenly through the ultramarine paste and applies it to the canvas in three curving strokes. To make the shadow on the side of the sapphire, he mixes orpiment yellow with the azurite. Lastly, for the sparkles of light from the girdle of the jewel, he daubs tiny filaments of lead white.

He stands back to look. He's done it, turned the task around. The ring was inspired. The eye goes to it first. A sapphire on a gloved hand confers a kind of elemental majesty to the subject. It makes even Espettia a little fascinating.

"They'll be happy, surely," says Azalea from behind. It's midmorning already and Zorzo only half noticed his staff arrive and set quietly to work. They've all gathered to look at the finished painting.

"Janek, write to Lippi, tell him his daughter is ready for him. What is that?" Janek is holding out a note.

"A fellow brought it from the Ca' d'Oro."

Zorzo rips it open and reads. It's from Carlo.

Meet me at lunch, the Orseolo. The favor you asked—I have news.

★ ★ ★

"My father, God bless him," says Carlo, "turns out to be quite a gossip. He seems to have it in for Jakob Fugger and his 'unnatural' wealth, and relished spreading dirt. The wife, the fragrant Sybille, gets more interesting by the day."

"How so?" Zorzo has decided to keep to himself that he's seen her at Mestre and found out where she lives.

Carlo has bought oysters and a flagon of wine. The Orseolo tavern, just behind St. Mark's, is his favorite locale of the moment, fashionably tatty and down at heel, a meeting place for gondoliers originally, but now for all sorts.

"In as much as her short, pretty life has led to a trail of disasters, starting with the fact she was mislaid as a girl."

"Mislaid?"

"She fell off a boat as the family were going over to Denmark. At night."

"Really?" This is a choice piece of information, no doubt explaining her fear of water.

"She's eleven. Her brother jumps in after her, no one notices they've gone. They wash up on some island in the Baltic. Uninhabited. Winter falls—"

"Winter? How long were they there for?"

"Wait and I'll tell you. There are thousands of islands in that corner of the world, so many to search. So winter falls and if it weren't for the furs they fell in with, they'd perish. They try and live off berries and seaweed but they nearly starve. When the freeze comes and the sea ices over, the brother, who's older and this saintly character apparently, this savior, attempts to walk across it to the mainland. He falls through the ice, of course, and only just makes it back. By the time they're found, almost eight months after they were lost, they're feral, like wild animals. Apparently it's a famous story in Germany. It reminds me of something from, I don't know, a legend one of you fellows might paint."

"Incredible." Zorzo is already picturing the scene on canvas.

"Anyway, years later, Fugger and Sybille meet. I mean to say, they are of the same town, they live barely streets apart, but Sybille has been locked away in the family home ever since the island disaster. Her family are wealthy; her father was—is still—the chief burgher of Augsburg, but that is not what draws Fugger. He's double her age, but he pursues her like a fighting dog until he's done the deal. There's only one problem: the brother, I think he's called Edwin."

"What problem?"

"This saintly Edwin is against the marriage. He thinks it will ruin his beloved sister. And Fugger hates him from that moment. He's eaten up with jealousy, because Sybille and the brother are inseparable. I mean, they would be when they've almost died together a hundred times on that island. Firstly, Fugger doesn't allow Edwin in the house—" He pauses. "Is it Edwin or Edgar? I can't remember. Edwin Artzi. Anyway, Fugger won't have him over the threshold, this angel who tried to walk on ice to save his sister, or even for them to meet. Then, when they persist in doing so, Fugger uses his influence to banish the poor soul, on pain of death, from Augsburg, from the whole region. There are some who say he went further than that."

"Meaning?"

Carlo arches his brow. "Put it this way, Edwin Artzi has not been seen for two years." He draws his finger across his neck.

"This is a true story? Really?"

Carlo laughs. "Who knows? I like it, though—the intrigues of these Bavarian mine-diggers with more money than they'll ever be able to spend. Don't look so astonished. The Fuggers of the world can do as they please, far worse than see off a tiresome sibling. According to Father, Fugger has a whole team of assassins at his fingertips. One poor soul, who made the mistake of stealing some deed or other, was thrown off a watchtower in Stuttgart, headfirst. Your face, it's a picture."

"I'm just having trouble believing all this."

"And there was a farmer who refused to sell him some land and was locked with his family in an outbuilding and burned to death. The law won't touch Fugger. He owns it, like everything else. My advice, don't involve yourself with him. I prefer you living." Carlo laughs. "Anyway, fate is having the last laugh. Four years married and no children. The richest pair in Christendom and not one little Fugger." He notices someone at the door and screws up his face. "Don't I know that man?"

Vittore di Fonti has come in and is looking around for someone. He's self-consciously garbed in what the youngsters are wearing about court, a square-shouldered doublet and scalloped hat, and tries to look at ease in the boisterous tavern. He clearly isn't.

"The doge's adviser on matters artistic," Zorzo murmurs to Carlo, who pulls a face.

Di Fonti spots whoever he's looking for, gives a little wave and goes over to two men seated in one of the booths. One is in his twenties, wealthy, Zorzo presumes by his dress. The other is older, disheveled with unkempt hair and grubby hands, but otherwise nondescript. Zorzo assumes he's the other's manservant or groom, but it's to him, not the well-dressed one, that di Fonti presents himself, almost scraping the floor with his bow. The disheveled man does not reply in kind, restricting himself to a wary nod.

"Who is that fellow?" Carlo said.

The Orseolo isn't well lit and the group is half-obscured behind a pillar, but when the man turns his head and light catches against the side of his face, Zorzo can see his nose has been broken, half-flattened to one side. Zorzo feels his heart quicken.

"I have a notion," he says, "it is Michelangelo."

Carlo frowns. "The sculptor?"

"And painter." Zorzo is crestfallen. He'd hoped Bellini had been mistaken about the painter being in Venice. No matter that Zorzo's spent half a life waiting to set eyes on the creator of the *Pietà* in Rome and *David* in Florence, the last thing he needs at the moment is competition of his status.

"Doesn't he work for the pope?" Carlo's saying. "He looks like a beggar." Then, peering more carefully, "I hadn't realized Michelangelo was so old."

"He's not, that is to say, he's only a few years older than myself." The man with the broken nose looks well past his prime, but that fits with what Zorzo's heard. It fits also that his eyes are half-ruined, the lids buckled and stained with paint. "It's him, I'm sure."

"No, that's a beggar. A blind beggar."

"He's not blind, Carlo. A blind painter would be of little use."

"Why are his eyes like that? His whole face is covered in muck."

Zorzo wonders if he should give his friend a lesson in how painting frescoes takes a toll on men, even the healthy ones. He knows firsthand how inhuman it is on top of a scaffold, how your gaze is always up and paint forever dripping into your eye, how light is scarce, how you ache with nausea and cramps, how you must piss and shit in your trousers sometimes and how you work in almost constant fear of the scaffolding collapsing and taking you with it. You're worrying nonstop about whether the stucco has the right freshness, or if the brick is damp or unstable, and whether, after all the torment, your painting, for which you had to mix colors by the shovel load, will even read from the ground. "It takes quite a lot of courage to do what he does," Zorzo says. "I was up a scaffold for a month and it half killed me. He's been up one for two years."

"Courage? To paint pictures?" Carlo laughs. "You'll not make me sorry for you. Who's the pretty boy?" He nods toward the third man at the table. He has one of those faces that mark him out as high and mighty: languorous mouth, mocking eyes and sharp cheekbones—a fellow who makes no attempt to hide his sense of self-worth. Zorzo shrugs but thinks he might be the artist's lover.

"Well, if it is Michelangelo, I'm going to go and talk to him. We need an artist to paint our hall, a mural to hide the damp."

"No!" Zorzo exclaims, holding Carlo's wrist to make the point, wondering how it's possible to be such a buffoon, how self-obsessed to think the great Michelangelo can be propositioned in a tavern "to paint a hall."

"Look how everyone stares," Carlo says, gesturing around the room. Word must have spread among the customers as many have their eyes trained on the three men in the booth. After all these years, Zorzo is still surprised, and gratified, by the notion of a painter being famous. When he was growing up, the idea would have been absurd. "I'm in the wrong business, clearly," Carlo grumbles.

Zorzo feels like asking Carlo what business he is in exactly: son of wealthy landowner? Callous womanizer? Princely layabout who will never, in his life, have to worry about money?

Carlo shoots up. "I'm going to talk to him. Introduce myself. What's the harm in it?" He goes over to the men. He pays no heed to di Fonti or the young aristocrat, but extends his hand to Michelangelo. The artist leaves it hanging there a moment, regarding it, before eventually shaking. "Contarini," Zorzo hears Carlo say, loud enough for the whole tavern to hear.

Zorzo is embarrassed now as well as frustrated. He should be talking to his fellow painter, finding out what Michelangelo knows, but Carlo will lose him the chance, and all credibility. Zorzo decides to go over and gets up, before sitting down again.

He doesn't know what he's going to say or how he's going to say it. He's heard so many varied stories of Michelangelo that he's not sure which are true. Certainly, even as a youth, the prodigy's name was being dropped in society like a jewel, discussed in reverent tones usually reserved for great men long gone. He's rich, richer than any other artist in the world. While everyone else fights for commissions, Michelangelo works only for popes and emperors, and on the largest scale. And Zorzo has always been able to see why. When he first encountered the artist's *Pietà* in old St. Peter's church—the basilica they've now knocked down to make way for a new version—he felt almost helpless in its presence. Christ, sprawled on his mother's lap, a thin, dead man, a sack of bones.

Artists, or rather those who gather around them, people such as di Fonti, are always debating which is the nobler craft: painting or sculpture. On the one hand, sculptors can't catch the glow of armor, the shine of hair, the shock of lightning, the burning of a city, crowds, woods, meadows. On the other, painters are limited as they can only show one side of a figure at once—and of a story. But for Zorzo the test is how a piece makes you feel: if it quickens your heart, opens your eyes or chills your blood; if it makes you want to go out drinking, or sends you home to brood in the dark. Michelangelo's work makes a person do all these things at once.

Zorzo knows that side of the artist, but wonders how many of the other tales are true: that he's tightfisted, that he refuses to pay his share to the guilds, that he's too mean for fires, that he scrimps by grinding his own paint, that he never changes his clothes or washes, that he's unsociable and argumentative, that he fights with his patrons, walks out on jobs and rails at how little he's valued. Even his broken nose is said to be the result of his snide tongue.

Zorzo downs his cup of wine, and Carlo's too, to pluck up courage, gets to his feet and goes over.

"The man is an animal," Carlo says, coming back and intercepting Zorzo halfway between the tables, "and smells like one too. My mother wouldn't have such a creature in the house." As if that was the reason Michelangelo wouldn't paint their hall.

"I told him I was with you, and that you are the finest artist in Venice."

"And what did he say?" Zorzo says, noticing that Michelangelo is looking over. Those unfriendly, pinched-together, paint-embedded eyes are staring straight at him.

"He didn't seem to know you. Where are you going?" Carlo says, but Zorzo sidesteps him.

"Signor di Fonti," Zorzo nods, "sirs. Giorgio Barbarelli."

Michelangelo, whose gaze remains sullenly fixed on Zorzo, gives a faint nod. "Michelangelo Buonarroti. A pleasure."

He doesn't sound pleased, but what Zorzo is certain of, and relieved by, what is clear from the way the old painter looks at him, with a competitive smolder in the eye, is that Michelangelo knows exactly who he is.

Zorzo still doesn't know what he's come over to say. Michelangelo obviously met with Caspien in Rome, surely learned about prince orient, Fugger and the commission, whatever it might be; and Zorzo's first thought is to try and throw him off the scent. He thinks of inventing a story, of how Caspien can't be trusted, or how prince orient is just a plain brown, before realizing the best course, the one his father would always want him to choose, is to become friends first and, that way, get the information he needs.

"You know, when I first saw your *Pietà*," Zorzo begins, "I stood in front of it for hours. Then I came back the next day and the one after that. I just couldn't believe it."

Michelangelo gives a weak smile. Close up, he's even grubbier. His hair is filthy, matted and bald in places, his clothes stiff with dirt, and he smells of stale oil.

"That it had been carved from a single piece of marble," Zorzo goes on. "That's right, isn't it? The detail. Those emaciated legs and drooping pectorals, the ribs, the skin bunched under the arm. Exquisite." The famous painter is looking at him blankly and Zorzo doesn't know whether to go on. "Your Christ was as real as anyone in this room. He'd lived and died. And you were twenty-two?" Zorzo isn't trying to flatter for the sake of it. He wants to start a conversation, gain more insight, but Michelangelo seems to have no interest in talking. The pretty young man at his side is smirking. Zorzo takes a breath, broadens his shoulders, laughs, then says in what he hopes is a more commanding tone, "As you can see, I'm an admirer." Something else his father taught him, that vanity is a road to nowhere. "I'd be so honored if you'd come to visit me in my studio. I live on the Campo San Francesco della Vigna. There's a red house—"

The young aristocrat gives a snigger and says under his breath, "Oh dear."

"If it's all the same with you," Michelangelo drawls, "I'd rather not see the workings of another artist's life. There's no reward in it. And besides, we are short of time in the city."

"Venice is not exciting," the young sidekick puts in. "It's like a stay in the countryside. Only wetter."

Zorzo feels his cheeks heat up with embarrassment. The exchange is worse even than the one he had with Carlo's father. Thankfully, Tulipano has appeared at the tavern entrance, red-faced and out of breath, motioning toward his master—and Zorzo has an excuse to go.

"Well, it's been a pleasure to meet. I hope you survive the rain," he says. The older painter gives a nod, almost inscrutable, and Zorzo goes over to his apprentice.

"You said to tell you when anyone left Fugger's palazzo," Tulipano says.

"Yes, and?"

"The wife has gone to Mass at St. Mark's. With two other members of the household. By foot. I followed them there. The service has just begun."

"Well done. I'll head there now. You go back to the palazzo and keep your eye on it for the rest of the day, see if the husband goes anywhere." After Tulipano has gone again, Zorzo returns to Carlo. "You'll have to excuse me. An issue in the workroom. But I'm indebted to you." He leaves money on the table for the wine and Carlo's oysters.

"Make sure you keep me informed," says Carlo, giving a wink. "This Sybille Fugger has got to my imagination."

To Zorzo's too. He takes one last look at Michelangelo in the corner and rushes out, vowing to himself two things. Firstly, however famous he might become, he'll never become rude or self-opinionated, particularly not to strangers. Secondly, he'll redouble his efforts, triple them if need be, to beat everyone to Fugger—and win prince orient along with the commission.

8

The Heiress

The cathedral is filled to capacity. Worshippers are crammed onto pews, or standing, ten-deep in places, in the nave and aisles or bundled along the colonnades and side chapels. Barely an inch of the mosaic floor is visible. Instead it shifts, like velvet quicksand, with the skirts and coats of the congregation.

Zorzo hangs back in the main portico scanning the people until he spots, at the front, close to the baptistery gates, a figure he recognizes, blond-haired and taller than everyone else: Tomas, the colossus who had the golden tureen. He has the look of a bodyguard, eyes stagily pivoting this way and that, alert to everything. Sybille is seated near him, in a green dress and gabled hat. Her clothes have the intense, almost mineral color of malachite, or emeralds, a hue made more vivid by the velvet of the material. Next to her is the sullen housekeeper, Frau Bauer, who Zorzo saw overseeing the unpacking of barges when he first went to the Palazzo Pallido.

Zorzo goes to the left, along the side wall, and installs himself behind one of the twelve large pillars that hold the building up, and from here he has a view of the back of Sybille's head. She's looking around the church in such a way that Zorzo's sure it's her first time seeing it.

He realizes he himself hasn't been inside St. Mark's for a couple of years and has forgotten how bizarre it is. Whereas the outside, with its patina of sculpted treasures and golden fairy-tale domes, is cheerful and eccentric, the interior is like some dread cavern under the sea, vast and dim, like Neptune's lair: walls of rock crystal, porphyry and iridescent ceramic rising to a ceiling of burnt gold. To enter it, even in daytime, is like walking into night. There are so many shadowy alcoves it sometimes appears like a maze, one where you can be lost not just in place, but in time. You can find yourself in an anteroom or side chapel, dimly lit by candles or the gleam of an icon, and it feels as if you've slipped back to centuries past.

"A religious horror," was how Zorzo once heard someone describe the place, in reference to the relics the church professes to own: a piece of granite that Jesus preached from; an executioner's block on which John the Baptist was beheaded and still infused with his blood; and, most sacred of all, locked up in the heart of the building—wherever that is—the relic that gives the cathedral its name, the remains of St. Mark himself. "His bones were stolen from Alexandra on a moonless night," Bellini told Zorzo as a child, his version of a bedtime story, "and smuggled out of the city in a cart packed with cabbage leaves and pork. The pork was so the Muslim guards wouldn't search it." Stealing the remains of a saint and putting up a cathedral around them is a good subject for a painting, Zorzo's always thought, but he wonders if they're really here, and if they truly belonged to St. Mark; or if, like everything else in Venice, it's a piece of elaborate theater.

After prayers, there come cymbal strikes and priests cast censers forth, incanting, and clouds of incense hang for a moment above the crowd before dissolving. Zorzo watches Sybille and wonders what she makes of it all. The churches of northern Europe, he knows, are different from Italian ones. Cathedrals are pared down to their elemental forms, while the messages that are delivered are plain and dreadful. "God-fearing" is the term that comes to mind when he thinks of Germans and Scandinavians, rain-tossed cities, iron skies, lands of impenetrable forests, harvests hurriedly gathered before brutal winters set in. The painters of those regions are made of the same cloth, men like Hieronymus Bosch, suffused to their core with guilt and violent darkness. He watches Sybille, composed and neat, a green jewel in a sea of pink and earth tones, and he tries to imagine how different she must have looked when she was saved from a Baltic island after nearly a year gone wild.

Once the Psalms are read, the public begins to form a line to take the Eucharist. Sybille gets to her feet, but rather than join the queue in the main aisle she goes to one in the little chapel of the north transept. Frau Bauer remains seated, watching her. A group of Venetians allows Sybille to jump ahead of them, no doubt on account of her dress and hat, which mark her out as a visitor to the city.

Zorzo steps out from his hiding place but halts when he sees Tomas looking in his direction, before realizing the man would hardly recognize him across a crowded cathedral, after just one brief passing in a harbor inn. Zorzo pushes along the cross aisle and joins the line behind her. After she's taken her bread and wine, she'll turn and he'll finally be able to see her clearly.

A cry erupts and people in the rows closest to the door jump up. There are groans, and, row by row, churchgoers leap to their feet, many fleeing to the side chapels, as floodwater invades the building. It spreads outward from the entrance, pouring across the tiles, lapping against the pews and pillar bases. "Close the doors," someone yells and some men try to do so, only for a stronger wave to crash against them and throw them back open. A woman shrieks. The soles of Zorzo's feet are soaked as cold lagoon water seeps up from below. A mild stampede begins. Half the congregation makes for the main doors, while the rest goes the other way to the outer walls.

Zorzo's first thought is of Sybille, her fear of water, but she's no longer in front of him. On the other side of the church, Tomas and Frau Bauer are scanning the crowd. But for her forest-green dress and gabled hat, Zorzo might not find her again. She's pressed against the corner of the north wall, almost in darkness, hiding, so it seems, close to an open side door, where more people are exiting. Zorzo waits to see if she'll go to the others, but she pivots on her heels and, in the rectangle of light formed by the exit, her hat turns one way, then the other. She picks up the hem of her dress—and disappears from sight.

Zorzo rushes out. She's wading along the flooded path beside the church, then climbs the steps onto drier ground. He's on the point of calling out to her, before realizing he has no idea what to say. She darts along the rear of the prison, over the bridge of San Zaccaria and into the back streets of Castello—in the opposite direction of her home. She stops at a crossroads on the Rio de la Pleta and refers to a slip of paper from her pocket, before peering through the door of a shop and entering.

Zorzo approaches, ready to turn about if she reemerges. It's a *macelleria*, and the butcher at his block, having studied whatever is inscribed on her piece of paper, is giving directions. In the half-lit room and surrounded by meat, the color of her clothes is more intense than ever. Green against bloodred. Behind her, cuts of flesh hang from hooks, sides of beef and mutton with ribs opened out, pigs' heads, a red deer with its back legs hacked off and a bloody saw beside it.

Sybille puts the paper back in her pocket. "I'm obliged," she says to the butcher, her voice blunt and harsh after the singsong timbre of the Venetian. Zorzo spins back into the adjacent doorway as she exits and continues on, down the narrow path and across a bridge into the light of the piazza in front of the Arsenale.

For a moment, Zorzo can't decide what to do. He hates the idea of spying, shadowing like this again—it's underhanded, and he knows she's not going to lead him straight to prince orient or this commission—but still the need to see her face, to make contact, is impossible to resist. He wonders what conversation he could start up. "I have seen a hat like that before, in Munich," or "That church dates back four centuries," or "Do you not remember me? We met in Augsburg. It is one of my favorite cities in the world." No, if he begins with a lie, he'll be caught out in the end. Eventually he hurries on in the direction she went, across the bridge and into the piazza—and finds she's vanished.

He revolves on the spot, but the square is empty, as are the three side streets that go off it.

"What do you want?" a voice comes from under the white arch on one side of the square, the Porta Magna, the entrance to the navy docks. Zorzo cranes to see. Sybille is standing behind it, chest rising and falling. "I'm armed," she says and Zorzo notices the gloved hand of her silhouette brandishes a little stiletto dagger.

"I—" He scratches his forehead against the shame of being found out. "I mean no harm." He grimaces against the blandness of the statement.

"Have you been following me?"

The sun, emerging after the deluge, glares against the dove-white marble of the arch and Zorzo has to shield his eyes with his hands. "It's just that I know you, though you don't know me." The phrase slips out before he's thought about it. It makes him sound even more suspicious. Her neck freezes in a tilt, her ear turned slightly toward him, though she remains in the shadow of the arch.

"You know me how?"

Zorzo ventures a smile. "In Mestre, last night, we stood on the quay together. I was setting off at the same time, and I couldn't help overhearing your husband's name, Fugger." A pause, before reiterating, "I was right beside you on the quay."

"You know his name?" Then, "*Our* name?"

"Of course," remembering what Carlo said at the Ca' d'Oro, "Jakob Fugger is—well—he is a legend, is he not?" Sybille gives a grunt, but says nothing. "Then I saw you coming from the cathedral. It was madness with the flood and—I wanted to introduce myself, but you took off so quickly. You didn't hurt yourself, did you?"

She puts her shoulders back and steps out. For a moment she pulls the halo of light around the archway with her, until she breaks free of it.

Zorzo feels an emptying of air from his throat and he fumbles a bow. His first impression is that the features of her face are indistinct, unformed, not entirely legible, as if drawn in light pencil, especially next to her clothes that have the hard colors of minerals and pine forests. But he's wrong; her face is full of color too, ones harder to define, subtle tones like those that lurk in pearls or the necks of seashells. And there would be perfect symmetry to it, her face, were it not for the scar that trickles from the corner of her right eye, like a faltering tearstain. She keeps hold of the dagger. It's not much larger than an oyster shucker, but pin-sharp.

"I thought you were one of my husband's scouts." She pivots her eyes down at his clothes. "But obviously not."

"No, I—I've never met him. I've just seen him that once in the harbor, and not clearly."

"And why would you want to come and introduce yourself? And stalk me across Venice? Apart from the fact you know our name." There's a petulant bite to her voice and Zorzo wonders how often she's petitioned—for money or favors or access—as the wife of Jakob Fugger. He remembers also what Carlo told him, that she's an heiress in her own right.

"Well, because of your husband, I must confess. I have an interest in meeting him—from a business point of view."

"Oh." She gives a mirthless chuckle, before stowing her dagger in a pocket in her sleeve. "I was told whichever way you throw a rock in Venice, you hit a merchant."

There comes the clatter of a boat bell and Sybille turns to look as a large coal barge creeps up the canal toward the water gates of the Arsenale. A bargeman stands atop the heap, white eyes, red mouth in a sooty face. He calls out and the water gates open.

"I am no merchant," Zorzo says. "Far from it. I am a painter, lowly as that is." He offers a winning smile: a habit of his, hung over from his adolescence, that he wishes he didn't have. "Of canvases, that is to say. Worlds of make-believe."

He wonders if he sounds ridiculous, but his smile, or what he's just told her, has an effect. Sybille blushes; the hidden reds break out across her cheeks and enliven the edge of her scar. "A painter?" she mutters. "I've not met one in person."

"Really? Surely you have painters coming and going all the time?" He means, *being as rich as you are.* "That's why I followed you, to make sure the opportunity does not slip by a second time. I already regretted not introducing myself on the mainland. A painter is nobody without commissions." Sybille doesn't engage, or seem to understand. Like her face, her eyes have colors secreted in them too. They appear pale gray, but lapis blue stands guard behind.

"What I'm trying to say is, I've heard your husband is looking for a painter."

Now she gives a jolt of surprise. "No." Then, less sure, "Really? I hadn't heard it. But," she adds, surely with bitterness, "you could be better informed than I."

"I am Giorgio Barbarelli." He bows, glancing from the tail of his eye to see if the name means anything. It doesn't. "Or Giorgione, as some call me. Or Zorzo, which is my nickname."

"So many names. And you obviously know who I am."

The way she says it, with airless indifference, while making no attempt to leave, gives Zorzo a curious pang. "It is a pleasure. You speak Italian like one of us."

"Hardly, but polite of you to say so. What is this place?" she asks. "What's inside? This arch and these odd red walls that go on and on into the distance..."

"They go around the Arsenale. Where the navy is. The republic's world-conquering fleets." Zorzo wonders if his passion for Venice might be the thing to charm her, entrap her into conversation. "They build the ships in there too. Five thousand workers, a city within a city, one that never sleeps. A new warship every day." Sybille has her eye on the coal barge as it creeps into the enclosure and Zorzo wonders how often she's seen the procession of her husband's goods, the minerals slaved out from his many mines. "But you're right," he pushes on, "the place has a strange feel, at night in particular. If you come up here then, a cloud of bronze light hovers over it, and with the sound of a thousand hammers and saws still at work, it seems like the encampment of some ghost army."

"I can hear it now," she says, "the painter in you." Zorzo laughs. He can't tell if she's being disparaging. "It was interesting to meet you. Good day."

"While you're in Venice," Zorzo improvises to stop her from leaving, "why don't *you* meet with artists, make a commission yourself?" If she's the type that flees on her own, as she did just now, Zorzo thinks that alluding to her independence might pique her interest.

"Make a commission? With you, I suppose?"

"With any of us. Venice is the place. We're overtaking Florence. And I can tell how much you appreciate art." Sybille faces him, still as stone, but for her eyes. "How you dress. All those subtle layers of greens, the malachite coat, the pine-needle gown, the olive chemise, the emerald about your neck. And then that," he points to the gold and gemstone ring she wears over her left-hand glove, "vivid pink, in contrast to it all. What is it, sapphire? The eye goes straight to it." Zorzo presses on, more and more sure of himself. "I know everyone else—in Venice, at any rate, I can't speak for your city—wants to exhibit themselves in mixes of colors, frills and drapery. Understatement is an art us painters have to live by, survive by. You admire paintings, I know you do. You lose yourself in them."

Her eyes stop moving and they seem almost hard green now. There's a taut silence between them, just the sound of the Arsenale's water doors closing.

"Please, come to my studio and look. It's close to here, in that direction, on the corner of the Campo San Francesco della Vigna. It's the only redbrick building in the square, red like the walls of this ghost encampment here. If you have never been in one, a painter's studio is a wonder of the world."

"I think I'll make do without." She straightens her coat. "I must go or I shall be missed." She makes to leave, but Zorzo stops her.

"Wait, you were lost."

"No."

"It seemed—I thought you were looking for something."

"Not at all."

"I know every little lane of the city."

"You're mistaken. I wasn't looking for anything." She's lying, obviously; her temples and the skin around her scar redden with it. "It was nice to meet you."

"Can I just ask?" Zorzo might never see her again and has nothing to lose. "By any chance have you heard of prince orient?"

"Prince?"

"Orient. It's a color."

"A color?" She shakes her head.

"A rare mineral. One that is new to the world. Your husband will certainly have come across it. In one of his mines?"

She shakes her head again. "It means nothing to me. Goodbye." She retreats across the square.

"The corner of San Francesco della Vigna, the red house." When she takes no notice, he calls, "Does he usually have you followed by scouts?"

Sybille stops but doesn't turn around, just tightens her gloves against her hands, before continuing again.

Zorzo lets out a sigh, angry with himself for resorting to an outdated version of himself, to juvenile methods, to his so-called charm, that almost certainly came across as vulgar to a woman of her class. And then to call after her like that would have been the final insult. *I was told whichever way you throw a rock in Venice, you hit a merchant.* Zorzo thinks a painter might as easily be struck. He still wants to follow her, though, to find out what was written on her paper, what she was looking for, but he suppresses the urge. If she catches him spying now, it will surely be the end of his quest.

But when he turns to go he sees, on the far bank of the canal, a blur of green: Sybille is still there, looking his way.

9

Hero of Thermopylae

That night, Zorzo sits at his desk in his *studiolo,* drawing by the light of a candle. He dashes off a series of impressions of Sybille: her hand stretching from the carriage in Mestre, palm to the sky; then gliding across the quay toward the lagoon, frightened but upright, her white dress trailing through the dirt. He draws her in the shadow of the Porta Magna, stiletto dagger unsheathed at her side. He pauses, pencil resting on the dagger blade, and recalls the story Carlo told him at the Orseolo. He fetches up a new sheet and sketches the scene: the frozen Baltic, a deserted island, the brother's hands reaching up through the smashed ice sheet, Sybille stepping out from the shore to save him. He stares at the drawing, chest rising and falling. He can almost feel the cold, biting winds, the isolation, the terror.

He puts the drawings to one side and takes to his bed, only for the pictures to give rise to a series of dreams overnight.

Haunting vignettes: a fight for survival, fear of water, a deserted island world, Jakob casting out Sybille's brother. The scenes invade Zorzo's mind in such a physical and jarring way that when he wakes all he can think of is finding out what she was hiding yesterday, what place she was looking for.

So, rather than go next door to the workroom and look at the canvases he asked to be put out, possible pieces to send to Fugger, he exits the red house and hurries back to the butcher's shop.

"Good morning," he says, relieved to find the same man at the counter as yesterday, only for his smile to falter when he realizes he hasn't worked out what he's going to ask. "I was wondering," he looks around the shop, embarrassed by the task, by appearing predatory, even to a stranger, "do you have brisket for a stew?" Zorzo's father's favorite. If he spends money, the butcher won't mind sharing information.

"I have neck," the man gestures, "or rabbit cooks up well." There are half a dozen hanging behind him, stripped to flesh and sinew.

"Neck. Enough for seven of us." He may as well give his *garzoni* a treat.

The butcher packages everything up and Zorzo clears his throat. "A lady came by here yesterday. Dressed in dark green. She asked you directions. Not a Venetian, a German lady."

"She's betrayed you?" The butcher makes a choking sign with his hand.

"No. Not at all, the opposite. I'm—trying to find her."

"Find her? You should be more careful. She struck me as someone you'd best not misplace." He laughs and wipes his hand on his apron, leaving smears of blood.

"Do you remember where she was trying to get to?"

"I do, because it was odd." He pauses, for effect, one of those people who relishes telling a yarn. "San Isepo, the monastery. I told her she wouldn't get in, even if she were a man. She said she had business there."

"San Isepo? That's..." Zorzo has a vague recollection of a little walled compound in the far reaches of the city. He's not sure if he's ever gone as far as it on foot.

"East, as far as you can go, almost falling off the end of the city. Not what you were expecting? Still want your neck?"

Zorzo can ill afford the expense. "Of course."

He takes his meat and hurries to San Isepo, though he feels guilty for doing so, ludicrous even, but somehow convincing himself that the more he knows about Sybille, the quicker he'll find a way to Fugger, to prince orient, the commission—and find a way to pay his debts. He walks at speed, so he can get back soon, and in another corner of his mind, he remembers the story of Odysseus, and the call of the sirens from the rocks of Scylla, and how their promise, to reveal the future, turned out to be a trick.

The butcher is right about San Isepo: it's as remote a place as there is in Venice, at the very tail end of the city. Barely anyone lives in the area leading up to it. There are no tenement buildings, no palazzi, just wharves and warehouses, largely locked up and left, amid pockets of vegetable patches and scrubland. It's quieter than the rest of Venice, or rather—as with Poveglia—only birds can be heard, flocks of screeching gulls. The air feels different too, fresher and saltier. There is a pair of trees—oddities in Venice—bent at an angle over the years by ocean winds, and after those, there's a little bridge, the last one of Venice, going over to the final island and the monastery.

Zorzo crosses the bridge and circles the building: high, plain walls sporadically illuminated with small squares of candlelight. At the front, facing the water, is a decrepit pontoon; it looks as if boats seldom arrive or leave. If Zorzo didn't know the city was actually behind him, one of the busiest, most vibrant places on earth, he might imagine he's on a deserted stretch of coastland, that San Isepo is one of those faraway fortresses that nobody knows about, like the citadel of a paranoid king. Monks inside start up a chant and the walls of the building seem to hum. The wind sends the sound twisting out to sea.

Zorzo can't imagine why Sybille wanted to come here.

Going into the red house, Uggo says to him, "A lady is waiting for you. In your *studiolo*, sir. A Signora Fugger." A mischievous smile, a flutter of the eyes. "Very striking, sir, if I may be so bold."

"On her own?"

"With a boy from her house." Uggo points to where one is waiting on a chair at the foot of the stairs: Johannes, the young groom who helped Sybille in Mestre when she was nervous about the sea.

"How long has she been here?" Zorzo is amazed she came, having appeared so dismissive at the Arsenale.

"She knocked soon after you left."

"And you've been helpful to her? Did you offer refreshment?"

"I offered, in my best voice," Uggo says, demonstrating it, "but she wanted only for the fire to be built up: she was cold. Oh, and—" He pauses dramatically, palms up, and whispers, "She asked if you were married."

"What?"

"I think it might have been to do with the mess in your room. I tried to clean it up, but she seemed very," he can't find the word, "very anxious, sir. In any case, I told her you have neither wife nor children. That you are currently unspoken for."

"All right, Uggo. Take this to the kitchen." He gives him the packet of meat, which is now seeping blood.

"Not one of your rivals chopped up, is it, sir? Not young Tiziano, I hope." Zorzo wipes the blood off his hands on an apron by the door. "She's *very* striking indeed, master. I'm saying so you can prepare yourself. Perhaps splash a little perfume—"

"That's enough. Can a patron not pay a visit without tittle-tattle starting up? Good morning," he calls over to Johannes and ascends. At the top of the stairs, some of the other *garzoni* are peering through the workroom door. "Nothing to see," he tells them, closing it and going into his *studiolo*.

Sybille turns to him and he halts on the threshold and blinks in surprise. She looks different from yesterday: less stern in the eye, more at ease, almost smiling. "I took Mass at San Zaccaria," she says. "It is close by so I thought… Is it a bad time for me to call?"

"Not at all, not at all." He gives a bow and—to allow himself time to adjust to this version of her, to steady his nerves—goes over to the fire and stokes it. He has so many questions, but doesn't know if he can pose any of them. He wants to ask her for an introduction to her husband. He wants her advice on what would be best to send Jakob Fugger to get his attention, and whether she really knows nothing about the commission. He's desperate to find out about San Isepo too, what she was doing there and why she couldn't talk about it before.

"I prefer San Zaccaria to St. Mark's. It's a less frenzied atmosphere," she says. In contrast to the hard, mineral greens she wore before, she's dressed in shades of brown—rich earthenware umbers, cinnamon and tiger's eye—colors that are warm and inviting, like everything about her today. The neck of her dress is cut low, the top of her chest visible beneath a silk net, and Zorzo wonders if the way she's dressed is somehow for his benefit.

"So you wanted to see a painter's studio, after all?"

"Yes." She gives a little smile and a shrug, presumably to acknowledge her change of heart. She glances at the window. She must have pulled the drapes across them while she was waiting, as they were open when Zorzo left the room. She goes on, "Yes, to see your work and also," she pauses, clears her throat, "give you some information."

"Really?" Zorzo is even more surprised. He was not expecting to see her at all, but even less to be given something useful.

"It appears you were right," Sybille says. "My husband *is* in the market for a painter."

"Can I ask how you found out? He mentioned it to you?"

"No. We don't—" A shout from the canal below makes her start. She snaps her eyes to the window again before she realizes it's just a gondolier calling. "We don't usually speak about such matters." Over her tightly drawn blond hair, she wears a velvet cap sewn with tourmalines and adorned with a pair of pheasant's feathers, and in the gloom, with only light from the fire, she has the quality of such a bird, an exotic in human form. A shape-shifter. "I found out because a painter came to our house to be interviewed and I met him briefly in the hall."

"I see." That interviews have started is not good news. "What did he look like?" His first thought is Michelangelo. Those hostile, paint-cracked eyes seem still to be glaring back at him.

"He was old. Exceptionally old. And he was with another person, a rather florid gentleman with red hair."

"Bellini and di Fonti," Zorzo says, realizing it can't be anyone else, but to make sure, "How did you know he was a painter, the old fellow?"

"His hands, like yours. Color here between the fingers." Zorzo notes, for reference, that Sybille misses nothing. "In Augsburg, you see, it's only a certain type of person who visits my husband. Money borrowers and accountants."

"Did you speak to them at all?"

"The florid man seemed very pleased to be in our house. He doffed his cap to me, asked who had been the architect of the palazzo and how old it was. I told him I didn't know, that it was my first time in Venice, but that one part of the house was old and the other new. He told me the banqueting hall was famous in the region and that he'd always longed to see it."

Her gloved hand is resting on the table and Zorzo realizes the drawings he made of her last night are sitting on top. "And is it famous?" He tries to sound casual, while panic tips through him, that she went through his pictures while she was waiting. The top one, of her stepping from the shore toward her brother's hands reaching through the ice, is the most incriminating.

"It's vast and incompressible," Sybille continues, pulling a face. "It's tiled, all of it—floors, walls, ceiling—in dark green ceramic. I can't go into it. It's nightmarish. Anyway, Tomas came to collect them and they went up to my husband's room. I stayed in the hall until they left, less than half an hour later. The interview must have gone badly, because the old fellow's face was red, and the florid man was saying in his ear," she gives a kind of scowling smile, "that money is no guarantee of taste."

Zorzo is consoled that, at the very least, Bellini will be no competition. "By any chance," he says, changing position, so her eyeline does not fall upon the pictures of her, "did you hear anything more about the commission? Anything specific? The nature of it?"

"I'm afraid not. But I'll listen harder." Her voice drops an octave. "I'll listen harder and tell you what I hear. Would that be helpful?"

"Incredibly helpful." He smiles, as a kind of prickle sets through him. He's certain she's being flirtatious, certain also she's not a natural at it. Zorzo never thinks of himself as being attractive, and yet that seems to be the general view. Even Isabella d'Este, a former patroness who made a point of never being complimentary, begged him to "take his handsome eyes off her, or suffer the consequences." Even if Sybille isn't—how he hates the phrase—taken with him, something has brought her here.

"Your husband doesn't go to Mass with you?"

"No. He takes it alone," she replies, before adding, "I'm not a prisoner in Venice, you know. I can do as I please." There is something defiant in the way she says it and Zorzo wonders if it's true and, if it is, why she pulls drapes over the window and why noises outside make her jump. "Besides, I told him that neither his man, nor our plain-speaking housekeeper here, need accompany me about the streets. Johannes is all the help I need." Beneath the silk net at the top of her dress, her chest rises and falls. For some moments, there's just the sound of the crackling fire. "Well, are you going to show me where you work, what you produce?" she says.

"Of course, absolutely." He's relieved she's asked, as he can get her in front of the *Knight and Groom* and see if it might be worth sending to Fugger, as a demonstration of his skill. "Watch the hem of your gown."

He leads the way across the landing, opens the workroom door and enters, only to find she's lagged behind. All his apprentices are looking around from their stations. Zorzo pivots and finds Sybille standing in the entrance, like a pinned butterfly, a shaft of sunlight catching against her. The workroom has windows at either end, in grids of diamond-shaped leaded glass, and throughout the day the configuration of light continually shifts, overlapping forward and back, every passing hour settling in a new way. But at this precise time in the day, if the weather is right, it comes like a bolt from Olympus, lighting up the interior with an almost phosphorescent intensity, catching against every speck of dust in the workroom and illuminating all the work, as if, Zorzo is fond of remarking, God is making his inspection. It turns the gold and garnet shades of Sybille's gown to an even more profound hue and casts a smoky quartz halo around her.

By the expression on her face—almost alarmed—Zorzo can see she's never been in any space like this, where things are made. Her eyes dart about, from the shelves of color pigments to the plaster cast of a torso, from a stuffed owl to a human skeleton.

"Come in, come in," he says and wonders if she'll take his advice, or let her gown drag on the floor. She lifts it, by just a fraction, and glides in. The apprentices offer little bows or smiles to her, which she reciprocates with a kind of muddled imperiousness.

At the sight of Azalea, Sybille stops. "You have girls?" she says.

"And there'd be more if their fathers would let them."

"Signora." Azalea stands to attention like an eager cadet, glittering eyes reflecting back Sybille's golden-brown dress.

She glides on to the end of the room. "So many of you. I would never have known. This is how pictures are made?"

"Yes. It's a collaborative business."

"Not a trophy you expect to see in Venice," says Sybille, nodding toward a set of stag's antlers that hang amid the plaster casts and models. Despite its size and drama, Zorzo has never much cared for it. Tiziano bought it at a flea market at the studio's expense. "Our hall is full of such souvenirs." The antler's shadow turns across her face as she walks around it. "Jakob must have a hundred of them lined up."

"That he's hunted himself?"

"It certainly wasn't my doing. And this is one of your paintings?" she says, turning her gaze to Espettia Lippi's portrait.

Zorzo hurries over. It's the one thing he didn't want her to see. "She's a young lady we struggled to come to terms with, but it's finished now. Teodor," he calls over, "this needs to go to Lippi today. See to it." Zorzo knows that the count is away from Venice for a month, that there'll be no chance of being paid what he's still owed straightaway, especially as the picture will doubtless be returned with notes, but he'd rather set the process in motion—as well as appear in demand to his guest. "I want to show you this painting." He guides her over to the easel where the canvas of the *Knight and Groom* is placed.

"A soldier," she says blankly, squinting at where light, painted in white lead, reflects against the curve of the larger figure's armor. "Should I know who it is?"

"No. It's not historical, strictly speaking. I'm trying to capture a mood more than anything. An intimate moment. A warrior and his equerry before battle. That said, in my mind at any rate, the knight is a hero of mine. He is Leonidas."

"Of Thermopylae?"

"You know your Greek history." He wonders how far her knowledge spreads, and if she's able to put it to use.

"Why a hero of yours? I always thought of him as rather empty-headed, a career warrior. A bit of a brute."

"He's often shown like that, if he's remembered at all, but in my view it misses the point. He sacrificed himself—for everyone, really."

"Is that a fact?" The tone is mocking, but the smile genuine.

"If he and his three hundred men hadn't blocked that mountain pass and fought to the death—well, imagine." He hopes to sound well read and interested in the world, rather than a know-it-all. "The Greeks obliterated. Socrates was born a decade later. Well, he would not have been. Aristotle neither, nor Plato, Homer nor Euclid, not to mention their illustrious descendants in our own age. We would not be here talking, that is for sure. And for that matter, nor would Venice stand. It would be marsh and water. Thanks to one man. But as I said, the story is just an aid for me. The poignancy of the moment, the relationship of the two figures, is what matters." He pauses before he asks, "Do you think it would appeal to your husband?"

"Why?"

"I thought of sending it, on loan, to make him aware of me." At once she looks alarmed. "It's a thing us painters do."

"Oh, I see." Various worries seem to battle back and forth across her face.

"It's just that, regarding any commission, any interview, if your husband doesn't know who I am—I mean to say, these matters are time limited."

"I understand, I do. I would be careful, though. He hates to feel people pushing. You don't want to end up like the gentlemen earlier." Her manner has changed, the playfulness gone. At once, she seems guarded, distracted, in the grip of some turmoil. She fidgets with the scar beneath her eye. There's a divot where the flesh must have been torn apart and Zorzo wonders if it was from an accident. "Can you give me something to drink? A brandy?"

"Of course. Paulino, bring over the bottle there." Everyone is staring at Sybille and he motions for them to get on with their business.

"This is Calvados, if that suits?" Paulino says, rushing over with a bottle and glass.

Sybille makes no reply, just holds out her hand for the glass and waits as he pours the drink with a hand he can't quite stop from shaking. Zorzo watches as she drinks it down. Her golden-brown dress seems to come from the heightened world of a painting, or from a dream, not from muddy real life. A rust color comes up into her cheeks; it burns from under her skin, prickles across her face, picks out the line of her scar, and a tear wells up in her eye. "Why don't you let me give it some thought for a day or so?" She turns from him and dashes away the wetness with the back of her hand. She's back in control of her thoughts again. "About the best way to approach Jakob. Would that help?"

He wants to say a day or so may be too long; that commissions have dried up, bailiffs are circling; that everyone in the room depends on him; that his foreman and his three children are about to be turned out of their house; that Paulino, though barely seventeen, is the sole earner for his family after his father went blind; that even Teodor has spoken of leaving the workshop and joining a mercenary army. He wants also to address whatever is going on with her.

"Of course, any help at all. Or perhaps..." He has nothing to lose by asking. "You might recommend me to him yourself?"

Sybille laughs, before realizing Zorzo is not joking. "That would not be wise." She doesn't explain why, just sets the empty brandy glass down on the table. "I should go. I will find out all I can. Do you ever go to San Zaccaria? Do you know the church?"

"Better than any." Zorzo spent months there assisting Bellini with the altarpiece.

"Perhaps we could meet there? Would you be free to tomorrow?" Zorzo can barely hide the surprise from his face. "Or maybe that doesn't suit you?"

"Tomorrow would be ideal."

"Three o'clock?" She looks panicked, as if she's suggested too much, gone too far, until she thinks about it and her brow unfurrows. "I'll be there. Goodbye. I'll show myself out." She looks about the room, nodding a general farewell.

Zorzo goes after her. She's halted on the landing at the top of the stairs.

"Can women never be the heroes? Like your Leonidas?" she says with her back to him. "Are we doomed to be in service only? Secondary characters?"

"No. Absolutely not."

"So why are we not the subject of paintings?"

"You are. Many." Zorzo is too much on the spot to think of the best examples—Antigone? Or Penelope? Or Diana or Judith?—but Sybille's shaking her head anyway.

"You'll be my friend, won't you?" she says, facing him at last, showing her livid eyes and burned cheeks. "I realize we barely know each other, but tell me you will."

"Absolutely."

"I have no one in Venice, you see," she mutters. "So few friends in the world at all."

She turns and reaches out her hand to Zorzo's but doesn't quite follow through and their fingers only brush together. She starts to take her hand away, before she changes her mind and wraps her fingers around his palm and clutches tight, her hand hot through the satin of her gloves. Something integral shifts inside him, like a boulder dislodging from the earth, letting off some internal, long-buried heat.

"I must go. I'll see you tomorrow. Three o'clock. Johannes, are you there?"

Zorzo watches Sybille descend in a glide, like a magnificent creature of the deep, her gold-brown dress glittering against the dark hall. Uggo opens the front door and she and her boy disappear from view, the pheasant feathers in her cap the last things to go.

Uggo looks up at his master inquisitively.

"Don't ask me what just happened," Zorzo says to him. "For I have no idea."

10

The Commission

Zorzo arrives at the church of San Zaccaria as the city's clocks strike two, an hour earlier than Sybille said, just in case. He finds it deserted, between services as he thought. It's a couple of years at least since he was here so he takes the opportunity to reacquaint himself. The point of triumph—the interior is otherwise strangely gloomy—is still Bellini's altarpiece. His old master painted it at the turn of the century, brilliantly positioning the scene—virgin, child, saints and musicians—within a structural arch of the building, so it seems as if you're gazing through it to an alternate reality beyond, one that's actually more alive and enticing than our own. Though Zorzo had left Bellini's studio by then, his old master hired him back for a few weeks, to "bring a July mood" to the picture. Zorzo repainted portions of the sky, brought a quality of summer light to the scene and reimagined the Madonna's gown as a bold sweep of azure blue. He got a lot of praise for this, or rather, Bellini did.

Zorzo starts when a door to one side of the chancel opens and nuns file in behind the columns of the ambulatory. He can only make out moving fragments—habits, hoods, young faces, clasped hands—until they're lost from view. A woman gives the cue and the others start singing, recanting a Psalm. A choir, with ten different parts moving in and out of each other, like the coming and going of bells. Zorzo wonders if he's allowed to be here, if he's trespassing, but a smattering of other Venetians start arriving and taking seats.

He positions himself in the back corner, where he has a view of the door and the whole interior, and waits. He fantasizes about what color Sybille will appear in. She was moon-white in Mestre harbor, then dark jade at St. Mark's and tiger's eye in his workroom. The sound of the choir reaches up into the roof and stays there, and against it Sybille's voice loops through Zorzo's head, the agitation that came over her when Zorzo suggested contacting her husband: *I would be careful. He hates to feel people pushing.* And then the curious, almost desperate, lament on the landing: *Can women never be the heroes?*

More people arrive—an old lady, a pair of young men with the threadbare look of students, a drunk—but no Sybille. An hour passes, then another, the choir disbands, the congregation too, leaving Zorzo alone once more. The church becomes cold and dark, Zorzo does another circuit and worries jostle for space in his head. He wonders if something has happened to her, an accident with water, perhaps; or if she suggested the plan because Zorzo was becoming too assertive about sending a picture to Fugger and she never intended to come at all. He becomes concerned that he's wasting precious time when really he should be in his studio, working out if there are other ways to get to Fugger, that he's letting his judgment become clouded. By what, he isn't sure. By lust, perhaps. Caspien and Carlo described her as having a rare beauty. Both parts of the phrase may be true, but particularly the first. She's rare, a contradiction of things, both blunt and mysterious, soft and hard, frightened enough to jump at sounds and close drapes in the daytime, but defiant too.

Zorzo finds himself in front of the other celebrated painting in San Zaccaria: a presentation of hell, a warning to the souls that come to the church, antithesis of Bellini's summer-soaked vision. Death stands watch as the damned fall headfirst into the abyss, to be consumed by fire, or snakes or each other; all of it rendered in dirty colors, that look as if they've been muddied with blood itself. Zorzo tries to imagine—a diversion from thinking about Sybille—the dark days of the Middle Ages, when plague ruled, and Satan haunted every corner of the world, and how it must have struck terror into people. Now, in the age of trade, with ships all but circling the globe and knowledge pouring from printed books, he wonders if the brand of primal fear that the painting once spoke to still exists. For many, most, who live outside cities like Venice, it probably does. It puts him in mind of Bellini's doom-laden pronouncements of a few days ago: *All those sculptures and essays, all our wicked thoughts—that declare man is the center of it all. Not God.* The memory is unsettling enough to propel Zorzo out of the church, and he's halfway home when he stops and turns—and goes to Cannaregio instead, to the Fugger residence.

Reaching the pathway at the rear of the Palazzo Pallido he stops dead. A window in the tower at the back of the house is open and, hazy in the gloom beyond it, he sees Sybille. She's in view for a few moments, in a cerulean-blue gown, her face concentrated but certainly not in any way upset, or impatient or aggravated. Zorzo first feels a turn in his stomach, a twist of hurt, before another thought strikes him: that she's there against her will, perhaps locked in. In his mind, a person in a tower has eerie connotations: a tower is where innocents are locked up, like the two English princes an ambassador once told him about, heirs to the throne who mysteriously disappeared. She appears again briefly, to throw out three scrunched-up pieces of paper, which drop into the canal, before she leaves the room. She wasn't locked in. Zorzo hears the door slam and catches another glimpse of cerulean blue from a lower window and his sense of hurt pride returns.

He begrudges the fact that she's inveigled his thoughts and continues to do so, that she's appeared in his dreams two nights running, as the protagonist, not a secondary character, an exquisite and unsettling presence that casts itself over everything. In the past, when Zorzo's friends have despaired of infatuations, bemoaned being "under a spell," he has felt relieved, amused even, knowing he'd never fall in that way. He hadn't with Leda, except for a brief spell of suffering a few days ago when he discovered her lover. And before her, his affairs with women—all of whom were fascinating and independent-minded—invariably came to a natural, good-natured end, in which neither party seemed to lose. Which is why he's remained friends with them, good friends. Now, though, when he should be working, he's at the back of a house, spying like a jealous lover on a woman he's only spoken to twice, a woman who is married—married to a man who, if not dangerous, is powerful beyond belief.

The discarded papers sit on the surface of the water, with the outgoing tide starting to carry them away. One has opened up enough for Zorzo to see it's a letter, presumably started by her, because the writing—in green ink and heavily slanting script—stops abruptly halfway down. Zorzo's impulse is to jump in and get it, but he stops himself and thinks a moment, before deciding he'll try. Keeping his eyes on the back of the house, and even as he's sure he's being ridiculous now, he lowers his legs into the canal up to his knees and reaches for the half-open one. He almost has it in his grasp when there's a shunt of metal and the back door of the palazzo opens.

Zorzo jumps out and backs into a doorway. There are voices,

and as he waits to see who'll emerge, he watches the discarded papers drift away. A man comes out, carrying a portfolio under his arm. The door shuts behind him with a bang; he crosses the little bridge and shuffles up the street. It takes Zorzo some moments to realize he knows him, though he hasn't set eyes on him for years. He's dressed in disheveled clothes, untucked around the belly, and has messy, dark ginger hair. Zorzo's initial surprise turns quickly to jealousy, this time of a professional variety. His stomach swills with it. What is *he*, Lorenzo Lotto, doing in Fugger's house, armed with his portfolio?

"Lorenzo?" Zorzo says and the man halts and looks up.

He's so wrapped up in his thoughts it takes him a moment to realize who it is. "Giorgio? Is that you?"

"It must have been five years. How are you, friend?"

"Five at least. They've summoned you too?" Lorenzo says, motioning toward the back of the house.

Zorzo conceals his battered pride with a smile. "No, I was on my way to see a friend." He points up the path and spots Sybille's discarded papers disappearing from sight along the canal.

"It's so good to see you, Giorgio," Lorenzo goes on. He's never used Zorzo's nickname like everyone else, always Giorgio. "I'm surprised you recognize me. Everyone thinks I look like an old man now."

"You look the same," Zorzo replies, even though Lorenzo, at barely thirty, is not aging well. He's always been a fretter, particularly about his success, or perceived lack of it. On the other hand, he looks like a Viking warrior—stocky and pale, with tousled ginger hair and beard. Zorzo wants to ask straightaway about Lotto's visit to the palazzo, but must small-talk first. "Where've you been all this time?"

"Where haven't I been? Treviso, Ancona, Fermo, Recanati." He pronounces the names as if listing a series of illnesses. "Lotto has spread his wings. But I do come back from time to time to see my mama and papa."

"And you've been busy in those places?"

"Busy, yes, I suppose so," Lorenzo says with a worried smile. "My time in Treviso did well for me. My portrait of Bernardo de' Rossi brought attention for sure." He gives a bashful chuckle. "And I painted the altarpiece for the church of Recanati, and one thing led to another, as it does, and now I've settled in Rome, if *settled* is the word. Sorry, sorry," he mutters to a couple trying to pass along the pathway behind his portfolio. His forehead is beaded with perspiration, despite the cold. "I've changed my style a good deal," he says. "It's very different now. It is more—what is the word—dramatic."

"Well, I always thought you were one of a kind." Zorzo chooses the phrase because he knows that when they were both starting out, a rumor used to hang about that Lorenzo copied him. Zorzo hadn't agreed. Either way, his colleague has never made his mark in Venice, the city of his birth. Perhaps his work is too subtle for the cognoscenti of the city, men like di Fonti. Or maybe Lorenzo himself is the problem.

"I've just put the pieces together," Zorzo says, deciding he must now find out as much as he can. "I realize what you meant before, about them summoning me too. You mean the Fuggers? You were meeting them?"

"Well, just one, Fugger, that is."

"Jakob? Regarding a commission?"

Lorenzo chuckles uncomfortably. "I—I'm not supposed to talk about it. I had to sign a paper, promising my—what was the word they used—not discretion, but—"

"Silence?"

Another nervous giggle. "Well, I suppose you could call it that. But—there's nothing to be silent about. They'll not offer it to me, not in a thousand years. You would have more chance than I. But you've not been called, you say?"

"Why don't we walk on a little? Are you going home?" Zorzo knows Lorenzo's parents live not far from the red house.

"I don't know, Giorgio, really. The whole business has put me into a spin."

"Aren't we old friends?" Zorzo says. "Didn't we go through everything at the same time? Are you hungry?" He knows how much Lorenzo loves his food.

Lorenzo scratches the back of his neck, considering, before eventually saying, "Well, there's a place in Santa Croce that sells *pasticcini*, the best in town."

Santa Croce is much further than Zorzo would like to go. "Then what are we waiting for?"

"But wait, you said you were on your way to see someone?"

"She can wait." Zorzo casts a final look at the palazzo tower.

"Ah. There's still a trail of them coming after you, I suppose," Lorenzo jokes, reading Zorzo's comment the wrong way. "The ladies, I mean."

Zorzo smiles back, though he's more determined than ever to be seen as anything other than Caspien's "career bachelor."

Lorenzo leads the way over the Rialto and across to the other side of the city, eventually arriving at an alleyway, where a little barred window punctuates a long wall. Sugary odors drift out from the dark interior. "Hello," he calls, before confiding, "I've been coming here since I was a boy." Zorzo was expecting a shop at least, but it's a monastery, and a nun appears in the shadows behind the bars of the window. "Good afternoon, sister. Do you have *struffoli* today?" The nun nods. Apart from her walnut-skin hands and the belt of her habit, she's a dark shape. "Two of those, then. No, four, I'll take some home for Mama. Six, actually, in case we have guests. And a slice of *torrone*. Two slices. Delicious also," he says aside to Zorzo. "The almonds come from Sicily. Very sweet. My mother says I need to build myself up, that I've grown thin. I don't know if she's right."

Zorzo doesn't either. The belt of fat that settled on Lorenzo as a teenager has filled out and will probably be there for the rest of his life.

The nun passes everything through the window and Lorenzo pays her. "It's like confession," Zorzo says, "with pastries instead of pardons." The men take a seat on the steps of the well in the center of a square and Lorenzo puts his folder down.

"So, how did the interview come about?" says Zorzo. "And why has it put you in such a spin, as you say?"

Lorenzo indicates that his mouth is full. "Eat," he says, finishing his first *struffoli* and shoveling in the next. Zorzo's not hungry, but obliges. "So, I told you I was in Rome. And I've found myself working for Bramante, the architect, who you must know?"

"Who built the Tempietto?" It's a building, even a decade on, that everyone talks of with a kind of religious fervor. A small but perfectly formed classical temple put up on the spot where it's said St. Peter was crucified.

"Precisely. Well, he may be a genius of an engineer, but as an employer, I can tell you, he leaves a lot to be desired. I've worked for him for two years and he's barely paid any of what he owes me. It has driven me to the edge of reason. He ignores my letters and I can't afford my rent or food, let alone what I have to spend on materials. Anyway, you know all this. You're in the same profession. Should I have another pastry?" he says, eyeing up the extra ones he bought for his mother. "Why not?" He tucks in.

"You don't deserve all this trouble, Lorenzo, really you don't. So, Bramante is involved with this commission?"

Lorenzo brushes the crumbs from his shirtfront and goes on. "Well, in the summer, when I confront him, face-to-face, about his debt to me, he starts with this long story instead. He says he's been commissioned to put up a building, a very expensive, very daring, very *everything* building, in Rome. It won't just be the biggest building in Rome, but in all Europe. And of course he needs artists for this unforgettable structure. He goes, 'You'd be ideal for the project. I'll put in a word with Julius.'"

"Julius? Pope Julius?"

"None other. So I prepare for *months*, working through the night, every night, drawing up ideas, reams' worth of ideas. In the daytime my hands are tied: because I'm designing trompe l'oeils for his apartments, which incidentally have left me half-blind and more than a little mad. Anyway, after all this, after working myself to the bone, he says, 'The meeting won't be in Rome, but in Venice. Can you get there?' Still no mention of my overdue wages, nor how I'll afford the journey. Regardless, I come and nearly die getting here. Those damned Tuscan roads. And I arrive to discuss this so-called commission of a lifetime and find these strange men, no sign of Julius at all—*he's* still in Rome—no Bramante either."

"So there's Fugger and who else?"

"Well, Fugger is monosyllabic, but he has a sidekick, some cardinal or other, who does the talking. Soderini, he's called. Very slick. He might be a man of the church, but he was pure salesman, like some hawker on the Rialto. They want a portrait, as an altarpiece, full-body, immense, three times life-sized at least. Of St. Peter. They have drawings already, or 'guidelines' as they called them, which they wouldn't show me."

"I don't understand. What is Fugger's connection?"

"He's the one paying for it, this building to end all buildings."

"Fugger is?"

"That's why the meeting was in Venice. Fugger won't go to Rome, apparently. He's the backer, not Julius. Pope or not, he's as good as bankrupt." It's almost amusing how Lorenzo has gone from silence to spilling every secret imaginable.

"Sorry, am I being stupid? What is the building?"

"Oh, I thought it was obvious. The new cathedral. The basilica. St. Peter's of Rome. *The* St. Peter's. After tearing the old one down, the new one will reach the heavens. And the building will go up around this 'astonishing new painting.'"

Zorzo laughs, he doesn't know why, maybe from desperation. He's known for years the old church came down, and that one would replace it in time; and that it would have to be the greatest church in the world as it would be at the very center of Christendom. He's known all this, but not that it had a financier and architect already, and, quite soon, an artist too.

"They barely even looked at my work," Lorenzo rattles on, tapping the side of his portfolio, "barely spoke to me at all, before announcing they're 'still holding out for their first choice.'"

"Who is?" Zorzo almost doesn't want to know the answer. "Michelangelo, I suppose?" Lotto shakes his head. "Not Tiziano?" If his old student were being sought, it would be a body blow to Zorzo.

"Worse. Much worse: da Vinci."

"What?" Zorzo coughs on his last mouthful of sweet and it takes some moments to get himself under control again.

"And how do I know? Because he came out before I went in. The legend himself."

"Da Vinci, here in Venice?"

"Exactly. What chance does anyone else have? They're all arriving in town, you know? Every painter in Christendom from Rome to Flanders. It's like an infestation."

"Wait, wait." Zorzo puts up his palm. Facts are coming too fast for him to take in. "Are you sure it was da Vinci?"

"He introduced himself, but I knew anyway. The mane of silver hair, the magician's beard, the *very* obscure sense of humor. He asked me if I knew Venice, and I said yes, I was born here, and he said could I recommend a costume shop in the city. He'd been invited to a ball and wanted to go as Death."

"As Death?"

"A skeleton beneath a shroud or something, with a sickle in his hand and empty clock dials hanging from his belt. He said the motif of the party is 'men who've changed the world.' According to him, the host is a bore and they'll all be dressed as Charlemagne or Marco Polo. But if any character has truly changed the world, he said, it's you-know-who. And he laughed and I have no idea what he found so funny."

A memory surfaces in Zorzo's mind, a man in a cinnabar-red coat who'd come to visit Bellini's workshop when Zorzo was sixteen or so. He was demonstrating something, sketching with his left hand before passing the chalk to his right and carrying on. *You work for this charlatan?* he joked to Zorzo about Bellini. Deep voice, glittering eyes, buccaneer's face and a manner so easy and calm Zorzo has never forgotten it.

"It is quite a story." Zorzo's itching to know if Lorenzo has heard of prince orient, but decides against mentioning it to anyone else, and asks instead, "Can I see your drawings?"

"For what they're worth," Lorenzo sighs. He passes over the folder and unties the ribbon. "They're how I would imagine St. Peter, but the first thing they said when I went in was they didn't want to see actual representations of him, that they'd prefer almost anything else. Another incomprehensible turn. At least you might appreciate them."

He's done a huge amount of work, good work too, bringing his version of St. Peter to life in a dozen meticulously detailed drawings. They must have taken months to complete, especially given he'll only have brought the very best ones to the interview. He's a brilliant draftsman; the quality of his line is as sensitive and unconventional as his personality.

"I suppose I might be able to use them for something," Lorenzo says, peering over his friend's shoulder. "He doesn't *have* to be Peter. Rub some lines from his face, he could be Christ. Or a middle-aged Apollo."

"Of course you'll use them. Good work is never wasted." Zorzo means it when he says, "You're one of the finest artists in Italy. I've always thought so. Don't forget it."

He returns the folder. "You'd better get the rest of your sweets back before they're all gone. Though I'm sorry you wasted a trip to Venice, I'm glad it meant our paths crossed. By the way, was Fugger's wife there?" he says before he goes. "Very striking, you wouldn't forget."

Lorenzo's face lights up. "Yes, when I came in. She was talking to da Vinci. What a creature she is. Exquisite. Like a white egret. I suppose it's his wealth. Why else would a woman like her marry such a man? Goodbye, friend."

Zorzo gives him a hug, squeezing him tight. For all his oddities, he's fond of the fellow. It's only after Lorenzo has shuffled away that Zorzo realizes how agitated he is. He hurries on and flags the first gondola he sees.

"Castello," he says to the boatman and jumps aboard. "As close as you can get to Campo San Francesco della Vigna."

"Rodolfo, isn't it?" the gondolier asks.

Zorzo does a double take: having never encountered him until a week ago, the same man who took him to Poveglia has cropped up again. "Zorzo, and you are Tullo."

"I knew it was an unusual name. You're a Venetian?"

Zorzo is caught off guard, partly by Tullo's chattiness, but also the abstract question. "From Castelfranco originally."

"A lovely town, sir. I visited it with my sister." Zorzo had misjudged the gondolier, thought him only sullen and bad-tempered.

"Castello, then." Tullo casts off, pushing down on his oar until he picks up speed along the canal.

As soon as he gets back to the red house and into the workroom, Zorzo takes some paper from the desk, ink and a pen and scribbles a note. "Tulipano, take this to Cannaregio, the Palazzo Pallido. Give it to Johannes, the boy who came with Sybille Fugger yesterday. *Only* to him, do you understand? He's to pass it to his mistress. Is it legible? Read it back."

"'I waited today. San Zaccaria, tomorrow, the same time. Urgent.'"

Zorzo wonders if it sounds too rude, but decides it will do.

There is no point in not being direct. He folds the paper and seals it with wax from a candle on the worktop. "Off you go."

As soon as Tulipano has torn off, Zorzo retrieves more sheets of paper, along with pencils and chalk. "I don't want to be disturbed," he says, slamming the door to his *studiolo*.

He's not going to wait for Sybille's consent or sanction on the matter. An altarpiece for the new St. Peter's cathedral will be the commission of the century. Bellini, Lotto and da Vinci have already been seen, probably Michelangelo too. For all he knows, Tiziano could be in the running too. No, Zorzo can wait no longer. He's going to make a painting to send to Fugger. Lotto said they didn't want to see a picture of St. Peter, so he'll paint the man himself. From his imagination, he'll paint Jakob Fugger.

11

Sirocco Winds

On the first sheet of paper he sketches Fugger, as he was on Mestre harbor: in silhouette at the edge of the sea, his back turned, decked in priceless blacks and looking toward the towers of Venice as if he owned them.

On the second sheet, Zorzo keeps the same outline of the man but draws it against the Lusatian Mountains, the mouth of the pitshaft where prince orient is being brought to the light. Dashing off more sketches, Zorzo pictures him as an industry baron, intimidating and plain-speaking, presiding over factories and furnaces; as a road builder, overcoated against the winter like a general, as his army smashes through the Urals; as a fearless engineer. Zorzo works and works, wondering until his head aches how to capture the man, how to get his attention, how to intrigue and flatter, in such a way it does not seem obsequious.

Zorzo draws into the night and starts again as soon as he

wakes. He pictures Fugger at the gates of his banking house; and with Lady Fortune, a sly, smiling-eyed personification of wealth. He sketches him with the pope, and with the Holy Roman Emperor, and with three Eastern potentates below a traveling star. He places him before palaces and cathedrals, as a god in human form, as Zeus, and as Vulcan, manning the fires of the underworld.

"Sir, it's past two," Janek says in the afternoon. "You told me to tell you."

"Yes," says Zorzo. The time to go and meet Sybille has come around quickly, too quickly. Today she'll come, he knows, because she sent word back via Johannes, a note even more brief than Zorzo's to her. *Agreed, three o'clock. S.* Written in the same green ink, the same slanting letters, as the note she tossed into the canal.

He wipes the tiredness from his eyes and looks down at his drawings. Twenty or so are strewn in front of him, but none are right. Despite Lorenzo Lotto saying the men didn't want to see a version of St. Peter, Zorzo still wonders if he's on the right track, making Jakob Fugger the subject. *Be personal,* was always Bellini's advice. *Make your patron believe they're the most important person in the world.*

He wonders why he hasn't put Sybille in any of the drawings. He takes the one of Fugger at the mouth of the Lusatian mine and sketches her outline beside her husband. He goes even further and puts a child between them, a girl, and then an infant in her arms. He looks at the drawing, *the family,* before he rubs out the infant, then the child, then the wife.

By the time Zorzo has stopped fiddling around with ideas and got into his clothes, he's running late and has to rush through the afternoon crowds to San Zaccaria. He can't help but notice how warm it is in the streets compared to recent days. Balmy sirocco gusts—which often at this time of autumn bring the last of the year's heat from North Africa—whistle across the city's piazza and down its canalways.

He arrives at the square and finds Sybille pacing near the steps of the church, with Johannes close by. She's a vision of red. Her long, voluminous cape is the color of dragon's blood or overripe cherries. The sight of her sends an eddy of heat, a dose of the sirocco, through Zorzo. While he was working, she fell away from his thoughts, for the first time since setting eyes on her in Mestre. Now he wonders how it will be possible to think of anything else. In this moment, he could almost forget about the painting of Fugger, the commission and prince orient, and keeping the business afloat, the bailiffs and his father's ring. She, not them, is the most vital thing in Venice.

"Signora Sybille," he calls and she looks around.

She tells Johannes to stay where he is and comes over, just as a gang of choirboys spill into the square and she gets trapped among them: two dozen laughing innocents in snow-white surplices and she in her dragon's-blood cloak, pushing through. The ache inside Zorzo—up his spine, and into his neck—is at once a violent delight. Sybille Fugger cannot be passed over, ever.

"You should not have sent me that note," she says, bearing down on him, the wind catching against her cloak, making her appear like some vengeful deity of ancient Greece coming in to land. "Have you any idea of the trouble you may have caused? What if it had been given to my husband?"

"I'm sorry, I—"

She ushers him out of sight down one of the alleyways that go to the lagoon, even though there's no one in the square but her groom and the last of the choirboys entering the church. "He'll think straightaway that—I don't know—that I have something to hide, or that I'm having an affair with you. It has happened for far less."

Zorzo had misgivings about sending it, but not as grave as this. Though the phrase she uses, *having an affair*, gives him another curious twist of longing. He pauses before saying, "Signora, I'm sorry."

"I told Jakob I'd heard of a painter, Giorgione," she goes on. "Against my better judgment I brought it up. I suggested he seek you out, that you were a young star in Venice. I didn't say we'd met. How could I?" Her forehead and neck have turned the same burnt red as the rubies sewn into her gown. "But if he'd seen the note—his men read my mail, you understand, I have no privacy—he'd have realized we were in alliance."

"So he didn't see it, then?"

"Luckily my boy received it," she motions back to the piazza, where Johannes is standing by, "and brought it straight to me. On this occasion. But understand, you risked everything."

Zorzo can barely remember a time when he received such a scolding. Even when he was fourteen and put a hole through one of Bellini's finished canvases after a practical joke went wrong, the explosive telling-off he got didn't chasten him as much as this. "Signora Fugger, please accept my apology. It is no excuse, but I came here yesterday, as you suggested. When you didn't appear I became concerned. In the meantime, I learned your husband had been interviewing more candidates, that the commission was much larger than I'd thought, and I regret impatience took hold of me."

"So was it concern for me, or impatience for your own advancement?"

Zorzo wants to say both, but what she's insinuating is true: it was more the latter.

"Did you stop to think there might have been a reason? It was precisely because there were people in the house, because my husband was interviewing, that I stayed behind. For you, to gather information for you."

Zorzo hangs his head. "Truly, I have nothing but shame for myself. It's no excuse, but when I found out that one of the painters being seen was Leonardo da Vinci, who is a hero of mine, of all of us, a kind of madness came upon me. I am so sorry."

The speech, and the way he puts it, has the effect of washing away some of Sybille's fury. The darts of red dissolve from her forehead and neck, and her breathing evens out. After a pause, she looks down and says, "Da Vinci, yes. I didn't realize myself until after he'd gone. I was impressed with that."

Keeping the conversation light, Zorzo says, "Jesus Christ himself appearing in one's hall would be scarcely less miraculous."

"My advice is to go no further in this matter."

"This matter?"

"With my husband. The danger is too great. He's vindictive. He has the mind of a murderer. And make no doubt, if he suspected there was something illicit between us, you would be the recipient of his killing thoughts, not I. There must be other commissions, other colors. Look to those."

Zorzo never knew how seriously to take Carlo Contarini's stories about Fugger, about him having people disposed of, thrown off buildings or burned alive, but he hasn't forgotten them. On the other hand, what Sybille is suggesting is devastating, especially in the light that she herself just recommended him to her husband and is now reversing course. He wonders if he should tell her that this is not an ordinary commission, nor an ordinary color, that securing either would guarantee fame down the ages. And even if it didn't, it would pay his bills many times over. It would ensure the return of his ring at least.

From behind, the organ strikes up inside the church, and then the choir. The clear, sharp sound carries over the city. "Johannes?" Sybille calls back and the lad appears at the mouth of the alleyway. "Go back to the palazzo and wait for me near the back door, so we can go in together. I'm going to walk the long way around."

"Madam?" he says, silhouetted against the light of the piazza. "I should—"

"Don't worry about me. I'm in safe hands. Go. I shan't be long."

The boy is still reluctant, but nods and disappears from sight.

Sybille continues up the path; Zorzo follows and they come

out onto the Riva degli Schiavoni, the wide promenade that runs almost the length of the city. The wind is stronger here. It has set waves rolling across the lagoon. Sybille shields her eyes with her red-gloved hand and scans left and right, at the people along the path. "There," she says, "out of the wind." She leads the way to the little arched colonnade below the prison. They stand in silence for a while. Like two days ago in his workroom, Zorzo has the sense of her being gripped by some unspoken torment, something dreadful and great beneath the surface.

"Why are there always ships anchored in the middle of the lagoon?" she asks. "That one hasn't moved since I last came this way." She's pointing at a galley that's a hundred yards out, a Byzantine of some sort, immense with fin-shaped sails.

"Under quarantine. Forty days they have to anchor there. Plague. Venice is always the first in line. The whole world threads through this city."

"Plague. It's a wonder my husband comes here at all." She continues the conversation, though Zorzo's certain her mind is elsewhere. "And does someone watch the ships? What's to stop their crews—I don't know—coming ashore at night, in secret?"

"Coast guards. Many eyes are on them."

Sybille nods and there is silence again between them, before she says, "I am sorry I was so agitated. I meant what I said about the note, but there was something else." She fingers the scar below her eye. "On our way here, we saw a terrible sight."

"What? Where?"

"In St. Mark's. In the *piazzetta* just along there. Johannes tried to hurry me on, but I felt I had to watch. Out of duty, having never witnessed such a thing. A public hanging."

"Good God." Of all the things she might have said, this was the last Zorzo expected. He knows where the republic carries out its official executions, and that many people go to view them, including Bellini, who has a bloodthirsty streak, and that the corpses are left rotting for weeks on end. "I find them barbaric, especially where they're carried out, in our government square, but I'm one of the few who thinks that way." Then, recalling what Sybille just said, "Why do you say duty?"

"I couldn't imagine what this fellow had done. He looked like anyone—not young, my father's age, well dressed. He seemed, I don't know, gentle?"

"Well, appearances aren't everything," he says. "For all we know he may have put a whole family to the knife."

Sybille turns to him, flushing. "I don't believe it. I saw his eyes as they pushed him up the steps of the gallows and tied the rope about his neck. He was no killer. And so it proved. I asked the lady next to me in the crowd who he was. He was a professor at the university. He was a printer of books."

Though Zorzo's put in mind of Bellini's gloomy pronouncements a few days ago, about ill omens and powers that be, he doesn't understand why she seems so personally affected.

"Zorzi?" comes a woman's voice. "What are you doing skulking by the prison?"

It's Leda. She's dressed in her finest and has her assistant, Hakim, at her side with his notebook at the ready. She rushes over to Zorzo, holds out her hand—not to be kissed or touched, but as an affectation—and only then notices Sybille. Her smile freezes in surprise.

"Leda Sitruk," Zorzo says quickly, to save embarrassment on all parts, "this is my colleague, Frau Sybille Fugger. She's visiting from Augsburg." It's the first thing to come into his mouth.

The women appraise one another—just for a moment, though it seems like an age to Zorzo, the way their eyes are like packs of cards being shuffled—before they shake hands, barely touching fingertips, Leda's gloves of bright apricot leather against Sybille's vermilion satin. The contrast in the way they dress—Leda bodiced into as many colors as possible: lime green, sapphire, burnt pink and turquoise; Sybille in restrained, exquisite variations on deep red—could not be more absolute.

"Signora Sitruk is one of the only female merchants in the city," Zorzo offers. "She manufactures buttons for practically everyone." The moment he says it and notices Leda grit her teeth in annoyance, he realizes it's the wrong boast to make in this company.

"It's a hobby, really," Leda trills. "My father is the governor of Cyprus. But I hate to sit around and do nothing with my time." Zorzo knows this is a barefaced lie, that Leda's father, at best, has a position on the island's council. The status of her family changes according to whom she's speaking with—though she's never gone as far as governor before.

"How incredible," Sybille replies, "to run a business for yourself." She says it so blankly Zorzo can't tell if she means it. Her eyes are darting at all the little embellishments of Leda's outfit, the ribbons, buckles and feathers. "Look out!" Sybille suddenly calls.

A gull screeches, the shadow of it wheeling over them; there's a sound like a child's foot striking a puddle and a glossy white and brown deposit splashes onto Leda's collar, then drops lumpily down onto the bosom of her dress. "You poor soul!" Sybille exclaims, straightaway taking Leda to one side, producing a handkerchief from her pocket—a piece that probably took a lacemaker weeks to sew—and wipes the muck from the dress. She shakes it onto the ground, before using the sleeve of her shirt to mop up the rest until the stain is gone. "Velvet is difficult," Sybille says. "You must get to it straightaway."

Leda seems completely thrown by the unexpected act of kindness, almost put out by it. Zorzo can't help but compare the two women. One came along in a cloud of ego, pretending to be a governor's daughter; the other just moments before had been troubled by nothing less than an unjust hanging. She seemed cool to the stranger at first, but jumped to her aid the moment it was needed. It was almost sisterly.

"You shouldn't be allowed in Venice," Leda says to her. "You're far too beautiful. And considerate." She gives her dress a body-revealing tug, the body that Zorzo used for his Venus, puts her shoulders back and turns on her smile again. "Don't get carried away by the wind, you two." She curtsies at Sybille before turning to Hakim. "Quickly now, we're late." The boy hurries to her side, pencil once more at the ready, and they turn up the street, past the prison, in the direction of San Zaccaria.

"What a striking lady," Sybille says, though in such a way that Zorzo can't tell if she's sincere. "You are lucky to live in a city where there are flowers of every type. In Augsburg we are all just plain daisies. I must leave you too, and get back home."

They stand in silence and the sirocco wind teases against the sails along the embankment.

"I can't stop you from seeking out Jakob," Sybille says eventually, "if your mind is made up. But no more notes to me like that. We've never met, understand? You do not know me. And I warn you, for your own benefit, dealings that men have with Jakob very rarely end in their favor. So, do what you must, but know," she pauses, considers a moment before looking at him directly and saying in a quiet, firm voice, "know that if I had my way, I'd keep you as my secret and nobody else's."

Up the path, San Zaccaria's organ and choir fall silent. Zorzo feels a shiver down his spine. The sirocco wind has found its way into him, found an opening and is needling against the bones of his back, against the scapula and clavicle and into the base of his skull. He can't believe what he just heard.

I'd keep you as my secret and nobody else's.

On the one hand she's filling him with fear about her husband; on the other she seems to be alluding to something illicit between them.

"I have a great deal to reflect on," he finds himself saying glibly. He needs time to think about what is happening. "Shall I walk you home?"

"No, no, there's no need." She says it so abruptly that she has to add in a softer tone, "I know the way. Goodbye, then, for now."

She gathers her dress up and hurries down the path, the way Leda went, back toward the church, and Zorzo goes the other way, along the embankment to St. Mark's. He wonders what he must do now. How can he go home and carry on planning a painting for Fugger after what Sybille's just said?

He goes to the gallows between the columns in the *piazzetta* and looks up at the newly hanged man. His face juts at an angle and is the color of a gray autumn day. And diarrhea has spilled out against the lining of his cloak; but other than that, Sybille was right. He looks the essence of ordinary. A well-to-do man in his fifties, as harmless as any of the fellows who are crossing the square. A gust of sirocco sets him swinging slightly, unleashing the faintest ammonia stench, the beginning of his very end.

Zorzo turns and looks at the front of the Doge's Palace and remembers his father, how he stood by his side on this very spot the day they came to Venice, when Zorzo was about to start his apprenticeship. "You'll paint there one day," his father said, nodding at the palace. Zorzo, believing none of it, grinned up at him. The old fellow, pale as flour, hands bloated and misshapen from endless mishaps with chisels, tried to keep his back straight against thirty years of stonemasonry, a lifetime of crippling work. "Mark my words, you will."

Then he sees her, Sybille, in the distance, her red dress unmistakable. She lied. She hasn't returned home, but gone the opposite way. She went back to the embankment and is halfway along it, halfway around the southern shore of the city. And she's not taking a leisurely stroll. Her vermilion cape flutters against the gray sky, occasionally rising and falling when she hurries over a bridge. Eventually it becomes just a hazy spot of color, before even that is lost among the buildings at the end of the island. There is only one place she can be going to: San Isepo. Zorzo wonders how it is that every time he meets Sybille Fugger, he's left with more questions than answers.

"No, no, if you have people here, I'll not interrupt." Zorzo stalls in Leda's hallway.

"Come up," she says, "we were about to eat." She nods her head back to the murmur of people on the first floor. "A ragtag of misfits, none of whom bite. You're alone, are you?" She raises her eyebrows, hoping for some tittle-tattle about the woman she met earlier.

"Most definitely alone. I just wanted to set eyes on a friendly face." And steady the nauseating, around-and-around wanderings of his mind. "Is your—*gentleman* here?"

Leda tilts her eyes at Zorzo and gives a warm smile. "Captain Berotti, he is. And though you'll think he's an oaf, which he is, he'll be a reminder to you of what I deserve: not a lionheart such as you. Is that for me?" She means the parcel that Zorzo's holding. "Marzipan?"

"What else for the bone queen?"

"I've missed your offerings." She gestures for him to enter.

Upstairs, there are a dozen or so people just beginning dinner. A fatty lamb smell hangs in the air, even though the windows are open. The still-warm wind inveigles its way into the room, making the candle flames on the table dance.

"Bring another chair," Leda says. "This is Zorzo, my first friend in Venice."

In the gloom, various faces turn, while Captain Berotti brings a chair. Zorzo has the impression he's moved in—having presumably left his inconvenient family—even though Leda always insisted she'd never live under the same roof as a man until she had a wedding band on her finger. Zorzo wonders if Berotti had known, or cared, he had a rival. Leda introduces the others and Zorzo recognizes a couple of them in passing. There's an actor called Felicio, who speaks with a declamatory lisp and likes to call himself Leda's wicked sister, a pair of impoverished nobles, the slow-burning black sheep of a banking family, a father and son of new money and a designer—or embroiderer—of collars and cuffs. As Leda said, a ragtag bunch, but a self-regarding one too, and Zorzo wonders if he should just make an excuse and go.

"How is he, our tall Giorgio?" Felicio, the wicked sister, asks.

"Full of the joys of winter," Zorzo replies. He reaches for the red wine, fills his glass to the top and sits.

Leda's guests eat, argue, make speeches and deal observations. Zorzo lets the conversation wash over him. He drinks hard and steady. Images of Sybille in her vermilion cape on the steps of San Zaccaria repeat in his mind over and over until his head feels like hot, wet cement.

I wish you could be my secret and nobody else's.

He has a choice, he sees it clearly now, between Sybille and the next step of his career. An affair with a married woman—or everything else, all that he's worked for, and all that is to come: prince orient, the commission and success, success like Bellini has, that will last for decades.

Occasionally he looks up and finds Leda watching him from the other corner of the table, concerned. She makes sure the wine keeps coming, though barely drinks herself. She's a practical, daytime person and Zorzo sometimes wonders why she has such wastrel friends. It's probably because she feels, deep down, she's lucky to have any. Despite her successes, she ranks low in Venetian society.

After dinner, a young man on the other side of Felicio—long, pale face, thin, black beard—who's barely uttered a word, places a little bottle in a pool of light on the table and raises his brows. The conversation halts, eyes pivot to the bottle, the corners of Felicio's mouth twitch into a smile and Berotti looks over to the maid, who makes a point of seeming not to notice.

"It *is* what you think it is," Felicio purrs. "From a friend of ours who ships amber from Persia."

Zorzo knows what it is: laudanum, opium tincture. There's a steady flow of it into the city and it's begun to appear more and more in the salons of certain types of Venetians. Zorzo tried it once, with Carlo Contarini, of course, who hated to miss out on any new fashion. The young noble was violently sick and Zorzo spent most of the evening nursing him. "Swear on your life to never tell a soul," Carlo muttered afterward—pallid cheeks, drooling mouth, bloodshot eyes—not about him trying the drug that the church decrees as heretical, but his inability to stomach it.

"Who will taste?" Felicio says, taking out the bottle's tiny cork.

The guests were obviously forewarned and more than half volunteer. Leda abstains, along with the youngster and his father (though both look as if they'd like to). The way the man with the thin beard solemnly administers drops into everyone's drinks is like some ungodly communion, Zorzo thinks.

"You, sir?" the man with the beard says, coming to him last.

Zorzo shrugs. "Why not?" He holds out his glass and receives his medicine.

Soon the room becomes stranger: voices deepen and conversations grow more earnest and excited, one quickly overlapping the other. Dark shadows creep about the room as the last of the day's light abandons the windows. The wind blows through them still, but grows colder by degrees, until Leda gets up and closes them. This doesn't stop the noise of the sirocco, though: it sighs against the glass, makes the fastenings rattle. It whistles down the chimney so that the fire dances and pops. The opium-takers grind their jaws and widen their eyes.

"In the year 1084 an earthquake dislodged the campanile of San Angelo," the embroiderer says a little later, when talk turns to "violent acts of God." "There was a slow and regular thunder beneath the earth and the whole city trembled. In 1223, a shock came on Christmas Eve, in the middle of the night, that sent every church bell in the city ringing at once. Can you imagine being woken by that? By God's own voice."

The discussion dances around from subject to subject: the founding fathers of Torcello, war with the Genoans, the doge's would-be mistress and his never-ending tenure of the crown. Zorzo loses the thread again and again. He edges his chair ever deeper into the shadows, feeling as if he's on a ship ebbing back and forth and the people at the table are grimacing marionettes swaying in the wind.

In his drug-altered state, Zorzo imagines Leonardo da Vinci

as a bearded ghost always just out of sight. Then the ghost is arm in arm with Sybille, whose train is trailing through the mud. A young prince orient walks alongside them, in a jeweled gown and turban. Zorzo longs, until his heart aches, to have time to make his mark on the world, render it more significant, more magnificent—even if only by a fraction—than the one he was born into. He wants his name to be remembered.

Berotti, who's spoken even less than Zorzo and drunk much more, stands up, swaying, says good night and stumbles to bed. Leda goes down to show Felicio and the last of the others out, leaving Zorzo in the room alone. He gets to his feet, goes to her mercury mirror and looks at his reflection. "Our tall Giorgio, who all the ladies love," he mutters, recalling Carlo's phrase at the Ca' d'Oro. He can see the boy he once was, the same age as the choristers that Sybille pushed through at San Zaccaria, a boy who might one day find wonder. Then a cold, hard thought comes to him. He gave himself the wrong choice before. It's not between Sybille on the one hand and prince orient and the commission on the other. It's between all these things—and the realities he should actually be facing, beginning with bankruptcy.

"Stop this," he says to his reflection. "*All* of this business, *all* this spying and losing sleep. Phantom colors and unreachable commissions and siren calls. Stop it, right now." He watches his lips move as he promises himself. "Or *everything* will slip through your fingers. You have work to do. In *this* world."

"Are you being followed?" Leda says, returning.

"What?"

"When you came did you notice a man in a dark green cap outside?"

"No." He goes over to the window and looks both ways down to the street.

"He's gone now. I saw him earlier. Well dressed. Waiting in the doorway opposite. I thought he was locked out and asked if he'd lost his key and he ran away."

"Young?"

"Twenty or twenty-five? I couldn't see."

Zorzo stays at the window, his breath condensing against the glass and the warmth of it coming back against his face. On the other side of the pane the wind whistles harder than ever and he can just make out the trill of hundreds of ship bells ringing from the city's quays.

"Marzipan?" says Leda, unwrapping Zorzo's gift. He shakes his head and she eats a piece, then another. She wraps the packet up, puts it away in a drawer, takes it out once more and eats two more pieces. "Are you going to tell me what's wrong?"

"Wrong?" asks Zorzo.

"The look you have about you: like an abandoned dog. Is it that woman I met?"

"Of course not."

"Why of course?" Zorzo opens his mouth to reply, but nothing comes out. He tries a smile, but it's unconvincing. "Oh dear, you're lost. Well, I hope she deserves you."

"No, no, it is the end, not the beginning, whatever it is. It is the end of the chapter. And it was a very short chapter at that."

"Wait," Leda says. She goes out and returns with a lute, wiping the dust from its neck. "I failed, in your wish for me to learn. Play a little?"

He does as she asks and Leda sits next to him and rests her head on his shoulder. He can feel the mechanisms of his body, the tension in his bones, the skipping, irregular beat of his heart. Sybille's voice whisks around his head like the sirocco wind.

He wakes at dawn on Leda's settee. There's something different about the room, something has changed in the air, but he can't tell what. He sits up and at once it's very clear what he has to do.

"About time," Uggo says, wiping the sleep from his eyes, when Zorzo enters the red house. "We were about to send a search party."

"It's a new day, Uggo, and a good one. I'll need you upstairs later. I have an assignment for you."

"But can you afford me?" jokes the boy as Zorzo tears up into the workroom.

"We have a lot of work to do today," he announces to the room. "Azalea, go to the *biblioteca*, see what pictures you can find of Augsburg, views of the city, from a distance ideally. If you're able to bring any back, do so, if not, make your own sketches. Janek, could you prime a canvas, two-foot square, no, three feet by two. Teodor, help him. Uggo, you are going to model. I need you in a smart coat. Find something in the store. It has to look good from the back. I'll be drawing you from behind."

"From behind?" the boy says in mock indignation. "You'll find my front is more alluring."

"Quiet, everyone," Zorzo calls out when the others start laughing. "I need you all to concentrate, do you understand?" His tone is graver than ever. "For your own good. To keep this workshop going. Competition is fiercer than I've ever known it. Everyone is chasing fewer opportunities. Last night, I'll admit, I felt almost overwhelmed. Today is different. If we don't want to waste all the work we've put in; if we're to survive, if we're to stay together, we cannot fail at this task."

No one is smiling now. "What is the task, sir?" Paulino asks.

"We're going to win this commission," he says. "We're going to beat everyone. We're going to convince Jakob Fugger that we're the only ones for the job." He stops and listens.

"What is it, sir?" asks Janek.

"I've just realized what's different. That damn wind has stopped."

12

Augsburg's Child

"This is the idea." Zorzo gathers everyone around to look at the large compositional cartoon he's drawn up for the painting they're going to make. Azalea has returned from the *biblioteca* with a naive street map of Augsburg, elevations of two of its famous buildings and, most usefully, a kind of bird's-eye view of the city. It's terribly drawn, its scales confused and angles mixed up—a poor imitation of Barbari's peerless *View of Venice*, an aerial perspective printed a decade ago that Zorzo reveres—but is informative enough for what Zorzo needs.

"A boy of thirteen or so," he nods toward Uggo, "stands in the foreground, on the brow of a hill looking down on the walled city of Augsburg. The inference is that this is Fugger as a youngster. Maybe there'll be a clue, a little detail of his coat of arms somewhere, but we're not stating it literally, just implying it. We want to give a feeling of his personality: ambitious but learned, brave but respectful, an adolescent on the cusp of greatness, who even as a youth has the town, and the world, at his feet and for the taking." He looks around at his *garzoni*, to make sure they're following. "I have no idea if Fugger ever had such traits, or possesses them now, but who doesn't want to be presented as heroic and fascinating?"

There are murmurs of agreement. For the time being, Zorzo has decided to keep to himself the dire warnings that Carlo spoke of and Sybille alluded to, that Fugger might be the antithesis of heroic and fascinating. That he could be responsible for cold-blooded murder.

"This," Zorzo circles a section with his finger, "will be Augsburg. It doesn't take up much space on the canvas, but the city must be immediately identifiable. Otherwise the picture fails. Paulino, you're in charge of it. It needs a mathematical mind." He hands over the drawings Azalea brought back. "Make the best sense of these you can. There's a pair of towers with onion-domed tops and a hexagonal church. Feature those more overtly than the rest. They make Augsburg unique, I presume. All good?"

"Yes, sir," Paulino says, blushing as usual.

"The third element, and where we begin," Zorzo gestures around the sides and top of the picture, "is landscape. And atmosphere. The rest of you will help me with this." Zorzo invariably likes to start from the outside, from the periphery, first capturing the mood of a picture's world—the time of day, the time of year, the weather, the light—and work gradually inward, often coming to the human subjects last, to the mood, weather and light *within* them. "It's midwinter but the sky is bright, crisp." He stops and thinks about it before going on. "No, it's far on in winter, the end of February, beginning of March, almost the cusp of spring. There are tentative shoots," he shows where they might be, "the first birdsong in the air, very timid." He thinks through his plan, making sure he hasn't missed anything, then claps his hands. "Good, everyone has understood. Onward, then."

They all set to work at once, beginning with transcribing Zorzo's cartoon onto the primed canvas.

That evening he places the painting on an easel and stands back to look, while everyone gathers around. "Good." He nods. "Good work, everyone." Most of the colors of the countryside and sky are blocked in. Augsburg is reading well, particularly with the addition of red umber to the roofs of the civic buildings. No color has been added to the boy yet, neither to his clothes nor face—what little we see of it—but his tunic is drawn in some detail and his form has believable weight. The composition, in color as well as shape, is harmonious still, while the *concept* of the picture—that phrase Zorzo can't bear—is clearly coming through.

"Right," he says, "we need to find the right color for the lad's coat. It has to sing out. That peridot green, do you remember it?" he says to Janek. "That I used in *Mary and Assisi*, in the banner that drops from the dais. Though a grade lighter."

"Yes, yes." Janek understands and warms to the idea immediately. "The same as *David*'s coat, under the breastplate."

"That's right. The color has to charm, particularly as we see little of the fellow's face. While I work on sketches with Uggo in his coat, grind whatever we have. Help him, Tulipano. Give me a couple of alternatives."

"Yes, sir." They both nod.

"Paulino, continue with the city. How is the light striking those roofs? And against these windowpanes? And are there people on the street?" Zorzo thinks about it. He knows how tricky it is to describe general human movement in a city, especially from a distant viewpoint. It can be more of a distraction than anything. "Draw up one or two and let's see. Azalea, Teodor, stay on landscape. The foreground verdure here needs to be more specific, more intriguing too. Much more. The shrubs don't have to be German. Italian will do. Go through the reference files," he says, pointing to where homemade books of drawings are kept on every imaginable subject. "Alternatives, please."

At noon the following day, Zorzo calls another halt to check on progress. Like a magic trick, the canvas has all but come to life. The weather, landscape, the city have propagated across it like organic matter. Only the figure in the foreground is not fully realized yet, but approximated in abstract planes of green, like a ghostly, out-of-focus presence that's on the point of materializing. "So now to the vital part of our mission: our hero, this boy of ours. He is where the emotion is. No matter we barely see his face." A thought comes to him. "And though it's cold, the boy doesn't feel it. Even as everyone else in Augsburg's teeth might be chattering, our young Fugger is too warmed through with the success that will come."

He cleans his brushes and starts up again. He works almost in silence, biting at his lip, finding the way to reveal the character of the boy from just his back, adding details to the clothes he wears, making sure they read as understated, beautifully made, a fraction too large for him. He's so engrossed with the task of bringing the boy to life he barely sleeps that night, taking just an hour here and there, just enough of a break to ensure his hand stays steady. His *garzoni*, despite being given permission to rest, do not allow themselves even that. At one point, early in the morning, Zorzo stands back to look at them. In an illuminated sphere, they crouch over the main table of the workroom, with their talisman before them, a canvas that will lead—Zorzo has sworn—to victory. They're all aware that excitement of this sort, this brand of almost crazed concentration, doesn't come often. Only the older apprentices will remember the week-long interment—Zorzo's humorous word for it then—before the delivery of Castelfranco's altarpiece in time for Easter. Indeed, there's been so little coming and going through the front door these last two days—only one rushed errand to fetch missing materials, and to buy army-camp quantities of cereals and wines—Uggo jokes that neighbors will think the household is stricken with the plague.

The final detail Zorzo applies, onto the silver tip of the boy's swagger stick, is Fugger's symbol of entwining lilies. He puts down his brushes, rests the painting on the easel by the window and stands back to examine what he hopes is a finished canvas.

"Still there's something missing," he says, "an element I can't place. And this is too bare." He means the empty space of foreground greenery to the left of the boy. He blinks at it, eyes red from lack of sleep, before something else catches his eye out the window. Sybille is crossing the square with Johannes in tow. Her gown and gloves are pink today, amaranth, the color of a blush or cherry blossom.

"One of you go downstairs. Tell Sybille Fugger I'm not at home." Some of the apprentices exchange looks. "What are you waiting for? Azalea, you go." She's closest to the door and rushes off. Zorzo steps back into shadow, while on the square Sybille disappears from sight. A moment later there comes a knock. Zorzo cranes his ear to the sound of the front door opening and the conversation that ensues, though he can make little of it out.

When Azalea returns to the room, she's ashen-faced.

"What is it?" asks Zorzo. "What did she say?"

"I told her you weren't at home, sir."

"And?"

"She said she saw you through the window. I told her she must have been mistaken."

"And she believed you?"

Azalea is clearly unsure. For a moment, Zorzo's brain freezes: he has no idea whether to chase after her and explain, apologize. He can't remember a time in his life when he pretended to a woman, or to anyone for that matter, that he was not at home. It's the sort of thing Carlo Contarini does.

"Has she gone now?" he says to Paulino, who's next to the window.

"Almost. She's crossed the square to the Calle de Cavallo."

Zorzo goes over and peers out. She's retreating up the street, her blush dress cheerful against the drab day. It's almost painful watching her retreat, like a dream of something slipping from his grasp. He wonders why she came, whether she had something important to say about her husband. "Let's not break our concentration, agreed?" he asks, more for his own benefit.

"Let me see it again," he says, returning to the canvas, disregarding the look on everyone's face, particularly on Uggo's, who loves a piece of drama. "And stop smirking," Zorzo says to him. "This is a workroom." His tone is sharp enough to make everyone focus. He stares at the picture, clutching his forehead, and tries to work out what is not right.

"The hunt," Zorzo mumbles to himself, looking around at the stag's head that caught Sybille's attention. "Of course, the hunt." At once, the notion is so obvious he can't believe he didn't think of it before. "Paulino, those French prints, you know the ones, *la chasse de Bretagne*."

Paulino is already one step ahead. He mounts a table and searches through a stack of folders until he finds the one he's looking for. He jumps down, opens it and lays out the pictures along the tabletop: a dozen woodcuts, ancient and frayed at the edges, hunting vignettes, forests, trappers, dogs, deer.

"This is it," Zorzo says, alighting on one particular image, a stag that rears up from the crest of an escarpment, head turned to the sound of horns. He takes the picture and places it alongside the canvas. "We transpose it here." He describes the shape with his finger. "At a distance to the boy, midground, but as a counterpoint to him. The boy and the stag share the same world. They're equals." Everyone nods in agreement and work commences again.

By lunchtime, after the three most intense hours of all, Zorzo finally puts down his brushes, hangs up the painting again and nods. He's pleased with the finish: it's not perfect, but somewhere between a preparatory cartoon and a completed canvas. He's found in the past, with new patrons especially, "raw work" like this will invariably pique interest, start conversations. And besides, if a painting is to be given free of charge, as this in effect will be, it can't appear to have taken months.

He goes to his desk, takes up a sheet of paper, scribbles a note, a little absentmindedly, signs and seals it. "Leave the picture to dry a little more," he says to Janek, "and in an hour, pack it in a crate, one of the shallow ones there. It doesn't matter if the oil hasn't completely set. Once that's done, Tulipano and Teodor, take it with this letter to the Palazzo Pallido in Cannaregio. Don't leave it unless you've established without doubt the master is at home. I've made that mistake before. Go in an hour, understood? And make yourselves presentable. I'm going to get some rest."

Zorzo retreats to his *studiolo* and lies down, though his blood is racing too fast to sleep. The pressure of the last two days has tipped his thoughts into a ragged jumble. He regrets having to lie to Sybille, frets again as to why she came. He's never understood her motives. From her appearance at the red house, dressed up, to her secret visits to San Isepo. Underlying all these concerns is the conundrum of Fugger himself. Zorzo takes comfort in the fact the picture is still drying and he has an hour to change his mind. He doesn't change it, though, but waits until Tulipano and Teodor pass across the landing, a slim crate under the latter's arm, and when he hears the boys exit with the painting, his heart finally calms.

He doesn't sleep, and as soon as his men return, he gets up and intercepts them, empty-handed on the landing. "You left it, then?" he asks. "Did you check he was there?"

"We were told he was," Teodor says.

"And who did you give it to? It wasn't the housekeeper?"

"We passed it to a young man who came to the back door," Tulipano tells him. "He was helpful and seemed pleased to accept it. He said he would take it up straightaway."

"Well done, good work. Have you ever seen me in a state like this?"

Teodor chuckles but Tulipano looks concerned. "No, sir, never," he says, as if his master might be in need of propping up.

"Good, we can rest now." He pats them both about the shoulder and goes back into his room. Only for new anxieties to set about him. He thinks he should have double-checked the canvas before it went out. He fears that Fugger won't understand it, that the meaning might be too subtle, that the canvas is *too* unfinished, that the colors are not lucid enough, or just not the right ones for Fugger. Everyone has a different taste when it comes to what shades and combinations catch their attention. He wonders whether he should have taken the picture himself to Cannaregio, or if—while rushing—he didn't sign the note clearly enough. He even has an absurd fear that all the painters of Venice, of Italy, have come up with the same notion and Fugger has been inundated with obscure gifts.

All these worries subside, to be replaced by just one: that he is entering a dangerous world, allowing himself to be drawn into a trap, into a game he doesn't understand, where other people make up the rules—people who lie about where they're going, what their motives are, or who punish those who cross them by throwing them from watchtowers or burning them in their farms. Perhaps the reason Sybille came earlier was to tell Zorzo that her husband suspects something already. Perhaps they were even being followed all along.

"You're losing reason," Zorzo says to himself, lying back on the bed. "It's only a painting," he affirms, knowing in his soul it is so much more than that. This time, though, from sheer exhaustion, he falls asleep.

"Sir, sir," someone whispers in Zorzo's ear the following morning. He opens his eyes. "There's someone to see you," Paulino says.

"Is it Sybille Fugger?"

"No, sir. It's a man. He's waiting in the hall."

The way he says it, a little startled, makes Zorzo sit up.

Going downstairs, he decides it must be Johannes and that there's nothing to worry about, but Uggo, by the front door, looks startled too, unsmiling, head bowed, as if he's been told off. He nods toward the back of the hall, the dark part of it, and Zorzo turns. A thickset man stands up from a chair. It takes a moment for Zorzo to realize who it is, the blond colossus he first saw in Mestre.

"My name is Tomas," the man says. "I work for a gentleman called Fugger. He has an interest in meeting you. Can you come now?"

13

Blind Angels

Roman grandeur is the phrase Bellini would use to describe the interior of the Palazzo Pallido. The great hall that Zorzo is ushered into is vast and unwelcoming, walls and floor all in marble and onyx. Windows have been left open, bringing in chill air, while their corresponding shutters are closed, making the space darker than it should be. It's daytime, but there are candles shivering everywhere.

"Are you armed?" Tomas asks.

"No."

"Would you mind?" Tomas nods at one of his men, not Johannes, but another Tomas—a slightly lesser version—who goes about patting Zorzo down. Zorzo can't remember the last time he carried a weapon in Venice—probably as a young man, as an affectation.

"Please," grunts Tomas, motioning for Zorzo to follow the other footman up the staircase. "They're waiting in the salon."

Zorzo ascends, drinking in the surroundings, which somehow manage to be both more sterile and more opulent than the Ca' d'Oro. He's spent enough time—*just* enough—in very rich people's households to know that they have a particular quality: a sense of quiet excellence pervading everything, of things being managed at every level. No matter what it can't buy, money guarantees supreme overseers, housekeepers and supervisors who are efficient but never formal (formal staff are the preserve of the averagely wealthy), who make a place run like a machine, while appearing as if no effort is being made at all. It's the same here: everything shines, odors are sweet; everyday sounds—feet on the stairs, doors opening and closing, fires crackling—have a patina of luxury. It is not the house, Zorzo convinces himself, of a man who gets people thrown from towers.

"This way, sir," the footman says. Zorzo looks down at Tomas, who's stayed at the foot of the stairs. Tomas nods at him and Zorzo goes into the salon, the door clicking shut behind him.

It's a large room, dark like the hall. A man is writing at a desk at the far end, his back to Zorzo, while Sybille sits at a table in the center, her back very straight. Zorzo's chief worry had been what to do when he crossed her path. She gives a shake of the head, slight but emphatic, a reminder to Zorzo: "We don't know each other."

She's dressed in gray—the color of mercury or moonstone, the colorless color—and would be almost lost in shadow were it not for the whites of her eyes, which stay fixed on Zorzo. She wears gloves as usual. Her gown is buttoned close at the neck, and her hair is drawn tightly back from her forehead and tied behind.

"I'll be with you shortly," the man at the desk says, raising the back of his hand but not turning around. "Herr Fugger is just returning. Make yourself comfortable."

Zorzo goes to the table but remains standing.

"I am Sybille Fugger."

"Giorgio Barbarelli. At your service." He gives a bow and a gulp of air makes an uncertain passage down his throat.

Sybille pointedly casts her eye to the seat opposite her, on which Zorzo's canvas rests. Her opinion on it—on Zorzo having produced and sent it to her husband—is unreadable in her face. It's surprising to see the painting again, in a new setting, even after just a day. He notes that some of the colors are brighter than they should be, particularly the green of the foreground trees, which is too limelike. Augsburg seems very slightly tipped on its side, though the stag was an inspired addition: it brings a touch of danger. Most importantly, the boy in the picture is a success: intriguing, strong, relatable.

Zorzo looks around the room. At the far end is a closed double doorway decorated on either side with a statue of an angel. They catch the attention more than anything else, medieval curiosities that loom forward from their pedestals, hands stretched out into the room, with curling shoulder-length locks and blinded-out eyes.

"Giorgione is the name they give you, is it not?" says the man at the desk. "*Big* Giorgio?"

"Tall."

The man puts down his pen, closes his book and stands up. "Francesco Soderini—of Volterra," he says, without coming over. "You were kind to come and meet us." He scans Zorzo from head to toe. It's a look, Zorzo thinks, that Soderini probably gives to men who have been summoned to do his dirty work. His neat appearance is in keeping with his clipped voice. He wears a floor-length cassock of black silk with a silver crucifix about the neck. His hair is blond, parted on one side and slicked against his square skull. His eyes are blue, very clear and direct. Soderini seems like an Italian name, but he looks the essence of German.

"You're a Venetian?" he asks, staying his ground by the desk.

"I have adopted the city as my own, but no. I came as a young boy, to be an apprentice in the workshop of the Bellini brothers." Zorzo shoots a glance at Sybille, but she doesn't return it.

"I come from a small town called Castelfranco. It's no more than a day's journey from here."

"Just a day, and yet—" Soderini makes a motion with his fingers, to indicate the city, but continues to study Zorzo, smiling. His eyes are so intent they seem to touch Zorzo, finger the cloth of his doublet, run along his shoulders, push around in his hair.

"I see Herr Fugger received my—" What was his painting? A gift? A bribe? "—my work."

The cardinal comes over and offers his hand. Zorzo isn't sure of the protocol, whether he should kiss it. "Shake," breezes Soderini. "I am not a holy relic." Zorzo does so and finds the hand cold and muscular, surprising to the touch, like a snake.

"I came to Venice as a boy too," he says, "with my uncle, who had business here. He didn't like it. He said it made him seasick. And in my ear he told me over and over that it was sinful. Did you choose your profession or was it handed down to you?"

"It was my choice."

"Your father didn't paint?"

"He was a stonemason."

"And he still lives in Castelfranco?"

"No, I have no family left." He's unable to resist another glance at Sybille, which Soderini notices.

"We had a team of stonemasons working on the cathedral in Volterra," Soderini goes on. "Storm damage. The dust came with them at dawn and followed them away at night. Like ghosts, they were. It got into their very bones, I believe. There is a point when you cannot wash it away, no?" Silence. "So you were wise to find a profession distinct from your father's. And you have, what, thirty years?"

"Thirty-three."

"Christ's age."

Zorzo gives a bemused smile. The blind angels watch him from either side of the door.

"Ah," the cardinal says, remembering something. "Can I ask

you a question?" He goes back to the table, retrieves a battered sheet of paper and holds it up. "On my way from Volterra, this came into my hands. It had been put up in the market square."

"What is it? A pamphlet?" Zorzo can't see it properly from where he's standing.

"A piece of sedition. A filthy thing. It would have the reader believe our great church is fallible, that we somehow are the enemy. Somehow wrongdoers. When in fact those who invented these lies printed the paper, put it out around the market squares of the country; they are the ones against nature."

"I can't read it. Is it Latin?"

"No, no, our common language. But my point is: to produce such a thing, with this engraving at the head, these images all around, it struck me they would need artists." He nods at Zorzo. "I mean to say, *pictures* drive home ideas in a way words never can." He says "ideas" with sarcastic bite, as if such things cannot be trusted.

Zorzo grasps what Soderini is getting at. "You're probably right, but I can assure you I've never been—no one has ever tasked me with—"

"Of course not, of course not. I thought it interesting, that's all. The world of today. Sit," he says, putting the paper down and indicating two chairs by the fire. Zorzo does as he's told, though the cardinal remains on his feet. "So, our secret escaped?"

"Your secret?"

"Our reason to be in Venice." Sybille clears her throat and Soderini briefly regards her before acknowledging the painting. "We presumed you didn't send it on a whim? That you're not just a casual admirer of Herr Fugger? That you want something out of it? Out of him."

"Well, in truth—" Zorzo starts to say, but Soderini isn't finished.

"Do all you painters know? In Venice and wherever else? Does word get around that quickly between you? I imagined a more competitive distance between you, tighter lips, like us cardinals have. Anyway, I'll assume you all do. I suppose you'd find out soon enough, but Herr Fugger is so private, you see, so scrupulous about that." Soderini's teeth bite together, resting there, and he looks around again at the painting.

"I confess, I did hear about the commission," Zorzo says, "but only because I feel it my duty to know everything that is going on in the city."

"And what have you heard? About the commission?"

"A work for the new basilica in Rome. A large piece, in keeping with the stature of the proposed building. Of St. Peter himself, at the centerpoint of Christendom."

"I'll be frank, your name was not on any of our lists," Soderini goes on, "and certainly not our short list. I went to San Rocco and saw your painting there, after Frau Fugger brought up your name." He pauses a moment, and Zorzo can't tell if there's suspicion in the way he says it, that a link between her and Zorzo might be concerning. "You'll excuse me, but I didn't have much time and it was getting dark. I wondered at first if it was part of a larger piece. The composition is so," he searches for the word, "spare? I mean to say, the scale of it. Little more than two faces. And, I must admit, the atmosphere is bleak."

Zorzo feels like pointing out that surely Christ on his way to his crucifixion is as bleak as a subject could be: a man who has to drag a timber cross up a hill, in the knowledge that he'll be nailed to it through the ankles and forearms and die in excruciating pain. Instead he says, "I find no fault with your description. But as for scale, I have of course produced much larger work than San Rocco." After what Lotto said about the commission, Zorzo is prepared with examples. "There is the altarpiece for the cathedral in my hometown, and additionally—"

The door opens and Tomas puts his head around.

"Is he back?" Soderini asks, to which Tomas nods and goes again. Soderini holds his palm up to Zorzo. "One moment."

Zorzo notices Sybille clasp her hands together under the table. Half a dozen attendants file in and Zorzo, not knowing what's going on, gets to his feet. They open all the windows, as wide as they'll go, before closing the shutters behind them and fastening the latches. The room is almost pitch-black for a few moments, before candles are lit in every quarter, on tables, cabinets, torchères, wall sconces, ceiling chandeliers. A man brings a bucket and cloth to the table and wipes the top, thoroughly, with vinegar solution. Sybille holds the back of her hand to her nose at the smell but looks accustomed to the activity. One of the men stokes the fire while another throws on a torso-sized log and gets the flames going with bellows so that, even on the other side of the room, Zorzo can feel the heat against his face.

"Sir?" An attendant approaches Zorzo, indicating he wishes to check him for weapons. He holds out his arms, resisting the urge to say he's already been searched downstairs. Sybille's face remains impassive, as if to say this too is a common occurrence, and Zorzo wonders how completely her life was overturned when she met Fugger. Soderini is also patient, with one eye on the men who are double-checking that the room is secure. They inspect the balconies through the windows, and inside two little antechambers, and open the double doors between the angel statues and look there too. Zorzo can't see the room beyond, but from the chill, damp air that creeps out, he has the sense of a much larger space.

They all exit at once and more come in their place, carrying things for the table and setting them down: wine jugs, goblets and majolica serving dishes of various sizes, all of which are given a further wipe with vinegar solution, especially around the handles. There's a painting, Zorzo thinks, treasure arriving at the table of some dread potentate. The scene must reside somewhere in the Bible or in mythology, Herod's banquet, perhaps, or King Solomon's. Pungent smells come from the covered salvers, particularly the largest one, decorated with an image of Neptune speeding across the sea on a chariot.

There's the sound of footsteps slapping up the stairs. Some of the footmen freeze, cocking their ears to the door, before it swings open and Fugger enters. He's soaked through: cape, doublet, stockings, all drenched.

"Jakob." Sybille gets to her feet, startled. "What happened?" Fugger stalks over to the hearth and the footmen scatter like chickens from a fox. "Jakob? Tell me what happened."

"Get out," Fugger says to the servants. "Everyone."

"Tomas?" Sybille collars him as he comes in. "What is this?"

"Your husband had an accident, my lady, when he was embarking at San Isepo. The gangplank was not set properly—"

San Isepo? The monastery that Sybille went to visit and is so secretive about. Did Zorzo hear that right?

Fugger unhooks his cape, casts it off and it drops on the floor like a sack of wet sand. "You." He collars Johannes before he has a chance to slip away with the others. "Bring me a towel, and a robe." Fugger unpeels his doublet and, when Johannes tries to help, Fugger freezes. "Stand away. Do not come near me with your hands. Ever."

"Sorry, sir." Johannes picks up the discarded cape. "Any robe in particular, sir?" he asks.

"Out!"

Johannes hurries off and closes the door behind him.

Fugger stays in front of the fire, his back to the room, heaving up and down. It's stocky, muscular for his age. "Who is that?" he says, nodding the back of his head in the direction of Zorzo.

"Barbarelli, of Castelfranco. Giorgione as he's called."

"Do I know him?"

"The fellow who sent the painting."

The fire crackles and there's a shower of sparks. Fugger turns, a dark shape against the flames, and studies Zorzo. "This is the man?"

"Good afternoon, sir," Zorzo ventures.

There's a further pop and sprinkle of sparks, more violent than before, and smoke curls around Fugger's shoulders. "I'll congratulate you," he says coldly. "You caught my attention."

For a moment, Zorzo feels proud of himself, that his scheme produced an effective result, which often it doesn't. "And my wife recommends you. She claims you're the best painter in Venice. There's a thing. I didn't know she had the first idea about painters, let alone Venetian ones." Though he half smiles, his tone is surely malevolent. Under the table, Sybille's hands are fists now, the fabric of her gloves strained against the knuckles. Finding her in the room when he arrived, Zorzo wasn't sure if she would be on his side or not, after he'd gone against her advice; but it's clear in her face, she's concerned for him.

"I wouldn't say I—" Zorzo starts to reply but Fugger puts up his palm.

"Don't waste your modesty on me. I've no patience for it. Feel honored. She wanted to meet you in person." His voice, which is quiet and low, has the same slight accent as his wife's, a German dialect that seems to have been eroded by its voyage across the Alps. He motions at the painting. "You've been to Augsburg?"

For a moment, Zorzo wonders if he should lie. "I've not had that pleasure, not in person. Though pictures have allowed me to travel there."

"And I am the boy? That's the point you're making? The boy and his city? Unless it's a commentary on our tragic infertility? My unborn heir?"

"No, absolutely not. I promise you, no." Zorzo is horrified: such an interpretation never occurred to him, and he's reminded how only very wealthy people have no qualms about sharing their secrets in public.

"Do not fret. I am joking with you." Fugger could not sound less jocular.

Johannes returns with a robe that Tomas takes and hangs

around Fugger's shoulders before sending the young man away. The garment is a floor-length drop of ink-black velvet and silver sable, an object of almost incalculable value; but against it, Fugger's face is ordinary. It's the sort you'd pass in the street without noticing: unremarkable mouth, small, inanimate eyes, the left one dropping a little lower than the right, receding hair, the norm of middle age.

"Have you heard reports of an outbreak here, Signor Barbarelli?" he says. "I mean, being a resident here?"

"An outbreak?"

"Plague," says Fugger. "A friend of the cardinal sailed past the island of Lazzaretto yesterday and said it sounded like hell itself, the groans and sighs in the air, the smell of burning flesh. Lazzaretto is where the pest houses are, isn't it?"

"Yes, but a hospital too, for everyday illnesses. If there is any danger of plague, warnings come swiftly and effectively. All the bells in the city ring at once. Venice takes no chances. It has learned the hard way."

"Well, as long as you don't have it." Fugger goes to the table and lifts the lid off the largest dish. Beneath a cloud of steam are calves' livers, hot and whole, each one as large as a child's forearm.

"Cardinal, will you eat?" Soderini raises his palm to decline. "You?" Fugger says to Zorzo.

"I have eaten already," Zorzo says, though it isn't true. He was advised by his father to share food if offered, but he's always had too much imagination for livers: eating them feels like devouring a creature's soul.

"My wife won't touch them either," Fugger says, wiping the handle of his fork with his napkin before serving himself and sitting to eat. "Her father, on the other hand, can't get enough of them. He devours them cold, at night, when he can't sleep—isn't that right, my treasure? And they're human ones too," he adds, for Zorzo's benefit, before turning to the cardinal. "So you've started the interview? What have you found out about our painter? Is he any good?"

"I was just trying to explain," Zorzo puts in, happy to change the subject to business, "that scale is not an obstacle for me. In any respect. The opposite, in fact. Test me, by all means, and I will prove it. I was going to suggest—"

"How would you describe your style of painting? Your approach?" interrupts Soderini.

"I would describe it as Venetian." If they're interviewing in Venice, Zorzo decided on the way here, they must appreciate the art of the city to some extent. "Venetian in its purest form, by which I mean to begin with atmosphere—" He pauses. Fugger has cut his liver in two, unpursing a naked stench, like hot urine, and for a moment Zorzo has to hold his breath against it. "What the world in the painting *feels* like. Is it warm outside, or humid or stormy? Day or night? Spring, autumn, winter? Are there birds singing, or the sea calling, or is there silence? And if there is, is the silence tranquil—or ominous?" Sybille is listening intently and Zorzo notices her hands unclasp and relax onto her lap for the first time since he entered the room. "Then, when I turn my attention to the heart of a painting, the humans within it, the vital element, I know already a little of how they're feeling: hot, cold, anxious, content—"

"—regretful, resentful—full of fury," Fugger finishes the list.

"It's our duty as painters not just to replicate form—that is, what someone looks like—but understand their mood, the way they're thinking; not in a grand way, but how they felt when they woke, how their day has been, to catch a moment, catch what can't be seen."

Soderini exchanges a look with his host before saying, "And how, specifically, do you do that?"

"Color. It's all color," says Zorzo. "That's where it begins and ends. Venetians understand. Color is mood, love, sorrow, life.

Color is what the world is built of. You would know that, sir," he says to Fugger, "more than any of us."

Soderini cocks his ear, with concern, perhaps, at Zorzo's directness and familiarity. "Really?" says Fugger. "How so?"

"Your mines." Zorzo didn't know if or how he was going to bring the subject of prince orient up, just that he had to find a way. "The greatest colors in the world come from them. We would be nowhere without lapis lazuli, or copper red, or lead white. And," his throat is dry, his pulse at once racing, "prince orient."

There's a clack of metal on china as Fugger puts his knife down.

"What do you know of prince orient?" Soderini asks.

Zorzo keeps his eye on Fugger, but he returns to his food. "Only that it may be in your possession, and that there is no color like it in existence." Fugger chews on his liver and gives nothing away. Though frightened of pushing too far, Zorzo goes on. "I suppose it is reserved for St. Peter? For your commission?" He has the sense he's right, in the way Soderini looks to the host for a signal of how to respond. Fugger just revolves his hand in the air, as if saying, move the conversation forward.

"Would you describe yourself as devout?" Soderini asks.

The question catches Zorzo out. "Yes."

"It's important, Signor Barbarelli, for you to tell us what you believe, not what you think we'll want to hear."

"I am devout, without question." Zorzo knows they could hardly prove otherwise, unless they cross-examine someone like Leda Sitruk.

"Have you ever painted hell?" Soderini continues.

"Hell?" Another unexpected question. He never has, unless he counts his studies of the classical underworld. "Not that I have been aware of."

"If you had, what would your vision of it be? Imagine there's another giant fresco, facing our St. Peter, that the congregation must contemplate as they leave."

Zorzo has to think about it. "War? War that's never-ending. A loveless world. Loneliness."

"War? You have a low opinion of it? You don't think any worth waging," Soderini asks, "even wars in the name of our savior?"

Zorzo has to consider again, frightened of falling into traps. "You're right. Some wars are unavoidable."

"You suggested, when you paint, you capture not just what someone looks like, but how they feel and think. How would you depict Satan? Would *he* feel and think?"

"I—" Zorzo smiles, to stall for time, and reaches around in his head for a suitable answer. "Wouldn't Satan be even more fearsome if you believed he was real, if he had humanity of sorts—character? If he was, in his own way, fallible."

Soderini fixes Zorzo with his clear blue eyes. "Satan is fallible, no question. He is the very quintessence of fallibility."

There's silence for a while, just the sound of Fugger finishing his last piece of meat. Soderini looks at him—raised brows, tilt of the head—as if to say, what do you think of the applicant? Fugger replies with a shake of the head so slight as to be almost imperceptible.

"Thank you for coming to talk to us," the cardinal says. "And for sending your work for us to see, which now we should—I'm not sure of the protocol here—return to you?"

"No, the painting is for Herr Fugger." Fugger wipes his hands with a napkin, cleaning his fingers one by one. "You have no more questions? I feel I have not—"

"Honestly," Soderini says, "the scale of what we need is unprecedented."

"I can do this work. There is no question."

"But apart from that—" Soderini starts to say.

"I may not yet be the most well-known painter in Italy, but

the timing is auspicious. My star is in ascendency. And I have an ocean of enthusiasm." He winces at his own turn of phrase. He sounds like an apprentice again.

"And apart from that, we are far down the road with another candidate. Goodbye. It was kind of you to think of us." Soderini offers his hand, but Zorzo is not ready to shake it.

"Let me present you some preparatory drawings at least. I will make them for you free of any charge. I'll produce them at scale. In days, I could have them for you." Soderini goes over to the door and opens it for Zorzo, while Tomas puts his shoulders back as a reminder of his presence. "I have painted it already in my mind. You'll come through the door of the new basilica—which of course will be the greatest church the world has ever known—and in the twilight his eyes meet yours. This St. Peter, a hundred feet high but one of us, a fisherman once, flesh and blood, barefoot, plain and modestly clothed, fingers raw from salt and nets, skin coarse from rough seas and hot sun. And he stands in a land we know too, that's there in front of us every day, that you'll see, sir, on your way from here to Volterra. The Tuscan hills that roll to the Tyrrhenian Sea become our peaks of Galilee, silvery olive woods, cypress groves, vineyards and stone farms, all beneath a kind June sun. The atmosphere, the mood, the temperature, the familiarity are vital to make us believe this Peter is flesh and blood. A doubter, trepidation in his eye, fear too, of the unimaginable task ahead. The apostle who'll save the world, who'll build the church, all churches—but who's one of us. I know how to capture that face."

"Signor Barbarelli," the cardinal says, becoming irritated, "you forget yourself."

"Give me *any* subject to paint and I will prove my worth."

"Signor Barbarelli—"

"Any scene from the Bible, or from history, or from life. Or let me paint you, sir, as you are today," Zorzo says to Fugger, "or you, your grace."

"Desperation," Fugger laughs.

"I am in need of a portrait."

The voice has such a different tone to the others that for a moment everyone wonders where it comes from, until they realize it's Sybille. At once, four pairs of male eyes pivot toward her.

"My father," she says, straightening her back, "has long asked for a picture of me and I would like to oblige him."

For a few moments a charge hums between the occupants of the room, until Fugger shunts his chair back and gets up. "Goodbye, Signor Barbarelli."

Zorzo hovers, his unease matched in Sybille's eyes. "My gratitude for the opportunity." He bows, gives her one last glance and is about to leave when she too gets to her feet.

"I must insist," she says, tapping her knuckles on the table and turning to face her husband. "I have my own money, sir. Plenty. I would like a portrait, for my father. You have your own project. You wish not to employ this gentleman, even though he was kind enough to make a picture for you. In spite of his initiative, and his skill, and standing, all of which are considerable. That is well and good, but I have my own wishes."

As he waits for someone else to speak, Zorzo feels removed from his body, as if he's watching the scene from above, these curious humans in this cold room where windows are opened and shutters closed. Fugger studies Zorzo in a way he didn't before, too long for Zorzo's comfort.

"Did you say you were married?" Fugger says.

"I didn't, but—no, not married," Zorzo replies.

"Children?"

"Well, as I said—"

"You can have children without being married. Just as you can be married and have none."

"No, no children."

"And do you think you can find in my wife—how did you put it?—how she feels and thinks? Catch what can't be seen?"

Zorzo wonders if the question is a trap. "I will do my best. Whatever is required."

"If the painting is to be for her father, perhaps don't catch too much."

There's another excruciating silence, before Fugger shrugs. "Very well. As she wishes. Cardinal, arrange the business side of it. Find out how much this painter in ascendency requires." He gives a wave of his hand, to dismiss Zorzo, and goes over to the fire, putting his back to the room.

"Goodbye," Zorzo says to him and bows. He wants to share one last look with Sybille, to read her face, to see if she's as anxious as he is, but dares not.

At Tomas's instruction, Zorzo waits in the hall. After a short while, the cardinal exits the salon and disappears to another wing of the house. He leaves the door ajar and Zorzo strains to hear if Sybille and her husband are talking, but he can make nothing out. After half an hour Soderini returns, goes back in and it's quiet again until Sybille emerges, closes the door and descends to the hall. Zorzo gets to his feet. She keeps her distance, though, staying at the foot of the stairs. "Thank you," he says to her.

"Keep your eye on the salon door," she replies in a hushed tone.

Zorzo glances at it and back to Sybille. "I did not expect you to be on my side, after what you advised at San Zaccaria."

"Watch the door."

"Yes, I can see it from the corner of my eye." Zorzo pauses before adding, "I'm sorry I could not welcome you the other day. I'm sorry that—"

"That you asked your apprentice to lie for you?"

"It must have seemed juvenile. It was inexcusable."

"I know *inexcusable*. That was not it." There's a kind of kinetic silence between them. "My father would be happy to have a painting of me, but in actuality has not asked for one. It is for myself. *My* portrait. I've chosen where I shall place myself, in the white chapel." She points to where a little flight of steps goes down to a door. "And I've decided who I shall be."

The turn of phrase catches Zorzo by surprise. He almost asks, *Shouldn't you be Sybille Fugger?*

"The cardinal will be down soon," Sybille says. "Good evening." She bows and disappears into the back part of the house.

Zorzo waits for hours, until dusk begins to fall and the colors in the stained glass gradually mutate to murkier, heavier versions of themselves and then all become twilight umber. He wonders if he understood correctly what he is meant to be doing. Frau Bauer comes up from the kitchens and shuffles toward the staircase. She stops when she sees Zorzo and he gets to his feet again and offers a smile. He may as well have thrown a bucket over her, the way she glowers back, little round eyes in a bloated face, pasty, pea-green skin, the color of a body pulled from the sea. She could be undead, Zorzo thinks as she ascends the staircase, panting, some vengeful being of German folklore, an immortal fishwife of Valhalla. She slips back into darkness and another hour passes before a twinkle of lantern light comes along the landing and much lighter footsteps descend to the hall.

"Sitting alone in the dark?" Soderini chuckles, as if it was somehow Zorzo's choice to be neglected all afternoon. "We have a contract." He sets it down with his light, a quill and ink. "If you sign here."

It's Zorzo's turn to chuckle: he's never before been asked to sign an agreement without even a cursory offer of negotiation, and certainly not without a chance to read. "The terms are—?"

"The best we can offer. The figure there is in Guldengroschen. We feel it is fair. Five days to finish the canvas. Payment on completion, providing we are satisfied. The other conditions, listed here, you will find as standard."

"Five days? That's—" How could he put it? Ludicrous? Impossible?

"You'll appreciate Herr Fugger is a busy man and prefers the house not to be obstructed for too long with ephemeral matters. Please, sign."

He's hasty, Zorzo's sure, not because he's attempting to be devious, but because he doesn't take the matter seriously. Even so, Zorzo must read the document. He tries, but the light is so bad and his brain so muddled with everything that's happened, so leaden from waiting and the cold, he can barely make sense of the words. Zorzo is passingly familiar with German currency from a former client and knows the fee is not particularly generous, given Fugger's wealth. It's certainly well below what he was paid by the doge, but there'll be enough to get his father's ring back and return the workshop to a secure footing. "Is there any chance I might have some of my payment up front?"

"Herr Fugger does not do business that way," Soderini replies without hesitation. "But obviously," he gestures at the immense space, "he's as good as his word."

"Of course," Zorzo finds himself replying. He wonders if he should press for expenses at least, but concludes, if the painting must be finished quickly, he won't have that long to wait anyway. "Perhaps, then, if you're happy with the results—and dependent on this other candidate—there's a chance you might consider me still for St. Peter's?"

Soderini's reply is one a lawyer would make: "I couldn't possibly say."

That is not a flat *no*, Zorzo decides. He takes up the quill and signs the contract.

"May I begin tomorrow?"

14

The White Chapel

"What's she like, sir?" Uggo asks Zorzo on their way to Cannaregio the next morning. "Is she very aloof? Ladies who look like her usually are." He does an impersonation of one, putting his nose in the air and shoulders back. The lad is helping Zorzo with his box of materials and the canvas his *garzoni* prepared last night.

"I don't know if aloof is the word. A little unreadable, perhaps."

"She's a sphinx, is she, sir? She riddles, does she?" He waves to a passing porter. He seems to know every third person on the street.

"That is at least partly true."

"You should watch yourself, sir, with those eyes she has for you."

"That's enough, Uggo."

"Don't get caught up in a riddle, sir, not with a married lady."

"Enough. There are no riddles. No eyes for me either." Uggo pulls a face and mimes buttoning his lip. "Is that man following us?" Zorzo says. "Don't look now. Half a street behind, in the green beret?"

When they turn the next corner, Uggo slips a look behind. "I see him."

"He's familiar. I can't think where I've seen him before."

Once they've reached the wide road at the back of the Ca' d'Oro, Uggo whispers, "He's definitely following, sir."

Zorzo stops, turns about and quickly advances on the man. "Can I help you?"

The man, realizing he's been discovered, halts. He's well dressed, conspicuously so, nothing like a thief at any rate. Zorzo now notices there are three more fellows with him, rougher looking.

"Giorgione, isn't it?" says the leader.

"That's what my friends call me. What of it?"

The man advances and Zorzo realizes who it is, the surly youngster who'd been with Michelangelo in the Orseolo tavern. Not only that: the green cap he wears suggests he's the man that Leda spotted waiting outside her house. "Rodrigo Sordi," he declares as if the name can be looked at but not touched. "You're a friend of the Fuggers, then?"

Zorzo glances over at Sordi's companions, all doing their best to look intimidating. "Not friends," Zorzo says. "I have a small matter with them."

"Really? A small matter?" Rodrigo draws closer and screws up his face. "That regards a certain substance? A mineral, yes? We all know about it. I gather it has come into your hands."

"No."

"Whatever price you have been offered, we will triple it."

"I have no price because I have no substance." His tone is

sharp enough for the thugs to take a step forward and make a point of showing they're armed.

"Everything all right, sir?" Uggo says, coming to Zorzo's side.

"Everything is fine," Zorzo assures him. "You stay back." He says to Rodrigo, "Is it necessary to stalk me like this? Come with these men? Or follow me about the streets at night? You needed only to say hello. But no, you have the wrong information. Though you're free to ask Jakob Fugger directly."

Rodrigo's top lip curls. "Jakob Fugger is a man of exceedingly ill manners—and even iller judgment." He adds for Zorzo's benefit, "Especially in who he chooses to do business with. We spend two weeks traveling to this damp hole, only to find," a flick of his fingers at Zorzo, "a Venetian dabbler has got his hands on the prize."

Zorzo shakes his head and turns to go, before deciding he can't let the insult pass unanswered. "Do you have any skill of your own?"

"Skill, sir?"

"Any talent? Or achievements to your name? Being born wealthy and pretty does not count. Do you enrich the world at all? Or do you just ride for free on the success of others?" With that, Zorzo turns his back on Sordi and carries on.

Uggo follows at his heels, mouth gaping open in sheer delight at the encounter.

"There comes a point, my lad, when one can be polite no more. But I'm glad our paths crossed, for now I know."

"Know, sir?"

"That there's one less person to worry about. And possibly the most significant person at that." He can't help but grin at the unexpected turn of events. "Fugger and Michelangelo clearly do not speak. That's where belligerence gets you. Which is why, my friend, we should always be good-tempered with men who might pay our bills." Uggo looks up at his master and nods. "In fact, we should be good-tempered with everyone. Whatever harm came from that?"

"Very philosophical today, sir."

"I'll take everything from here," Zorzo says when they get to the alleyway at the back of the Palazzo Pallido.

"Don't I need to help you set up?" Uggo hates not to be part of a scheme.

"I'll manage." He wants to keep Uggo, and all his *garzoni*, away from Fugger as much as he can, away from the palazzo's cold rooms of Roman grandeur. "Get back now, and no dallying. Here." He gives Uggo a coin. "Don't tell the others—"

"That I'm your favorite?" He gives one of his trademark winks. "You watch those sphinx's eyes, sir." He heads off, polishing his coin on his breeches.

Zorzo waits until he's out of sight, then bundles everything into his arms, crosses the little bridge and uses his teeth to lift the knocker and let it strike against the palazzo's back door.

"Follow me," the footman says. He leads Zorzo up the rear stairs, across the hall and down the steps Sybille indicated last night.

"It's Johannes, isn't it? You came to my house."

At once the youth looks terrified. "That's right, sir." He nods and reddens. "Careful of your head." They get to the end of the corridor and Johannes hesitates. "I'm sorry, sir, but—"

"What is it?" Zorzo has noticed the boy's hand is shaking.

He drops his voice to a whisper. "Our going to your studio, sir, and to San Zaccaria, was not—the master of the house had not been made aware of it."

Zorzo immediately realizes his mistake. "I'm so sorry, of course. Of course. We have not met." He clutches Johannes's shoulders, to reinforce he can be trusted. He wonders what Fugger would do to the boy if he found out. From now on he must watch everything he says.

Johannes nods and opens the door. "This is the chapel."

It's a startlingly bright room. A rectangular box in which everything—floor, walls, altarpiece, pediments and arched ceiling—is marble and also white, or rather white with gray, and occasionally red, occasionally black veins lacing through it. There are arched windows on three sides, high up, and though gray October murk sifts through them, once it has rebounded off the walls and floor, it seems to find new strength, creating a brilliant luminescence.

"We brought this table down for you, sir," Johannes says, setting Zorzo's case on top of it.

"The room is older than the rest of the house, no?" He nods at the left-hand wall where various ancient sculptures are set in recesses: medieval effigies, long-ago knights, some lopsided by time.

"Quite possibly, sir."

"The surviving part of a former building, maybe. It's a quirk of Venice. Newer buildings consuming older ones. Perhaps the palace was all white once. That would explain its name."

"You may be right, sir. If there's nothing else you need, I'll tell the mistress you're here." He bows and goes.

Zorzo listens to the footsteps recede into the building, and exhales. It takes him a moment to realize his hands are also shaking. He's got what he wanted. He's here, in Fugger's house. He's beaten everyone to it. He has a commission and is surely now closer to prince orient than ever. Yet along with the exhilaration there are still ungraspable fears, that he's passing a point of no return, entrapping himself. For a decade, like everyone in Venice, he's heard stories of ocean-crossing explorers. Their tales percolate ever more through the city: the strange, dangerous lands discovered, inhabited by cannibals, fantastic creatures and carnivorous plants. Whenever he hears them, he wonders what it would be like to travel there. Now he's entering just such an uncharted territory, the world of Sybille and Jakob Fugger: a realm that will be fascinating and, he hopes, lucrative, but one where he must not only scrupulously guard what he says but have one eye over his shoulder always.

He puts up the easel and fastens the canvas upon it, then opens his case and takes out the tray of pigments. The sight of them steadies him a little. He lays out the colors in rainbow configuration, from reds through yellows, greens and blues to indigo and violet. He wants the entire spectrum in front of him, to resist at all times choosing obvious hues. He's learned over the years, more with every painting, not to fall into the trap of being too literal, of making exact copies of the colors in front of him. Often, unexpected tones emerge in a face once a painting has begun, when a particular light strikes it, or when a distinct shadow falls over it.

He wonders which pigments will best bring Sybille to life on the canvas, which will be her signature colors. She seems to dwell on every axis of the spectrum, from mysterious bone white to royal green, from hot-blooded garnet to gentle coral pink, from repressed gray to fiendish, incandescent red. Sybille is somehow *all* the colors.

"This is the place I spoke of last night," comes a quiet voice behind him and Zorzo turns to find she has slipped in without him noticing. "The light here is very particular. Very strong. Isn't light the most important thing for painters?"

"For all of us, no?" The reply almost gets trapped in his throat; he's so struck with her dress. *Midnight blue.* A profound, intense tone like emeralds or a deep, hot, starlit sky. The color is somehow unexpected on her, miraculous even. It brings her to life in a way that no other has. It's already coaxing unknown tones from her face: violet in the shadow of her jaw, epidote green above her mouth, lemon yellow in the sclera of her eye, blood orange at her temple. He's relieved he's brought Caspien's ultramarine with him, that he went to Poveglia at all. There'll be no better way to use it. She's let her hair down and dressed it away from her face, also changing her appearance. It drops to her shoulder blades in a faint, undecided curl. Zorzo still can't quite work out what color it is. In the shadow, it's light brown, like fire agate, but mercury blond and silver white where it catches the light.

"And this is the backdrop I have chosen." She indicates the left-hand wall. "I'll stand against these dead men with their swords." Zorzo smiles at her turn of phrase, how she characterizes the house's ancestors. "I am permitted to choose my own backdrop?"

"The wall is ideal." A new fear has come upon Zorzo, the most palpable yet: how will he be able to paint her without showing his desire? Must he work against instinct and keep it from the canvas, so her husband—or whoever may look—will not guess?

"What is it, Frau Bauer?" Sybille says.

The housekeeper is standing in the doorway, glancing around, as mirthless as a jailer, with her iron ring of keys resting against her massive thigh. Her presence seems to steal light from the room, as much of it as there is.

"We are quite settled, thank you," Sybille asserts. Without making any reply, Bauer turns away up the stairs once more. "Jakob wanted her to watch over us during the sitting," Sybille says in a low voice to Zorzo. "I told him she has lice, which appalls him, and she's found herself all but stranded belowstairs."

"And does she, have lice?"

"For all we know."

The way she stares at him, still and with the slightest of smiles, but with a kind of wild heat in her eyes, is thrilling and he can't wait to begin describing her in paint. "So, I'm intrigued," he says. "Yesterday you told me you decided who you wanted to be. Does what you're wearing give me a clue?"

"When I came to your workroom, I complained that history had too few heroines and you told me I was mistaken. I was, I realized straight after. I've been overlooking them all this time."

"So there's one you have in mind?"

"You also gave me the idea that I could become someone else, like you described your knight of Thermopylae," she continues excitedly. "And then I recalled the troupe of players that used to come to Augsburg when I was a girl; and how one actor in particular, a boy who played the female parts, always presented these invincible women. Queens and empresses. I'd seen the actor in the flesh, a scrap of a fellow that you wouldn't look at twice. But when he put on a crown, or held a scepter, transformation. In the body. In the voice, just magnificent. I always thought how lucky he was, to be able to put on a costume and become someone else. And you reminded me of him, made me realize I could do the same. Here, in my head, and here, in my heart, I will be Zenobia." She pauses. "What? You don't think I can?"

Zorzo makes a mental note of the dark ruby color that has come up in her cheeks, though she's misinterpreted his look. "You've caught me out. The name is familiar. She was of ancient Greece?"

"Zenobia of Palmyra. She stood against Rome, led legions against it, conquered Egypt. Ruled in her own right. I would be her. Then, in years to come, someone somewhere might come across your picture—maybe in a century or more—and they'll look at it and they'll know I once walked the earth. A woman of importance."

"But—you have walked the earth. You *are* walking it. You're here with me now." Sybille looks back at him and for some moments their eyes are riveted. The chapel, the entire house, seems to fall silent until Zorzo says, "So, shall we begin?"

She takes her position against the wall of sculptures and Zorzo takes his in front of the canvas. "Stand a little further over to your left." He motions. "I want you beside that particular statue, if I may." He points to a skeleton in ceremonial robes, a crown on its head and spare curls of hair down to the shoulder. "It will be as if those mortal remains are leaning over, about to whisper in your ear. Turn your body away from the window. That's right. Keep your hips facing that direction, but turn your chest toward me. Good. And your head around a little further still. That's right. Can you feel the light on it, just touching the bridge of your nose?" Sybille nods. "Are you comfortable? Will you be able to hold that position?"

"I can stay still for days on end. My brother and I used to play at being dead. I always won."

Her brother. There it is, the first mention of him, dropped casually in conversation, but momentous to Zorzo. Surely he's the sibling that she was marooned with as a girl and that her husband had disposed of, if Carlo Contarini's insuations were to be believed. "Just one brother?"

"Yes. Why?"

Zorzo notes a defensive tone to her reply. "It's just that you haven't mentioned him before," he says, before realizing it's a misplaced comment, given they have only met each other on three quite brief occasions.

"One brother is plenty," she says, and Zorzo is lost as to what she means. In any case, she signals, with a hardening in her eyes, the matter is out of bounds and Zorzo changes the subject.

"Would you take off your gloves?" He tries to make the request sound casual even though it feels as if he's asking her to strip naked. He's never seen her without them, except once at a distance, through a carriage door on Mestre harbor. She looks surprised, too: a purple blush creeps up from her neck. "Otherwise your hands will be lost against your robes. They tell a story just as much as the face."

She peels off the left-hand glove—skin of faultless chalcedony—before clenching her jaw and removing the right one and putting them both to one side. Zorzo tries not to let the surprise show in his face. Her right hand is damaged. A scar runs from the back of the index finger across the knuckles to the wrist, a glossy, mangled line, the skin pinched together in places in white or pink mounds, a sister to the one on her face. And her two longest fingers are colorless compared to the others, and inert.

"Good. Could you hold the hand here?" Zorzo demonstrates, placing his palm against his chest. "The other one, I mean. With the mark upon it." He wants the damaged one on show. He's never forgotten an argument that a fourteen-year-old Tiziano once started with Bellini. When the master painted out a faint harelip on a subject's face, the precocious youth declared that if Bellini truly wanted to capture the subject, he should have left the scar intact. All the other apprentices were aghast at the youngster's rudeness, but Zorzo not only agreed, but has emulated his junior ever since.

"Do I have to if I don't want to?"

"A painting is a wonderful thing." Zorzo smiles. "If we don't like what we see, in a brushstroke it's gone."

Sybille holds it up stiffly, but Zorzo shakes his head. "Would you mind?" he says and comes over and takes her hand, tiny compared to his, and hot to the touch. The back of his thumb brushes against the raised flesh of her scar. He arranges her fingers, so each has its own particular shape. "Like spider's legs, as one of my masters once put it. Does it feel all right?" She nods.

"Usually I begin a painting from the outside in. Not today. Today I start with you."

He returns to his position, takes up a slim stick of chalk, the dark red one that Caspien had gifted him, and, looking at her far more than at the canvas, makes a series of marks to describe the structure of her body: a line for her shoulders, her hips, her spine, her clavicles, neck ligaments and arms. He divides her face into a faint grid of lines, tilted horizontals across the hairline, the eyes, the mouth and corresponding verticals down the center of her face and either side of the ears. He does the same for her hands, breaking down the configuration of bones to their bare axes.

From light and burnt ocher, magenta, lead white and a touch of cerulean blue, he mixes a series of skin tones and starts applying them to the canvas, in blocks that mark the facets of her form where the light strikes them, the carpals of her hand, her cheekbones, the bridge of her nose, her forehead.

"Do you usually speak with your subjects when you paint them?"

"It depends who they are." He's thinking of Espettia Lippi, who sat for five days talking nonstop to everyone but him. "I like to. It usually puts the sitter at ease. And myself."

"And do you—?" Sybille gives a little shake of the head. "Do you paint naked figures?"

"I have."

"Men?"

"To the great extent." Zorzo wonders what Sybille would make of the fact that Leda posed nude for him for a week and there's a painting of Venus to prove it. "As apprentices we took it in turns to be models. We learned quickly not to be shy. And it was necessary. You can't understand what happens beneath clothes, beneath skin even, until you've studied the body a great deal." He squints at the canvas, having gone too far with one of his marks. He wipes it off with the back of his hand and tries again. "Some painters go to much greater lengths. They'll stop at nothing to understand how a body works."

"Such as?"

"Cadavers. Cut up. Muscles, tendons, ligaments, organs, all unpacked like the contents of a trunk."

"Good grief. Who does that?"

"Not I. To my shame, I'd be too squeamish. Michelangelo, though, has no qualms at all. They say he has a team of people that source him cadavers. He strikes deals with hard-up families to purchase dead relatives; and always has a room set aside just for human dissection. In fact, he spends so much time with the dead, I've heard his gut is in permanent revolt." He stands back to study what he's done. "So that is the shape of you." To anyone else it might seem like nothing more than an arrangement of abstract pinkish and brown forms, but he's happy with his progress, with the composition. "And now to breathe life." He begins with Sybille's hands.

Beginning a brand-new painting is always an uncomfortable process. He has described it to his *garzoni*: *It's like walking into a cold sea. You're hesitant, you shiver against it, but unless you take those initial steps, you'll never be able to swim. Or feel the joy of the ocean.*

For the first part of the day, Zorzo pauses again and again to consider the marks he's making, the colors and angles he's choosing, the arrangement of light and dark throughout the picture. Soon, though, he gains in confidence, as always, and Sybille begins to come alive on the canvas. Zorzo finds himself hurrying to keep up with the speed of the manifestation, brush in constant motion from the palette, to the canvas, to linseed wash, forever being wiped clean on a cloth and returned to the palette again.

"I saw your face when you came into my workroom," he says after three hours of working. "The surprise. I was the same." He's painted the hands and face in detail, while leaving the dress and background as sketches for now. "I was twelve when I arrived at Bellini's. The odor of the room struck me first, the concoction of wet gesso, oils, linseed and gum arabic. And the assortment of curious objects, the skulls and maquettes, plaster casts, painter's dummies, wooden arms, likenesses of feet and hands, all different scales. And the particular landscape of sounds: nails being tapped into frames, pestles grinding against mortars, the swish of canvases being cut. Are you sure you don't need to rest?"

He's asked several times already and her reply is the same: "I'll tell you when I do." She's right about standing still. Zorzo has never known a person to be so physically self-controlled.

"To begin with, I cleaned, swept, fetched food, lugged crates. I slept in the corner on the floor, and when I was offered my own bed in the attic, I said no. Nothing would take me away from that workroom at night, with my newly found kingdom of colors around me."

Sybille's eyes are alive with concentration. She's intent on every word he says.

"Colors took me over. Completely. I volunteered for every job that would teach me more about them. I hurried around all the pharmacists and *vendecolori* of the city, comparing materials, inspecting, touching, smelling, turning everything to the light. Even the names of materials seemed to have this enchanted quality: porphyry, malachite, verdigris. Like names from mythology. I wondered how I'd managed to take it all for granted until then. An example: do you know there are about a hundred different yellows?"

"No!"

"I swear. Once, I was tasked to go with the head *garzone* to the Dolomite hills in search of a particular yellow."

"Where do you find yellow in the hills?"

"That is the trick. It's like hidden treasure. We traveled for days, following an old map made by Bellini's father, finally reaching a valley, a very wild and steep place. We dug down into the hillside with a spade. It took a dozen or so attempts, but we found color in the end: seams of ocher, from light to dark."

"I could not imagine."

"You probably crossed those hills coming into Venice and didn't know what was beneath you. And I fetched colors from stranger places than that," Zorzo goes on. "We used to go to the meadowlands west of Padua to collect particular wildflowers and grasses, vines, berries too—berries make true magenta. We tracked down certain insects, for even they have colors locked inside. Beetles, ladybirds, crickets. Or we'd go to the seashore to grub for mollusks and shells. You've seen a sea urchin, haven't you? Ugly-looking creature, with all the spines. They can be deadly too. But what if I told you, in the right hands, they produce indigo. And there are certain shells that make navy blue or iridescent silver. You're smiling. It's altering the line of your neck."

"Sorry." She reverts to a straight face. "I can't remember a time when I heard such tales. As a child, I think. It's so unusual, all of it."

"Well, colors from creatures, and from the earth, are good enough, but it's minerals that produce the marvels—for me at any rate—the tones that turn heads, the ones that the rich covet, that man will keep searching for until the end of time. A color, the right one, an exquisite one, can turn a good painting into a masterpiece. Blue from cobalt, blue as vivid as sky. Orange from potassium, the color of fire. Rich green from serpentine and olivine, red from hematite. The rocks, when you see them, look so ordinary. I worked almost two years solidly in a corner of Bellini's workroom grinding those plain-looking stones. First with a pestle and mortar to a coarse powder, then with stone rollers on marble slabs, reducing, thinning, pulverizing, and lastly on sheets of glass until it was just fine dust—and the color had revealed itself. I learned that everything has a color hidden within it."

It's as if she's fallen under a spell when Sybille murmurs, "It's the essence of that thing."

"Yes! You've put it far better than I've been able. The essence. Color is the purest form of things, of us even."

"And what is your favorite, I wonder—the color you couldn't live without?"

"That is a good question. I might have answered ultramarine, but now—well—"

"Prince orient?" Sybille whispers.

Zorzo starts at the sound of the phrase on her lips. The mystery of the color is inextricably tied up with her. It seems it always has been. "I'll need to set eyes on it first—but let's hope."

Later in the afternoon, he stands back and studies the canvas.

He's pleased with the work so far. The likeness is good, the face and hands have believable form and weight, and Sybille has an air of mystery. There is just enough of a sense of her that any viewer would want to know more. The trick with a portrait is to capture a fleeting moment, but at the same time, the essence of a person, and their grandeur, whether they possess it or not. In just one day, Zorzo has managed it, much more than he did with Espettia Lippi after months of laboring. He hasn't added any ultramarine to Sybille's dress yet, but has painted in the shadows of the robe, to show the folds and falls of material. And he's made three-dimensional sense of the marble statues in the background, which bring gravitas to the canvas. "Would you like to look?"

"May I?" she says, and he motions for her to come around his side of the easel. When she sees the picture her expression shifts. Zorzo waits for her commentary, but she opens her mouth and says nothing.

"Not what you were expecting?" he asks finally.

She holds her head back and tries squinting at it. "No, it's very skilled."

"That bad?"

"It *is*. It's just, perhaps," it takes her some moments to find the word, "more *decorative* than I was expecting."

"Decorative?"

"I thought it would be more unique, more personal."

Zorzo lets out a gasp, at that bluntness of hers again. "Well, there are certain parameters we have to work within—"

"Of course."

"And I have only just begun."

"You're angry with me?"

"No. I—" He clears his throat. "When you came to my studio you said you knew nothing about how paintings were made."

"Which is true, but am I not permitted to have an opinion? Seeing as you invited me to look?" She runs her hand down the length of her painted likeness. "I look rigid. And the dress takes over the picture. We won't be able to see what this woman is feeling. Oh dear, you *are* angry. Your temples have gone red." She's smiling now, teasingly. "There's no quiet life with me."

It takes Zorzo a few moments to remember how much he values directness, and how charming she's being, even as she disparages his attempts. "Well," he says, smiling back, "your comments are noted. And a quiet life is not what I seek. What's wrong?"

Sybille has turned her head to the sound of footsteps approaching from the hall. The tendons in her neck stiffen, the door opens and Fugger stands on the threshold, taking in the scene. Sybille fidgets with her hands, as if anxious about their nakedness, before secreting them in the folds of her dress, which her husband notices.

"What is it?" she asks coolly. When Fugger makes no reply, just stands there, peering at everything, she says, "We are making good progress." And then, "My father will be so grateful for it."

"I'm leaving now," is all Fugger manages, before nodding at Zorzo and retracing his steps.

Sybille watches him, until his boots have gone up the stairs and disappeared from sight, before she lets go of her breath.

"Leaving?" Zorzo asks.

"For San Isepo." She keeps her voice low, as if her husband might still somehow be listening. She takes up her position once more. "He goes every day, at this time." The change in her mood is palpable, the playfulness gone, a charged intensity in its place.

"What is at San Isepo?" Zorzo asks, just to see what answer she'll give.

"The monastery. He takes Communion in private. He'll not take it elsewhere in Venice." She's still listening for something, her head turned to the window now. Her shoulders have seized up.

"Why there?"

"Only his precious Abbot Agnello will do. He christened Jakob here in Venice. The city was his home as a boy."

There come sounds from outside, the ones she must have been expecting, a murmur of voices from the landing bay on the lagoon side. "One moment." She hurries over to the window and stands on her tiptoes. She has to hold her eye close to the stained glass to see through. A man calls and there's the noise of a boat casting off, a sway of water. Zorzo looks over her shoulder—at the spots of light from the boat's lanterns shrinking away.

"They're on their way," Sybille says, more to herself than to Zorzo.

"Who's he with?" He can just make out the shape of three more people on the boat.

"Tomas and some of the others. They wait outside the monastery walls for him." She stares intently, her breath quick and ragged, chest rising and falling. As her husband's boat glides toward the horizon, she calms and says, "Can we pause for the day?" She turns from the window and faces her companion. "Perhaps you'll take some supper with me upstairs?"

"Supper?"

"It's when food is eaten," she says and then, in response to his expression, "there is nothing to be frightened of. They'll be gone at least two hours."

"I didn't mean—" he starts to say, even though it's precisely what he meant. He finds himself searching outside for the spots of lantern light from Fugger's barge, but they've disappeared. He wonders who else in the house might have their eyes on him with Sybille but presumes she wouldn't suggest it if it wasn't safe. He's intrigued by what she might really have in mind, a chance for intimacy, perhaps. "I shan't eat, but—a drink to end the day, why not?"

"Good." She stares at him, a little too long for Zorzo's comfort, before turning and exiting the room. "Follow me."

15

Black Lilies

Zorzo presumes they'll go to the salon or one of the other receiving rooms on the *piano nobile*, but Sybille leads him up the back staircase, two flights, to a landing from where they enter a room at the back of the house. The walls are paneled in dark red velvet. A fire has been lit, and wine and food, including a roasted pheasant, have been left on a table in the center.

"I come here every evening. It is my sanctuary," Sybille says.

"I've never seen lilies that color." They're in vases everywhere, enormous flowers, deep purple, almost black in color, except for their vermilion hearts, which match the hue of the walls.

"Zantedeschia," Sybille says, taking one of the two seats at the table. "Black Stars. They send them from a hothouse on the mainland." Zorzo can barely imagine how expensive it must be to import such blooms in October. The cost of a batch could easily be more than one of his *garzoni* earns in a year. "Lilies

are emblems of the Fugger clan, but I keep them up here not from patriotism, far from it, but to block out the smell of vinegar. Jakob has the house scrubbed daily. You saw it with your own eyes. He washes in it too sometimes. The same in Augsburg. I've all but forgotten what it's like not to hold my nose."

Zorzo goes over to the window and looks out. The city below is a thousand faceted segments laced through with waterways. He realizes he's in the room from which Sybille threw out her half-written letters that day, just before he met Lorenzo Lotto. "It's for cleanliness," he says, "the vinegar? I noticed how particular your husband was about the plague."

"It's abject, his terror of it. Well, nobody welcomes such a thing, but his fear goes beyond the rational. No one can touch him. No one can touch the things he will touch." She serves herself some game, with red-currant sauce. "Is it money, do you think, that makes a person behave so? The paradox of being able to buy everything, except a guarantee of life? Though he tries even that." She eats before saying, "Like his private monastery in San Isepo. He pays a fortune for it, keeping the place running all year even though he barely comes to Venice. All for his personal salvation."

On the wall behind her, there's a painting—the only one in the room—of a young man sitting among classical ruins. It's beautifully rendered, in a style like Bellini's, Zorzo thinks: highly detailed and crammed with rich colors. They shine out particularly against the dark red walls of the room.

"I've seen him glare at rocks," Sybille goes on about her husband, "the ones he axes from the ground all over Europe—with actual jealousy. How dare they live forever, and he not? Anyway, you understand."

"It makes sense," Zorzo says, wanting to know more than ever why Sybille herself visited San Isepo, and so secretively. "Great rulers of the past did the same. They built themselves tombs the size of cities, so they could continue to rule even in death. Maybe if I was as rich, I would do the same."

"I doubt it. Sit down, you are making me nervous hovering there." Zorzo does as he's told. Sybille watches him directly, unblinking, studying his face. Midnight-blue gown, red velvet room, black lilies. "Pour me a drink."

He half fills two glasses. "It's an arresting painting." He nods to the canvas. "Does it live here?"

"No. It travels with me. Always. It is my brother."

"Really?" Zorzo is thankful the subject has come up again naturally. Carlo Contarini described Sybille's sibling as a saint, her young savior, and the picture gives the same impression: a smartly dressed youth with cerulean-blue eyes sits with his hand resting upon a pile of books. A dove, perched on a column behind him, makes a counterpoint to the youth's luminous face. A row of lit candles below the painting gives it a shrine-like feel. "Who's the artist?"

"It was painted in Wittenberg is all I know. Now that you've opened my eyes to your world, I feel foolish I can't tell you more. There's no signature."

"Well, Wittenberg is an important city. I wonder if it's from Cranach's workshop. Or even by Cranach himself. It's good enough." Zorzo's more interested in the story of Sybille's brother. "I can see the likeness now." Zorzo can, just a little. He makes sure to keep his voice very even, to not give away what he knows, when he asks, "Does he live in Wittenberg?"

"No. He studied there."

"And then returned to Augsburg?"

She pauses before saying, "No, he never came back."

Zorzo wants to ask what she means—if he didn't come back because he went elsewhere, or because he's dead—but her face has become unreadable and he can't tell if the subject is out of bounds. "You'll pardon me, but I heard a little bit about the story, you and your brother on the island?"

"Really?" This genuinely seems to take her by surprise. "What did you hear?"

"That the episode is famous in Germany. That you came off a boat and were stranded, for almost a year."

Silence for a while. Sybille has sat up in her seat, on her guard. "What else?"

"That when the sea froze, your brother tried to walk to the mainland and fell through the ice."

"No," Sybille interrupts. "It was I that went."

"You?"

"*I* fell through the ice." She pauses, her mouth open, brows arched, eyes wide, as if she's there again, on the island. "Edvard couldn't do it. I did."

Edvard. Not Edwin or Edgar as Carlo tried to guess. The image Zorzo had in his mind, that he sketched, is wrong too, of the brother's hands reaching through the ice. He must replace it with this new version: Sybille setting off across the ice sheet, and Edvard watching from the shore. "It must have been a terrible ordeal."

"That's what people always say, about the island. Of course that moment was, yes, the whole winter, in fact. We were lucky to survive. I fell from the cliff too, when I was calling to a boat passing in the distance, the first we'd seen since the accident." She glances at the painting of her brother. "But when spring came, and summer, it turned almost," she touches the scar below her eye as she searches for the word, "it turned miraculous."

"In what way?"

"You'll laugh at this, but we created a kind of Eden. We made ourselves king and queen. There was a cave in the hill and it became our palace. We passed laws—"

"Laws?"

"For our imaginary subjects. In our world, and remember we were still children, everyone was equal, man and woman alike. What was the word I heard just recently? Utopia. That's what we made on that island, our miniature realm." Her eyes shine with the memory of it, before they cloud and darken once more. "It's a shame we couldn't sustain those good intentions afterward."

"Yes. Did I hear also," Zorzo treads carefully, wondering if he should be asking, but now needing to know, "that your brother is no longer—" He doesn't want to say the word out loud.

She jolts in surprise, her fork held midair. "What?"

"Alive?"

"Of course he's alive." She seems affronted by the notion, before she laughs. "Why wouldn't he be?"

"I'm sorry, I—I misunderstood. Please go on." He shakes his head, having to repel another mistaken notion from it. "You were saying about the island. You fell from the cliffs. Is that how you came by your scar?"

Sybille gets up abruptly and goes to see to the fire. She shoves the burning top log with her heel.

"Usually I tell a tall tale," she says, "but why should I carry on defending him? Why should I keep pretending to the world my husband's not a monster? I am sick of doing so." She speaks in an even, quiet voice. "My eye: Jakob struck me with a boot-scraper as I tried to leave my house; before my hand was trapped in a door and crushed."

Zorzo's so taken aback he stops breathing for a moment. One surprise is following hard on the heel of another. He opens his mouth to reply, but no words come. He can't think of a question that doesn't sound banal. "When?" he asks.

"Last year."

"Only then?"

"All scars seem old, don't they? Even fresh ones."

"Have there—" Zorzo stammers on. "That wasn't the first time he's shown violence?"

After a pause, Sybille murmurs, "No." She looks as if she's about to cry and Zorzo gets up to console her. "Don't," she says, putting up her palm. "If you show me kindness, I will crumble. Please." She waits until he sits back down, before carrying on. "We were arguing that day, Jakob and I. Actually, about my brother. We are always fighting about him. Edvard has everything that Jakob lacks: charm, humor and looks too. Such poise with it," she goes on, "such ease. Really, the painting there doesn't do him justice. Jakob could never bear to see everyone's head turn when Edvard entered a room.

"Well, that day, I was traveling to see Edvard. I had news to tell him, you see. He lives close to Ulm, a day's ride from Augsburg. Jakob had barred him from our house, made it as good as impossible for him to even come back to his home city, so why shouldn't I visit him? It was almost Christmas and I wanted to wish Edvard well and tell him my news. Jakob forbade me from going."

"To see your own brother?"

"I snapped, finally, and told him I would go anyway. I packed a bag. Then, as I put on my coat and went to leave the house, he struck me with that cursed scraper. Still I tried to go, but he pulled me back. I remember the front door open and snow tumbling through it. I kept trying, but he got his fellows to help and they dragged me upstairs to a bedroom at the back of the house that had bars on the window. They pushed me inside. I made a final bid to get out. That's when the door was closed against my hand. I felt something crack. I must have screamed, but can't remember. I was locked in."

Her shoulders are trembling and Zorzo goes to her, lays his hands upon them so she can really feel them, so she knows *he* at least cares about what happened.

"He did come to say sorry. Two days later, on Christmas Eve. A threadbare apology. I pretended to accept it but didn't tell him the saddest thing of all. That I had been pregnant. That was the news I wanted to share with my brother before anyone else." Her voice is so low that Zorzo has to crane his neck to hear. "You see, I bled the morning after Jakob locked me in that room."

She touches the base of her stomach. "Shock had done its work. Jakob, himself, had snuffed out the life of his heir."

Zorzo takes her damaged hand and touches his finger against the scar, gently tracing the line of it. He wants to tell her how sorry he is, or ask how he can help, but everything he thinks of saying seems to belittle the tragedies she's been through. "Please tell me," he says finally, "that you saw your brother in the end."

"In secret. Always in secret from that moment. I found a way to get letters out of the house and Edvard and I set meetings for when Jakob was away, which is seldom, but occasionally on a matter of business, or out hunting. We arranged to meet in out-of-the-way places. In small churches usually. More often than not, I was too scared in the end to risk it and left poor Edvard waiting, but sometimes we succeeded. Actually," her face softens, a smile spreads across it, "just before Jakob and I left for Venice, my brother and I spent a whole day together."

"Really? So recently?"

"It seems a lifetime away, but yes, just two weeks ago. It was like the old times." For a moment she's lost in the memory of it, before her smile vanishes. "No one knows Edvard and I met. You must not mention it."

"Of course not."

"Obviously not to my husband; but not to anyone else either. Nobody in his house. Not even Johannes. I can't trust any of them."

"It would not enter my mind."

She takes Zorzo's hand and holds it tightly between her own for at least a minute—until the city clocks strike the hour. "The time," she gasps, letting go of him and getting to her feet. She rubs the wetness from her eyes and straightens her dress. "They'll be getting back soon. You should go."

"I'll not leave you like this."

"Well, you must. Or you make matters worse." Zorzo wants to kiss her, but she's not looking at him anymore. She's staring at the painting of Edvard. "Go, please." When still he doesn't move, she goes over and opens the door. "Tomorrow we continue," she says.

Zorzo takes in a breath, lets it out again before nodding and exiting the room, only to be stopped by Sybille's forceful whisper.

"I mean it," she says. "Not a soul can know I met my brother. It would end in more cruelty."

Before he leaves the palazzo, Zorzo returns to the chapel to have one last look at his painting.

He stares at it as the story Sybille just told him tumbles through his mind. She was right earlier, he thinks, the woman in this picture is decorative. She is rigid. It's clear, even at this early stage, that this is not the heroine she described. The figure on the canvas is not an empress or a lioness; not Zenobia of Palmyra, who stood against Rome, conquered Egypt and ruled in her own right. Zorzo is not doing Sybille justice. In the picture, at least, he must change her destiny, right the wrongs that have been done to her.

He mixes more off-white, a large amount of it. He leaves the drawing of the background intact, but as for Sybille, her face, hands and dress, even the shadow she casts—he paints over it all.

16

The Pageant

Zorzo wakes and at once is alert. It's not yet dawn; the room is still dark and the house silent. A memory has surfaced, perhaps pushed out from a dream: the time he was humiliated by Bellini in front of all his fellow apprentices.

He was seventeen and believed—or had been led to believe—he was the star pupil of the studio, the boy who could do no wrong, a boy with charm, who everyone looked up to, and not just figuratively, for he was already tall.

Buoyed by this perceived success, he took it upon himself to produce in secret his "first solo work of art." Tiziano of course did the same in the red house recently, but with a more successful result. Every night for weeks, Zorzo locked himself away, painting a Madonna and child. When the day came to show it off, he sent invitations to Bellini and his team for "a viewing" at one end of the studio. Zorzo, lying in bed, shudders at how immodest he was.

Bellini stared at it for a couple of moments before he said, "If you're going to use your time, and my time, on self-aggrandizing, I advise you not to plagiarize so inelegantly. This composition is Masaccio's, not yours. He painted his a hundred years ago and yet his Mary still lives and breathes. Yours is crude and garish. The child, Jesus, is stillborn and your colors are ones you find at the bottom of a swamp." He tapped his finger against the edge of his eye and said in a voice that still gives Zorzo nightmares, "Open your eyes. Look at what's in front of you. Now take it down."

Zorzo usually had a clever reply for everything, but there was nothing to be said that day. He was popular among his coworkers, and they were as stunned as he was. He took down the canvas and was certain it was the end of his career. In fact, it was the beginning. He got up the next day with the sense he was starting again from scratch. The rest of his life was an immense empty canvas before him. It was daunting but exhilarating. He could paint it how he wanted.

He feels the same today. Whatever happened in his dreams, a revelation, set in motion yesterday evening, is now working through him like a wash of cool water. He's more grateful than ever for Sybille's comments. The painting he started to create wasn't distinct enough from what everyone else is doing, or even from his own body of work. The canvas may be large, but the story he started to tell upon it lacked ambition. Of course he would have made it good enough, but shouldn't he be trying to make it unforgettable?

As soon as he hears movement next door—someone, probably Paulino, lighting the workroom lamps—he slips out of the red house and makes his way through the empty streets. It's the time of day when Venice is most like a dream, *the strange world caught between sea and sky*, as Bellini likes to describe it, *this city made in color, not in line.* The canals have a stillness, as if they need sleep too—from the effort they make all day, keeping the city moving.

The Palazzo Pallido hasn't woken for the day either and Zorzo has to knock three times on the back door to get the attention of a taciturn porter. He goes to the chapel and neatly, methodically, arranges his things, before mixing quantities of grays and light ochers as the day starts to rise through the windows. He's decided, while he waits for Sybille, to carry on working on the background, on the frieze of medieval effigies of knights and ladies. He takes his position in front of the canvas, picks up his palette and his brush.

Open your eyes, look at what's in front of you.

Zorzo starts to paint the effigies in detail. Along with the statue of the skeleton with the crown—the one he placed Sybille beside, in the center of the wall—there's a man in battle garb and chain-mail hood, and two sets of couples, man and wife kneeling together, eyes closed, hands conjoined in prayer. They're the sort of sculptures seen in all churches that Zorzo usually takes for granted, like everyone does. He studies them with greater care today, and it dawns on him they are more than just weathered stone, more than symbols; they're the remains of living, breathing people. The men in tight-fitting jupons, low-slung belts and ankle boots, and their wives in kirtles and trains, had once had dreams and fears, had children and friends from childhood, times of joy and episodes of pain. They walked under the same sun that Zorzo does, endured the same winters. As he paints them and imagines the households they once inhabited, and the arc of their lives, an idea comes to him of how to portray Sybille. Not arbitrarily in front of this collection of statues, but as part of a story that connects her with them.

He imagines that she, until a moment ago, was a statue herself, a conqueress of times past, a Zenobia long ago consigned to the realm of the dead, perhaps unjustly. She has now been granted life for one day only and is hurrying from her burial place. Maybe, just where Zorzo stands, someone is waiting for her, perhaps a lover she had lost when she died, the only true one she'd ever had, and she's darting out of the picture toward them. Even if nobody but Zorzo understands this meaning, it would make Sybille irrefutable.

At once he's too impatient to wait until she comes down and presses on. He sketches this new interpretation directly onto the background he's created, trying to capture motion in her body. Without rubbing anything out, he dashes off various versions, one on top of the other.

Sybille enters just after the house clock strikes nine.

"Take your place," he says, almost breathless. "I can't keep up with my excitement. I have found a way to capture what you spoke of yesterday. I ask just one thing: permit me to work in silence."

The request, or the way Zorzo poses it, or both, seems to excite his subject. She gives a smile, touches the tip of her tongue against her top teeth and stands in front of the statues, remembering her position precisely.

"That's right," says Zorzo, "but turn to me, as if I've just appeared and you need to speak with me. In fact," another unexpected idea lights up in his head, "look straight at me."

She does as he says, and suddenly the idea of it, of her looking directly out, engaging with whoever is there, strikes Zorzo as revolutionary. It makes the viewer *become* the lover she lost when she died, and for whom she's defied even the grave to return to. He can think of barely a handful of paintings where the subject confronts the viewer in such a way, and those all men. It's an unwritten rule that Zorzo has found himself following with everyone else, that women, if not shown in profile, must be glancing to one side or another, that their story cannot break the walls of the canvas, but must be contained within them. When Zorzo painted Leda as Venus he went even further and had her close her eyes. But where does this practice come from, he wonders now; why is it necessary to trap the subject in the picture? With the back of his hand he scrubs out the overlapping sketches he just made, and in their place draws a face twice the size it was. Sybille complained yesterday that the dress took over the picture, that you couldn't see what this woman was feeling. She was right about that too. And if she's going to stare straight out, he resolves, and if her face is going to dominate the canvas, let's see *everything* that's happening in it.

Now he peers into it as he's never peered into a face before. He imagines he's on a cliff, staring down at the ocean. At first he would only notice the surface of the water, the reflection of sky against it, the undulations made by the breeze. And then he'd see through to the underwater realm, the chasms and seamounts, swaying forests of kelp, shoals of fish and shale dunes. Just so, he peers through the surface of Sybille's cheeks and eyes and forehead to the multicolored depths below.

Over the following three days, Zorzo works at unprecedented speed, with an energy he hasn't possessed in half a decade, building definition in every quarter of the canvas. Although bold, he could not have imagined that his decision to have Sybille look straight ahead would reap such rewards.

There is some conversation between them, after all, spells of it throughout the days. Zorzo asks questions about Sybille's life and, although her answers are often spare, her eyes seem to round out the stories. They allow Zorzo into the realm of her mind.

He travels through it and can see into the rooms she's inhabited, the spaces she's passed through. A nine-year-old girl, in her bedroom in the burgher's mansion in Augsburg, looks over the rooftops of the city and dreams. A twelve-year-old on the deck of a ship, on a cold Baltic night, her brother at her side. The shock of the sea, of life changing course utterly and parents lost across the ocean. The courageous girl who sets off over the ice only for the sea to try to take her once more. As summer blooms, sister and brother at the mouth of their cave, their designated palace, from which they've built their kingdom. Then, watching from a carriage window as they're returned to Augsburg, dressed in finery again, but in their eyes a tiny wildness that will always be there. An eighteen-year-old bride, small against the Gothic arches of Augsburg's cathedral, advances past the city elders to the altar. In the hallways of the Fugger mansion, the new mistress is presented to the army of valets, grooms and housemaids. The twenty-one-year-old wife waits as Jakob trawls back from the winter hunt and wonders when he'll come to her bedroom. She sees guests arriving, *his* guests, bankers and mine-builders, carrying their importance across their shoulders, welcomed with hot wine and fighting talk—and wonders if *she* will ever conquer again, or find meaning in her life, as she did that summer on the island with her brother. The twenty-four-year-old lady, in the paneled gloom of Augsburg's finest glove maker, consoles herself with luxury and tries on five exquisite pairs and orders twenty. The wronged wife takes to her bed after her husband has beaten her. She wakes and everything—sheets, nightgown, stomach and legs—is drenched in blood. Her baby is gone. The twenty-six-year-old woman hurries to a forbidden rendezvous with her brother and they spend a day together in secret. Then she sits in the pink damask interior of her private carriage, as the caravan from Germany makes its lurching progress across the Alps to Venice.

Zorzo can't remember a time when a picture so successfully emerged from his psyche onto the face of a canvas. Every mark he makes, every color he mixes, every spot and line and dash, adds a little more to the success of the whole.

Although Jakob Fugger can be heard in the house occasionally, he doesn't appear in person again, or come to check on progress. Since Sybille told the story of his cruelty, Zorzo has been bracing himself for the moment he meets the man again. He knows he'll struggle to keep his contempt to himself. But the moment doesn't come. Fugger's absence is as incomprehensible as it is disturbing. One of the first things Sybille said about him was how a note from Zorzo would make him think she was having an affair with him. But the two are left to spend days together. Zorzo wonders if Jakob is testing his wife somehow, even secretly monitoring her. More than once Zorzo casts his eyes around, searching for a hole in the wall or the ceiling, behind which an eyeball may be watching. He frets that their voices may be carrying up through walls, or via chimneys.

Every afternoon, at precisely the same time, Fugger's boat sets off from the palazzo's front pier and Zorzo unknots and steadies. Sybille does too, for a little while. She always stops and goes to the window to look at the retreating lanterns of the barge. She might say something lighthearted, or they might chat for a while, before she becomes preoccupied again, her gaze often returning to the window. By that point, light is waning anyway, and Zorzo doesn't carry on for much longer.

At the end of each day, he asks if Sybille wants to look at the canvas, but she says she'll wait. It's not until the third evening, an hour after her husband has gone, that she says, "Now, perhaps?"

Zorzo clears his throat and tidies a space in front of the easel and she comes around to look.

She looks stunned for a moment and Zorzo thinks she doesn't like it. She laughs, her shoulders drop and a kind of light seems to shine from behind her face. "There you have me. There is a fighter of a woman." She clutches Zorzo's hands in her own and holds them against her, tightly, so he can feel the drive of her heart. He puts his arms around her, looks down at her mouth, as her lips slowly part. He's on the point of kissing it when he checks himself, realizes the door is wide open, that anyone could come down and find them. He lets go, but their eyes remain locked. Zorzo feels transfigured.

"What fortune," he says, "that our paths crossed."

"I think the same. If you had seen me but two weeks ago,

on our journey to Venice, how agitated I was. How beset with worry. Almost feverish with it."

She looks down at her damaged hand, runs a finger along the ridge of the scar, and Zorzo says softly, "Tell me."

"Crossing the mountains, we stopped for the night. As everyone slept, I climbed out of my carriage and stood at the edge of a ravine. I was shaking. I'd never been among those peaks before. The moon was out, paler than ever, and everything below it was colorless. It was just—what is the word—monochrome. White moon, black sky, white stars and these black mountains with white peaks that went on and on forever. No sign of anyone, no life anywhere, just this shrill breeze and endless monochrome. I could have thrown myself into that wind, off the edge of the ravine. I've never felt so lonely. So bullied. So anxious. So worthless. Not one thing to look forward to. Not one light on the horizon. Just dark, grim tasks ahead of me. And then, Venice," she sweeps her hand over Zorzo's tray of pigments and their reflections scatter across her face, "and color at last. And you."

Zorzo steps closer to her and Sybille's chest rises and falls. He leans down, his mouth close to hers, but again he stops himself from kissing her. "I was on an edge too—" he starts to say before the sound of footsteps comes along the corridor: Frau Bauer along with a housemaid, who has a bucket and mop. Zorzo goes to clean up his materials. The women enter. When the maid sees that her mistress and the painter are still there, she stalls and looks to her overseer. Usually the room is empty by now. Making a point of ignoring Sybille and Zorzo, Bauer motions at her lackey, who blushes, curtsies and begins mopping the room. The delicate odors of oil paint and linseed are subsumed by vinegar solution.

Zorzo checks his jars have been properly corked and that the brushes are dry and clean, but every time he glances up, he finds Sybille's gaze still upon him. His heart is beating so fast and hard it seems to rap against his ribs. Yes, little more than two weeks ago, as Sybille was standing alone on an Alpine crest contemplating a grim future, his own was just as unsure: bailiffs, debt, the looming collapse of his workshop, the fear of letting down his *garzoni*, the loss of his reputation. Little more than two weeks ago, he was standing in Leda's salon, humiliated, another love affair over. Now he has a commission, which may lead to a greater one, or to a new color, a color everyone is clamoring for. And somehow, possibly more significant than all of this, is Sybille. He's heard other painters talk of their muses and he's been half envious, half disbelieving that such people exist; quasi-divine individuals who bring luck, change fortune and draw out genius. And, as all muses seem to, might Sybille become—somehow, in some way—his beloved?

Keeping his voice low so only she will hear, he says, "I don't want to leave you."

"And I don't want you to leave."

They stand, not moving, until the maid draws closer with her mop, the odor of vinegar with her, and Zorzo gets his coat. "Good evening, then, Frau Fugger. Until tomorrow."

Zorzo walks home at double speed, almost in a run. He can't keep up with the whirl of his thoughts. *How lucky, lucky, lucky, I am,* he thrills. *How lucky all of us are, to have our time alive, here in this world, our period on the stage, to have this great pageant unfold around us.*

He hastens through the evening crowds, along the side of the lagoon now, and his thoughts are like the lantern lights springing to life on the hundreds of ships in the channel. *How lucky we are, to have this panoply of people. The great ones living and the illustrious dead. Whose canvases can transport us anywhere. Whose music can make us jump to our feet and dance, or hold each other and weep. Whose buildings ascend to make it seem as if our dreams are coming true. Whose ships set sail for every corner of the world; whose maps grow and grow, every year with yet more discoveries, more realms, mountains, cities and seas. More ideas. The living and the dead, all alive, their pageant for us. How lucky, lucky we are.*

"Sybille has changed everything!" he says out loud, jumping across the top of a bridge. "This painting changes everything. Now is my time. At last, my time."

"Greetings, dear Uggo," Zorzo says, rushing into the red house and planting a kiss on each of the boy's cheeks.

"Been drinking, have you, sir?" the boy says.

"On success. Vats of it. And I mean to drink more. Until I can't stand."

"I wouldn't advise it, sir. You make a very clumsy drunk."

"My brave young scoundrel who has a quip for every moment. Is everyone here? I need to speak to my troops." Zorzo hurries up the stairs and into the workroom. "Good evening, Paulino, still at work? Good for you. Come and take some wine with me. Come, all of you. Let us toast to the turning tide, our burgeoning business. Paulino, I command you to stop that sketch immediately and fetch our best bottle. Bring two bottles of Eleanor's wine."

"Really, sir?" Paulino says, taken aback, like everyone else in the room. "I thought you wanted to keep it until—?" Zorzo has told them more than once that Eleanor's wine—four priceless bottles from a vineyard planted by Eleanor of Aquitaine—is being saved for his wedding day.

"You're right, Paulino. You're always right." He pinches the lad's cheek. "Fetch the *second* best, and we'll toast with that."

"Yes, sir." Paulino sets to the task, disappearing down the back stairs.

"Sir, what's happened?" Azalea asks, coming forward.

Zorzo turns in a circle to look at the room. It's alive: sketches he thought he'd grown bored of, half-finished paintings, trays of color, pestles and mortars, framing tools, skulls and busts. They all vibrate with power. "All I know is that each and every one of you is remarkable. Without you, I'd be—"

Tears have wet the rims of his eyes and as he half laughs, half sobs, Teodor jokes, "Watch out, storm coming in." A happy cry goes up among the others and they all press around their talisman and give him pats of support.

Paulino returns with cups for them all and two bottles. Zorzo uncorks one and holds it up in the air. "To our new beginning. The turning tide." He pours.

An hour later, when the wine has been drunk, and Zorzo has played his lute for everyone and his heart has steadied, his apprentices begin drifting off to their beds. Paulino is putting out the workroom lights when Uggo appears, wiping the sleep from his eyes.

"Sir, this just came for you."

He hands over an envelope and Zorzo opens it. Her handwriting, her slanting hand in dark green ink, and the single sentence—*I'm downstairs in the square.*

17

The Chinese Room

"Do I need to give a reply?" Uggo asks.

"I'll come down with you."

They descend, Uggo drooping like a sleepwalker—once sleep has come upon the lad, there's no enlivening him—while Zorzo couldn't feel more alert suddenly. The boy goes back to his cocoon of blankets by the front door, and Zorzo exits.

The figure of a man is cutting across the square away from the red house: Sybille's groom, Johannes.

"I'm here," comes a quiet voice. She's in the shadow by the wall. "I sent him back. You'll have to watch over me." Her mantle and hood are a deep shade of purple, an imperial color against the murky night. "The conversation we had before left me," as she searches for the word, she gently wrings her hands, gloved in purple also, amethyst satin, "too exhilarated to sleep." She continues sotto voce. "In fact, I feel I may never sleep again, that after a decade of one long, bad dream, I've finally woken." Then, inclining her head toward the red house, "Will you invite me in?"

"In?" The word gets trapped in Zorzo's throat. There are so many reasons to say no. Fugger for one. And Tomas could probably strangle a man, even one of Zorzo's size, with just one of his colossal hands. Then there's the fact that his *garzoni* know Sybille's married and he'll be setting a poor example. He didn't even allow Leda to stay the night, not that she ever would have. There are countless reasons to convince Sybille to go home, but none as compelling as the need to have her with him, here and now. A breeze tiptoes across the square and Sybille's cloak moves like burning indigo in the gloom. Tyrian purple, as chosen by Roman emperors. "Of course," Zorzo says, "follow me."

Inside the hall, he closes the front door quietly, bolts it and takes a candle from the nightstand, before opening another door. He motions Sybille inside, toward a little flight of stairs. He's not going to his *studiolo*, where he usually sleeps, as it's right next to the workroom. As he's closing the door, he notices Uggo is watching, bleary-eyed, on the point of falling back to sleep, but aware of what's happening, that Sybille Fugger has crept in for the night. He blinks at his master and gives a smile that's so faint it's almost invisible, and at once Zorzo has an almost unbearable pang: at his love for the lad.

"That smell, what is it?" Sybille asks, going up first.

"Cedar. From your part of the world. I'm storing it for a friend. You had black lilies and I have forest timber." Sybille glances around: a spacious room that ascends to the rafters of the building. There are bundles of timber here and there, amid workroom ephemera, large frames, moldings and plaster casts. "It was intended for my father to move into. It was the only way I could convince him to leave Castelfranco for Venice, when his health… I planned to give him his own annex, where he could do as he pleased. I built that myself for him to sleep in." Zorzo points to a timber closet in one corner. "He never got to come in the end. Shall I light the fire?"

He half expects Sybille to ask why, or what, they're doing in a storeroom, why they don't go to a salon, or a bedroom, but she says nothing, just takes off her mantle and lets it drop over the back of a chair.

Zorzo kneels down at the hearth. Three years ago he set kindling and logs ready to light for his father's entrance and they're exactly how he left them, though veined all over with cobwebs. The kindling is so dry he barely has to touch it with the flame of his candle for it to go up with a flash of orange.

"The walls," Sybille gasps as the room lights up around her, "what is that?"

She means the mural that circles the space at chest height, a panorama in the oriental style.

"My father used to tell me stories of Marco Polo when I was a boy, the lands he visited, you probably know the tales. My father said he had no regrets about staying put in Castelfranco all his life, but I wanted to take him on a grand journey. So..." He gestures around the room. In shades of red cinnabar and burnt brown are palaces with curved roofs, pagodas and water towers, in a landscape of conical mountains, *Cunninghamia* forests and curling rivers. Little details of it, a roof here or there, the armor of a mounted knight, are rendered in gold leaf and catch against the firelight.

"You made all this for your father?"

She comes over and stands before him. Her eyes are wide, and wild, like the sea. The line of her collarbone slowly rises and falls. Her breath is shaky, the only sound in the room but the crackling fire. She rolls off her gloves and Zorzo knows, from the base of his spine, there's no turning back now. He takes the gloves, lays them carefully down. She nods. Their lips touch, and as they kiss a flame of burning pink, the color of a summer thunderstrike, lights up through him.

★★★

"The first day I set foot here, thirteen years old, climbing off a rickety ferry with my father, who hadn't seen Venice either until then, everything changed. Everything. How could it not?"

Zorzo's voice is low and even. He's naked with Sybille, a blanket half-pulled over them, cocooned in the timber closet, on a plump hay mattress that has never been slept on before.

"It was as if we'd been plucked up and dropped into the future," Zorzo goes on. "We walked through the city in a trance and when we came to St. Mark's and saw the Doge's Palace we didn't know whether to laugh or cry. From pictures, I knew where kings lived, in castles, thick walls, slit windows, towers, all defense and fortification; but here, suddenly, was a royal place from the imagination: rose-pink, nothing but windows, as light as air, not putting up barriers to the world, but letting all of it in."

Sybille rests her head against the curve of his neck.

"I love this city. Everything about it. Each day I'm amazed all over again. So much more so than my friends who were born here. Did you know, the first settlers—it must be a thousand years ago now—chose this boggy lagoon, not because it was easy to live here—disease-ridden all summer, bitter all winter—but the opposite: because no one else would come. It was a refuge from war. They were fishermen first, but soon became craftsmen, and then traders, before they drove a million piles into the mud and created, from nothing, the greatest city the world has ever known."

Sybille holds on to him tighter than ever and he takes in her balmy, febrile scent.

"There are people here," he goes on, "the so-called clever ones, that believe the Venetian state is a thing to be mocked, or distrusted or fought. They make fun of me, put me down as a wide-eyed country boy. They're the misguided ones. I'd direct them to the great chamber of the Doge's Palace. Have you heard of it?" Sybille hasn't. "A gigantic room—it spans the whole length of the building. You almost can't accept it's real. It's where the city council meets, to look after their people, and to dream of greater things to come. In a thousand years, Venice has never lost its way. It never diminishes. And I'm convinced in another thousand years it will be the same."

Sybille disentangles herself from him. She lies looking at the ceiling, at the play of firelight across it, before sitting up against the bedhead and arranging the blanket to cover herself.

"What's wrong?" asks Zorzo.

Her eyes are focused on a point in front of her. She looks upset, maybe even angry. "You really believe that?" she says eventually. "That city councils meet to look after their people and to dream of greater things to come?" Surely, there's sarcasm in the way she parrots him.

"I suppose I do, yes. What is this?"

"It's a rather childlike view, isn't it?"

Her tone is more than mocking; it's curt. Zorzo sits up too. "I'd say children have generally a healthy view of things."

"Healthy, perhaps, but aren't children, by definition, unsafe in the world?" For a while, there's silence between them and they both stare out into the middle distance of the room. Zorzo can't believe how quickly the temperature has changed, how the warmth of the evening has dissipated completely. "If Venice is as perfect as you say," she goes on, "which I doubt, it's alone in that respect."

"So what is it that you believe?"

"That people are slaves for the most part. Blind. Bound. Drudges to do the bidding of the tiny few."

Zorzo finds himself laughing, at how the conversation has veered from his childhood reminiscences to the gravest subject imaginable. "You are a philosopher, truly," he says, smiling, trying to steer back to where they were before. "I shall not be able to keep up with you. The tiny few?"

"Don't pretend you don't know who they are. The Church of Rome, and those in its thrall. A handful of others, my husband chief among them. Perhaps myself too, by extension. It's because so few people hold the reins of the world that stakes have grown so high recently, in this 'age of light' we live in. It's why war is coming. And soon."

Zorzo opens his mouth to reply, but nothing comes out. He blinks at her and recalls Bellini's pronouncements on the way back from the Ca' d'Oro, about ill omens and the powers that be watching them. "War?"

"Think what's at stake. The world now, look at it. The time of print. Fifty years ago, the total number of books on this earth was barely in the hundreds. Now it's in the hundreds of thousands. Presses in all quarters. Pandora's box opened. Knowledge everywhere. Opinions far and wide. Man has all but gone around the earth. Mysteries solved. Of course the pope's Church is going to fight for its existence. It has the world to lose. Its whole architecture is being torn down, brick by brick. That's why they're building a new St. Peter's, why they want painters like you to fill it with pictures of their choosing."

"Painters like me?" She's probably not aware how dismissive she sounds, she's so focused on the points she's making.

"To keep the story turning in their favor. Protect what they've invested in for centuries."

Zorzo knows that Sybille has a sense of right and wrong, a conscience, but he is only just discovering how deep her thinking goes. "I never thought of it like that, what you say about books."

"With each one that's printed, the Church of Rome and the rest of the tiny few will push back a little harder. They'll fight to the death. You know the pope is a war commander first? That he carved out his life on the battlefield, not in a monk's cell?"

Zorzo lies down, facing her, and takes her hand in his. He's no longer hurt by the taunts she made just now; the opposite: he's newly fascinated. He can't help comparing her to Leda, counting money at her desk and believing her small empire is the center of the world. He closes his eyes and listens to her breath, feels the heat from her hand, catches the scent from her neck.

"What are you doing?" she asks.

"Thanking whichever god it is I believe in—for making sure I followed you that day from St. Mark's."

Sybille folds herself over him, kisses his forehead, his nose, his mouth...

Zorzo wakes with a start and sits up. Sybille's no longer beside him on the bed.

"Are you there?"

No reply.

Her clothes are gone, and the fire burned out. It's not yet dawn. Zorzo lies back down and tries to think of her, to recall the rapture of last night, her body against his, but his ears are tuning on the noises now coming from the main part of the house, his *garzoni* setting up.

He gets up, puts on his clothes and descends, opening the door into the hall quietly, so as not to disturb Uggo. He'd rather not see the boy's face, in case there's judgment upon it. But Uggo isn't there. His bed is folded up. Zorzo stares at the front door, at the bolts that have been pulled back, for Sybille's departure presumably, and wonders what state of mind she was in when she left. He decides to go out, rather than face his staff: if word has spread, they'll all have their own opinions by now, from an impressed Teodor, to a censorious Paulino. He puts on his coat, but as he reaches for the door handle, it gives a sudden jolt and Uggo steps in.

"Sir?" he says. "You're awake?"

"Did you see her leave, Sybille Fugger?"

"I told her I'd take her home, sir, and she said there was no need. She insisted, in fact. But I trailed her anyway, just to be sure, back to Cannaregio. You know what they say about the hour before dawn being the killing time?"

Zorzo has never heard the phrase before and thinks Uggo has confused it with another one. "When was this?"

"Less than an hour ago."

"And how was she? In good spirits?" The question comes out before Zorzo thinks about it. He wonders how Uggo is supposed to reply. At any other time, he could imagine the boy quipping, *By the look on her face, I'd say the night's passions were a revelation, sir.* But Uggo is unusually sober this morning.

"If I'm honest, sir, she looked a little fraught."

This sends a cold shiver through Zorzo, but he smiles and says, "It was kind of you to go after her." He buttons up his coat.

"Where are you going, sir?"

"Back to work," Zorzo says, going out. "There's still a lot to do."

It's not work that's troubling him: it's Sybille. She is more than one kind of person, as she showed last night, switching from tender to fiercely opinionated. He wonders if the woman who rose at dawn and rushed home without saying goodbye is another version of her altogether.

18

Malachite Ceramic

He hurries across the square. Rather than go straight to the Palazzo Pallido, he turns south toward St. Mark's. He needs the comfort of open space around him, to gather his thoughts.

Once he's moving with the rising sun flickering on his face, bringing out all sorts of pinks and oranges from the city's façades, memories of last night start pouring through his mind. The ecstasy that was hoped for, but never expected. Sybille's astonishing yielding to intimacy. For Zorzo, uncovering her was like coming across hidden treasure, a magnificent thing that has lain out of sight, a hidden city under the sand.

He comes into the piazza, into a great block of sun, and stands there. "I love her," he whispers to himself. "I do."

He holds his hands to his head and could almost laugh. *This is happiness*, he thinks, and St. Mark's Square, the greatest rectangle in Christendom, unpeopled in front of him.

Then people come, youngsters, navy cadets, swaggering, arrogant, clutching bottles. They must have been up all night. They're making fun of one of their number. Someone steals this cadet's cap and the others toss it to one another and the poor lad tries to catch it. Zorzo moves away, toward the water, and as a breeze comes in from the lagoon, it carries a bitter scent. He's still there, the hanged man between the columns of the *piazzetta*, his head at right angles to his body, his coat even more jarringly fine against his yellowy black skin. Sybille was right: it's almost impossible to imagine what crime he could have committed.

When Zorzo arrives at the Palazzo Pallido by the back door and heads past the kitchens, he hears Sybille and her husband arguing in the hall upstairs. He halts, his first terrifying thought that Fugger has found out about last night. He glances over his shoulder to the exit, wondering if he should slip away until he can find out more. But then he notices a pair of cooks, one cleaving the heads off rabbits and smirking at the other, signaling, surely, that the row is domestic and not grave. Zorzo ascends a little further, until he can hear clearly.

"I'm not asking you, woman, I'm telling you," Fugger is saying. "It's of no consequence whether you like it or not. It's decided. I thought you hated all this water around you anyway."

Sybille notices Zorzo hovering below. "There are people here, Jakob. Please lower your voice."

"What people? What do I care?" Then he notices where she's looking.

"I'll return later," Zorzo suggests.

"No," Fugger barks. "Come up." When Zorzo doesn't immediately move, Fugger snaps, "Come up, for pity's sake, where I can see you!"

Zorzo does as he's told, although he would just as well take Fugger by the throat and tell him what he thinks of men who abuse their wives. The three of them stand for a moment in silence, Fugger looking Zorzo up and down before saying, "You have until tomorrow noon to finish. Understood?"

"Yes, sir."

Fugger continues glaring at the painter, as if he's noticed something he's missed before. *He suspects*, Zorzo's sure in that moment, before Fugger says, almost casually, "And I hope you've done a good job, if you want to please her father." He turns on his heels, ascends to his salon and slams the door behind him.

Sybille shares a petrified look with Zorzo before hurrying down into the chapel. "He is mad," she says under her breath. "It is lucky you came when you did." Shaking all over, she holds the back of her hand against her cheek.

"What happened?"

"There is some report or other of plague in the city. Who knows if it is to be believed, but we're leaving. I suggested traveling had more risk and we should stay where we are. But we go the day after tomorrow. Can you finish by then?" she asks distractedly. It's clearly not the first thing on her mind.

"I'll do my best. Leaving?" Can he tell her he's devastated? Ask if she feels the same? He waits for her to calm, to show him some warmth, acknowledge, in her eyes at least, the night they just spent together.

"He asked who it was." She nods at the painting. "Who I was running toward so happily. I might have suggested it was him had I not feared he'd strike me for insolence."

Zorzo takes Sybille's hand and tries to kiss it, but she pulls it away. "Don't. I can't. I'll go and change."

All day Sybille is distracted. She can't keep still, or remember the position of her arms or feet or the angle of her head. Every time Zorzo corrects her she clenches her jaw, or fists, but says nothing. Her eyes are red around the edges, not just from lack of sleep but from a private stress, and her pupils never steady, not for one moment. Zorzo is completely thrown off balance by her behavior. He can't understand how she could have spent the night with him—which alone would be an earthshaking act, given her circumstances—and now be so remote. Perhaps she feels guilty and is pretending it didn't happen; or maybe the house is oppressing her and she'll return to normal when she's out of it. Zorzo doesn't know how to ask. He must be soft, he thinks, and first put her at ease.

"How many people have married in this room, do you think?"

Sybille gives a weak smile, but says nothing.

"I can't resist a wedding," Zorzo goes on. "Is anyone ever unhappy at one? Even if they know the marriage is doomed. A wedding is like the first warm day of the year, wouldn't you say? Nothing but hope. After it, everyone might revert to being sworn enemies again, but for that day, peace."

Sybille gives another perfunctory smile but adds nothing to the conversation and Zorzo decides to carry on in silence.

He starts making mistakes. When he's touching up the line of her brow, he puts too much paint on the brush and a drip falls down the canvas, against her cheek like a black teardrop. It's the most subtle part of the painting, built up, layer upon layer—in soft pinks, off-whites and Egyptian blue—to give her skin translucency. As he attempts to clean it, he ends up making the mark worse. He tries to divert his attention to the dress and the background, but, like picking at an unhealed scab, he keeps returning to the damaged area.

"I'll have to wait until the morning to fix it," he says in the end and puts some cloth over the top of the canvas to avoid looking at the mistake.

In the afternoon, the moment Sybille hears her husband's boat depart, she breaks from her position and hurries over to the window. Zorzo peers over her shoulder as the barge retreats. He hopes she might relax a little now, but she's wringing her hands and seems more agitated than ever. He puts his palm, very tenderly, against the small of her back, just so she can feel the warmth of it, but at his touch, she stiffens, before moving away.

"I have to get out of this dress," she says. "I can't breathe. Meet me upstairs. In the room I took you to before. You know the one? Take the back stairs. I need to talk to you." Before he has time to respond, she's gone, a bustle of ultramarine hurrying to the hall.

Zorzo turns back to the window. Fugger's barge is ebbing into the distance, almost out of sight. He cleans his brushes and, as always, makes sure the phials of pigment are corked for the night. At length he turns the easel so the painting faces the room, carefully removes the cloth he placed over it earlier and stands back to look. He's relieved. Now the paint has dried and settled, the damaged area doesn't look so bad. Though Sybille appears to have a blackening wound down her cheek, he's confident he can rectify the issue in a matter of hours. What is more gratifying is that the picture works. His hunch has paid off. The canvas has drama and immediacy. There's a sense of mystery to it, as he'd hoped, in her relation to the background of statues. More unexpected, and perhaps the thing that elevates the painting the most, it has a quality of danger. This is a person who, though alluring, we're not sure we can trust. In any case, Zorzo is confident there will be no hindrance with payment, especially now he's been tasked with finishing ahead of time. And as soon as he receives the money, he'll go straightaway and retrieve his father's ring.

He goes up through the house. Every corner of it creaks against his passing. Though there are pools of lamplight here and there, mostly it's dark and he gets temporarily lost. He finds himself on an unfamiliar upper landing and has to retrace his steps until he eventually discovers the door to the salon she meant.

"Are you there?" he says, giving a little knock. There's no reply and he enters. The room is empty, cold too. It looks different today. No fire lit, nor food waiting. The lilies have gone, though the vases remain, still with their water, dirty and stagnant. The window is open and a trail of fallen petals leads to the window ledge. Some of the stamens have burst into little pools of dark indigo. The flowers must have been thrown out in a hurry, for when Zorzo goes to close the window, he notices stems strewn against the lower ledges of the building and at the side of the canal below. He closes the casement.

"You found it all right?" says Sybille from the doorway. Clasped in her fist is a set of heavy-looking keys. She's changed from her dark blue gown to a silver floor-length cloak. Only in paintings has Zorzo seen a woman like her. She's extraordinary. The cloak is embroidered—in what must be a million silver beads—in a swirling pattern that looks like a cornfield in a storm. It would have taken seamstresses months to create, be worth a fortune, and she wears it as if it were a common housecoat, thrown on.

"What is it—?" He coughs against the sudden dryness in his throat. "What did you want to talk about?"

"Jakob has forced my hand, with his plan to leave Venice. I have so much to do." Sybille half circles the room and the silver beadwork of her gown stretches and curls. Again, Zorzo feels as if he imagined last night, that it hadn't really happened, that she's forgotten. She looks at him and says, "I know where prince orient is, and I can get it for you now. You can see it tonight and take it home with you."

Of all the things Zorzo thought she might say, this was not one of them.

"He keeps it in a safebox in the ballroom, a metal cabinet where he stows precious things. He discussed it with Cardinal Soderini the evening after da Vinci was here. I didn't tell you at the time because that was when I was trying to get you to leave the whole business; you remember, at San Zaccaria? One of these keys opens the safe."

For a moment Zorzo feels a wash of relief, of triumph, that his instincts were right all along and that his plan is paying off. But the news has come in such an odd way, hurriedly and without fanfare. And it seems too obvious to point out that he can hardly steal the prince orient, that surely it would be missed. "You said you have much to do?"

"If we get into the cabinet, and I find the material for you, will you help me?"

"With what?"

"Not a small matter. Not a palatable one either. There's risk, but little to you—if you do as I tell you." She freezes, holds up her hand and turns her ear to the door. "Did you hear something?"

"No," Zorzo says, though he's too dazed to notice anything but her.

"They've barely gone. It's too early."

She exits back along the landing and listens from the top of the stairs. Zorzo's skin prickles about the shoulders and the room seems oppressive. He finds his head turning to the sole painting in the room, his eyes meeting those of Sybille's brother, Edvard. The young man's face, as pale as the dove on the perch beside him, seemed elegant and composed before. Today, Zorzo detects a hunted, fearful man. Edvard's gaze seems to say, *Get out of this place, run from it as fast as you can, forget prince orient—or your life will be overturned as mine was.* Zorzo tries to imagine how Fugger has people dealt with, the ones that cross him. He notices blood on the canvas. Three spots of it seem to bleed into the breast of the dove. He's about to look closer, to see if it's real or painted on, when Sybille comes back.

"It's not them," she whispers. "No one here but us. Follow me. I'll show you."

Not waiting for him, she descends the back stairs. Zorzo goes after her, at a remove, following her down one flight and along an unfamiliar passageway into the main part of the house.

"Quickly," she says, her hushed voice echoing around the repeating tiers of stairs and landings. She stops at the entrance to the salon, the room in which Zorzo was interviewed. "In here," Sybille calls and goes inside.

Zorzo knows he must leave the Palazzo Pallido. *Not a small matter, not a palatable one either*, she said, but in a manner that implied it was far from either, that it was dreadful. He feels stranded, a tiny thing against the red marble pillars of the chamber, held by some invisible force. He orbits the gallery and puts his head around the salon door. It's dark inside. Sybille is standing beside the double doors at the far end, beneath one of the blind angels whose hands reach out to the room. "Come in," she murmurs. "There's nothing to be afraid of." She motions toward the double doors. "It's in here, in the ballroom."

Zorzo can feel sweat pool in the small of his back. "Sybille, let us leave this matter now." Can he say he's frightened of her, long keys held like daggers in her hand, silver gown shimmering, pale face floating above, that she reminds him of a siren of Greek mythology, a creature to tempt men to their doom, that still she hasn't answered his question, explained what help she needs or acknowledged, in any form, the night they just spent together? "I'll not go in there. Come, leave it now. I'll return in the morning to finish the painting."

"Just look. What harm is there in that?" Then, more impatiently, "I risked everything getting these keys. I had to steal into Tomas's room when he was in the house. When he's out of it, he keeps his door locked. He could have caught me, but I risked it for you."

This might have been gratifying to hear any other time, what she's done for him. As well as the fact she's offering the prize that Zorzo has long sought. "Sybille, this cannot be the way to do it—"

"At least come and look at your color. I thought it was life and death to you?"

Zorzo wonders if he does what she asks, if he goes into the room, perhaps this new coldness in her might dissolve. He crosses over to her. She gathers herself and knocks on the ballroom door, softly, to check that no one is inside, then turns the handle and opens it. Cool air creeps out. The scene feels surreal, preposterous, as if fictional characters are enacting it. They enter.

Zorzo was expecting a large room, but even so, the size is shocking. It's extravagantly high. It's as cold as a catacomb and as echoey, due to the dark green ceramic that tiles the entirety of the walls and floor. Zorzo's heard accounts of porcelain interiors, in Constantinople and Granada, but never set eyes on such a thing in Venice. The tiles have the color of a forest at night, and are veined with spidery traces of gold that come and go as you cast your eye around. There's something Germanic about it, a chamber from a dark tale of folklore, or a place where grand poisonings take place. A long table seems to hover midair, like a floating carpet, and two dozen high-backed chairs are set, not around it, but pinned against the walls.

"It's here," Sybille says, leading Zorzo over to a waist-height trunk of metal, centered like an altar at the far end of the room. She starts trying the keys, one by one probes them back and forth. The rattle of metal, echoing against the malachite walls, makes Zorzo almost nauseous with anxiety. "I can feel the mechanism inside but it won't drive home," she's saying.

The trunk frightens Zorzo, the gravity it seems to possess—a slab of scarred metal, strengthened by iron bands and fist-sized rivets. It seems to smell of furnaces and gunpowder, to have an elemental, indestructible quality, as if it's endured through time, been hauled through ancient wars. A great part of him longs to see if truly it contains prince orient, but his instinct to flee from live danger is more overwhelming. "Sybille, truly, I do not like to be in this room. Tell me, what help do you need?"

"I mean to end him," Sybille says.

"End him?"

"My husband. Tomorrow." She's almost matter-of-fact in the way she utters it. "Have I tried this one?" she says of one of the keys. "It looks too thin." Zorzo can't believe what he's hearing, what she's suggesting so casually. "At San Isepo. He goes alone," she continues. "Just him and the abbot in the monastery's chapel. No Tomas, no other men watching over him. There, an end to him. It is planned in every detail. For a year I have planned it. It's the reason I came with him to Venice."

Dots of dark color dance in front of Zorzo's eyes, and the room tilts away from him. How has it happened? He was seeking a color, just that, but now he's in a new land, where violence is in the air. She wants him to help her kill her husband. Is that what she's always wanted? The only thing? Is that the reason Sybille persisted with Zorzo from the start, why she came to see him, why she insisted, even against her husband's wishes, that Zorzo paint her portrait? "End him?" he repeats, clinging to the hope he's misunderstood.

"I'll need you only to get me away afterward. Get me away quickly. Nothing more serious than that. Why do these wretched keys not work?"

"No, Sybille. I cannot. Of course I cannot."

"You don't want your color?" She's scornful now. "I thought it was a miracle, that it came from the stars. That it will make your name for all time."

"But you think I would murder for it?" He's asking himself as much as her. In the moment, he wonders whether murder is the only price there is.

"And I tell you again. It's I who will do it. I need help to leave this island, that's all."

"What has happened to you since yesterday?"

"Time has happened. It has run out."

"Did it mean anything to you? The night we spent?"

"This has nothing to do with that."

"But tell me all the same. For me, it was…" He shakes his head as images of her flesh, her ecstatic eyes, tumble back and forth through his mind. His eyes return to the sight in front of him: Jakob Fugger's indestructible trunk and the treasure it contains. Prince orient and Sybille are still entangled. "I've thought nothing through, about you and I," he mutters, unable to marshal his ideas into a plan. "You are married, you live far away from here." He knows he sounds like a lovesick adolescent, but goes on. "I thought at least a friendship had begun."

"Do you want the color or not?"

"Of course, but not in this way. Not here in this room."

There's silence for a moment and there's more than disdain on her face. There's hatred. "And you fancy yourself as the hero of Thermopylae? I'll find someone else, then. I'm leaving. You know the way out."

As she turns to go, Zorzo takes her by the arm and she slaps him.

"You too. Men's hands on me always. Get out."

As Zorzo reels and cups his palm to his cheek against the burn, there comes the sound of footsteps approaching across the next room. The door clicks open and a corridor of light creeps across the floor. Sybille hides the keys in the folds of her gown.

"Who is it?" she says to the silhouette in the doorway. "Tomas, is that you?" It's him for sure: his immense frame all but fills the opening. "Has something happened? Did you not go to San Isepo?" Why is she asking that? It makes her sound guilty. "Tomas, is it you or not?"

"Madam," he replies blankly and Zorzo has no idea how much the man has heard or what he's thinking. "Herr Fugger cut his visit short today."

"Signor Barbarelli asked to see the ballroom," Sybille goes on, crossing back to the door and in control of her voice again. "The chamber is famous in Venice, isn't it? I take it that's allowed? Him looking?"

Zorzo goes in her wake, but even when he's close to Tomas and can see his face properly, he can't get a reading from it. "It is a remarkable room," he says in a voice that he hopes sounds passionless. "I've heard about it since I came to Venice and always wanted to look for myself."

"Good night, then, Signor Barbarelli," Sybille says breezily. "I'll see you in the morning. Last day."

"Good night." He nods at her, and at Tomas, who stands to one side, but not quite enough for Zorzo to be able to get through the door without turning at a slight angle. Certain that Tomas is following him with his eyes, he strides across the salon and exits. He doesn't go down the main stairs—he's too terrified of coming face-to-face with Fugger—and instead circles the landing to the back stairs they just used. He halts halfway down. There's another man below, though he's half the breadth of Tomas.

"Sir, is everything all right?" the figure says and Zorzo realizes it's Johannes. He tries to steady his breath. "Everything is good," he manages. "Home now."

He slips past Johannes and carries on down, through the kitchens and out. Halfway along the passage to the road, he stops and vomits.

19

Pharaoh's Eye

He storms through the streets. He needs a drink, a number of drinks, but all the taverns he passes are cramped and noisy. He has to have air around him, to breathe again. He comes out onto the Campo dei Santi Apostoli, which is large and all but empty, and finds a place tucked away in the corner by the canal. He orders a bottle of wine, fills a cup and drinks it down in one go, then fills the cup again. The innkeeper makes some joke about Zorzo being thirsty, which he ignores. Then, for fear of the innkeeper starting a conversation, he takes the bottle and goes and sits on the steps outside. On the opposite bank, a group of men are standing next to two great blocks of stone, talking loudly, passing a bottle between them. Zorzo wouldn't notice them, but the blocks, which are as tall as the men, have been carved, one in the shape of a hand, the other, a wrist with a bracelet around it. It's a surreal sight, gigantic body parts sitting beside a canal. Like everything that is happening tonight, it seems to belong in a dream.

I mean to end him.

The phrase opens up Zorzo's head again and panic tumbles out. Sybille Fugger: silver gown, ivory face, carnelian lips, malachite room. He drinks hard. He has no idea if Tomas believed her story about what they were doing in the room. Either way, he will have told his master and Fugger will be coming to his own conclusions. Zorzo thinks he cannot possibly go back there now. Even if he'd finished the picture, surely he must face the fact that payment is lost—prince orient too. He can't help wondering if he should have been more courageous, in the moment, when it was in touching distance.

The voices on the other side of the canal grow more animated and Zorzo looks over. The men are discussing how to move the carved monoliths to another part of the city. They're young and dressed in workers' garb, except for one. He's older than the rest, wears a wide-brimmed hat and a velvet coat of dark Persian pink. There's something familiar about him, and the unusual color of his coat. Eventually, they give up on their discussion, leave the monoliths alone and set off up a path away from the water. It's only then that Zorzo realizes who the man in the velvet is. His hair gives him away, long locks of gray curling to his shoulders, and a beard to match.

"Signor Piero?" Zorzo calls, scrambling to his feet, but the man doesn't hear. "Signor Piero," Zorzo tries again, before deepening his voice. "Leonardo da Vinci."

"Someone wants you," says one of the youngsters, pointing over the canal, and Leonardo squints to see.

"It's Giorgio Barbarelli, sir. We met when I was an apprentice, in Bellini's studio."

"Barbarelli, you say?" Leonardo can't place the name.

He's so much in shadow, especially beneath his hat's wide brim, Zorzo can't make out the features of his face. "Or Giorgione, as some call me now," he says, stepping right to the edge of the water.

On the other side, Leonardo gives a jolt of surprise. "Giorgione? *The* Giorgione?"

"Yes."

"And you say we've met before now?"

"As a youngster. You gave me good advice."

"Dear me, I hope you didn't take it. I know your work. Gabriele Vendramin and I are great friends, even though he's as mean as a snake. I saw your landscape below a bolt of lightning there: *La Tempesta*. What a painting. What a treasure. And *Venus* as well, sleeping in the forest. That was you, wasn't it? I don't mind admitting I was jealous when I came across it. And even more so now. No one told me you were tall and handsome too. Damn you."

"It's dark here, that's all. I'm not so pretty in the light," Zorzo replies, making Leonardo laugh. "To hear you like my work, a man such as you, is beyond imagining."

"Now *you* flatter. I'm a slave to a wage, that's all." His friends find this very funny. "What do you do now?"

"In work?"

"Tonight! What do you do tonight? I go with these fellows to a ball. Can we call it a ball? Far too grand. The stonemasons' guild is to be pulled down and built again. We're mourning the old and celebrating the new. Though our plans to arrive with two pieces of old Egypt," a wave to the carved boulders left behind, "are abandoned."

"Old Egypt?"

"The last remains of an immortal, salvaged from the Nile. A third section, even larger, of a pharaoh's eye and forehead, arrived happily at its destination a month ago, but the two pieces sitting there have just been jettisoned by an angry shipper over late payment, and none of us can agree on how to carry them across Venice. But all this is by the by. Will you come with us?"

"Yes, I'll come. Of course I will." He's looking for the nearest bridge across the canal when an idea comes to him. "May I fetch a couple of my men first? They'll not hound you, I promise, but would delight in laying eyes on you."

"Fetch them all. Hound me. The stonemasons' guild. We'll see you there."

Leonardo carries on with the others and they resume their conversation, while Zorzo hurries back to the red house.

He's never forgotten the day, aged thirteen, barely a month into his apprenticeship, when he first heard of Leonardo. Bellini's brother, Gentile—Zorzo's other master—returned from Florence, having spent a month with the artist. He described—as if recounting some incredible tale of passion—leafing through Leonardo's sketchbook, being overwhelmed by the range of interests, how on one page alone Leonardo had drawn, in spare marks of chalk, the study of drapery about a Madonna, the penumbra of a shadow, a human skull, a cow's heart, a war machine for hurling mortar and a fetus in a womb, all accompanied by minute notes, some written backward. "He's left-handed, right-handed, has eyes at the front, the back, the sides."

Over the years, like a prospector always on the lookout for gold, Zorzo picked up, whenever and wherever he could, facts about Leonardo. He put the great copper ball on top of Florence's cathedral dome and came up with a design to divert the Arno. He's flamboyant and likes to wear rose-colored tunics. He's an animal lover and buys caged birds at market just to set them free. He writes poetry, backward, and mathematical equations, speaks a dozen languages and is admired for his singing voice. *Perhaps someone will have a lute*, Zorzo thinks, *and we may make some music together.* Leonardo's brilliance, Zorzo concluded long ago, is not simply in the answers he gives, but the questions that no one else thinks to pose: why the stars are visible by night, not day; how water makes its way up to mountaintops; how hands work, and eyes and throats.

Meeting the artist could not have come at a more fateful moment, he decides. He's grateful now for what happened at the Palazzo Pallido, as it has thrown him into the path of his hero. Leonardo can be the beginning of a new chapter. Zorzo can begin the task of putting aside the madness of the last two weeks; absorb the loss, forget Fugger and Sybille and prince orient. Since he first heard the names on Poveglia, they have brought nothing but disquiet. Perhaps he and Leonardo can collaborate, if the maestro truly has such a high opinion of him.

"Where's everyone else?" Zorzo says, getting back to the workroom and finding only Teodor, in front of a mirror again, though at least working this time, sketching a self-portrait. "Where's Paulino?" It's Paulino in particular he wants to introduce to Leonardo, for he will appreciate it the most. The lad is perhaps even more obsessive about da Vinci than Zorzo is and it will bolster his confidence.

"He went to help his father," Teodor replies. "He didn't say when he'd be back. The others have gone to dinner."

Zorzo knows Paulino's father has all but lost his sight and often needs looking after, so he waits for a while, but after an hour, frightened of missing out himself, he puts on a fresh shirt and goes out again. He doesn't tell Teodor where, deciding it wouldn't be fair on the rest.

Inside the cavernous hall of the stonemasons' guild, he searches for Leonardo's velvet coat among the throngs of revelers who are drinking and chatting, pressed into chasms between blocks of stone, pieces four times the size of the ones left on the canalside, granites, sandstones, limestones, marbles. He spots the Persian-pink coat and rushes over only to find it's someone else, the jacket a different shade of red.

He carries on looking, back and forth, coughing on the cold dust that seems to hang everywhere at head height, sorry that his father had to endure it all his life.

Eventually he goes to sit in the corner of the room, to carry on his vigil from there. He finds his gaze resting on a piece of rock at the back of the room. Its abstract form is familiar and he angles his head to study it: it is an eye, the one that Leonardo spoke of, that belongs with the hand and wrist left on the other side of the city. There's a pupil, brow, forehead and—just above—the edge of a crown, a king's *pschent.*

Judging from its size, it must weigh fifty tons. He goes to examine it. Quartzite, "one of the hardest and heaviest substances on earth," he recalls his father saying about a much smaller statue they once saw together in a palace in Padua. Quartzite, and yet hands—thousands of years ago, long before the days of steel and saws—have fashioned them into human form.

Zorzo runs his hand over the smooth, softly rounded cornea, the rutted, more textured brow, and against the back of the stone, the rougher side, where there are still marks left from the quarrying. It looks white, but unexpected colors leap into the night: violet, realgar orange and verdigris green, colors that have come from a time further back even than the pharaoh.

He stands back, far enough for him to imagine the whole statue. He tries to picture it, in the desert sands of North Africa, at the time it was completed. A pharaoh, high as a cathedral, shoulders back, head straight, while this eye and its twin face perfectly forward. They used mathematics for that, Zorzo learned in his studies, so the pupils always pointed straight, in the direction of eternity. He tries to think of the man who inspired the statue, inspired thousands—tens of thousands—of his countrymen to prize incomprehensible tranches of rock from the earth and haul them to their place. The direction of eternity. Even alone, maybe with all but two other parts of its body lost eons ago beneath the sands, this eye at the back of a wharf in Venice, in the ordinary present day, has found it.

"Giorgione?" a voice calls and Zorzo thinks, of course, now Leonardo appears, to share this moment, to toast the pharaoh's eye.

But it's not Leonardo. It's one of the youngsters who'd been with him by the canal. "The old man asked me to pass you a message." The fellow's a slightly older version of Uggo, with the same cheeky air about him.

"Yes?"

"He said to say he was sorry he missed you. That he had a thing to do before leaving Venice. He said if ever you were in Milan, his door is open to you."

"Thank you. I'm sorry too."

The lad disappears and Zorzo sinks. At once, the fears he's kept at bay since he left the Palazzo Pallido start rolling back, more lurid and unmanageable than ever.

I mean to end him. My husband.

The phrase rattles through his head like poison. Sybille intends murder. Why can't she run away from Fugger? What has pushed her to this conclusion? It can only be what Carlo Contarini spoke of: the reach of such a man. But whatever her reasons, she tried to involve Zorzo. To bribe him to do her bidding. Murder.

He stays until the revelers have filtered away and the canalways outside are emptied of boats.

"It's the end of an era," a guildsman who comes to tidy up says. He looks around at the building, "All this will be gone in a month."

Zorzo goes home, locks the front door behind him and makes sure it's bolted, top and bottom. He hugs Uggo, holding on for a while, then goes to bed.

The following morning, a note arrives for him.

Arsenale. As soon as you can. Sybille.

Then, in capitals: *I BEG YOU.*

20

The Red List

Zorzo gets his coat and is about to leave when an idea occurs to him. He riffles through the credenza in his *studiolo* until he finds the tied-up burlap bundle at the back. He undoes it and takes out the dagger and sheath. He's forgotten how heavy the weapon is, and how sharp the blade. It's almost as shiny as the day he bought it. He usually only arms himself when traveling inland at night, but last evening's conversation, along with Tomas's appearance in the ballroom, have put him on his guard. He fastens it to his belt and goes, putting on his coat as he hurries from the house and across the square.

There's a storm coming, which invariably means floods too, and Venetians, bellwethers by nature, are preparing: bolting down hatches, sandbagging doorways and hauling possessions to higher floors.

He hurries along the waterfront. White-tipped waves wheel

across the lagoon, breaking against the piers and bridges of the shorefront and sending all the boats moored along it bobbing frenetically, a thousand ship bells ringing at once. Cries go up from the decks of the Byzantine galley, the one Sybille pointed to ten days ago, still anchored offshore. Its sails have been put down, but it rolls back and forth against the wind.

He reaches the end of the promenade and enters the square in front of the Arsenale, where he first spoke to Sybille. She's waiting close to the Porta Magna, eyes turned skyward toward the drums of thunder. She wears a mantle and hood in dark turquoise, the color of the sea—a wild, winter sea, such as it is today. It's stamped in diamond patterns, making it look like a coat of scales. She could be a sea creature, or some dread ocean goddess arisen from the water.

"We may be caught out," Zorzo says, nodding at the sky. It pulses with a kind of violet light. Rain has started to patter from it.

"I have little time. Look inside." She deposits a sack in his hands. It's small but very heavy. "Your desire. Prince orient."

"What?"

"I managed to open the safe after you left. And I was lucky to get the keys back before anyone noticed. Look inside," she repeats.

Zorzo opens it to find a bronze casket with a handle on top in the shape of a pine cone.

"A pine cone is the symbol of Augsburg," she says, "that's why Jakob has it." Zorzo finds it an obscure thing to mention in the circumstances. "It's locked," she goes on, "and I don't have the key. But I'm sure you'll be able to find a way to break it open." She pointedly takes it back and ties it up again in the bag. "I will bring this to you later, along with the money my husband agreed to pay you. How much was it?"

This is a new, yet still bewildering version of Sybille: the deal-maker. Before Zorzo has a chance to reply, she says, "Whatever it was, I'll double it. I'm sorry the painting could not quite be finished, but it will still be treasured. I will bring you the money and prince orient if you will do me one simple favor in return. Find me a pair of boatmen. Two gondoliers who you trust. I need two for speed. Men you can rely on, that is the most important thing. I cannot use anyone from our household. Do you know someone?"

"Sybille, slow down, please. To begin with, I can't take that box if it's stolen."

"Well, you must. It's lost otherwise, forever. And besides, I can't return it to the safe now. You *must* have it. And you *must* produce something sublime with it. You say prince orient comes from the stars. Well, do justice to them."

"Sybille—"

"You deserve success," she says, "truly—from my small understanding, at any rate. My only regret is I shall not see the color itself. Will you arrange the boatmen for me? Are there any you trust?"

"To go where?"

"To the mainland. I leave Venice tonight. Alone. There's a bridge that goes over to the island of San Isepo. Bring whomever you find and meet me beside it an hour before dusk—and I will give you this. I hate to suborn you, make bribes after everything you've done, after everything we've—after you and I..." She pauses, on the point of tears, before pressing on. "The night at your house was as unexpected for me as you said it was for you. I'll not forget it. I promise you that. But now, you must pardon me, I need to be sure of my escape. Can you help with what I ask?"

Even without prince orient, the money, if her offer is serious, can't be denied. It would solve his debt and he could get his father's ring back, but he can't go along with such a plan. "Sybille, you cannot proceed with what you spoke of yesterday."

She stares back at him. "I can. I will. My husband dies tonight.

I've one day left in Venice, and in Germany the task will be impossible. So it must be tonight. And San Isepo is the only place."

"Sybille, stop. The task does not need to go ahead in either place."

"And I tell you it must. I beg you, can you find someone for me or not?" The storm clouds reflect an unearthly green light on her face, revealing the wetness in the corners of her eyes.

"I'll not assist in murder, no. You have to put an end to this business, immediately. There are other solutions, Sybille. Leave him. Do not seek his permission. Just go. I understand you're worried about him finding you. But you have—"

"It has nothing to do with him finding me. He *cannot* survive. That is final."

"I was saying, you have family. Your parents in Augsburg. No? Your brother in Ulm."

"Leave him out of it. You know nothing about him."

Her desperation is tipping over to anger and Zorzo makes sure he keeps his tone even and calm, despite everything. "I mean there are people that can help you. *I* can help you. But not murder. There must be another way."

"And I tell you there is not. If I do not stop him, he will do great harm, harm beyond imagining."

"I understand. I do. Everything. You've been mistreated. It's horrific."

Sybille's eyes turn vengeful green. "This is not for me. I do not think of my marriage. Who cares for my misfortunes? They mean nothing. This is for my fellow man, not for me. Never for me." Zorzo is lost now completely. Even in the context of yesterday in the ballroom, her tone is hysterical and grandiose.

With a swishing sound, the rain turns from patters to a torrent, bouncing against the cobbles, unleashing a rising mist. Sybille gives a little gasp, swings around in search of shelter, but ends up turning on the spot. Two gondoliers hurry into a doorway as the square is lit up by a flash of lightning.

"There, look," says Zorzo. A porter at the entrance to the Arsenale is motioning for them to come in undercover. "Quickly," he urges, and they mount the front steps beneath the arch and run into the complex.

For a second, Zorzo halts, startled by the size of the place, as he always is: basins of water lined with ships, wharves going off in all directions—to infinity, it seems. They take cover under the roof of the nearest one and stare out at the curtains of water lashing down, as galleons—even large, four-masted ones—kick against the walls of their dock.

"You're wet through," he says, "and you're not leaving in this condition. There's a fire there."

There's a furnace where a blacksmith's working, hammering out nails, and Zorzo goes over to it and waits for Sybille to follow. He unties her cloak and hangs it from a beam above the fire. "Let it dry. Stand closer to the fire; you're shivering. For a short while at least."

She does as he asks, though like an angry child. Across the Arsenale work forges on despite the deluge. Below hissing clouds of smoke, furnaces burn in every wharf; armies of dockworkers dart about the work sheds and quaysides like ants, around the upturned skeletons of hulls, against the calling of foremen, tapping of hammers and shearing of wood. The Arsenale is sky and scale and industry. It's like a backstage to Venice, the inner workings of the city—or its alter ego. Sybille watches it all, and the furnace light burns back and forth across her face.

"For your fellow man?" Zorzo asks finally. "Is this to do with what you said at the red house?"

She clenches her jaw, tries to steady herself. "I've told you my husband is dangerous, but I haven't made it clear enough. It's not everyday danger he poses. It is on another scale. It is diabolical." She fixes Zorzo with a stare, to make sure he grasps the difference. "He was once a reasonable man. He was learned. He had an inquiring mind. I do not recognize the person he has become. My husband has an enterprise, with Cardinal Soderini, and numerous others. It has been in gestation for two years. Shortly they will start to put it into practice, and what has been just words will become actions."

"An enterprise?"

"Have you heard of the Inquisition in Castile?"

"The Inquisition?" The question might have seemed obscure any other time, had Bellini not mentioned it only a couple of weeks ago, in his barge coming back from the Ca' d'Oro. The other pronouncements he made then—of hares in the city, of wicked thoughts, of artists being watched—have stayed with Zorzo ever since. "I've heard—some reports."

"My husband and his group mean to set up their own translation of it, outside of Spain. On a much greater scale. In all our lands. In Florence, in Rome, in Venice, in Augsburg—and everywhere else. It is the reason he came to Venice, to meet and solicit. The business of your commission and St. Peter's is but a small part of it. A cloak that hides all else. Why that look on your face?"

"I believe you." He has no reason not to, but wonders how she's arrived at these conclusions. "Go on."

Another intake of breath. "I don't know when I started to watch Jakob closely," she continues, "to pay attention to the people around him, all the wheels and pinions that go off from his businesses. Three years ago? Four? But the more I looked, the more alarmed I became. I'll spare you all the details but one." She pauses and clutches her neck, gathering her thoughts. "In March this year a delegation came to Augsburg. I watched them arrive. Wealthy, middle-aged men. Wielders of power. There were some names in the air I recognized. A Jaggiellon, a Medici, one of the Welsers—usually Jakob's enemies—along with innumerable grim-faced cardinals who looked as though they'd come from battle. And finally the pope."

"In Augsburg?"

"Jakob won't go to Rome. It's the center of all the world's disease in his opinion."

"The pope went to visit your husband? Pope Julius, you mean?"

The question irritates Sybille. "You do know who Jakob is? You understand that he rules the continent? In truth, he does. He owns it. Not emperors or governments, not even popes. He props them all up. They've all arrived at our door, the power-mad and money-poor, the vain, the entitled, the oafs who can't stop spending beyond their means. It's almost comical to see them fumble when they greet him, not knowing whether to bow, to a lesser man—a lesser man with so much more than they'll ever possess. Yes, Pope Julius came to visit my husband."

She checks whether her cloak has dried, before carrying on. "I don't know if you've come across him in person." Zorzo shakes his head. "He came in, shrouded in this tatty, oversized cowl, like Death himself. Scars everywhere. What a coarse creature he is. Everyone greeted him in that way wealthy men do, affecting nonchalance, while jumping inside, totting up the riches that might now come their way. And they went up to Jakob's room, purring like lions—and shut themselves in for two days."

"And," the notion sounds almost comedic, but he asks anyway, "you listened at the door?"

"No. But after they disbanded I found notes, on Jakob's desk. It wouldn't cross my husband's mind—not then anyway—that I'd look, let alone understand anything, not the burgher's daughter. One page stood out: a list of names, three dozen or so. Some were underlined or in capitals or highlighted in a circle. I was familiar with a few in passing, but I made my own copy and investigated. There was a printer from Basel called Froben, and a bookseller called—my memory plays a trick with the name—Lachner? Wolfgang Lachner? There was a preacher and scholar of Wittenberg, another from Cologne, others from Amsterdam and Antwerp. There was a common thread: scholars, academics, translators, philosophers. It was a death list. *A red list*, as they call it."

"I—it sounds," he presses his fingers to his temples, "almost unbelievable."

"This endeavor cannot proceed without my husband's investment. Mountains of money will be needed."

Zorzo can't place why what she's saying, though theoretically logical, has an air of the fantastical. "Money? To kill these people?"

"To buy governments, judiciaries, opinions; to unroll—what would it be called: a religious police? Turn the world on its head. Everything controlled, everything censored. And the killing would not stop there. They'd do away with tens of thousands more: the followers of other faiths, nonconformers, anyone whose values rub against theirs."

"Sybille, please, stop." She's making the speech like a priest at a pulpit, as if she's repeated it often, and Zorzo wonders who has her ear. The words don't seem to belong to her. "You'll murder your husband for these notions? Because of a list you found? Those names could mean anything."

She glares at him furiously and her top lip quivers. "There are more things in this world than your pictures and paints. You're safe on your little island of glass blowers and spice merchants. You don't know war, or horror. You talk of your hero of Thermopylae, but you haven't understood the story. Just because you find the idea unpalatable, that handfuls of men meet in rooms and carve out the lives of a million others, does not mean they don't." The blacksmith is looking up, at Sybille's raised voice, enough to silence her. She snatches back her cloak and puts it on, tying it at the neck. "I am leaving now. You cannot understand what you have not seen. You will have your pigment. And your wages. Double your wages. Are you able to find me a pair of boatmen or not?"

The skin around her eyes reddens. She holds her breath, to

try to stop herself from crying, which makes it worse. Her mouth turns down and the tears come. Zorzo goes to her but she pushes him back, scrubbing the tears away with her fist. "Will you help me?"

"On one condition. That you'll take no action until we meet later. That we'll talk again at San Isepo. That in the meantime you try to calm yourself. If you promise that, I'll bring two boatmen to the bridge you speak of." A plan is already forming in his head of how to help her in a better way, to use the gondoliers to convey her from Venice before she does any harm—not after it. She claims that escape on its own is not an option, but there must be a way to convince her otherwise. And if she won't listen, he'll physically prevent her if he has to.

"Thank you. There's a warehouse close to the bridge with a red tiled roof. It's empty. Tell them to meet by the door to it, an hour before dusk. You know as well as I when Jakob sets off."

"But before you leave, tell me where you will go, once you get to the mainland?"

"To Augsburg in the first instance. It is my home, just as much as it is Jakob's. Everyone forgets that. There is some recompense, some elegance in having no children. It's cleaner. Everything comes to me. I will use the money to unpick the damage Jakob's done. I will obliterate this Inquisition—and try to do some good in its place."

Though it seems too obvious a thing to ask, Zorzo must: "And you're not frightened of being caught? That the law will likely see things differently from you?"

"I'll not be caught, if I carry it out as I intend. As I told you yesterday, I have been planning this long before I arrived in Venice. And once I'm away, if you will help with that, the laws of this city will have no bearing."

There is silence for some moments before she puts her arms around him and holds on, her head against his chest. He embraces her back and she clutches even tighter. In that moment he could forget his fears, her recent anger, the strangeness of their last two meetings—return to how they were in the red house. Before she goes, he says, "One last question: how do you intend to do it?"

"That is where money has come in useful. Have you heard of the killing machine that fires a shot of gunpowder in the blink of an eye?"

"I've heard of them, but never seen one. They're rare, I suppose?"

"German engineering, born with the new century. A flintlock pistol. They're worth their weight in diamonds, those tiny machines. After he heard what happened with Jakob, how violent he'd been with me, my brother took me to a gunmaker and made sure I bought one." She gives Zorzo a farewell kiss and says, "He gave it to me that day before we set off for Venice."

21

They Will Fight

"I'll be with you in a minute," Bellini says to Zorzo, not looking around, brow corrugated with concentration as he applies minute filaments of dark umber to the canvas he's working on. "Sit." He nods toward a chair by the window.

Zorzo goes over but doesn't take a seat. He's numb from the conversation with Sybille, and soaked through, having hurried to his old master's studio through the storm. Peals of thunder are still tumbling about the city, and through the workroom's large window, the sky has turned from violet to a kind of livid jade-green.

He glances around the room, which is more like a manufactory than an artist's studio, there are so many people at work: two dozen or so, at least six of whom encircle their master, like altar servers around a cardinal, each one ready to fulfil a particular task. Zorzo can't see the painting itself, but against the back wall a pair of models are posing for it. One is costumed in a friar's robe and has his head thrown back and mouth open in a pretend scream. The other is his attacker, dressed as a soldier, plunging a pretend knife into the first man's heart.

"That's enough for today," Bellini says, passing his brushes to one of his assistants who straightaway sets about cleaning them, while the two models stretch their arms and share a joke about how old they're getting. "I need alizarin for the assassin's tunic," Bellini says to another apprentice. "Use the madder root up there. Grind it well, mind you. And malachite, half as much."

"Yes, Signor Bellini."

"And carmine lake too. The best we have. No counterfeit. Have it all in hand by the morning. Cloth!" Impatiently, he waves his paint-splattered fingers at a third assistant. He cleans his hands, dismisses the remaining *garzoni* with a shake of his fingers, before motioning Zorzo to come over. "My new *Martyr Assassinated*, almost finished," Bellini tells him, gesturing at the picture. On a country road two clergymen are being murdered. Zorzo knows Bellini has painted the subject more than once, the death of Peter, a friar of Verona. "How do you find it?"

Zorzo is in no mood for giving critiques, especially not to Bellini, who can be prickly, but out of courtesy he makes a show of studying the picture. In truth, he finds the scene too sanitized, too reverential, not truly violent. Peter has a dagger in his heart and is screaming, but there's no blood coming from the wound, when in reality it would be spurting out, drenching everything. Zorzo feels like saying Bellini should get his hands dirty for once, like Michelangelo would; instead he offers, "It's wonderful, sir, and disturbing, in all the ways it should be."

Bellini grunts, no doubt detecting a lie. "I've seen more of you in this last month than in the forty previous. You're not a spy, are you? You're wet. Come here by the fire."

Bellini shuffles over to it, takes a seat and uses his cane to evict a sleeping cat from a second chair.

"I shan't trouble you long." Zorzo stays on his feet and clears his throat. "When we last spoke you said a curious thing, about 'the powers' that are watching us. I can't remember exactly how you put it, but you talked about how thinkers and writers and artists and so on were undoing a thousand years of rules. The phrase I remember most was, 'Our wicked thoughts, that man is the center of it all. Not God.'"

"I said that? I should be a philosopher. Do you think I'm wasted as a canvas filler?"

"What did you mean by it exactly?"

"What did I mean? Let me think." He taps the other chair with his cane and waits until Zorzo sits. "I suppose I meant that the world has bent itself out of shape since I was young, to make it almost unrecognizable. How old are you?"

"Thirty-three."

"Well, I have half a century on you. Things were simple when I was your age. The only choice we had to make was between heaven and hell. In these times, though," he whistles through his teeth, "we can be scholars, we can be mathematicians, engineers, believers in reason, believers in art, or in this, that or the other. Our heads spin with all our choices."

Zorzo nods in agreement: what Bellini is saying chimes with Sybille's thinking. "You mentioned also the Inquisition of Castile," he says. "Was that because you think such a thing might be set up here in Italy? The same sort of," he searches for the word, "tribunals, I mean."

Bellini narrows his eyes at his old student, seeming to appraise him in a new light. "It is more than possible." His voice is quiet and precise. "It may have begun already."

Zorzo swallows. "And you know about Castile? The Inquisition there? The things that have happened? Can you explain them to me?"

"Yes, I know *all* about Castile." Bellini gives a crafty look around, to check none of his men are close enough to hear. "I have friends in Spain who keep me informed." Then, graver, "I have lost friends too." There's silence for a little while and Bellini studies his old pupil. "You're intelligent enough. You understand what I'm talking about."

"Go on."

"When it was set up, thirty-odd years ago, they said it was for the sake of peace—"

"They?"

"Isabella, I suppose, the Spanish queen, and her husband. The Inquisition was to be a practical act. That's what they claimed, for 'prosperity' to unite 'the disparate parts of the realm,' and so on and so on. It was no such thing. The Inquisition was created to instill fear and make profit from it. That's all."

"Profit?"

"Isn't that what everything comes to in the end? The first executions were in Seville, as I learned from my friends' letters. Moriscos, I believe, who hadn't sufficiently embraced the rules of the true religion, were burned alive as heretics. A month later, more executions. Then weekly lists were drawn up. The charges become vaguer: blasphemy, insufficient prayer, witchcraft." Bellini chuckles. "What on earth is witchcraft anyway? Before anyone knows it, death courts are convening everywhere, Avià, Córdoba, Jaén, Toledo, Segovia, Las Palmas, each with their own quota, and executions became a daily staple. There's nothing like a public burning to sharpen the mind."

"And you believe the rest of Europe will follow this course?" He's shocked that what Bellini is saying tallies closely with what Sybille was suggesting. A part of him thought, or hoped, she was exaggerating, or misinformed.

"Look at your face. Aren't you supposed to be a strapping fellow? You look like a frightened rabbit."

"You were saying?"

Bellini tosses a log into the fire and prods it with a poker until it catches light. "Our days may be numbered already, or yours might, my rabbit. As I told you before, I'll have shuffled away before the apocalypse."

"To be clear, it's money they need in your opinion?"

"What else? And they'll find it. That's why, at the back door of every church in the land, salvation is sold. Even starving paupers will part with their last *soldi* for it. Indulgences, I mean. I am a religious man, as you know. I'd prefer heaven to torment, but those practices are pure scandal. They'll not cease, though. They'll worsen."

"And—what should we do about it? We must do something."

"There's the irony. There is only one thing: pray."

"Tullo?"

The boatman squints up at the quayside. "Zorzo? How are you, sir?"

"I am well, I am well. Is your boat out of action?"

Tullo is scooping water out of the hull. "From the rain earlier. If you're in no hurry, I'll have this dry in an hour. Where are you headed?"

Zorzo reminds himself of his plan, to meet Sybille and convince her more forcefully to flee her husband, rather than attempt anything foolish. To be sure, he'll go with her for the first part of the journey. He has a fear he'll not talk her out of it, but either way, having some form of escape will give a safeguard against the worst. "To the mainland, later. To Mestre. I will pay well. Double the rate."

"I'd be happy to. I could do with the money. I've had a terrible fortnight. No one on the street. And now with this talk of an outbreak, plague. Have you heard?"

"A rumor, yes."

"Some dockworkers in Dorsoduro fell sick, and two of them have perished already. They'd been unloading a Byzantine, illegally, not knowing half its crew was already stricken. Apparently the ship is a floating morgue. A horrific scene it must be. What men will do for money, eh?"

Not for the first time today, bile swills in Zorzo's stomach. He's sure it's the same ship that he spoke with Sybille about, the galleon with fin-shaped sails anchored out in the Giudecca. "Well, we must all be on the lookout," he says. "And, Tullo, can you find another gondolier? Someone you work with, who you trust? For the sake of speed."

"At twice the fee, of course?"

"Naturally. Money is not an issue." His hands have become sweaty with agitation and he dries them against his tunic. "So meet me at San Isepo an hour before dusk. Or a little earlier. There's an empty warehouse with a red tiled roof, by the bridge. You know San Isepo?"

"I know it, east, east, east." Tullo gives a whistle, as if he was talking of the far Indies. "Will you be going alone?"

Zorzo is caught out by the question. "No, there's a lady."

Tullo mistakes the hesitancy for Zorzo hiding a secret, a different secret at any rate. He gives a knowing smile. "Of course. I'm discreet in all such matters." He holds out his arms, as if saluting a childhood friend. "I look forward to it, sir. San Isepo. I'll be there in good time."

Returning past St. Mark's cathedral, Zorzo notices a service is just beginning. The organ has struck up and the last of the churchgoers are pushing through the door. *Of course the Church is going to fight for its existence; it has the world to lose*, Sybille said when she came to the red house and Bellini said almost the same thing. At once Zorzo needs to test this idea, see for himself, so he enters behind them.

He hasn't been in the building since the day he followed Sybille there. It's even fuller than it was then; even more like Neptune's undersea lair, as the air is damp and hazy with the vapor from all the rain-sodden clothes. Zorzo leans against the back wall and studies the scene, watches and listens to it as if for the first time. How the congregation hangs on every word of the bishop's monologue; how, when prayers begin, every member genuflects as one, a sea of bending backs all the way to the altar; how everything is accompanied by nagging shakes of high-pitched bells and clicking censer chains.

At the denouement of the spectacle, when everyone starts forming lines to take Mass, Zorzo steps forward from the wall to look closer. He notices an old lady, a tiny thing, almost breathless from the effort of just getting on her knees. When it's her turn, when the cardinal comes with her portion of wafer, *"the body of Christ,"* she looks up devotedly, adoringly. Any other time, her face might be plain with age, but here, in this moment, a light shines from it. It shines from the faces of all the waiting supplicants, whatever their age. Zorzo can imagine them all noticing the picture of hell on their way out—like in San Zaccaria, there's one here on the back wall—and not seeing what Zorzo does, a dramatic piece of mythology, but a grave warning, an all too real promise of what life would be like without their church. And even if not everyone heeds these warnings in Venice, a city of open minds, he imagines they would in all the other churches of Italy, of Europe, the thousands upon thousands of worshipping places, most of them in out-of-the-way lands, where the books and ideas Sybille and Bellini spoke of have barely started to chip the old superstitions away.

Zorzo's old master is right: there is so much to lose. Zorzo looks from priest to priest, faces stiff with concentration, incanting as incense froths everywhere and—recalling something else his tutor said—he wonders where in St. Mark's they sell indulgences.

"How did you find me?" Leda grins down from the gallery.

"Hakim told me. What is this place?" Zorzo's voice echoes around the empty building.

"Isn't it almost incredible? Wait, we're coming down." She and the two men she's with—one of them Berotti—descend. "What do you think?" she says, sweeping onto the ground floor. "We might take it."

"This house? For you?" Another glance around. "Are you pregnant?"

"Zorzo." She swipes him, both pretending to be indignant and actually being so. "You don't have to have children to live in a house like this." He's forgotten how touchy she gets on the subject of offspring. She might be the least maternal person he's ever met. "Besides, the captain has his." Then, in a lower voice, "He's leaving his wife for me, you know? Don't look at me like that. She's a gorgon by all accounts and it was not my idea anyway. Zorzo, you're soaked through."

"I'm fine." He left Sybille three hours ago and still hasn't been home. After Bellini and the cathedral, he continued wandering the streets, his heart setting off in a gallop every time he came back to one particular thought: that the world is bigger than him, that he is insignificant to the great, grinding turn of history. "You look lovely."

Leda holds out her arms to show off her outfit, another multicolored concoction, and one that makes the most of her hourglass figure.

"This is Signor Rachidi," Leda says, indicating the second man, using her Venetian voice—which Zorzo always had a soft spot for—in which she tries to disguise her Cypriot vowels. "He's letting out this beautiful house."

"I'm just the agent," Rachidi clarifies. He's baby-faced, with a ready-to-please manner. Berotti stays in the background, looking more like an old, hungry wolf than ever.

"Did you see the lower ground floor on your way in?" Leda goes on. "Immense. I know there are no windows, but I could get fifty workers in there. And store everything. No more back and forth to the warehouse. Business would boom. And did you see the river entrance? So grand. And there's a parade hall. I could throw banquets. And robe rooms. It has—" She calls over her shoulder, "How many robe rooms did you say there were, Signor Rachidi?"

"Three."

"Three. Just for robes." She gives a throaty laugh. "It even has a *triclinium*." She whispers aside to Zorzo, "I have no idea what that is. Do you know?"

"It's what the Romans used to call a dining room," he tells her.

"How did you get so clever? When I'm such a simpleton." She doesn't mean it: she's always ranked herself above Zorzo. "But the best of all…" She leads him to a window at the end of the room. "Look."

"At what?"

"The Grand Canal, obviously." There's a sliver of it between two buildings. "We'd practically be rubbing shoulders with the Contarini." She arranges Zorzo's hair, the way she used to. "Why are you here? Tracking me down in my new palazzo?"

"I need to talk to you. About something serious."

"Leda, are you coming?" Berotti demands.

She ignores him, but says to Zorzo, "Can it wait until later? Come upstairs with us."

"No, it has to be now. Just quickly. I—" He takes a deep breath. He hasn't planned what he's going to say. "I need to ask a favor. I have to—I'm going to—" He starts again. "I have an errand I must run. If for any reason something happens to me—"

"Happens to you? What's wrong?"

"Everything's fine. I've been meaning to ask you for some time, you understand, as an insurance, whether you would step in if… I'd hate to leave my *garzoni* on the streets. They've worked too hard."

"Zorzo, you're making no sense."

"Leda?" Berotti tries again.

"Wait," she snaps back. "What is this?" she says to Zorzo.

"A precaution. Keep an eye on the red house, that's all. Honestly, don't worry. I meant to ask you years ago. Because you and I are the same, aren't we: no parents, no children—but we have our families of co-conspirators." Then, remembering, "And one other thing. My father's ring is with Rosso, the bailiff."

"Zorzi, really." For Leda, debt is the original sin.

"I know, I'm sorry. It was an emergency. But make sure you get it back. Find a good home for it. Give it to Uggo when he comes of age. He would value it the most. But not, as I repeat, that there'll be any need to."

"Is this still to do with that lady?"

"No. Of course not. I just wanted to have the conversation. It's been on my mind. Now go, go and inspect your new domain. A view of the Grand Canal. I take my hat off to you. A good day to you all," he calls to the others. "Good day, Signora Sitruk."

Leda holds on to him, head tilted, eyes slitted, studying his face. "I'll put it down to your artist's temperament. But if you get hurt, I'll kill you." She giggles at her own joke. "Off with you now." She releases him, blows a kiss and hurries to catch up with the others. "I come, gentlemen. Lead the way."

When Zorzo eventually gets home, he finds everyone gathered together and Uggo on top of a ladder, prodding a broom handle between the rafters.

"What are you doing up there?" Zorzo asks.

"He's been trapped in here for an hour. Terrified."

Just then, a bird flies out, a tremulous dash of gold and green. It does a circuit of the roof, bashing its wings twice, tumbling and setting right before tumbling again. There's nothing so unnatural, Zorzo finds, so macabre, as the beat of feathers inside a room.

"Here, here," Uggo calls, trying to coax it to the skylight.

There's another frenzied zigzag before suddenly the room falls silent. Everyone freezes, ears cocked.

"Did it go?" Teodor says.

"I think so." Azalea turns in a circle on her heel.

"Bye-bye, goldfinch," Uggo chirps, sliding down the sides of the ladder in one go. "Expecting trouble, sir?"

"What do you mean?"

Uggo nods at the dagger sheathed on Zorzo's belt. "To keep us in our place, is it?"

Zorzo covers the weapon beneath his jacket before turning to the shelves, pretending he's looking for something when really he just wants to look, to hold his possessions in his mind for a moment. The sense of doom he's carried around all day settles at the sight of the jars and bottles of pigments neatly stacked side by side, beloved things. Colors collected over a lifetime, friends who'll never desert him—like the ones in the room won't—who'll mercifully outlive him, outlive even the likes of Uggo.

And now he's been given this chance to add one more color to his collection, one that may be the greatest of all. But this is not how it was supposed to happen. Coming by the color should have felt like a victory, a coup that no one else managed to pull off. A repayment of all the work he's put in. If he had won it fairly, he would have rushed back to the red house, proclaiming success, telling one of his men to fetch Eleanor's special wine to toast the moment. He doesn't even want to mention the subject to them. He feels only apprehension. It's as if the bronze casket with the pine-cone top contains some dreadful secret, like Pandora's box.

At once he has an idea that, after breaking the box open, he could just look inside it, just *see* the color, and then return it to Fugger. He discounts the notion, for it will tie him to her escape. Or, he keeps mulling, after setting eyes on prince orient he could send the box back without giving a name. But then someone else will get their hands on it and it will be lost forever. Soon his thoughts start spiraling. He wonders if he should be trying to stop Sybille at all, that really he should be abetting her, putting faith in her cause. If she's right about Jakob, and in light of what Bellini clarified, Zorzo would be doing a heroic service by helping end the life of such a man, especially as he's such a devil of a husband.

He carries on staring at the workroom shelves. Jostling for space among the pigment jars are a hundred more objects, friends also, precious possessions he's collected throughout his working life, many of them gifts. There's a jar of peacock feathers from the country estate in Mantua where he went, for the first time, as head assistant to the master; a headlike block of quartzite from a trip to a quarry in Umbria; a horseshoe from his father's mare, the animal Zorzo learned to ride on; a sketch of the infant Moses by Bellini that Zorzo picked out of the wastebasket as a boy; a Chinese paintbrush jar he bought when he sold his first canvas. There's one unexpected item on the shelves: a silken ball of green and gold—the bird they thought had got away. Its tiny, frightened chest pips up and down, while its eyes, miniature beads of dark opal, are turned on Zorzo.

"Let me help you," he whispers and slowly reaches up his hand. He closes his palm around it, a little purse of shaking bones, before a noise frightens it. It breaks free of his grasp, circuits the room, panic-stricken, before taking refuge again in the rafters where it hid earlier.

"Leave it," Zorzo says. "It will find the window in time." But Uggo is scaling the ladder once more. "Uggo, do you hear me? Leave it." The boy ignores him, balances his foot on the top rung and, holding on to a support beam, stretches across the pinnacle of the eave.

"Signor Goldfinch," he calls, making bird whistles, to everyone's amusement below, everyone but Zorzo.

"Uggo, come down from there."

"I almost have him," the boy chuckles, before hauling himself up onto the beam and crawling along it, until there's a crack of timber, the beam gives, snaps, and Uggo falls. There's a thump as his shoulder bashes the corner of a worktable. His shirt tears before he hits the ground.

"Uggo!" Zorzo runs over and drops to the floor; everyone follows. "Uggo? Uggo?" The boy is unresponsive and Zorzo's stomach turns to liquid, before Uggo opens his eyes and gives a smile.

"That hurt," he says, sitting up, to murmurs of relief. From above, there's a dart of color, of wings, and the goldfinch escapes through the skylight. "Are you crying, sir?"

"Of course I'm not." Zorzo dashes away the wetness around his eyes. "You're a fool, do you hear me? All of you are fools."

"I'm leaving now," he says from the door a little later, making sure his voice is soft. He's changed his clothes, put on a coat he keeps for traveling: a plain, heavy garment that never catches attention. "I'll be back soon. I didn't mean what I said. There are no fools here."

There's something in the way he says it, in how he stands there, eyes swimming slightly, brow furrowed, that catches everyone's attention.

"Where are you going, sir?" Paulino asks.

"Just to collect the money we're owed," he says, "and help a friend in need." He pauses a moment, looking from face to face, trying to appear unruffled, even as unaccountable terror rips through him. "So I'll see you all soon." He nods, turns and goes.

22

The Last Building in Venice

"This is Achille," Tullo says. "I've known him since we were this high. Very trustworthy."

Zorzo has just arrived at the warehouse with the red tiled roof that Sybille described, and found the two gondoliers waiting there. He casts his eye back along the path, but apart from some fishermen coming ashore, no one else is in sight.

"It's Giorgio, isn't it?" Tullo's friend says. "Barbarelli?"

"Yes. Do we know each other?"

"Achille, from Bellini's studio," the man says. "Years and years ago. You were arriving as I was leaving."

Zorzo's head has been such a jumble of thoughts it takes him some moments to place the man. "Achille, of course, I remember. I was there just earlier, at Bellini's. Achille. How are you?"

"It must've been eighteen years. Giorgio Barbarelli. I've followed your career, sir, seen how well you've done. Royal commissions. What a fine life you must be living. I hope I wasn't too much of a brute to you, sir. I was rather pleased with myself back then."

Zorzo is embarrassed to be called "sir" and be lauded by a fellow who was once his senior. He remembers Achille used to be striking looking, and confident with it—a little like Teodor is now—befitting of his name, but age, and drink, by the look of it, has withered him, physically, and taken the self-certainty from his eyes. Zorzo wonders how Achille has ended up doing favors for someone like Tullo and wants to ask if he still paints. He says instead, "If you were a brute, I don't remember. The Bellinis were the ones who terrified me." He and Achille share a laugh at this, and as the sound of it ebbs away across the lagoon, Zorzo returns to the here and now, and his preoccupations about what lies ahead.

"What is this place?" Tullo says, motioning toward the open barn door of the warehouse. Zorzo peers inside at the empty space and has the sense it was cleared out in a hurry, as storerooms often are in Venice, between shipments. The other warehouses nearby, which Zorzo passed on his way, are locked up for the most part, guarded by the occasional dog, which can be heard but not seen.

"Listen," Zorzo says, turning back to the gondoliers. Since he left the red house, he's been devising a new plan to put to Sybille. "I will make sure you're both paid the full amount I promised, but when the lady I told you about gets here, I'm going to try to persuade her not to go at all. But don't worry, as I say, you will be paid. You've both been very amenable." He's keen to stress this, not least because he has an inkling that Achille has fallen on hard times. "Wait here. Let me see if she's coming."

He goes to the water's edge, to get a better view of the path from the city, but Sybille is nowhere in sight. He looks the other way, over to the monastery, which is just a black shape against the dusk. The storm has gone from the rest of the city, but remnants of a charged wind still seem to whistle around San Isepo's belfry and chimneys.

He's about to turn back to the others, when he notices a boat passing around the eastern headland in the distance, catching the light of the sunset: Fugger's barge. Pressing back against the warehouse wall so he won't be noticed, he watches it disappear for a minute behind the much larger San Pietro church, before turning into the final stretch to San Isepo. There's Tomas and another man, and two men rowing, while the shadow of a person under the gondola's awning belongs to Fugger.

Zorzo goes back to the others and the three of them wait. To fill the excruciating silence he asks Achille about the work he's done since leaving Bellini's, though he is too distracted to take in much of Achille's answer: a long tale of how he painted signs for a while, how his family had always been boatmen and he was the odd one out, how his dreams of having his own workshop faded when his wife became pregnant, how he has four children now and was probably never cut out for the life of a painter. "Too much uncertainty," he says in conclusion. "What about you? Did you start a family?"

That question again. It seems to fill Zorzo with more regret and unease every time he's asked it. Luckily Tullo saves him from answering.

"There." The gondolier points to a woman in hood and cloak walking toward them at a swift, even pace along the side of the next warehouse. It's Sybille for sure, all in black, black as coal, dress, coat, gloves, collar. Even the fur about her cuffs is the color of a panther. She's a shifting shape of profound darkness. The only contrast, like a treasure of porcelain within the gloom of her hood, is the cup-shaped line of her jaw and the smaller carmine bow of her mouth. It's as if night, herself, were arriving.

Achille wipes his hands on his jacket, while Tullo says under his breath, "Now I understand your nerves, sir."

Zorzo goes to meet her. She's carrying the bag she had at the Arsenale. "You're here," she says, halting before she gets to him.

"I said I would be." Zorzo can't see her eyes, just two faint stains of light where they should be.

"And those are the gondoliers? What a good man you are. I've been waiting on the promontory there, next to San Pietro, for my husband's barge. It passed by minutes ago. He's inside by now. Alone."

Zorzo doesn't mention he saw the barge too. "Sybille, come in here." He gestures toward the entrance of the empty warehouse. "So we can speak for a moment. It's best the boatmen don't hear us." He goes in and she reluctantly follows. Large patches of the ceiling have come away, so the dusky light makes a dappled pattern on the floor. Zorzo goes over to some upturned crates, sets one straight and wipes the top with his hand. "Sit here."

"Why?"

"To talk for a moment."

"Talk? Why? To have me change my mind?" Her hand clutches the neck of the bag. Zorzo can see the shape inside it, the bronze box with the pine-cone handle.

He pauses before saying, "Don't sit if you don't want to, but hear me out. I have thought about this business. All day, I have considered it carefully, from your point of view. I have understood everything you've told me, and you must go no further. I had originally thought of suggesting you leave the island straightaway, flee your husband, but I now believe—and I'll explain why—you should return home and leave with him tomorrow as planned. I have told the men we will settle their bill and they may go home."

"No." Her voice, at once sharp, echoes around the rafters of the building and a couple of pigeons take flight through the broken roof.

"Sybille, listen to me."

"It's no business of yours." She lets the bag drop to the ground.

The box inside is so heavy it makes a hard thump. Zorzo peers over, just to make sure the lid hasn't been dislodged and the contents spilled out. She notices him looking and takes a step forward, as if standing guard over it.

"Just hear what I have to say, please. I have gone almost mad with thinking. It has been the strangest day of my life, but I have a plan. A possible way through. Just hear it, please, and decide afterward. I beg you, Sybille." He motions once more at the upturned crates, but she remains on her feet.

"Put up with your husband a few days longer," Zorzo begins.

"And I tell you I cannot."

"Just until you're back in Augsburg. Bide your time, in the knowledge you'll suffer only a little more. Less than a month. You say your brother is in Ulm?" When she makes no reply, he asks, "That's right, yes?"

"What of it?"

Zorzo feels his point must be obvious, but clarifies anyway. "Well, the two of you are very close, no? You saw each other the day before you came to Venice."

"I can't live with him, if that's what you insinuate." Zorzo notes how, on the subject of her sibling, her tone becomes defensive, and not for the first time. She's obviously aware of it too and says more reasonably, "He's set in his ways. In how he lives."

"Then your parents are close by, too?"

"Yes. Though old."

"And no doubt you have cousins? A wider family?" She shrugs. "What I'm trying to say is, go to them, your kin. That must happen first. Understand? Safety. And then—think who you can tell what you told me earlier. The list of names. The meeting in your house. All your fears about Jakob. Rack your brain as to who will have ears for it. I can't tell you who, but you're already sharing air with these people, Sybille. You say your husband rules Europe, but I do not believe he is the only one. There will be great men, or women, who have the same mind as yours. Doors open for you, Sybille. You're a Fugger. That is a great advantage. In time, you'll find the people you need. And you'll convince them. You'll look them in the face, you'll be reasonable, forceful, respectful—as you were with me—and they won't be able to deny you. Sybille, nobody wants to live in a world like the one you described to me this morning. But this is all by and by. Safety is what you need first. Forget murder, do you hear? Even if it were easy to do, which it cannot be, one mistake and you're done for."

Sybille has been standing in a dapple of light beneath the broken roof, but in the time they've been talking, dusk has thickened outside and she's almost pure shadow now. When she speaks, though, her voice has bite: "I'll not go back. Not for a minute more. Or it will never end."

"Listen, do not misunderstand me. I hate to even talk about your leaving. I shall miss you. I burn with it, truly. That has been one of the agonies, thinking what might have been—had we been thrown together another way."

Her shadow sighs and there's silence for a short while before Zorzo continues. "What you told me this morning, and what you said the night you came to me, have affected me so much. I tell myself I'll be immortal through my paintings. I won't. I know. And what's more, it's almost certain that I will be forgotten in a decade or so—while the great wheel of time keeps on turning. With you, it's different. You can influence, because of who you are. Because of your position. *You* have power. But I promise you, if you do what you have planned, I know in my very bones you'll do nothing but harm to yourself."

Sybille's still for a while. She's thinking, Zorzo can almost hear it.

"You say you're certain to succeed," he goes on. "But how can you be so sure? Just think what happens if you don't, if you go in there and you're caught. You're taken away, you're put in prison, or Jakob does what he wishes with you. You're removed.

Possibly dead. It would be the worst of all worlds, don't you see?" Even in shadow, he can tell from her stance she's starting to come around. "There would be no one to stop Jakob anymore. He'd be left to commit these atrocities unchecked. You will have made the situation worse, not better. And you will have sacrificed yourself for nothing."

She comes over and there's a tremble in her words when she says, "You're right." She feels inside her coat, which is lined in dark pink, the color of sea anemone spikes, a surprising tone against her cloak, and the darkening day. She produces a metallic object, a little larger than her hand. It's heavy; Zorzo can tell by the way she holds it.

"To think this little thing cost as much as my father's house in Augsburg," she murmurs, looking down at it, turning it in her hand.

Zorzo edges closer. The pistol is shockingly new, bright steel and brass, fiendishly intricate. In the way it snatches the last of the day's light, it puts him in mind of the golden tureen Tomas produced in the harbor inn in Mestre. "Can I see it?"

She passes it to him. "My brother explained it to me. That spring turns against a piece of pyrite. It makes an intense spark and ignites the powder in the pan, which flashes through a touchhole. That sets off the main charge in the barrel, and—it happens. It can be fired with one hand, even by a little bird such as myself." Whatever wildness has been taking hold of her, it seems to pass, and when her eyes fall on Zorzo once more, they are calm. She returns the pistol to the pink lining of her coat. "Truly, you are right. In everything you say. Thank you." She kisses him on the cheek and Zorzo notices how cold her lips are. "Go and tell the boatmen they're not needed."

"Good. Good, Sybille. You do well." He goes, but then turns back again. "I'm sorry to ask. I promised I would pay them for their time. I have almost enough on me, but I'd like to be generous, they've been so patient."

"No, no, you shall not pay anything." She takes out her purse and opens it. It's full of jewels, emeralds and sapphires, all twice the size of the stone Zorzo pawned, as well as a small fortune of gold—for her escape, presumably. "How much?"

Zorzo takes two of the smaller gold coins. "That will be more than enough. They'll be content. This is no night for journeys anyway. I'll speak to them, then I'll take you home. You are doing the right thing," he assures her, holding on to her shoulders.

He goes back to Tullo and Achille and hands over the money. "Thank you. We're destined to go on these strange escapades, you and I," he says to Tullo. He feels so grateful to him he takes what little money he has in his own pocket and hands that over too. "To buy some wine later."

"There she goes," Achille says and Zorzo turns to see Sybille escaping around the other side of the warehouse and hurrying toward San Isepo bridge. He daren't call out for fear of being heard by the men on Fugger's barge who must be just out of sight; but he must stop her. In Sybille's chaotic state, she's bound to fail, be caught at the first instance. He quickly runs to the warehouse, grabs the bag with the box of prince orient where she dropped it and takes it back to Tullo.

"Keep this safe for a moment, will you?" He wonders if he should tell them there's nothing more valuable in the world than what's inside, and whether he can trust them. He can, he decides. What choice does he have? His connection with Achille alone, he reasons, is surely guarantee. "Can you wait here?"

Tullo holds up his gold. "You've been more than kind."

Sybille is speeding across the bridge, her black dress giving off flickers of anemone pink. When she reaches the monastery, she circles the side wall and peers around the front of the building—presumably to check on Tomas and whoever else is waiting on the pontoon—before she doubles back and slips behind some bushes, down a stone staircase at the side of the building and then disappears from view.

Zorzo hurries across the bridge. He thinks of his workroom, his waiting *garzoni*. For their sake, he should leave this business now, once and for all, turn around, collect his casket of pigment and let the Fuggers fight their battle. He presses on, though, praying he can stop her before it's too late.

He follows the route she took, skirts the perimeter wall to the front and peers around the corner. The pontoon is fifty yards away, Fugger's barge moored to it. One of the gondoliers lounges at the front, skimming his finger back and forth through the water, while Tomas and the other men sit talking behind him. Zorzo gathers himself, retraces his steps and pushes apart the bushes covering the way to the staircase. His palms and forearms burn, from nettles, he realizes too late. He descends, careful of where the stone has crumbled. The steps turn a corner and arrive at a low door. It's ajar. Sybille must have tried to close it: he can see by the way the weeds are bunched up against its base. He shoulders it open and steps into a cold, dark space.

"Sybille?" he whispers in the darkness and his voice seems to take a moment to come back. "Sybille?" He can see nothing of the crypt, except for the little pool of light beneath his feet from the doorway. He moves forward and trips on the step down to the actual floor, which is flooded in inches of water. He listens, terrified of the sudden explosion that might come from above. How loud is a pistol? He's never heard one fired. There are hollow drips of water, remnants of the storm; while from above, barely audible through the thick stone, the Eucharist is being spoken. "Sybille?" His chest rises and falls; his hands and arms throb from nettle stings. He forges on, getting used to the dark, and portions of the space configure: pillars here and there, sections of curved vaulting, sepulchres. He spies in the far corner a pattern of dim rectangles: stairs going up. He wades over to them. Basements anywhere are grim, but in Venice doubly so. The sea always wins in the end. He wonders how often the tombs down here have been drowned beneath the tide and the skeletons levitated in their beds. He finds the foot of the stairs and ascends carefully, as the baleful, monotonous voice of whoever is administering Mass grows clearer.

He comes up behind a screen at the back of the chapel. At the far end, in a pool of light from a single, elaborate standing candelabra, a private Mass is being conducted. An abbot in surplice and stole—an ancient man, pale as dust—recites from the altar step. Jakob Fugger kneels before him, while three more priests attend, one bearing the monstrance, a second sounding an altar bell, the last curving a censer in a slow half ellipse so its incense falls around Fugger's head. The rest of the nave and chancel are in almost complete darkness. He scans from wall to wall in search of Sybille, longing for her not to be there, hoping she changed her mind, that she has now left the building again.

He keeps looking, to be sure, every moment growing more accustomed to the gloom. The church belongs to a long-ago epoch, when Venice must have been still young, still superstitious. Its walls are decorated with frescoes of people, real-height renditions of biblical figures and saints, every painted eye peering out at the knave. They've watched the proceedings here, in the chapel of San Isepo, for hundreds of years. Zorzo scans the cast of characters, the good people of history, each with a battered golden halo to denote it: Abram, Isaac, Moses, David, Saul, Elijah. On the side wall, behind the choir, standing among them, the only figure without a gilded corona, is Sybille.

Zorzo stops breathing and the whites of her eyes turn slowly, deliberately, on him. He can see she brandishes her pistol. She blinks slowly, steps forward to the edge of the pool of light. She waits for the abbot to notice her, stop speaking and for her husband to look up. She lifts the pistol in both hands, the grip against her chest.

"Sybille, no," Zorzo cries.

There's an explosion, his ears pop, the church is washed in phosphorescent light—each fresco seems to gasp—before the tide of brightness washes out. Stone crumbles from the ceiling. "Here! Murder!" Fugger shouts and someone overturns the standing candelabra; there's a cartwheel of flying lights, a crash of metal against floor, candles rattle across it and snuff out. For a moment the room is pitch-black and silent, before footsteps hurry from outside, the main door flies open and men rush in, Tomas first. "Sybille," Fugger gives a second strangulated cry. "Murder."

Zorzo watches her tear down to the crypt, an almost invisible sweep of black. The men rush to their master. Zorzo tries to see if there's blood on him, but the men are helping him to a chair. The abbot and his priests are looking on in horror. Zorzo edges back and slips down after Sybille, into the waterlogged basement again.

"Are you there?" It's too dark to see anything, except for where the door leading to the outside is half-ajar. "Sybille?"

"Did I strike him? I don't think I did." Her voice is shaking. She's standing by a lopsided tomb and there are little clicks of metal as she passes the gun back and forth between her hands.

"We have to go. Now." Zorzo moves toward her, but she sidesteps him.

"I must finish the job. It's my duty." Her voice is shrill and loud and Zorzo puts his finger to his lips to quiet her. "Sybille, please, leave this now." He keeps his voice low and steady even as rage burns through him.

"You don't understand. My duty."

Zorzo bears down on her and almost gets hold of the gun, but she lashes out. Her elbow lands hard against his jaw. There's a click of metal, a burn of sulfur, an intense light shakes in the gun's chamber, the room seems to silence, before air rushes in from all directions. Zorzo falls back, his head smacking against the corner of the tomb. Sybille shrieks. He feels a strange, almost calming sensation, a pounding heat against the top of his leg. He rights himself, grabs the gun in one hand and her wrist in the other and pulls her to the doorway. "Get out!" he hisses, kicking it open and dragging her up the stairs, even as she totters to keep up.

"I've hurt you, I've hurt you," she's saying.

His trousers are split open at the thigh and the skin scorched black beneath from the bullet, while blood comes from below his hair, from where he struck his head. He pulls her to the top, through the thicket of nettles, careless of her protests, and drives on, squeezing his eyes against the shock, his throat against the stench of saltpeter. He tosses the pistol into the lagoon. There's a whirl of brass and steel and it drops, gone. Never letting go of her wrist, he hauls her over the bridge.

Tullo and Achille are coming toward them. "Get back," Zorzo shouts. "Unmoor." For a moment they stand frozen. "Do it! Unmoor!" Zorzo can barely hear his own voice and it doesn't seem to belong to him anyway. The city and all its campanili slop back and forth and he has to crouch as he goes, to keep his center of gravity low, to stop himself capsizing into the sky.

"I've hurt you, I've hurt you," Sybille repeats over and over.

Zorzo pushes her on board. "Hold her," he says to the others, but they're still too dumbfounded for anything. Zorzo jumps in and takes Sybille by the jaw. "You stay, you understand? Here."

"Of course, of course. Where would I go? I'll never leave. What have I done?" Zorzo's fingers leave stains of blood on her face.

"Go! Mestre," he shouts, before peeling the material of his breeches from the face of the wound. The bullet has grazed his leg, not entered it, but sulfur has burned the skin away, down to the flesh, and trickles of blood ooze through it. "What are you waiting for? Go now!" Tullo casts off into the lagoon only for a thought to come to Zorzo. "Prince orient. The bag I gave you?"

"There," says Tullo, pointing to where it's stowed beneath the bench.

"Grief." Sybille has thrown off her gloves and her trembling hands hover above the wound. "What can I do? Tell me what I can do."

"Shut up." Then, "I pray you did not kill him. For all our sakes. Is it possible you did? Did you strike him at all?"

"I don't know. I don't know."

"Did you see blood?"

"I can't remember."

"Take that off." She undoes her cloak, gives it to him and with both hands he tears it in two, the thick black front and the pink lining beneath. The sensation is pleasurable, not just for itself, making waste of a great blanket of velvet and satin, a tiny revenge on Sybille. He wraps the strip around the top of his leg, twice, and knots it tight. He looks back at the monastery; Fugger's men have come out onto the pier and Tomas is scanning the island. Then their master exits too, unsteady on his feet, but apparently with no fatal wound. He's a long way off, but as Zorzo stares back at him, Fugger looks over. For a fraction of a moment, their eyes meet, Zorzo's sure of it, before he ducks from sight.

Once Tullo's boat has rounded the San Pietro church at the end of the island and started to double back along the eastern shore, Zorzo points to a pontoon and says, "Stop there."

"What? Why?" says Sybille.

"Be quiet!" Zorzo turns to the others. "I'll need someone to go back to my workroom, warn my fellows."

Tullo guides the boat over and Achille takes hold of one of the pontoon posts.

"Go to the Campo San Francesco della Vigna," Zorzo says to him. "Do you know it, just past the Canal Galeazze?" Achille nods. "In the corner of the square, there's a red house. There'll be a boy at the door called Uggo. Tell him you bring an urgent message from me and go upstairs to the workroom to speak to the other fellows. Paulino is quick-witted, find him."

"A red house, Uggo, Paulino," Achille repeats.

"I should go myself," Zorzo says, pushing himself up only to collapse. He presses his palms into his temples. Even trying to find simple words is a struggle.

"I can do it, no trouble," Achille is saying.

"Tell them to go to the house of Leda Sitruk. Immediately. Paulino knows where it is, in Cannaregio on the Calle del Forno. If you forget her name, say the bone queen. They must not delay, pack nothing up. Just leave. Understand? Tell them to wait there until they hear from me. Give them this, so they know it's me." Zorzo tugs his scarf off and hands it over.

"Shall I come back here?" Achille says.

"No, we have to leave. Go home afterward. Run."

Achille jumps out and sets off at speed.

"He'll do it all right," Tullo assures Zorzo, seeing the worry on his face, then casts off into the lagoon and turns the boat toward the mainland.

Zorzo takes up the spare oar, sits propped against the center thwart and rows with it, shaking his head impatiently at Sybille's attempt to help him. Over and over Tullo drives the oar down through the rowlock, which sets off in a rattle when the oar touches the seabed and returns. And with each repeating stroke, the dreadful minutes in San Isepo unspool in Zorzo's mind: the explosion of sulfurous light, the startle of saints' faces. Then, worst of all, Fugger just now, staring across the lagoon and, maybe, maybe not, catching Zorzo's eye.

"You'll be all right," Sybille is saying from the other end of the boat, still wringing her hands. Gradually the city recedes, all of it, swinging side to side—and Zorzo thinks the pain and the shock will send him mad.

23

The Mandolinist

"And what is our plan now?" Zorzo asks as they approach the lights of Mestre and sees how busy the harbor is. "Are we any safer here? We'll not find transport until the morning."

"To go where?" Tullo asks.

"Inland? Away from Venice?" Zorzo's pain has worsened; he can't think clearly or be methodical, and it's all he's come up with.

"My brother-in-law lives in Dolo," Tullo replies. "It's more out of the way. You could rest a night or two." Tullo promised to be discreet and has kept to his word. Witnessing the chaos at San Isepo, he could have refused to help. Instead he has kept calm and taken a protective stance over his passengers. He's unrecognizable from the brute who first took Zorzo to Poveglia.

"Dolo?" says Zorzo.

"Along the Brenta Canal. A few miles west."

"Miles?" Zorzo grimaces, before thinking through the idea. "Yes, Dolo. But stop at the harbor and find a second oarsman. No, find two. Money is no object." He motions at Sybille without looking at her.

"And get you to a doctor before we set off?" Tullo suggests.

Sybille nods in agreement, but Zorzo says, "No. Not needed. If that cursed bullet of yours had found its way inside me, perhaps. Dock there, fetch some men and let's go. Quickly. Agreed?"

Tullo does as he's told and soon they've moored and set off again with two more souls aboard. The gondola goes south at speed, hugging the shore, before turning into a wide estuary and then inland along one of many winding waterways that vein the Veneto.

The pain from Zorzo's burn is sharp. It feels as if pincers are plucking over and over at his raw skin. The ache carries up to his spine and out to his fingers, which he can't stop clenching, stretching and clenching again. His skull hurts too, from where it struck the stone, a different kind of discomfort, which turns all thoughts to a torpid fog.

Eventually, the background burr of the city evaporates, along with the odor of damp and rot. It's supplanted by countryside silence and clean, cold air. The throbs of pain from his leg and head take on the rhythm of the punters' oars, and with his eyes trained on the dancing reflection of the boat lanterns in the water, Zorzo's mind finally quiets—and he falls asleep. He drifts in and out of it. Hours pass, or seem to. He's aware of the boat passing up the river. When the oars cut the surface of the water, the plashing echoes around a canopy of trees.

"A laurelwood," Sybille says. She's moved to the dark space behind Zorzo and her voice is so disembodied it might belong to a hallucination.

"Where are we going?" he asks.

"Dolo," she replies.

"My *garzoni*?"

"They'll be all right. Your fellow, Achille, went to help. And when Tullo has dropped us, he'll return to make sure."

"Prince orient?"

The question seems to catch her out, but she points at the bag with the bronze box by his side, before saying, "We'll be there soon."

"He saw me, you know? Your husband."

"Saw you?"

"He was there and I was here." His eyes glaze over and he forgets what he's talking about. "Is this the Styx? Is he Charon? He's lean like him."

"That is Tullo, your friend, and there are two more behind you. We are going to the house of Tullo's brother-in-law. He's a carpenter and has a room we may lease for a day or so. This is the Brenta Canal."

They come from the trees and the land reveals itself: a wide valley, patchworked in fields, gradually rising up to low peaks on either side. On the ridges, cypress copses, all in shadow, could be watching giants. A palazzo sits on a bluff, asleep for the winter, and Zorzo thinks it's too small for Hades's underworld palace and must belong to a lesser god. He drifts off again and is only blearily aware of the boat coming to a halt and being assisted from it, of unfamiliar voices, terse exchanges of conversation, Sybille fussing, burning pain as he's helped into a house and put to bed in the dark.

When he wakes, breaking from a fretful sleep, as if coming up through ice to the surface, Zorzo is breathless and disorientated. His whole body is racked. In particular a grotesque pain throbs from his thigh. He pushes the cover down with his fist to look. There's a clean bandage strung around it, from under which patches of discoloration creep out, in blue, violet and hay yellow, as well as coal-black smears from the gunpowder. At once the events of the evening quickly spool through his mind. If truly Fugger saw him, Zorzo's life is over. No matter that he shouted out to Sybille in the chapel to stop. No one will remember that disembodied voice, only what they saw: a murderess escaping with her accomplice. He notices a dog is watching him—a rough-haired lurcher, sitting on his haunches at the end of the bed.

He and the hound are in a small cottage room. A fire is lit and through a half-open door comes the sound of turning wheels, shearing metal and the scent of freshly cut wood. Though the room is warm, the light sifting through the little window is harsh and metallic, like white lead. Zorzo cranes his neck to see out and finds it's snowing. Across the breadth of the valley, delicate, slow-moving flakes descend, dusting the ground.

He tugs back the covers and pivots his hips, only for pain to shoot up his leg. He clenches his jaw against it and the dog takes a concerned step forward.

"I'm all right," Zorzo says to him. He reaches his feet to the ground and sits on the side of the bed. He's far from all right. It's as if the skin is being ripped from his leg all over again, while a searing lethargy has set about him. Sybille is not there, but her bag with the prince orient in it sits on the floor. He opens it, takes out the bronze casket and puts it on his lap.

It has nicks and scratches all over, but otherwise looks indestructible. There would have been no chance of it breaking when Sybille dropped it. The lid is heavy, firmly locked, with no give to it at all. The metal feels thick and won't be easy to prize open, though by the same measure, the contents are at least safe inside. Judging from the hole, the key for it—wherever that may be—must be broad. An ordinary box, Zorzo thinks, neither particularly old nor valuable, and yet it contains a substance that may have arrived from the heavens, come down to earth in the very moment that Jesus Christ appeared, a pigment that every painter in Italy is in search of. He lifts it up and puts his nose to the keyhole but can only smell the metal of the casket. "If all else is lost," he thinks out loud, carefully putting it to one side, "I have you." He holds on to the bedstead and pushes himself to his feet, letting out a curse that makes the hound put his ears back.

"Do not fret," he soothes. On a side table by the door, Zorzo notices an open pot of ink, a pen and a couple of pieces of blank paper. They bear the faint indents of slanting handwriting where someone, Sybille obviously, must have written a note on top of them. Zorzo fears he is looking at the imprint of a farewell message for him. He scans the room but can't see one. He limps next door. A carpenter is working at a lathe, though there's no sign of her. "Good morning."

The fellow hears him, turning his head slightly, but carries on at his task. The workroom is smaller than Zorzo's own, without the multitude of colors, rather a monochrome of timber in all its forms, from planks to finished cabinets.

"The lady I was with?" Zorzo asks.

"Gone to Dolo, nearby, to send a letter," comes the gruff reply. Zorzo is relieved at least it was not for him, though he wonders whom it could be for. "And she'd better return," the carpenter goes on. "I lent her my wife's cloak."

"I'm sure she will," Zorzo puts in, though he's not sure of anything. The lathe turns. "And you are Tullo's brother? That much I remember. It was kind of you to put us up at short notice."

"He's my *wife*'s brother," the carpenter clarifies, "and since you arrived in the dead of night, I was left with little choice."

"We'll make sure you're paid well for your kindness." Another promise that's not Zorzo's to give. He tries to keep his voice sunny, despite the pounding in his leg. "I am Zorzo Barbarelli."

The carpenter glances back and though he's youngish, not older than Zorzo at any rate, he has a world-weary air, as if his face set into a scowl years ago and stayed that way. "Ignacio." He makes it sound more like a curse. "Beer?" he asks, coming over.

"Thank you."

Ignacio pours two cups, hands one over. "Glad to see you on your feet. You were undone last night and I had to help you into bed. You're not a light fellow, are you? Big Giorgio, they call you?"

"That's right. What is it you're cutting? Maple, is it? Such a sweet smell." Ignacio cleans the floor with a broom and Zorzo says, "A carpenter is a kind of magician, I've always thought. And you play the mandolin?" He nods to where one is leaning against the workbench.

"I repaired the neck, that's all. Though in the end the fellow never came back for it."

"Well, I play." Zorzo gives a helpful smile, to which Ignacio grunts, before pointing out the window.

"There she is now." He nods and returns to his lathe.

Zorzo feels a little jump in his stomach at the sight of Sybille striding along the raised bank of the river. She wears an old brown cloak, the color of dry mud. *If you've arrived at brown, you've made mistakes*, Bellini used to say. The color was always an anathema to him. Even if he were painting something that was actually brown, he'd change it. Zorzo has never felt the same: the right brown in the right place is as winning as anything. The cloak has an ancient look, an article from faraway times, the way it's clasped at the chest, rather than the neck, with a fastening of old bronze, a Celtic cross. Sybille pauses on a bluff, casts her eyes back along the valley, and as the wind catches against her hair, which is loose, Zorzo thinks she could be a Viking queen.

"I'll wait for her in here," he says, hobbling back to the room.

He sits on the bed and tries to work out what he's going to say. He hears Sybille come in and talk a few moments with Ignacio. Then she steals into the room, stands behind the door and Zorzo forgets his pain for the first time. Just as ultramarine coaxed unexpected hues from her face, plain brown does the same, bringing forth a new spectrum: rust, olive green, pine needle and burnt gold.

"You're a little better, then?" she says, standing her ground, barely looking him in the eye. "I put on a new bandage last night." The old one, the strip torn from Sybille's cloak, is discarded on the floor. "With some balm that our host made up. You met Ignacio. Very kind. The wound is not as bad as it looks. For that we must be thankful." Her voice trails away and she goes over and runs her hand through the scruff of the dog's neck. "You met Otto too? He's been looking after you."

"Otto? That's the dog's name?"

"Yes, why?"

"Someone I know, a kind lad, the apprentice to a—" He thinks back to Poveglia, where this journey started, and wonders where he'd be now if he hadn't met Caspien that day. Sybille hangs the cloak behind the door and Zorzo asks, "Is she here somewhere, Ignacio's wife?"

"Dead. Drowned, just up the river. A flood, two years ago. An awful business." She halts when she notices the bronze casket on the bed next to Zorzo. "Let me move that." She puts it back in the bag, which she places on the floor, out of sight at the end of the bed. It's as if the presence of the mineral is upsetting to her and Zorzo wonders if she regrets stealing it now, though surely that crime is nothing compared to the attempt of murder.

Sybille goes on. "You may not remember me telling you last night, but I sent Tullo back to Venice after he dropped us off, to check your *garzoni* were safely moved. To the house of Leda Sitruk, as you told Achille." She goes on, trying to be businesslike, though still not able to look at Zorzo directly. "And I tasked him, when he was done with that, to go and wait in the square in front of your house, to see if anyone…unwelcome appears. And to return here immediately if there was any sort of problem. I gave him money, a good quantity of it, for all his assistance, and to share out among your *garzoni*, until they hear from you again."

"That's kind of you," Zorzo says, to which she gives a mirthless laugh, at the irony of it.

"Leda Sitruk. She's the lady I met, isn't she? The merchant?"

"And a very reliable friend."

He doesn't mean it as a slight on Sybille, but neither does he mind that she takes it that way. Her eyes redden, on the point of tears, but she pulls herself back. "They told me in town a decree has gone up today: an outbreak of plague. Half the city is packing up and leaving. So now it is official."

There's silence between them for some moments. Zorzo's thoughts are for his *garzoni*, that they keep themselves safe from it, as much as from Fugger. "You were sending a letter?" he asks.

"What?" The question genuinely seems to take her by surprise and Zorzo nods at the paper and open inkpot. "Oh, yes. To my brother. To tell him I—" Whatever she was going to say, she stops herself. Instead she produces a sealed envelope from her pocket. "I changed my mind. I'll send it later." She puts the envelope on the table, along with her purse.

"You walked all the way to town, and then changed your mind?" Zorzo's tone is pointedly suspicious.

"Because I wanted to talk with you first." Her lips tremble. "I'm sorry, so sorry. I shouldn't have—why did I? Everything is my fault." She dashes at her eyes, though still no tears have fallen from them. "I have ruined you. You must wish you had never set eyes on me."

Zorzo remains silent. If she's expecting consolation, he'll not give it. Because she's right. He *is* ruined, probably beyond repair.

"Well, I have been methodical," Sybille goes on. "And I have a plan, of sorts, formed from scratch over this sleepless night and on my trek to Dolo and back. If you're in a fit state to hear it." Zorzo remains silent, and she forges on. "Before I continue, I must ask: did he see you, my husband? You said it last night. Did he know you were there? If he did, our options are—less favorable."

"I called out in the chapel, but there was so much happening at once he may not have noticed. Afterward, though, as we cast off, he looked in my direction and I'm almost certain he caught sight of me. But I can hope."

Sybille nods intently before replying. "I wish I could send the arrow of time back and reverse what came to pass last night, not for myself—I must stand by what I tried to do—but for you. I cannot change what happened, but I will put this right for you, Zorzo, if it's the last thing I do in this world. To begin, let me explain where *I* must go now. I say it first only because it may help you make up your own mind. I will head to Florence."

"Florence?"

"Rome was my first thought, for it is a city that Jakob cannot abide and has sworn never to set foot in again. I've told you as much already. But in fact—I realized in the dawn light—his dislike is as strong for its sister kingdom, perhaps stronger."

"Yesterday you wanted to return to Augsburg."

"That was before I failed. It's impossible now. So Florence. Jakob hates the Medici and the Pazzi and Salviati, their claims that their city is the home of banking. He'll have nothing to do with the town. In Italy, only Venice holds interest for him."

"But you mean to hide from him? That is your course of action?"

"I mean not to return to Augsburg, to Germany at all, to do the opposite of what I spoke of, to turn my back on my old life." There's a determination and pragmatism in her tone that's distinct from any Zorzo has noted before. "Do you know Florence?"

"A little, yes."

"I do not, at all, but is it not a practical town? An intelligent place? People talk of it as being the most remarkable city in Europe. Even if it were only half so, it would be sanctuary enough. And there are powerful people, aren't there, near equals of my husband, the bankers I just spoke of, who I would happily align with, to guarantee our peace and safety."

"Our?"

"This is the point I come to. The subject that is most pressing. Come with me, Zorzo."

"To Florence?" He laughs, scornfully.

"It is not the only proposal I have for you, but hear it first. How curious that, yesterday, you were laying plans in front of me and now I do the same for you. I would buy you a workshop there, twice the size of the one you have. Put it in your name. To be yours always, beholden to no one. I'd become your patron in chief. Money cannot solve all the problems of the world, but it can help with some. I have enough of it, without a penny from Jakob. My father was shrewd in that respect. He never liked Jakob, or approved of our marriage, and kept back a portion of his wealth for me in trust. What would you think of such a plan? Of coming to that city with me?"

"Sybille, it's impossible." He's not absorbing her plan, just thinking how little he can trust her. "Everything I've built is in Venice. And I won't leave my *garzoni*."

"Of course not. I would pay for them to join you. Whatever you need. Or all of you remain and I will do the same for you in Venice. I only suggest Florence as I imagine it would be good for your business. It must be a fine place if you can live there well, which I guarantee you would. And, well," she blushes, "I thought also, you and I might be able to make some kind of alliance together."

She looks at him hopefully, but he's unable to forgive her for what happened in San Isepo, to think of her in the same way he once did. "So—you suppose your husband *will* come after me, if I return home?"

"His battle is with me, I'm sure of it, with me alone—but there is risk."

"And what would *you* do in Florence, with your life? Continue your plan? The mission you've set yourself?"

There is a long silence during which Zorzo notices Sybille glower at the bag with the bronze casket on the floor behind the bed, as if the stolen box contained some portion of her troubles.

"I don't know." The corners of her eyes turn a kind of livid red and tears come at last. "I feel I've woken from a nightmare. I've been living in it for years and years. I've been lost, Zorzo. Truly. I hadn't even realized I was dreaming. But that gunshot in the crypt shook something from me. Your bravery, too. It broke the spell. All the speeches I've been making, inquisitions and red lists and plots and popes. I don't know if I care about those things as much as I've said."

She sits next to him and takes his hand between hers. He means to remove it—but it's a relief to have contact, to feel her warmth, her skin.

"I've abused you, Zorzo, in honesty I have. I took advantage of your kindness. And of your ambition. I went to your house that first time to make you my ally. Because I was scared. Because I didn't want to do this thing alone. I tried to put you off the commission, and meeting my husband, as I thought you were more useful to me away from him. Then, when you took the initiative and sought him out anyway, I changed my plan again, but always for my own advantage, not yours."

"Sybille, quiet now." She clutches tighter, leans her weight against him, and Zorzo finds himself softening. "If you used me a little, it was for a good cause. And no doubt I used you too. I had my own schemes." He says it not to console, but because it's true.

"No, no, I've done you wrong. I seduced you. Can't you see? How I've done you wrong." Her shoulders are shaking and the tears have burned scarlet lines down her face. "The fellows in your workshop," she goes on, "the way they love you, the feeling in the air there, how everyone is considerate… I've never had that around me. I'm always trapped in prisons. Men and their schemes. But you—just the light through your windows. And your kindness. What you do. Your nobility. You don't take, take, take, or give orders or snatch away. You *make*, Zorzo. You leave a mark. You *add* something of value. When you've gone from the world, it is there. If only I'd been born in Castelfranco on the street next to yours."

"Sybille, calm a little." He's moved by her argument, her palpable remorse, her desire to set things right. "When we've rested, we can think. Everything has its solution."

"Yes, yes. We can make a little paradise, Zorzo, you and I, in Florence or wherever it might be."

She turns and kisses him. He resists at first, but finds himself unable to hold out. They kiss for a long time, locked together in a way that makes a colorburst ring through Zorzo's body and mind.

Later, the three of them eat dinner together in Ignacio's parlor, pottage stew with rye bread still warm from the oven.

"Would you permit me to play a tune on your mandolin?" Zorzo says afterward. Ignacio gets the instrument and passes it over.

Zorzo tunes it, string by string, tightening the tuning keys until he finds the right tone for each. Before he begins, he says, "My father wrote this for my mother. She died when I was only ten, but it was longer than Orpheus had with his Eurydice. After she died, if he'd known the way there, my father would have gone to hell to fetch her back. To Orpheuses everywhere," he says with a nod to Ignacio, and begins to play.

Later that evening, after Ignacio has gone to bed and Sybille has fallen asleep in the chair by the fire, Otto resting his head on her foot, Zorzo finds himself thinking about her plan to move to Florence. And the more he does, the more the idea takes hold of his imagination. Perhaps this calamity might end up opening new doors, he begins to think, revealing new paths he would not have thought to take otherwise. Zorzo knows the two most famous artists of the day, da Vinci and Michelangelo, make a point of being traveling men. It would be an exciting challenge. He'd be exposed to a new raft of patrons. Unexpected doors would open. *The Venetian*, he could be known as. *Have you heard he's the master of atmosphere*, the talk might go, *and of color? You must employ him. He's quite unique in all Florence.* And going there wouldn't be like emigrating to some remote outpost. Sybille's right, Florence is the city many consider to be the Athens of its day, where ideas are born and hatch in their thousands before flying off into the world, where patronage of the arts is as serious a matter as statecraft itself.

Not all his *garzoni* would appreciate the move, but most surely would, especially if Sybille were backing the business. Even if it weren't twice the size, as Sybille suggested, they could move to a workroom in a sturdier building than the red house, where the roof isn't falling in, that isn't at the mercy of Venice's vagaries, the flooding and damp, the bitter winters and stifling summers. On the two occasions Zorzo has been to Florence (he was bashful of the fast pace of the city then, but that too would be reversed if he lived there), he was struck by how fresh the air was, being up among the hills, and how the Arno River, a spacious, fast-flowing channel that cups around the city, seems to cleanse it even more. In Venice any ugliness—whether from smell, disease or poor government—seems to fester in the unmoving water. In Florence, the Arno carries it away.

And then, of course and most crucially, there's Sybille. That could be the greatest surprise of all. A mighty adventure. Can Zorzo dare to think of a life together? It would mean keeping secrets, of Sybille shedding her former self, of starting anew; but she'd hardly be the first person in history to escape a violent marriage to do so. Together, it could even be possible for Zorzo to realize his great dream and have children.

What a union it could be, he thinks, what happiness they could find when things return to normal. Zorzo and Sybille, bosomed in the heart of Florence, the Arno carrying the last of their troubles away. Family trips up to the mountains of Tuscany, Zorzo with sketch paper and Sybille with a notebook of ideas. A new bloodline, a different type of dynasty, one fitting the changing times: broad-minded, daring, kind. *"Do you know the Barbarellis?"* the talk may go. *"They had a difficult beginning. You remember that business with Jakob Fugger? Well, now they're the golden family of Florence."*

Zorzo wakes in the dead of night and is alert at once. The noises of the countryside are clear and acute. The river passing sounds like knives being sharpened. The marsh rushes whisper and the laurel trees on the bank seem to groan. The house too, though sleeping, creaks. Zorzo can hear a mouse pattering in the attic, and even, he fancies, the tumble of dust on the floor where the night air comes in under the doors. A prickling malaise besets him. An image stands out in his mind, like a rusty nail in a wall: Fugger looking from the steps of the monastery and his eyes meeting Zorzo's across the lagoon.

He peers at Sybille. He can hear every other sound, but she's entirely silent. She sleeps curled up on her side, like a child, the blanket rising and falling against her. Zorzo turns the other way and tries to go back to sleep, even just for some moments more, but when he closes his eyes, Fugger is still watching from San Isepo's steps.

He realizes Jakob Fugger will *always* be watching. Zorzo and Sybille will be fugitives forever, looking over their shoulders to the end of their days. And given Fugger's influence, that end may come sooner rather than later. Even if he could guarantee their own safety, he can't do the same for his *garzoni*, or their families, or Leda Sitruk, or anyone he knows. Zorzo remembers a piece of advice Bellini's head *garzone* once gave him, when they were digging for madder roots in a wood after a storm and saw a great oak come down. *If a tree starts to fall, run toward it, not away; for when you face the danger front on, you control your chances better.* Zorzo reminds himself that all he, personally, has done wrong is accept a stolen casket of pigment. *That* he can return. The rest he can do his best to explain. Fugger must have intelligence. And, as Sybille said, he was once reasonable, learned and had an inquiring mind. Vestiges of that must remain. If Zorzo goes to him, reasons with him, face-to-face, explains what brought her to that point in San Isepo, enables the husband to see the world as if through her eyes, though he's unlikely to get a pardon for Sybille, he may just be able to convince Fugger to spare her life. As for himself, he may not be pardoned either, but at least he can ensure his *garzoni* are not pulled into the vortex.

He gets up, quietly puts on his clothes, goes over to the desk and writes a note on one of the blank pieces of paper.

I have gone to speak with your husband. I will put this right. Wait here until you hear from me. He notices the sealed letter to her brother that Sybille changed her mind about sending. There's something expansive, almost lavish, in how she's written Edvard's name, a more exaggerated style than her notes to Zorzo had; as if her sibling, alongside whom she's suffered so much, deserves a special kind of writing. Zorzo tucks his own message just beneath her purse. Then, realizing he gave the last of his money to Tullo, he opens it and looks inside. The emeralds and sapphires wink up at him, and he remembers his father's ring and is relieved that, should the worst happen, he left instructions with Leda to get it back. There's a quantity of money at the bottom. Sybille promised to pay him for the picture, but he feels very uneasy about taking money from her purse while she sleeps. If he succeeds today, if it's possible in any way, he can have his bill settled later. He freezes when she murmurs suddenly. Her eyelids flicker but don't quite open. Then she turns over and falls back to sleep.

Zorzo takes enough from her purse for what he needs, to get back, and for the ring. He slips it in his pocket and replaces the wallet. He retrieves the bag with the bronze casket, and tiptoes out. As he unlatches the front door, a low voice comes from the foot of the stairs.

"You're leaving?" says Ignacio.

"I must. Thank you for your kindness." Zorzo keeps his voice at a whisper.

"Does she know you're going?"

"So I might help her, she does not." He fixes the carpenter with what he hopes to be a trustworthy look. "I am no scoundrel. I do not run away. The opposite. We have found ourselves at sea, she and I, and I must chart a course back to safety."

It's sincere enough for Ignacio to nod, and motion for his guest to carry on. Zorzo opens the door. "What you said last night," Ignacio says, "about your father and Orpheus, going to hell and back to find their love again... I appreciated it." His face quivers, before he composes himself, gives a bow, a little gesture of the hand—and Zorzo exits.

He limps along the bank to the nearby copse of laurel trees and breaks off the sturdiest branch he can find. He looks west, in the direction of Florence, toward the hills, whose peaks are coloring pink against the dawn. He imagines for a moment what life might wait for him there, before turning the other way.

He makes sure the box of prince orient is secure at his side and, using the branch as a stick, sets off westward toward the church spire of Dolo. From there he'll find passage back to Venice. As he goes he reminds himself that he's not doing this for himself, but for everyone else. If he's unable to convince Fugger to leave Sybille alone, and to overlook Zorzo's own seeming involvement—both of which are unlikely—he must, *must*, ensure the safety of his *garzoni*.

24

Descent

It takes Zorzo over an hour to limp along the banks of the Brenta to the village. He keeps pausing to gather his breath against the pain; only to worry that Sybille will come, much faster, to track him down and persuade him back. For everyone's sake, and her own, that must be avoided.

He arrives at the riverside harbor as the village clock strikes nine. It's a scruffy, down-on-its-luck place. He'd not expected many boats to be waiting, but the quayside is all but deserted. There's a cargo barge, with a team of horses, which looks as if it has just arrived, and a single tatty-looking gondola. Zorzo can't find anyone aboard the barge, but the solitary gondolier has seen Zorzo and is beckoning him over.

"Where are you headed?" the man asks, overfriendly.

"Venice."

"Venice?" The gondolier whistles and Zorzo remembers what

Sybille said about the decree going up, that an outbreak has been declared. He expects resistance, but the gondolier says, "I can take you as far as the port."

The man's smile is insincere, and Zorzo's certain he's drunk, even though the day has barely begun. His boat is worse, battered and unkempt, with empty bottles and half-eaten food lying about. "The port is fine, but I have some haste. Is there another oarsman about you can share the task with? For twice the money."

"That will not be a problem," the man says and whistles to a group of youngsters on the other side of the pier. "You're needed," he shouts and one of them slopes over.

"I've walked all morning," Zorzo says, "let me buy provision for the journey." He nods toward an *alimentari* on one side of the harbor. "Would you like anything?"

The gondolier is taken aback by the offer. He makes a show of tidying his shirt, which is filthy, and says theatrically, "A quart of beer will get the oars moving nicely." He fishes around among his things and produces a cup, then glances aside as something moves under the stern thwart. He stamps and a rat scurries from the boat onto the pier and vanishes from sight. The boatman gives Zorzo a comradely roll of the eyes, and hands over his cup.

When Zorzo returns from the shop, there are two more waiting gondolas, smarter ones, each with a brace of more palatable-looking drivers. Zorzo's sure he'd get to the city faster in one of their boats. Also, the youth that has come to lend a hand has an unappealing look about him: angular, thin as a stick and an angry expression. Perhaps sensing Zorzo's hesitation, the first gondolier calls aloud, "Aboard for Venice!"

Always keep your promises, was Zorzo's father's rule and his son has followed it all his life. He hands over the beer and clambers in. "The throne is yours," the gondolier says, motioning toward a stool. "And would you mind paying in advance?"

Zorzo should really break up one of his coins: it's too much on its own. For expediency's sake, though, and from exhaustion, he hands it over. The gondolier wipes it on his coat and studies it, before giving Zorzo a reappraising look. "A gentleman, I see."

Hardly, Zorzo thinks: he's carrying stolen goods and last night was involved in an attempted murder. The driver finishes his beer in one, tosses his cup down; his helper jumps aboard and they cast off.

It's only when they've left the harbor, turned east along the canal and come into the light that Zorzo properly notices the face of the new lad, how sallow and sweaty it is. His neck glands look prominent and swollen; or it may be just his skinny frame that makes them seem that way.

"What have you got there?" the first gondolier asks, giving a sly look at the bag on his passenger's lap.

Zorzo realizes it's fallen open, revealing the top of the casket, the bronze model of the pine cone. He covers it up and clutches it tight. A warning look is the only answer he gives, to both the men. He checks he still has his dagger, just in case. He has the urge to ask them to turn the boat around, take him back, so he can choose a better boat. It's too late, though: he's on his way. He glances again in the direction of the hills, the blur of purple quartz on the horizon that seems more enticing than ever.

When the youngster starts coughing and hawking up phlegm, Zorzo turns the other way and buries his face in his jacket. He doesn't care if he appears rude anymore. He has not an ounce of sociability left. And for once, he doesn't ask his drivers' names.

Let it be over, he says to himself. *Let this day be over.*

Approaching Venice, Zorzo's gondola seems to be the only one going that way. The lagoon is so teeming with departing craft it looks almost like a city regatta. Venice's bells are all ringing at once, with a more urgent rhythm than usual, to declare the city is in a state of emergency; not the gravest, like an invading armada, but close enough.

The harbor piers are frantic, mostly with well-to-do families trying to get off the island, to places like Dolo, presumably. There clearly aren't enough boats for them all and angry scenes are breaking out. Zorzo notices one wealthy-looking young couple arguing with each other, and is reminded of when he first saw Sybille and her husband at Mestre, he chiding her for her fear of water. Was she frightened yesterday, in the boat? She didn't seem to be; but the night has become a blur of darkness, and of the river, and of Sybille's gloveless hands forever fidgeting.

Before he even disembarks, his gondolier is striking up a deal with a waiting family, and Zorzo leaves them to it. Shouldering through the crowd, he sees someone he recognizes at the other end of the port: a man tightening his belt and glancing at the sky before heading away, into an even busier part of the harbor. He carries a heavy traveling trunk and Zorzo's sure that it's Caspien, but he keeps losing him among the throng. "Caspien," Zorzo calls, but there's too much noise. Wherever he's going, there's no one with him, no sign of Otto. Any other time, Zorzo might think nothing of it, but has the sense, in the pit of his stomach, from the way in which the man moves, head down and shoulders hunched, that the boy has perished. "Caspien!"

He carries on searching for a bit, for Otto's sake, not Caspien's, keen for assurance that the boy still lives; but after trailing around for a quarter of an hour, through the din of fraught parents snapping at their children, he knows he can't delay longer. He turns into the city and heads south, toward the center, where the bells ring loudest.

Venice has become almost unrecognizable in just one day. Now the warning has officially gone up, the streets are as empty as the port was full. Only the poorest folk, who have no choice but to go to work, are continuing as normal, but they're wary, treading more carefully than usual. Many cover their faces with their sleeves or improvised masks and everyone keeps their distance. From behind closed windows and shutters, Zorzo's aware of families pressed together, restless shadows, watching and fretting as to whether this episode will pass—as most do—without significant horror, or if this one will be severe. A catastrophe is long overdue, a second black death, people have been saying for as long as Zorzo can remember. He wonders what he must look like: a solitary young man, hobbling along in torn clothes and a bandaged leg. He's reminded of the picture he drew in Poveglia, at the start of his quest, of the war-torn Aeneas tramping through Hades.

The Palazzo Pallido is being packed up. The water doors are open and Frau Bauer is instructing her team. They're loading up trunks onto three waiting barges. The back door into the kitchens, on the far side of the little bridge, is open too. As Zorzo crosses over to it he hears voices from the canalside. There's a band of young men there: a gentleman in a peacock-blue coat and four other fellows who are much burlier looking. The one in blue is recounting an anecdote, something rude about the city. The punchline, *"How would I know anything? I'm Venetian!"* sets the rest laughing. Zorzo realizes who the young man is: Rodrigo Sordi, Michelangelo's sidekick with whom he argued. Rodrigo glances over his shoulder at Zorzo and gives a mocking nod of the head, before Zorzo slips into the palazzo.

The kitchens are frantic with activity and the business of shutting up the house, pewter stowed, porcelain and silver sorted, numbers listed in a ledger before it's locked away. Zorzo passes through, bracing himself to be challenged by Tomas or one of the other men, practicing in his head the plea he'll make to at least be allowed to speak to the master. He's convinced that appearing in person will be proof of his innocence, for a guilty man would never be so brazen. In any case, no one notices him and he ascends the back stairs to the hall.

The space, usually so gloomy, is ablaze with light this morning; two great bronze doors, which have always been shut, on the ocean side of the palazzo, are wide open. There's a landing bay and, beyond it, the expanse of the lagoon. Reflections from it pour in and bounce off the marble. On the table in the center is the gold tureen that Tomas had brought into the inn on Mestre harbor, more shining and triumphant than ever.

Zorzo looks up. On the first-floor landing, the door to Fugger's salon is slightly ajar and there are voices coming from inside. There's laughter, a thing—like the light from the sea—Zorzo never thought to encounter in the palazzo. He puts his bag on the table, opens it and lays his hands upon the bronze casket, for the final time, somehow hoping, by holding it alone, he still might get a sense of the mystery inside.

He's about to continue up when the salon door swings open and Cardinal Soderini exits swiftly. "Good day to you all." He waves to whoever is left in the room. He doesn't notice Zorzo standing below and passes along the gallery into the back part of the house. Zorzo closes the satchel and tucks it under his arm. Three more men emerge, talking with one another, and descend. Zorzo feels unusual anyway, hot and foggy in the head, but the sight of these three, all of whom he recognizes, is like a strange hallucination.

The first is Vittore di Fonti. He is not so much smiling as beaming beatifically. Behind him is Michelangelo. He looks almost happy too, or at least not angry. He's smartened up and wears a clean shirt under a velvet coat. The third man looks more earnest. He's in his late twenties, possibly younger, with long, dark hair and the smooth, intense face of a doll. Zorzo has never spoken to him, just had him pointed out once across a room: Raphael Sanzio. *His* presence is the most surprising. In all this business of prince orient and the commission for St. Peter's, his name has not once cropped up. "He's the best painter of hands in Italy," Bellini once meanly remarked, as if hands were all he could do. Zorzo is so taken aback he forgets for a moment why he's here: that he's come to surrender, to plead at least for the safety of his *garzoni*, even if his and Sybille's proves irretrievable.

Zorzo broadens his chest, still in the habit of appearing winning to his competitors, though in fact he's lost everything, and says with a smile, "Good afternoon, sirs." The others pause at the foot of the stairs. Michelangelo gives a guarded nod, Raphael smiles, though has no idea who he's looking at, but di Fonti is alarmed. "Do not trouble yourself," Zorzo says to him, "I'm here on another matter. A personal one. Congratulations, sirs," he says to the other two. "I'm sure you're worthy conquerors. For my part, I am glad the war is over." He laughs. "I might hang up my armor now and become a mandolinist. Don't let me keep you."

Zorzo stands back. The others share looks and Zorzo doesn't mind if they think he's mad. "Good day," Raphael says; the others nod and all three stride toward the great rectangle of light, the waiting lagoon. They board their barge and a steward closes the iron doors behind them. Gloom envelopes the gargantuan space once more, creeping over the golden tureen and finally Zorzo himself. He can feel a drip of sweat down the back of his neck.

He ascends and finds the salon empty, but the double doors between the statues of the blind angels are open and a sickly green light, reflected from the tiles, bleeds out. Inside someone is rustling papers. Zorzo limps over and stops at the entrance to the ballroom. He's in luck—if luck is the word—as Fugger's in there, alone, at the end of the chamber, studying a map laid out on top of the metal safebox. What a painting, Zorzo can't help thinking, the richest man in the world, in a silken day coat, the color of an eastern sunset, alone in a malachite-green banqueting hall. Tomas is not there.

Zorzo clears his throat and says, "Herr Fugger?"

Fugger looks around and it takes him some moments to realize who it is, to switch from impassive to alarmed. "Tomas!" he shouts to the floor below. It's unnerving to see his face animated, in daylight, not the gloom of San Isepo, a usually slow-moving predator snapping to life. It's clear from his expression that Fugger did indeed see Zorzo at San Isepo, if not in the boat, somehow. "In here!" Like any predator, he doesn't actually sound frightened for his life. There comes the sound of men rushing up the stairs, like a roll of bass drums, and four men tear into the room.

Zorzo puts the bag on the floor, takes off his sheath and dagger, makes a show of dropping them and lifts his hands above his head. "I have, of course, not come here to fight."

Two men pat him down, a third inspects the dagger and puts it out of reach, while the last examines the bag. He takes out the bronze casket and studies it from all sides before placing it on the table. This is not how Zorzo was planning to return prince orient. He was going to produce it after an impassioned explanation and apology. He watches Fugger, waiting for the reaction, the burst of outrage that Zorzo made off with his precious mineral, but the banker glances at the box with no apparent interest and asks, "Where is she?"

Tomas comes in last and halts at the sight of Zorzo. He shakes his head and gives a mocking smile, at the audacity of the man, before taking up his usual position by the door.

"Frau Fugger does not know I am here," Zorzo begins, "but I do come on her behalf. To try to explain what happened to her, so you might understand the business in San Isepo."

"I know what happened, you dolt, she tried to slaughter me. Wait outside." Fugger waves away the other men, while Tomas remains. "Where is she?"

"Sir, when you hear what I've come to say, you may do with me as you will. If that means," he doesn't know how to say it, "if that means I'll be punished, so be it."

"Oh, you shall be punished, painter. Make no doubt about it."

"Firstly, I'm returning your casket. I'll explain, after everything else, how it came into my hands. But there it is."

Fugger apparently has no interest in the box. "Where is she?"

Zorzo reminds himself that running toward the falling tree is safer, that being truthful is the best course, that Fugger was once a learned man. Besides, he rehearsed what to say over and over. "While I was painting your wife, it became more and more apparent to me that she had fallen under the spell of a particular," he tries to remember the word he'd settled on, "a particular *conviction*. She developed such a belief in a certain cause, such fear on account of it, it took her over completely and I feel she may have lost some of her reason. Perhaps she cannot, or should not, be excused, but she is remorseful." Even if she isn't, Zorzo knows this must be stated.

"Where is she? Tell me." Fugger rounds on him, that face that has smashed through mountains to build roads to his ports, the hands that struck his wife with a boot scraper as she tried to escape, but Zorzo stands his ground.

"And I will. But let me speak first, about this conviction she had." He's decided on the angle he'll take, to make no mention of Fugger's cruelty to her, but to appeal to the reasonable person she claimed her husband once was. "She has a picture in her mind of—of—" He tries to get his breathing under control, to remember exactly how he planned to say it. "She has a picture of the way the world should be and she thinks, for whatever reason—and I know it sounds grandiose—that you plan, with your money and influence, to obliterate what she hopes for. She would have you change, that's all."

"What is this jibberish? Tell me where she is? Mestre? Men have been scouring the port all morning and nothing."

"I beg you, for everyone's sake, to hear me first. This is my one chance to speak directly to power, sir, to a god in this world. You, sir." He forges on with his planned argument. "When I was a student, my master, Bellini, had me sketch the faces of twelve Roman emperors. To give the pictures authenticity, I learned about each of them, their good deeds and bad, their triumphs and failings. I will make myself clear, I promise, and then tell you where Sybille is." He speaks quickly, so as not to be interrupted. "On the one hand there was Trajan and Hadrian and Marcus Aurelius. Good men. Bold men. They reshaped government, built universities, made systems of laws, fought poverty and ignorance. They were wise, and moral. Then, at the other end of the scale, there was Domitian and Nero and Caligula, who just stamped on freedoms, pulled down learning places," he gives a crafty glance at Fugger, before adding, "set up tribunals of fear, built palaces for themselves. They were men who didn't heed the past, care for civilization, who had no interest in culture, not truly, who were tyrannical and selfish. You have as much power as those kings, Herr Fugger, I have come to realize that. More so. And the question that Sybille had, that tormented her, that soured her brain to the point that led to yesterday, the question I would have too: which would you be, sir, a Hadrian or a Nero?"

Fugger is like a bull now, ready to charge. His forehead has turned almost violet. "Where is Sybille?"

"But which?"

"I dig for iron and copper and lend money against them, that's all."

Cardinal Soderini steps into the room, and is as alarmed by Zorzo's presence as everyone else is. "What's happening here?"

"We're trying to find out," Fugger growls, turning back to Zorzo. "What did she tell you about me? I long to know. That I am the devil incarnate? That I struck her daily? Did she tell you that's how she came by her scars? How she lost her unborn child? She said that to you?" Zorzo doesn't know what to say. "No need to own up. I can see it in your face. What other crime have I committed? Some extraordinary thing, by the sound of your speech just now. What was it? Answer me."

"She—" Zorzo's leg has set off in a shake. "She said you were involved with—" Zorzo believed her story, in the end, but now he doubts it all over again. "She said you and the pope and others had a plan to—a plot to… May I sit?" His leg is now juddering at double speed and he can't control it. He takes a chair. "She said that you wished to set up an Inquisition across the continent, as they have in Castile."

"An Inquisition. Do you hear, Cardinal?"

"I do."

"They've gone too far now, that knave and her. Now I understand it: her behavior all the way here, her oddness at every turn. All that secret letter writing she thought I didn't notice. He'd put her up to murder. There can be no doubt, can there? Am I right? *He* is at the root of this."

"It bears all of his hallmarks," Soderini agrees.

"We'll have to take measures," Fugger says.

"The time has certainly come." Soderini nods.

"But what? Capture him, put him on trial?"

"Trial?" Tomas laughs. "Execute him, I say."

Zorzo can't understand which person they're talking about. Capture who? Put who on trial?

For a few moments, Fugger is lost in some private thought, his chest rising and falling, until he goes over to the hearth and picks up an iron stoker. Zorzo stands, trying not to cower, though he's certain he's about to be struck, but Fugger bashes it over and over against the wall of the fireplace, smashing bricks, sending stone pieces hurling in all directions. Soderini jumps back to avoid one, while two of the men that Fugger sent away put their heads around the door. "Get out!" He stands, panting in front of the hearth still clutching the poker. When he turns back, Zorzo can barely believe what he sees: Fugger's eyes are livid red, on the point of tears. "And what's this she gave you?" he mutters to Zorzo, motioning at the bronze casket. "What's supposed to be inside, some proof of my damned wickedness?"

"No, it is…" Zorzo's suddenly unsure of himself. "It is the prince orient."

"The what?"

"Prince orient, the pigment."

"The pigment?" And then, remembering, "Oh, that. What's the connection with her?" Zorzo shakes his head, understanding less than ever. Fugger seems entirely unconcerned with it. "Get the keys to this box," he says to Tomas, who exits the room.

For a while Fugger, Zorzo and Soderini stand in silence, before Fugger says, "It would be a fine speech you gave just now, Barbarelli, but for one thing: Sybille is not remarkable, not in the way you think. She certainly has skills, a whole snake pit of them. Did she seduce you?"

"What?"

"Did she throw herself at you? Let you stab her in her house?" He's tapping the end of the poker against the tiled floor. "Don't look so holy. I presumed she would. At least you may have been worth it, unlike some of the others. You have some charm, 'the painter in ascendency.'" Zorzo shakes his head, more lost than ever. "She no doubt professed love to you," Fugger goes on, "like she did to me once, so convincingly. Don't misunderstand: she *can* love. She does, in fact, with limitless passion. Her shipwrecked darling, boy king to her desert island queen. The captain of her incestuous heart." He glowers at Zorzo, gripping the poker ever tighter, before he throws it down beside the hearth in a loud clatter.

Prickles crawl up Zorzo's back as at last he understands who Fugger is talking about. He traces his eye along the ground at the pieces of broken stone and feels as if the room were turning beneath him. "Her brother?"

Tomas returns, unlocks the casket and opens it. There's a small pile of folded-up papers inside.

"What are they?" says Fugger.

Tomas takes them out and goes through them. Zorzo can see they contain lists and columns of numbers. "Receipts, sir, for cloth."

"Cloth?" says Fugger.

Tomas reads some of them out: "'Three yards silk damask in emerald green; two yards indigo velvet; five yards gold brocade.'"

"For her dresses." Fugger does not take his eyes off Zorzo. "The beloved Edvard Artzi. The brother who pushed her off a boat into the Baltic Sea. Who's filled her head with poison ever since. Who knows, perhaps he even believes some of it himself. *I* set up an inquisition?" Fugger laughs. "There's no profit in that. No sense either. Only *living* people buy things. If I had my way, the whole continent would be booming. As for who cut her face and crushed her hand, and struck her pregnant stomach—I need hardly tell you. But seeing as the child was probably his, it was no doubt for the better. Where is she?"

After a long silence, Zorzo asks, "Will you hurt her?"

Fugger pauses before saying, "I should. She deserves it this time." A decade of troubles, of marital horror, seems to play back and forth across his face, before he pulls himself together. "No. But I'll not forgive her anymore."

"Dolo," Zorzo murmurs, unable to stop the word from tumbling out of his mouth, too overwhelmed to put up a fight anymore. "That's where she is."

"Is that far?"

"An hour beyond Mestre."

"Does she have money?"

"She does."

Fugger turns to Tomas and the cardinal. "If she has money, I suppose she'll be back. If not, she can find her own way to Germany. Get him out of here," he says to Tomas.

Tomas holds out his hand to the door and Zorzo walks toward it in a trance. He stops, turns. "All I wanted was prince orient, sir. It is why I made you a gift, came to your door, painted your wife. For prince orient. For me, color has power. It is everything." He's about to go, but dares himself to ask one final question. "Can I see it? Is it here? The real prince orient?"

Fugger shows his teeth. "You're lucky I let you go at all. Get out."

Soderini stands back from the door, staring at Zorzo as he departs.

He goes with the men down the stairs to the hall. He feels like an actor in a play who has forgotten his lines, though the play is incomprehensible anyway. Johannes and some other footmen are carrying things from different parts of the house and leaving them piled up by the double doors to the lagoon, ready to be loaded up. Among the items, turned on its side, is the portrait of Sybille's brother. He looks as angelic as ever. Close up, though, is a detail Zorzo hadn't made out before: the dove behind Edvard, that most peaceful of species, has a flap of torn-off flesh hanging from its claws. The speckles of blood Zorzo noticed on its white plumage are from where it has ripped apart its prey like an eagle.

"Sir?" Johannes says, spotting Zorzo and coming over. "I meant to ask if you received all your materials back all right?"

"I'm sure I did, thank you. What happened to the canvas?" Zorzo asks.

"There, sir." Johannes points to where a crate is leaning. "I was told to pack it up. It's going back to Augsburg. Is that right, sir?"

"Of course," mutters Zorzo. The crate is open in the center, and through the aperture, on its side, is Sybille's mouth, carnelian-red lips slightly apart as she rushes toward the viewer. Zorzo doesn't bother to say it isn't quite finished. "It does not belong to me anyway."

He turns away from them and goes with the men, down through the kitchens, and exits the Palazzo Pallido for the last time.

25

Leda

"You there!" a voice calls from the corner and Michaelangelo's sidekick, Rodrigo Sordi, steps forward. "How were the Fuggers?" His ruffians are hovering behind, looking Zorzo up and down. "I feel we got off to a bad start. Do you have a moment? I'd like to invite you to a drink of something."

"That's kind, but I can't now." Zorzo forges on, but Sordi's men block his path. He tries to sidestep them, but they won't let him pass.

"Truly, you look thirsty," Sordi says. In his peacock coat and jaunty hat, he has the look of an oversized children's puppet. His crooked smile tightens. "A refreshing drink." He gives a nod to his men and two of them take Zorzo by the arms, while a third punches him in the stomach. They drag him along the path into a little square and to the fountain in the middle. Rodrigo motions with his fingertips and the men kick Zorzo behind the knees, push his head down and hold it underwater.

Zorzo thrashes against them. He claws for the hilt of his dagger before realizing he's left the weapon behind. When he's pulled out again, he says, spluttering, "I don't have prince orient."

"What was it you said to me?" Rodrigo takes out a handkerchief and dabs the spills of water from his face. "About my pretty face? And how I just ride for free on the success of others?"

"If I offended you, I apologize—"

"I was born in a fifty-room palazzo on the Bay of Naples. The house was built on the site of Pompey's villa and bettered it."

"Good for you."

"I will inherit it in due course. And my family's fortune. As you say, my pretty looks may desert me, but I will have, until I die, the view that the most famous general of ancient Rome chose above all others. What will your view be? What will you have? Envy and some faded memories of other people's fine houses."

"And what about *after* you're dead?" is the only reply Zorzo can think of. "Hell eternal."

Rodrigo signals and his men push Zorzo's face down into the water again. This time, he doesn't try to stop them, or grab for air. He gives in to it. In the cold, murky silence he thinks of what on earth he can do now. He must begin again, return to the point before he traveled to Poveglia; to the day before he heard of prince orient, or Jakob and Sybille Fugger.

He's released eventually, and left on the steps of the fountain, dripping. From the corner of his eye, he sees a final flash of peacock blue—before Rodrigo and his thugs vanish from the square.

Zorzo tramps across the city to St. Mark's Square. It starts to rain and he sits on the steps of the campanile. He looks up at the Doge's Palace and tries to remember happier times, the day he was here with his father, when they talked about Zorzo's future—

but all he can see is the portrait of Sybille's brother, turned on its side, those rosy cheeks, those clear blue eyes looking out, that nub of bloody flesh beneath the dove's claw. *Such is the power of a painting*, Bellini's brother once said, *that the valiant may become villains, and villains the valiant.* He waits for hours, oblivious of the stares of passing people. The rain stops, or rather it transmutes into a damp mist that dissolves the pink palace to a blur and erases all the lines of the city.

He thinks back to the day at the Orseolo, when Carlo Contarini told the story about Sybille and her brother, the shipwreck and the deserted island. Now Zorzo has learned the actual truth, all the things he hadn't understood about her make sense: her agitation whenever the subject of Edvard came up, her sudden defensiveness, the way the ideas she spouted seemed to belong to someone else, the letter she walked miles to send before changing her mind. When she confessed in Ignacio's house that she'd woken from a nightmare she'd been living in *all her life*, it was her brother she was talking about, it was *he* she wanted to turn her back on. So much so, she even resolved against sending that letter to him.

Deciding he must make his way home, Zorzo eventually staggers up and turns in the direction of the red house. "No, Leda's," he mumbles, remembering where his *garzoni* are. His head pounds and he feels dizzy from everything that's happened. His mind is so muddled, such a fog of the mistakes he's made, the regret of it all, he can't think of the way. "North, east, south?" He points with his fingers, guessing, trying to remember. He stands panting, shoulders dropped forward, head hanging, overwhelmed by the prospect of moving, of the superhuman strength he'll need to get to the Jewish quarter and Leda's house.

"I feel ill," he whispers to himself and, though he's sure that the events of the last day have put him in this state, he can't help but fear the worst, that the plague may be setting about him. He can think of nothing but the gondoliers who carted him over from Mestre, the mate with the swollen neck who coughed all the way. He should have gone on another boat, with other oarsmen. Just that once, he should not have been courteous—he should not have kept his word.

"Signor Barbarelli, what happened?" says Leda's steward, Hakim, when he opens the front door and finds Zorzo on the step.

"Stand back." Zorzo motions. "I've been close to people who were ill, and if I have caught their infection, I do not wish to pass it on. Stand back," he repeats in a firmer voice and Hakim does as he's told. "Is your mistress in?"

"Of course, yes. And your apprentices are here, too. Shall I get them?"

"Just fetch the signora for now. Say nothing to the others. Nothing, you understand? I am not fit to speak with anyone yet."

Hakim nods and disappears up into the house.

Zorzo crosses over to the other side of the road and drops down onto a doorstep. He turns his ear to the sound of voices from an upstairs window, a familiar chat. Uggo is telling some story or other and his companions are laughing. For a second, listening to them, Zorzo is overwhelmed with relief, with joy, until he freezes and terror creeps back, fiercer than ever. Of what, he's not even sure, but there's a sense in the pit of his stomach that things have jolted so far out of place they will never be put back properly again.

"I'm here," he calls to Leda when she comes out. "Stay where you are, though." She ignores him, starts to come over, and he stumbles to his feet and puts up his hand. "I'm worried I have the plague." He says it to make sure she keeps her distance, but the moment the words leave his mouth he's sure they're true.

"That's dramatic of you. Where've you been? All these messages we've received. We've been worried, Zorzi."

"I shan't ask again, come no closer. Two men brought me to

Venice this morning. At least one was ill, I have no doubt. We were cheek by jowl, he and I, and he coughed all the way across."

"Come upstairs, Zorzi, and I'll get you something to eat."

"No." He says it in such a way that Leda freezes. "I'm sorry. Give me a day or two alone, to be sure I have no malady. That's what I've come to ask you, whether you mind if my *garzoni* stayed with you a few nights longer?"

"Of course not."

"Berotti won't mind?" Leda tilts her head at him, as if to say it is an absurd question. "Thank you. Tell them I am safely returned. I have gone back to the red house and they must leave me in peace. Don't mention it straightaway. I don't want them to follow me into the street. Can you do that? Exactly as I say?"

She's reluctant to agree. "If that's what you want."

"Let me check I have my key upon me." He pats his coat until he finds it in one of his pockets. "I will explain all. Thank you, Leda."

Zorzo pauses at the entrance to his workroom. He can't remember a time when it was empty of people during the day. Even at Christmas, or on Easter Sunday, there's always someone in one of the corners at work. Achille must have been convincing when he came, as the place has clearly been abandoned in a hurry. Paints are discarded half-mixed, jars of pigment left with their lids off—normally an unforgivable act—and brushes left to harden. He gets some blankets from the cupboard in the corner, the bedding of the apprentices that sleep in the studio, lays them below the window and collapses.

On the second day back at the red house, after a daytime slumber in the same spot, he wakes to find the room is growing dark. His mouth is dry and his throat feels as if he's swallowed glass. His joints ache and his neck is so stiff and sore he has to check there's nothing tied around it. He has a fever, while at the same time is so cold; even with all the blankets wrapped tight around him, his teeth won't stop chattering. He's fourteen again, in his spot in the corner of Bellini's workroom. *I must get up*, he thinks, *get on with my duties, or the masters will think I'm lazy. I have green jadeite to mix for the brocade of Leonardo Loredan's gown.* Shivering, he clambers to his feet, looks around at the empty room and realizes where he is, who he is. He remembers he no longer works for Bellini, but for himself, that he has his own workshop now. Holding on to the edge of the long worktable, he stumbles over to the shelves to look at his colors, to be sure. There are familiar bottles stacked up to the ceiling and pigments within them, quantities of powder, but none have color. All of them are plain brown.

"It cannot be," he stammers, teeth setting off in a faster click. He looks back at the window, at the encroaching dusk, and hopes lack of light is the cause of it. He holds his hands to his temples as he tries to remember where the flint and matches are kept. He riffles over the tabletop and through drawers before he remembers and goes to the credenza on the far wall, finds what he wants, lights a candle and returns to the shelves. At the sight of colors coming through—Egyptian blue, realgar orange, purple smalt—his heart steadies. "Smalt," he chuckles, taking up the nearest bottle and cupping it in his palms. "I have been so rude about you. Forgive me, do."

He's relieved for a moment before the reality of his situation dawns upon him. Whether passed from the gondoliers or not, there's no doubt anymore—that he's infected.

There's a knock on the front door downstairs and Zorzo freezes. He goes out to the landing and peers down. There's the shadow of someone's feet in the gap below the door and he waits for it to go away. He's concentrating so hard that when another knock comes—just a slight rap of knuckles—he drops the bottle of smalt, the glass smashes and a cloud of brilliant indigo dust turns about in the air in a curious drift before settling on the floor.

"Open the door," a woman's voice says, "it's me."

"Sybille?"

Zorzo dares not move, dares not go down, or step onto the fine layer of indigo. The handle rattles, turns and the front door opens. She stands there, in the brown cloak she was wearing that morning, its hood up.

His first thought is that she's come to explain, detail the misunderstandings, but another notion strikes him: "You took her cloak? You shouldn't have. It was his wife's." She doesn't answer, just advances like a phantom toward the stairs. "What do you want? I'll not have you here." He backs across the landing. "Stay away!"

"It is I, Medusa," she says, all breath, then puts down her hood and starts to ascend. Zorzo thinks he will go mad with terror, that it *is* Medusa, that her head is all writhing snakes. She comes up into the light and he realizes his mistake: it's Leda. Her coat, which he's seen many times before, is not brown, but pink, the color of a child's cheek. "I've been to the market." She has a basket under her arm. "Do you have a fire lit? I shall heat some milk."

"Leda, stop. You are kind, but you must leave." The sight of her, tidy in pink, brisk efficiency in her voice, brings Zorzo back to his senses.

"Why, are you entertaining?" She means it as a joke, but he shakes his head anyway. "Then I won't take no for an answer." She comes up onto the landing. "If you don't want to pass any malady on to me, isn't it better you stand back?" She pushes past into the workroom.

Zorzo studies her from the doorway as she unloads the contents of her basket. "Bread, honey, horseradish, beetroot, lemons—I nearly had to sell my body for these—onions, violet seeds, bread.

Quite a witch's brew. It's dark in here, Zorzi. And messy. And no fire lit. No wonder you shiver."

"Leda, I do not joke. If you stay, you will catch whatever I have and I'll not allow it."

She looks at him directly. "Zorzo, I'll not fight with you. Sit down and *I* shall do the talking." She undoes her cape and looks for somewhere clean to put it. "I only have to set foot in this room," she complains, "and your powders are ruining my clothes." She hangs it from the antlers of the stag's head, then goes to the hearth and builds up the fire. "I'm making you hot milk and violet. It's a Cypriot cure."

"It sounds disgusting."

She lights the fire and gets it going with bellows. Soon it is an inferno and the light from it shakes in every corner of the room. It shines against the bottles on the shelves and coaxes all the colors to brilliant life.

"Be careful of that canvas," Zorzo says, indicating the painting of the knight and groom, which is leaning against the wall close to the hearth. "Put it on the easel there. Keep it safe."

Leda does as he says, stopping to glance at it. She notices something about it and peers more closely. "I thought that was the reflection of the fire, here, the light against the man's armor. But it's painted." Not quite believing how the effect has been rendered, she puts her face to the canvas and feels the spot with her fingertip, touching the nub of built-up white and yellow pigment. "How incredible."

"It is one of my favorite pictures," Zorzo tells her, before he starts to cough and soon it becomes uncontrollable. Leda goes to him but he motions her away with an angry wave. He holds his sleeve over his mouth and hacks over and over. After a minute, the fit subsides and he steadies himself. "That doesn't look so good," he murmurs, studying the fabric of his cuff, which is speckled with red.

If Leda is concerned by it, she doesn't show it. "I need a pan."

She searches, grumbling more about the mess, finds one, pours the milk she brought into it, adds honey and violet seeds and puts it on the fire. "You need to go next door to bed. You can't lie on the floor like that."

"No. I want to be in here, with everything around me."

Leda purses her lips, unsure, but relents. "Very well. I'll make a den for you. And that part of the room shall be your domain. Mine shall be this section. Agreed?" He's too exhausted to argue. "Well, move, while I arrange it."

He sits in the corner and she clears the space below the large window and sweeps the floor. She lugs the mattress in from the studio and goes to find clean sheets downstairs. After more complaints about "the shocking disarray," she puts them on, along with as many pillows and cushions as she can find. "You can see out to the square now," she says, motioning for him to take his place. "You won't have to look at me all day."

"All day? How long do you think you're staying?"

She ignores the question. "I was forgetting." She produces a little package and drops it in his lap. Zorzo opens it to find his sapphire ring. "And next time you need money, I'll be offended if you don't come to me." She pushes it back onto his finger, over the pale band of skin where it always lived. "And I've settled your most urgent debts. I got Janek to bring me all the papers. What a mess everything was in. Janek's a nice fellow, but Zorzi, really, he has no head for business. He reminds me of a tortoise turned upside down—flailing a good deal but going nowhere. Now drink."

Zorzo sips the brew, speechless from her kindness, and she returns to the painting of the knight and groom. "I know you believe me stupid on these matters, but I can't imagine: how do you *paint* light?"

"Practice?" Zorzo says and Leda stays staring at it. "And do you recognize the boy? That's my Uggo."

Leda's eyes widen. "Of course. He's perfect."

"He's helping the knight get ready for battle. The glimmer on his armor is from the dawn light. A door has just been opened. Someone has come to say it's time. He knows he must be bold, must *appear* bold at least, but underneath, he's unsure. His life is hanging in the balance."

Leda's face lights up with an amazed smile. "You're right. Now I see it."

"Tell me about this one," she says later. "He looks lovesick." Leda has chosen half a dozen pieces of work from the racks, preliminary drafts of finished paintings, positioned them in the light and is going through them in turn. The one she's referring to is of a young nobleman at a window. His head is on one side, his cheek resting lightly on his hand, while a steward tries to get his attention.

"The model for that was Carlo Contarini of all people. Who I doubt has ever looked lovelorn in his life, but has a good face for what I wanted."

"It's so interesting how you use different pieces of people for different effects. What's this in his left hand? An orange?"

"A *Seville* orange. Known for being bittersweet."

"Like love? I see. Ha. That is clever. Everything has a meaning." She moves on to the next. "What scene is this?"

"That's the infant Moses. The pharaoh is offering him a choice between gold and red-hot coal. I know which you would choose, but you might not be right."

Leda gives him a sideways glance. "I've read the Bible. The instructions are quite clear." She turns back to the canvases. "Now this is one of my favorites. Who is he?"

"The model is my apprentice, Teodor. He's the Adonis of the studio. He's an archer here, who's been taken by surprise—perhaps by Cupid himself. What is it?"

Leda has frozen, having noticed a drawing that was tucked behind the others. A preparatory version of the canvas she modeled for, *Venus Asleep in the Forest.* "You gave that to me once and I was so rude. I said I wouldn't hang it in my house. What airs I had, Zorzi. I still do. It's shameful how I behaved."

"Shh now, none of that. No tears today. Let me gift it to you again." He pushes himself to his feet and goes over to get it. "Sketch or not, I preferred this version to the final piece. It's more immediate. She's sleeping, but so alive, don't you think? Here, it's yours." Then an idea comes to him. "Actually, wait a minute." He goes over to the workbench, mixes some burnt umber and a little of Paulino's bone black and, with just a dozen well-judged brush marks, paints a shape on the right-hand side of the canvas. "In adoration of her," he says, placing the picture in front of her.

Leda gives an excited clap. He's painted, in silhouette, a knight kneeling, sword and helmet at his side, head bowed toward the sleeping Venus.

He starts to cough again, worse than ever, in profound grating rasps. The skin of his face turns puce, particularly around his eyes where the veins engorge. He clutches his chest, scrambles over to the bed, juts his head forward and retches blood down the side of his leg. Leda goes and sits next to him and puts her arm around his shoulders. He tries to push her away, but she holds tight.

"I'm here," she keeps saying. "And here I'll stay."

26

The Colormaker's Song

Within a day of her being there, swellings in Zorzo's neck grow first to the size of walnuts, and then as large as crab apples. He can't help fidgeting with them. Their presence inside his body, hard as shale, seems like a mistake, an impossibility, as death itself should be—and yet there they are.

The buboes replicate themselves and soon he has them growing under his arms and his groin, while dark purple, almost black, patches come up on his arms and legs. "What a devilish color," Zorzo comments to his companion. He traces his finger around one of the abstract, cloudlike shapes. "There's a reason some people are afraid of it. Purple might be the color of emperors and kings, but it's *owned* by death. Everyone, every*thing*, passes through purple on their way to black."

"Don't look at them, Zorzi," says Leda, who's on top of the

cabinets, individually dusting every jar of paint. "It will make you feel worse."

"Worse?" Zorzo chuckles. "Does it get worse?"

It does. The aches in his head, down his spine, in his chest, even in his feet, become unendurable. His skin becomes as brittle as thin veneer and the growths eat through it and turn to pus-filled lesions. More and more unnatural hues come up on the surface of his body: engorged veins are ice blue, bruises are fringed in sand yellow and gamboge, his fingertips turn dark verdigris green. Leda persists in breaking her own rule by coming over to the bed to clean them with hot water. When she's close, for fear of contagion in his breath, Zorzo doesn't dare open his mouth.

The day wheels into night and the light in the window evaporates. The temperature drops outside, sharply, and the glass panes film up against it.

"I think it might snow again," Leda says, wiping away the condensation to peer out.

"It would be a mercy for this burning if it did," Zorzo says.

Downstairs, the front door opens and Uggo calls from the foot of the stairs, "This is a warning. I'm coming up."

"Tell him to go away." Zorzo sits up on the side of the bed so quickly that it produces a new coughing fit. He longs to see his *garzoni* and has missed Uggo's grinning face in particular, but for that very reason, he must stay away.

Uggo bundles in, snowflakes on his cap and shoulders, dressed up in a tangerine-colored costume. In one hand, he carries a pair of unlit lanterns, in the other a tambour drum, with a pie balanced on top. "Good evening, Signora Sitruk." He puts everything down and does a bow. "I know, I'm not supposed to be here, but we're missing one vital piece for our—" He finishes the sentence with a wink, before flourishing the pie. "And I needed to bring this from my mother. She's been baking since dawn. *Torta Pasqualina*," he calls over to Zorzo. "Your favorite, sir." He puts his nose to it. "Smell that. Still warm. How are you, sir? On the mend?"

Zorzo is trying to get his coughing under control. "No visitors," he splutters. "You have to leave. Kind as you are."

"I don't know if he has much of an appetite," Leda murmurs to the boy, "but it was thoughtful of your mother."

"Don't worry about her, miss. She'll do anything for the master, my mama. She'll run ten miles for him, she will."

"What's the piece you're missing?" asks Leda.

"It's there," Uggo says, going over to get Zorzo's lute. "Do you mind if we borrow it, my liege? We promise to be careful."

"What in the devil's name—" Zorzo starts to say.

"I must go. I'll see you in a moment, sir." He picks up the drum and lanterns he came with and is about to rush out when he remembers something. "Sir, do you like my costume? It's the color of fire. You'll see." He rushes away, thumps down the stairs and exits below.

"What will I see?" says Zorzo.

Leda goes over to the window behind his bed, opens one of the casements and invites him to look out.

Outside, the night sky over Venice is a matrix of falling white. Large, puffy flakes descend in a continuous reel, settling against roofs and pediments and architraves, making abstract, sharp shapes of all the buildings in the square, of the whole city. "All I can see is Uggo," says Zorzo.

The boy is on the steps of the fountain in the center of the piazza, lighting the lanterns.

"There," Leda says, pointing.

Many lights are capering up one of the side streets as a line of people advance. Uggo fastens the drum to his belt and starts to play, banging a forceful, steady beat. At first, Zorzo can't see who the people are, just that their lanterns catch the color of their clothes—and all the colors are different. At the front, Paulino is dressed in a peridot green. Behind him, Azalea is in golden brown and Naples yellow and her brother, Tulipano, in cerulean blue. Teodor is in coral pink and Janek is in crimson and violet. All carnival costumes, in vivid fabrics, with wide brimmed hats, elaborate headdresses, feathers and ribbons—and each person carries a different musical instrument.

Behind this first group, more lights follow. Many more. The people file into the square, and Uggo—beating his tambour ever more resolutely—marshals them into lines. Zorzo begins to recognize them. There are fellows from the various paint shops of the city, folk that Zorzo has grown up with. There are watercolor makers, the ink and charcoal men, Zorzo's suppliers of gesso, and of brushes. There are apprentices who used to work at the red house; and old colleagues from Zorzo's time at Bellini's studio, as well as ones working there still. There are boatmen Zorzo has befriended over the years and the two ladies from the bread stall. There's Uggo's brothers and mother, and Lorenzo Lotto.

Soon the square is humming with light, and with a hundred different colors. Uggo passes Zorzo's lute to Teodor, who kisses its neck and gets ready to play. Alongside him Azalea has an oud, Paulino a little citole fiddle and even Janek—who has always claimed to be tone deaf, which no one disputes, having heard him humming—has a timbrel. Uggo stops drumming and holds his palm in the air. There's silence for a moment, an enchanted quiet in which just a soft, Venetian wind blows and the snowflakes drift down. Teodor steps forward and announces, "'I Go Before You,' by Beppe Barbarelli of Castelfranco." He counts the others in and they start up the song, just instruments for the first stanza—before everyone joins in singing, the group as one, a chorus. Zorzo's hands shake, his mouth too.

"No, no," he gasps and fat teardrops spill onto his cheeks. He opens the window as far as it will go, so he can lean right out, but it's too narrow for him. "Let me see from here, let me see." Balancing himself against furniture, he stumbles over to the door they use for winching heavy materials up from the street. He tries to open it, but the bolts are too stiff for his shaking hands. Leda comes to his aid, snaps them back one by one and the door springs open. Zorzo holds on to the edge of the casing, half leaning out, careless of the drop beneath, of the cold, of the snow pattering against him, his face beatific at the sound of the song.

A man in a dark cloak and hood has come into the square and halted. Zorzo notices him peering around at the buildings, looking for something. He's distinct from everyone else: he hasn't come to join the singing, nor is he dressed in carnival clothes. He's somber. Hanging from his fist is a small but heavy-looking sack, of grain, Zorzo fancies. The man doesn't wait until the song ends before asking one of the singers a question. The singer replies with a gesture toward the red house, the front of which the man studies, before noticing the figure leaning from the first-floor window.

Zorzo stares back, fear dropping through him like an ice rock, unable to see the man's face below his cowl, but certain it's Death himself come to fetch him away. Zorzo is terrified by the little heavy bag he clutches and tries to remember what purpose grain has for going down into the underworld. He looks away, tries to concentrate on his *garzoni* instead, on Uggo's defiant, almost warlike expression at the front of the choir. But the moment of magic has passed for Zorzo. Death has ruined it, standing there, among Zorzo's favorite people in the world, glaring up and waiting for his moment.

The song finishes and Janek calls out, "Three cheers for the master!" and everyone hurrahs.

"Get well. We'll be back tomorrow," Uggo shouts and Zorzo waves back, while his chest heaves because he knows that, by then, the stranger with the little, heavy sack of grain will have claimed him. The people start to drain from the square, lanterns zigzagging, everyone waving, some laughing, others carrying on the tune. The figure with the sack does not move or make a sound. He waits until the piazza is almost empty, then steps forward. For a moment he disappears from view, before there comes a firm knock on the front door.

Zorzo holds his breath.

"Let me in," the man calls. "I have urgent business with Giorgio Barbarelli." Zorzo shakes his head and stumbles back behind the bed. There's a second, even weightier rap. "Giorgio Barbarelli, are you in?"

"Send him away," Zorzo whispers. "I'm not ready for him. Please send him away."

Leda goes out and he cocks his ear to the sound of her descending, and the conversation once she's opened the door.

She returns up the stairs, into the workroom, looking alarmed, and says, "He insisted. He knows you."

It's not death that enters behind her, but Cardinal Soderini. He halts, surprised by the room, frightened by it even. "I'm sorry to appear unannounced—" he growls, puts the sack on the floor and lets down his hood. His hair, usually neat and slick, is disheveled and sticking up. He has dirt on his face. "I am sorry also to hear you are unwell." His voice is trembling and he holds onto his neck as if to steady it. "What a state I am in. I fell over on my way from Cannaregio, down the steps of the Ponte Storto. They were covered in filth. My chain must have come off, the little gold crucifix my father gave me. When I realized, I hurried back to search but some thief had snatched it. I should have left Venice already. I should have been gone days ago. I've been holed up alone in Herr Fugger's house. May I?" he asks, taking off his coat. "It stinks of whatever was on the steps of Ponte Storto."

Underneath, his cardinal's robe is so intensely red it's as if a wave of pure blood has swept into the room. He motions to a stain on his coat. "Dog filth. The worst. They are not my creatures at all, and this city is beholden to them like no other. Do you have some water," he says to Leda, "to clean it for me?"

Leda resents the request, the insinuation that she is a maid, but takes it. "As I told you, his condition is bad," she says under her breath. "Really, this is not a safe place to be."

The cardinal replies with a petulant wave. "I shall be safe. Do not fret about me. I am vouched for." He touches his chest where his crucifix usually hangs. "Hold on a moment." He motions at Leda. "In the pocket there, a flask." She gives it to him and goes off to clean the stain. The cardinal peers around the room and finds Zorzo against the window, behind the bed still. "How are you, Signor Barbarelli?"

"I've been better."

"Of course you have. Of course. And you will be well again soon. I will pray for your recovery. You will recover, Signor Barbarelli. And if you do not, that is God's plan." He clutches at his bare neck. "My father's crucifix, I could weep. My most beloved possession. It was five hundred years old. It went in 1095 to Jerusalem on the first crusade and has protected its bearer ever since."

"I'm sorry to hear it," Zorzo manages.

Soderini undoes the cap of the flask and drinks. "For calm. You'll pardon me, I shan't offer any to you. So this is an artist's workroom? I always imagined a place of dark magic and so I find it."

Leda has returned with the cardinal's coat. "Is there anything in particular we can help you with?" she asks.

Soderini steps over toward the bed and stops. He takes an envelope from his pocket. "Herr Fugger asked me to bring this to you before I left Venice. A note." Despite the fact he has wished Zorzo well, his tone seems undercut with malevolence. "I was reluctant, I do not mind saying, Signor Barbarelli. For Jakob to be cordial with you after everything that happened, strikes me as...unnatural. Then again, anything related to Sybille Fugger and her brother is so. Edvard Artzi has always been a disgrace, the worst kind of scoundrel, maligning Jakob to anyone who'd listen, spreading vile rumors, but he surpassed himself this time. This story that he's fallen in with a circle of Wittenberg intellectuals, that he's grown a conscience, that he's fighting against injustices. Nonsense. It's jealousy, pure and simple. He hates Jakob. He can't bear his success, and that he took his beloved sister from him. Beloved?" He lets out a mirthless laugh. "That's a fine word for someone who inflicts almost perpetual abuse, has done so no doubt since the day she was born." He takes another sip and does up his flask.

"Anyway, Edvard is one thing, Sybille another. She could have broken her ties with him but she always scurried back, like an ant to a dunghill. Jakob found out they'd met as Sybille was packing up to come here. It has always been my counsel that Jakob should annul their marriage, but my friend is too kind. He defends her, sees her side, has sympathy. The island and all that. He forgives, over and over again, but she knows what she's doing. It's all just a grand and spiteful game for her. She is a lie of a woman, to her very bones."

Leda steps forward, not liking the direction Soderini has taken the conversation. Zorzo listens, jaw clenched.

"But he'll carry on suffering her, until the end, no doubt," Soderini goes on. "Excusing her transgressions. That she had an affair with her own kin. And do you know why? Why he forgives?"

All Zorzo can manage is a shake of the head.

"The poor fellow is still in love with her," Soderini says and lets the notion settle a moment in the sickroom air. "In any case, I am not a man to deny my friend's wishes, so here." He tosses the envelope onto the bed and stands back again. "I saw your painting of her, in the chapel. It is—" He pauses, his face turns to a scowl and he says, almost with hatred, "It is, in its own way, a masterpiece."

He takes his cloak, checks that it has been properly cleaned and puts it back on. "He said to give you this too. That you left it." He kicks the bag on the floor. "Good night, signor. Really, it is a shame I had to come. I would still have my father's crucifix if I hadn't." He gives Leda a terse nod. "I'll see myself out."

Once the front door has slammed shut behind the cardinal, Zorzo breaks the seal of the letter and looks at the note. He can discern two lines of writing, but they're a blur. He tries to focus, but the words slant and swim away from him. He presses his eyes shut, tries again, but it's no good.

"Shall I?" asks Leda.

"In a minute. What's in the bag? I left nothing."

Leda opens it up and takes out a heavy package with a waxed parchment wrapping, tied with string, and a battered label attached. She squints at the inscription on it, deciphering the heavy Gothic type before reading, "'Contains mineral powder. Keep dry and warm. Prince orient.'"

Zorzo tries to stand, but falls back down. "Put it there, in the light," he says, panting. "Open it." She rests the bundle on the tabletop and tries to untie the string, but the knot is tiny and hard, hitched so long ago it's fused into one. "Cut it," Zorzo says. "A knife, there."

Leda makes a single incision; there's a pop, a little cloud of dust goes up, the string recoils into a ball, leaving clean white marks on the front of the parcel in the form of a cross.

This time Zorzo manages to push himself to his feet. He gestures at Leda to give him space and totters over to the tabletop. He cups his hands around the package. Inside is a mass of crumbled rocks, warm to the touch, as if it still carries heat from when it struck into the earth. And as it moves, it emits a scent that makes Zorzo swoon. "What odor is that?" He puts his nose to the parcel and a memory surfaces, one that's never come back to him before, a moment he'd entirely forgotten, but that is now as clear and hard as a jewel. A day in his childhood, when he went with his mother to the pear orchard, the copse of fruit trees nestled just inside the walls of Castelfranco. It was late August, the sun was setting through the branches and that same odor—surely—was in the air: his mother's scent and the heady smell of sap rising, and of eternal, golden days ahead. He pulls back the overlaps of wax parchment and is about to see what's inside, when a thought comes to him.

"Is anyone still in the square?" Leda doesn't seem to understand and he snaps, "My *garzoni*, are they there? Quickly, look."

She goes to the window, cups her hands over her eyes and peers out. The weather has turned since everyone came to sing: a stiffer wind has picked up, and as it drives down the side streets and across the piazza, it makes the snow dance in raggedy tendrils. "The square is empty," she says.

Zorzo thinks for a moment. "Will you go and fetch them? They can stay down in the hall and I'll send this down to them. So we can look at the same time. We must share the moment, Leda. Are you sure they've all gone?"

"No one is there."

"Fetch them, please. We must be together."

"If that's what you want."

"Yes, it must be now." For a while he says nothing more. He casts his eyes around the room very slowly, as if he is seeing it for the first time.

"Zorzo? Why don't you sit down?"

She motions him toward a chair, but he waves her away. Inside, a curious change is turning through him. He feels light, poised, or rather the weight of sickness is lifting away. He's clear-headed. The room is sharp. It gleams. Everything is in focus, like one of those meticulous paintings the northern Europeans are so good at, where every object, each detail of a room, has clarity and believable mass. There's an order to it all. All Zorzo's senses are piqued. He can pinpoint each individual odor in the room, plaster here, cut timber there, linseed, bone primer. He can hear the quiet roar of the fire, snowflakes patting crisply against the window, the crackle of candles. He can hear, in neighboring houses, going-to-bed voices, low and benign.

"Leda, I think—" He looks at her, amazed. "I feel better."

"What?"

"Something is righting itself. I'm sure of it." He keeps surveying the room, to be sure he's not imagining the alteration. "We have won, Leda. Look at what we have. Prince orient. We are made. We may have lost the commission, but we have beaten them all in this. Prince orient is ours." He looks down at the line of shadow beneath the flap of the parcel. All he has to do is lift it and see. "You must go and fetch my fellows."

"Do you really feel better, Zorzi? Really?"

"Yes, in truth, yes. People get well from this, don't they? Or a fair portion do. I wouldn't be the first. I'm healthy, so why not? This treasure has done it." He rolls up his sleeve and runs his hand along the side of his arm. "This lump here, at my elbow—it's smaller, isn't it? Hasn't that dreadful color gone from it? It's shrinking, no? And this on my neck. It feels like the life has gone from it. We have won, my darling. In the end, everything is as it was meant to be."

Leda, disbelieving at first, is ecstatic now. "I shall get them, straightaway." She bustles around, looking for her coat.

"And buy some wine to celebrate." Another idea strikes Zorzo. "No, don't buy it. I have it already. My special case. We must toast our success with that. Find it before you go. Downstairs, directly below us, you know the second storeroom. In the corner, there's a tall trunk, inside it a wooden box, painted red. Bring that. It has sat down there for as long as I've been in the red house."

Leda laughs, blows a kiss to him with both hands and goes down the back stairs to look.

Zorzo has had the wine hidden away for almost a decade. He's always felt ashamed of it, embarrassed he was convinced to buy it, to spend as much as a tradesman or gondolier earns in half a year on four bottles of forty-year-old liquor that might, for all he knows, be undrinkable. He had just won the commissions to paint the doge and the altarpiece of his home cathedral and had become—he can see now, but couldn't then—impressed with himself, enthralled by the fuss circling around him, the attention, finding himself invited to balls and dinners, into grand rooms. At once there were new coteries of people in his orbit, ones he didn't realize even existed before, enablers, fixers for the rich, experts, lubricators of high society's wheels, purveyors of luxury. There was one fellow—Zorzo can remember everything but his name—an equerry of some kind, a palace official, who would very likely have ignored him if he had not become notable, but very charming and amenable, who convinced him to buy the wine from a dealer friend. He told Zorzo it was from a vineyard planted by Eleanor of Aquitaine, a private estate on the banks of the Loire, tended by monks, and which produced a liquid that was honey sweet and the color of gold. He convinced Zorzo that owning some of these rare bottles would be a mark of his arrival in society, a bold statement of success.

"Have you found it yet?" he calls down through the floor.

"I'm looking," comes the muffled reply.

Zorzo notices Fugger's note on the bed and remembers he hasn't read it yet. He takes it up and this time the words are entirely legible.

No doubt you are right—about the world. If I may choose what I am, I choose a Hadrian, not a Nero. Yours, JF

Zorzo's first feeling is of surprise, that the man is far from the monster he believed him to be, that he has listened, and understood, and gone to the trouble to let Zorzo know. Then he realizes the note is more momentous than that. That Jakob Fugger, one of the most significant individuals in the world, could reasonably change his behavior, or the way he thinks, or become a force for good, just because of what Zorzo said, strikes him as incredible. And even if Fugger's approach doesn't alter, he has at least understood. *He has listened.* That alone is remarkable. In that instant it strikes Zorzo that humans have a willingness to comprehend each other, and to share what they learn. It is the combination of these things that makes societies, and civilizations.

All at once, he cannot only see the room as it is now, see it with astonishing clarity, hear, smell, feel it; he can see it throughout its existence, from when it was a new house more than a century ago. He can perceive the traces of everyone who has inhabited it, all the little steps of advancement they've made, which may have been tiny at the time, but add up to so much more. Then the walls of the red house seem to fall away and he can see across the city, from high, like in Barbari's woodcut. He can feel the history of Venice, the majesty and success of it. He can fall back in time and wonder at the first settlers, the canal builders, the pile drivers, the visionaries; and all the men and women who have shaped it since: engineers, planners, politicians, artists and experimenters. And he knows the promise of what's to come. He can sense the other city-states of Italy—Genoa, Milan, Rome, Naples—and he could burst with sheer excitement at the scale of human endeavor. He can see further afield—to Paris, Tours, Granada, Prague and Ghent, even as far as the English shore—and every place is a wonder, indisputable proof of human brilliance. He lays his hand on the package.

As suddenly as the elation came upon him, like a wave it begins to ebb away, to turn foul against him. Inside, something collapses, something vital and structural, and beneath are banks of pure pain. The room elongates, the ceiling stretches up, the walls turn red, then brown, as if paint were being poured down them. There are doors all around, behind which little vignettes of his life play. He tries to see inside the rooms, to relive those moments of another time, but the doors start closing, slowly to begin with, but soon slamming shut quickly, one after the other—and the closing doors spiral into darkness above him. He's falling, into a vortex, down, down, toward an incontestable hardness, toward that unendurable pain. There is a sudden burst of pigment, like a firework in his head. The snowflakes outside are sparks of color hammering at the glass. He hears Leda come up the back stairs and tries to call out to her, but no sound comes. There is a void of power. He sees her shadow rise, stretch across the room, and her feet turn to him. Everything is dark purple. Then, like a candle being struck out, even that turns to black.

Leda sets down the box of wine and puts on her coat and hat. "I'm going to get them, then. I'll be back soon. Zorzo?"

His feet are on the ground, his knees twisted and his top half lying diagonally against the mattress. Fugger's note hangs from the fingers of his hand. No part of him moves. Only his hair shivers against the breeze through the window. When Leda realizes what has happened, her face turns to stone. She stands for minutes, not moving, before going to close the window. Below, a woman is standing alone in the square, staring up at the red house. All in black, she'd be well dressed were it not for the fact that her cloak is in tatters, her face dirty from traveling and her hair disheveled.

Sybille Fugger.

Leda's eyes meet with hers and at once there's an understanding between the two women. Tragedy has come.

27

The Marks We Make

In Rome, sixty years later, in January of 1570, on the *piano nobile* of a bare palazzo on the Quirinal Hill, sitting by a ceramic hearth, Leda Sitruk has talked for hours to her visitor, the Greek painter, Domenikos. As if taking Zorzo's point of view, she's told the painter's story, his life and death.

Domenikos has been transported, from the first moment: Zorzo's meeting with Caspien in Poveglia—and onward. He has not missed a single word. He's laughed, dreamed, cried.

"I suppose when I started speaking," she says, "you presumed I was Sybille Fugger and not who I really am?"

"I must admit, I did not guess."

"Back then, I wouldn't have either. I couldn't have imagined the woman I'd become. Zorzo thought I was a philistine. Interested only in money. And he was right, I was. Those last days together in his workroom marked the beginning of a great change in me. I left Berotti the next day. I didn't take the palazzo I had my eye on. It would have been folly. After two years, I sold my business, the one I told you about, hooks and fastenings, for a great profit. I went to Siena first. I had a cousin there, and it was far from Venice.

"At first I had no idea what I would turn my mind to, only that I wished—in whatever way I could, however great or small—to leave a mark too, as Zorzo had. Ever since our conversation, about his *Knight and Groom*, and how the light fell upon the armor, I'd begun looking at paintings, properly. Looking hard. But it was that picture there that set me on my eventual path." She points to the solitary canvas on the wall. "That he'd tried to gift me once, that I turned down and he gave me again, adding that figure in shadow, the kneeling knight. Take the light. Look at it now. You have my permission."

Her guest retrieves the candle from the table and goes over to the painting. "It was the first I owned, and the last I possess," she says. "I've left instructions with my children—yes, I had three boys, good souls, all flown with their own families now—I've left instructions with them for it not to be buried forever in one of their houses, but shared with the world."

Domenikos realizes the moment he sees it that he's seen copies of the original, a sublime piece, Venus sleeping in a forest. This "sketched" version is almost as complete as a finished picture. "It was this that set you on your path?" he says.

"The quality of its atmosphere; the way the moment is both fleeting and eternal; how, even with her eyes closed, she's a living, breathing, desiring creature; and the way it captures—the thing that every serious artist tries to grasp—the very mystery of a human being. When one day I finally understood, I knew straightaway what I must do. Print. Publish. I bought my first press."

Looking on the right-hand side of the picture, the silhouette of the kneeling knight that Zorzo added in his dying days, Domenikos can't help but feel new admiration. "So you published work on painters?" he asks. "It's curious, you'll excuse me, that I didn't better know your name."

"*My* name was irrelevant. Why would I detract from my subjects? But yes, to begin with, that was what I printed. In the end, my time making metal fastenings for clothes proved most useful in creating new varieties of printing machines, and of type, and in finessing ink, making it oil-bound so everything was fast and clean. I befriended painters. I had to. I traveled the continent, back and forth like a fanatic to meet them. I helped where I could, the youngsters coming through. I was one of the first to champion Tintoretto, you know? The first to print him. There were dozens of others, Cellini, Parmigianino, Correggio, Bronzino, Veronese. And I even came across Zorzo's hero, Leonardo. That was momentous. The curiosity of the man, and the kindness. Maybe he was just being generous, but he said Zorzo had left an indelible mark, that his loss to the world of painting was incalculable. My husband, a Spaniard originally, who passed on ten years ago, had joined my venture by then, bringing his fortune. He'd invested in Magellan's voyage around the world and opened my eyes even more. We were the first house in Italy to put out Copernicus: *On the Revolutions of the Heavenly Spheres*. Twenty-seven years ago and I can feel the earthquake still. We published Vasari's *Lives of the Painters*, Machiavelli's *Mandragola*, Thomas More's *Utopia*, Palladio's treatises of architecture. Works by Luther, Erasmus, Ariosto, Camões. How Zorzo would have loved it all."

"And Sybille Fugger? You said she came to the red house that evening? What happened to the painting of her? And the commission for St. Peter's, and prince orient?"

"The commission: it changed over and over again. In the end, I hear the altarpiece at St. Peter's is still to be painted. The portrait of Sybille: nobody knows. It was said that it never made it back to Augsburg. But I think Sybille kept it for herself and took the secret to her grave. Keep your eyes open, though, in case one day it appears."

"I will, absolutely. What a treasure it must be."

"And yes," Leda goes on, "Sybille came into the red house that night and it was the beginning of a friendship, of sorts, as we would always have Zorzo in common. Because of the plague, he was taken to Poveglia to be buried. The island had been cleared for the outbreak, and though funerals were not permitted, Sybille and I bribed the undertakers and we went with them and watched. I only saw her two or three times after that, but we wrote to one another where we could.

"After she left Venice, she managed to finally escape the clutches of her brother and I remember her writing that it was like pulling out a tooth that had grown infected. A thing that had to be done, but that brought indescribable pain, would never be replaced and ached still, even long after it was gone."

"And Jakob Fugger?" Domenikos asks. "Did he take her back?"

Leda shrugs. "They remained married, but in what form I can tell you little, for she rarely mentioned his name. Certainly, they continued childless. Eventually, when Edvard tried a final time to inveigle, she moved her life to the Harz mountains in the north of the country, to Rammelsberg, where Jakob had one of his largest mines. She felt safe there, high up, cut off, with an army of her husband's men around her. By coincidence, Fugger and Edvard died within a year of each other. The husband, I'm not sure from what, but Edvard's throat was cut after an argument in a tavern over a gambling debt. That's how life ends for some: a bad throw of the dice.

"Sybille always promised to write a paper for me to publish, on her 'uncommon' perspective, but it didn't materialize. The last letter from her came a week before she died. In it—this was four decades ago now, she was far from an old woman—she talked only of Zorzo. She said she'd dreamed of him every night for a year, so much so that she knew her end was coming. He'd stayed with her, she said, a constant companion; and although she regretted nearly all else in her life, her brief friendship with a painter of Venice had brought a kind of meaning, a consolation that made all the rest worthwhile." She pauses a moment and looks at her visitor very directly. "It's the marks we make that are important, Domenikos. The marks we make and leave behind."

Domenikos understands completely. "When I arrived, you said you wanted to pass on knowledge to me. It was this? To tell me Zorzo's story?"

"And to give you something. The most precious thing I have, more than that painting, more than anything I've possessed down the gallery of my years. I kept it to myself, you see, to remember him by. I ask you to do the same. Let it be your talisman. Your secret. Your power. And when, in the distance, your funeral bells begin to toll, when your time is all but over, pass it on to the next, the next great colorist in line—and in that way let it go, from painter to painter, down the centuries."

Domenikos's throat is parched and he has to swallow before saying, "Prince orient?"

Leda lifts the end of her stick. "The chest over there. Open it. Take out the casket."

Zorzo is walking through a forest. He can't remember starting the journey, or where he's come from. He doesn't know where he's going either, even though he's walking with purpose. He isn't sure if he's been in this land for hours or centuries or a fraction of a moment. The ground is mossy and soft and he can't hear his own footsteps.

A boy is standing at the edge of the woods, head tilted, squinting at the valley beyond, the further reaches of which are laced in sunlight. He jolts when he hears someone approaching but is relieved to find it's a man he knows. They stand at the edge of the wood, man and boy, regarding each other, before the boy says, "Hello, sir." He smiles shyly. "From Poveglia," he adds by way of explanation. "Caspien's boy."

"Otto." Zorzo nods, happy to see him, to see he's still wearing the coat he gave him. "This is a fine place." He peers at the valley, noticing spots of color here and there about the escarpments: coral, amethyst and verdigris green. Zorzo is about to ask where they are, but Otto preempts the question.

"A long way away in time," Otto says, "from where we were. In the future, I think, but it might be the past, or both at the same time. You can't really tell. But here we are, and here everyone comes."

Zorzo puts his hand on the boy's shoulder. "We should go," he says, nodding toward the valley, compelled to walk to where the sunlight strikes the other side. Otto agrees and they move out from under the canopy of trees.

"You'll know the answer to this, being a colorist, sir. What color is that?" Otto asks, pointing at the sky. "I often wonder. I never saw one like it before I came here."

Zorzo looks up and the shock is so great he freezes, gasps, blinks away a tear. He's never seen it either. "I know it, yes. That sky is prince orient."

The boy watches him, concerned. "Have I upset you?"

"No." Zorzo steadies himself. "No, my friend. I couldn't be happier." He points forward and they both continue on to the valley.

Domenikos Theotokopoulos leaves the palazzo that looks like a Spanish *palacete* and sets off down the Quirinal Hill toward the old Forum. He has a package under his arm, the box the signora gave him, containing a rare pigment, with a blanket wrapped around it for safety. He hasn't seen the color yet. The signora asked him to wait until after he left, and for daylight, before looking.

It's almost midnight now. Domenikos shouldn't be crossing an unfamiliar city alone, so late in the day, but looking at the view as he descends the slope it's impossible to imagine anything dangerous coming to pass. The snow has stopped falling but it has left the city entirely white, humming with light beneath a crisp, three-quarter moon.

He circles the base of the Capitoline and goes down into the oldest part of the town, the Forum Romanum, before turning up the Via Sacra. He passes through the Arch of Septimius Severus. The remains of the republic's senate house, the Curia Julia, are on one side; the temples of Saturn and Vesta on the other. The path is the same that Caesar once passed along, and Cicero and Augustus, Virgil, Horace and Ovid, people who invented the modern world. The proof and legacy of their achievements, and those of all the great men and women since, sits beyond, on the north shore of the Tiber, on the Vatican slope, the new basilica of St. Peter's, the grandest, greatest, most dazzling building in the world.

Domenikos stares up at it. Hammers are still tapping into the night. The city bells toll the turning of a new day. He clutches the casket to his chest and thinks how lucky he is: to have the skills he does, and the knowledge, the profound comfort of great minds behind him, and a lifetime ahead. How wonderful, he thrills, to be alive at such a time when buildings like St. Peter's can be magicked from the ground.

Leda is right: it is the marks that humans make that are important.

The marks their lives leave behind.

"We live," he cheers out loud and the sound echoes around the old buildings of the Forum before it hangs in the still, cold air.

He turns toward the Palatine Hill and, too excited to merely walk, he sets off in a run.

★ ★ ★ ★ ★